CAFÉ ROYAL

edited by John Murray

PANURGE
PUBLISHING

1996

CAFÉ ROYAL

first published 1996 by
Panurge Publishing
Crooked Holme Farm Cottage
Brampton, Cumbria CA8 2AT

EDITOR John Murray

PRODUCTION EDITOR Henry Swan
EDITORIAL ASSISTANT Janet Bancroft
Typeset at Union Lane Telecentre, Brampton, Cumbria CA8 1BX
Tel. 016977 - 41014
Printed by Peterson's, 12 Laygate, South Shields, Tyne and Wear NE33 5RP
Tel. 0191-456-3493

ISBN 1 898984 30 1

Copyright this collection Panurge Publishing 1996
Copyright the authors 1996

British Library Cataloguing in Publication Data.
A catalogue record for this book is available from
the British Library.

PANURGE PUBLISHING
Crooked Holme Farm Cottage,
Brampton,
Cumbria CA8 2AT
Tel. 016977-41087

PANURGE Anthologies Numbers 24 & 25

BARÈT MAGARIAN	*A Chance Encounter In The Café Royal*	9
JULIA DARLING	*The Bone Cafe*	13
PATRICK CUNNINGHAM	*The Haven*	16
JULIE CHARALAMBIDES	*Mrs Corallo*	24
DAVID WHITFIELD	*Plane Sailing*	33
CHRIS d'LACEY	*Routine Stuff*	39
SALLY ST.CLAIR	*Concerning The Kindness Of Aunts*	47
RON BERRY	*That Old Black Pasture*	52
SARAH CURRIE	*Astronomy*	82
DAVID ALMOND	*Jonadab*	85
CHARLES WILKINSON	*Treasure*	92
PATIENCE MACKARNESS	*Mushroom Soup*	103
WAYNE DEAN-RICHARDS	*The Dead Man*	115
ROBERT STONE	*An Uncommon Error*	118
CLAYTON LISTER	*Our Lady, The Virgin Lily*	133
NEIL GRIMMETT	*A Christmas Gift*	148
WILLIAM PALMER	*Even In Dreams, He Thought, We Lie*	155
MARK ASHETON	*The Entelechy Of Cyrus J. Porkbelly*	160
RHYS H. HUGHES	*The Troubadours Of Perception.*	165
MICHAEL KELLY	*Monstrous Regiments*	169
RICHARD BARLOW	*Things Of No Value*	179
SARAH SPILLER	*When Molly Met The Only Other People In The Whole World*	183
RICHARD C. ZIMLER	*The City For The Sea*	187
MICHAEL ZADOORIAN	*Mystery Spot*	194
First Person		
D. J. TAYLOR	*Success*	129
Editorial		
JOHN MURRAY	*Our Final Issue*	5
Photographs/Cover Photo		
PHILIP WOLMUTH		14, 67, 195
Subscriptions, Quizzes		15, 193
Contributors, Letters		4, 114

CONTRIBUTORS

FIRST PUBLISHED STORY
Mark Asheton is 24 and lives in Cardiff. **Julie Charalambides** is 37 and teaches Women's Writing in Bloomsbury. **Sarah Currie** lives in Surrey and is writing a book on ancient childhood. She did research on Roman murder at Brown University, USA. **Wayne Dean-Richards** is 33 and lives in the Midlands. He is working on a novel. **Clayton Lister** is 27 and lives in Reading. **Patience Mackarness** is 36 and teaches EFL in Bahrain. **Barèt Magarian** is 27 and lives in London. He likes sitting in Soho Gardens, watching the world go by. He is of Armenian extraction. **Sarah Spiller** is a TV reporter from Essex.
OTHERS
David Almond edited Panurge 1987-1993. He has a string of fine stories all linked thematically appearing in *Sunk Island Review, Iron, London Magazine and Critical Quarterly*. One other coming out with the *Edinburgh Review* won their Story Comp this year. He has two novels awaiting publication. **Richard Barlow** lives in Leicester and appeared in *New Writing 3*. **Ron Berry** is 76 and lives in the Rhondda. Author of five novels, four TV plays and a radio play, his first book is shortly to be reissued by Gomer Press. **Patrick Cunningham** is an Irishman living in London. A winner of the Hennessy Award he has also been in *Iron* and on the BBC. **Chris d'Lacey** was a winner in the Lancaster Story Competition 1995. He lives in Leicester. **Julia Darling** published *Bloodlines* with Panurge Publishing. This is to be serialised for BBC Women's Hour in 1996. **Neil Grimmett** has had fiction in *London Magazine* and *Iron* and lives in Somerset. **Rhys H. Hughes** appeared in Panurge 21 and lives in Cardiff. **Michael Kelly** has had stories in *Stand, Iron* and on Radio 3. He lives in Hull and West Africa. **William Palmer** has appeared several times in *Panurge*. All his Panurge stories will appear in *Four Last Things*(Secker) this year. His last novel was with Cape(*The Contract*) who are also doing his fourth novel in 1996. **Sally St Clair** was a winner in last year's Stand Competition. Born in 1953, she lives in Hampshire. **Robert Stone** lives in Ipswich and was in Panurge 19. He has also been in *Stand*. **D.J. Taylor's** latest novel is *English Settlements*(Chatto). He presented the awards for the Panurge Comp. 1994. **David Whitfield** is 30 and lives in Nottingham. His fiction has been in *London Magazine* and he has worked in a leprosy hospital. **Charles Wilkinson** is 46 and has had stories in *London Magazine* and *Best Stories 1990*. He lives in Watford and had a collection of poems out with Iron in 1987. **Michael Zadoorian** is an American who appeared in Panurge 20. **Richard C. Zimler** won First Prize in the Panurge Comp. 1994. He has a novel out with Gay Men's Press this year, *Unholy Ghost*. He lives with his lover Alex in Oporto. **Philip Wolmuth** worked in Syria and Palestine last year. **John Murray** has his fourth novel *Reiver Blues - A New Border Apocalypse*, published by Flambard in the summer of 1996. Flambard is disrtibuted to bookshops and libraries via Password Distributors.

EDITORIAL

Our Final Issue

This special souvenir edition containing about 100,000 words of new fiction, is the last issue of Panurge magazine we are very sorry to say. After twelve years and twenty-five issues we have finally decided to stop struggling with what is now an exhausting, impossible task. Like most small literary magazines we have always survived on a shoestring, but we also have the problem of being one of the very few UK outlets for stories, and the only one that regularly prints long ambitious ones. We are now getting about three times more submissions than we can comfortably cope with and *Panurge* is no longer tenable as a cottage industry run by a notional solo editor. Neither David Almond who edited the magazine 1987-1993 nor myself who has also just completed a six years stint (1984-87; 1993-6) ever envisaged it being inundated on the scale it is now, where we are clocking up some 4000 submissions a year. Our grant aid has remained scant throughout all that period and the subscription revenue is getting harder and harder to achieve as the years go by.

This also, by the way, explains why *Panurge* could never support an editorial team, and why, despite considerable effort on my part in the last few months, there is no one person or group stepping in with my departure. The economics of *Panurge* are such that for a 25 hour week rising to 50 hours near publication date, I pay myself a wage of £11 a week. It is not because I hate myself that I give myself these 1964 wages; it is because that is all there is to spare. Regional Arts Boards and the Arts Council consistently preach that magazine editors should pay themselves (not to speak of their contributors) the fair rate, but fail to put their money where their administrative mouths are, alas. Also and rather like the DSS, should you miraculously manage to bump up your subscription list, they keep their own contribution static, so that any extra revenue simply goes to pay for your extra print run.

However and to be honest, whatever the financial circumstances, I would still be finishing with the magazine at this point. My own writing has had to take second, third and tenth place in the last three years, as I have tried more or less single-handed to cope with the deluge. Confusingly I keep using the royal 'we', and some recent issues have had an impressive staff list on the title pages. But just like David Almond, I have done almost everything single-handed, bar the typesetting and a small amount of administrative work. It is Henry Swan who has done all my typesetting and thus I have called him my Production Editor, but I think that designation was less to flatter Henry, than to try and fool myself that I was somehow not alone. This also explains why David Almond did not wish to resume the editorship of something he worked on so brilliantly for six solid years. It was hard enough with 25 submissions a week to find time for his own writing; and it would be all but impossible under the present conditions.

People often compare *Panurge* to *Granta* in terms of its bulk and quality and attractive appearance, and there are those who might ask, well, if *Granta* can manage a phenomenal number of subscribers and run as a successful business, why not you? The answer to that is simple. *Granta* is a business success because it publishes exclusively established writers and journalists and is serviced by a coterie of London publishers and top shot agents who put their illustrious clients at the magazine's disposal with minimum fuss and maximum reward to

John Murray

themselves and their enterprises.

Panurge, by contrast, prints often brilliant work by people you have never heard of, and there is simply no way on earth of making any kind of commercial success out of unknown writers, all gathered together under the same roof in an anthology.

Last year I happened to talk at length with someone who had worked on the editorial staff of *Granta* when Bill Buford was in charge. She informed me that *never once* in all those years she was there, did Bill Buford ever accept *anything* from the unsolicited pile, no matter how excellent his colleagues thought it. I would be the first to agree that *Granta* is an excellent read, but in terms of editorial *courage* I would say it has almost none. To print the ready-made chapter proofs from a forthcoming Picador, amiably chucked at you by your mate from Picador three months before Picador publication. How much courage does that involve? How much risk? Whatever it says about *Granta*, it confirms literary agents in their truest identities. As literary pimps and literary procuresses, albeit of a charmed and effervescent kind. In keeping with this truth, the very worst manuscripts submitted to *Panurge* are those sent in by literary agents and especially those sent in by the big literary agents who are attracted by *Panurge's* reputation if not by its author fees.

Also and to apportion the blame fairly, short story writers are usually their own worst enemies. I would say less than a third of those who have appeared in *Panurge's* pages have ever consistently subscribed to the magazine itself. They better than anyone else in the world, know there is almost nowhere to send your stories once you've written the bloody things; so if they cannot support a notional lifeline, there is damn all chance that our target readers at *Stand, London Magazine* and the *Literary Review* will be persuaded to. And in fact, in 1996, they don't! One of the choicest ironies of the last three years is that the only reliable means of getting new subscription has been through putting promotion inserts in the *Writers News*, a cheerful market-oriented periodical for novice writers. Put inserts in *LM, LR, Stand* etc. in the mid-90s, and you get a response so derisory, you would have done better to give the money away to Amnesty International or scattered your several hundred pounds promotion costs as free fivers in the middle of Brampton, Cumbria. I am bound to be accused of defeatism at this point but let me point out that despite the obstacles I have *tripled* the number of *Panurge* subscribers in the past three years. Thanks to *the Writers News* and the *Panurge* fiction competition that is. The sad fact is that David Almond's few hundred subscribers were reliable core subscribers, and most of the ones I have won, have come and gone after a couple of issues. *Panurge* has rather too many words on the page and is too demanding a read for many would-be subscribers. Alternatively some short-term subscribers are writers themselves and are aghast and embittered at what they are expected to achieve to get between our covers. Hence they desert us in hundreds rather than dozens, and even ten reminders, even a free carriage clock or a handwritten plea from the editor will make no difference to their decision.

So there we are. It is sad to see a good magazine go and the short story market even more terminally hopeless than ever. However the real tragedy is not the folding of a single magazine but the fact that there is hardly any other magazine in existence seriously trying to look after short story writers. Hopefully

Editorial

the disappearance of *Panurge* will spur on someone somewhere to do something about an absurd situation. There ought to be at least three magazines like *Panurge*, not just one. I get three times as much publishable work as I can easily cope with, which is surely ample proof.

In any event, *Panurge* has lasted twelve years and has tried to sustain an ambitious formula that only good old *Passport* has ever tried to match. David Almond and I are proud of what we have achieved in the past twelve years. We broke all the rules in terms of what had gone before us, and yet for twelve years we staggered on to plenty of grateful applause from grateful fiction lovers. We both regularly printed stories that no one else would have had the nerve or the ambition to print. 12,000 word stories by debut writers. Virtuoso prose from unknown 19 year-olds (James Hannah, Panurge 23); ditto from unknown 78 year-olds (E. H Solomon, Panurge 21). Tough, demanding but excellent innovative work that would have made John Calder or Marion Boyars come out in sweats, never mind those charmers at Random House or Harper Collins who take counsel of the accountant rather than risk their necks and go for broke in the cause of literature of the enduring as opposed to the transient kind. It is so obvious these days it is hardly worth stating. Nonetheless here goes. If a new Joyce, Beckett, Woolf, Ronald Firbank etc. appeared on the scene now they would find precisely no one willing to print them in the UK in 1996. And that includes Fourth Estate, Serpent's Tail etc. who do a great job but have a partisan editorial taste as defined and exclusive as any of the big shots up the road. Hence *translation* publishers, laughably, are the ideal in these disgraceful times for UK literary publishing. Mike Schmidt at Carcanet will reprint three Eça de Queiroz novels in the same uncompromising list with the sure confidence that he will be unlikely to get his money back, never mind make a profit or swing any lateral deals or Frankfurt tie-ins and all the rest of the baloney. Yet he like everyone else is doing very little in the way of new fiction by new British writers. It is now rather easier to win first prize in the National Lottery than to get a first novel between covers. The literary agents have to be very choosy otherwise their ten per cents, their bread and butter, will dry up. Hence dozens of gifted writers are getting their talented manuscripts returned by both publishers and agents, frequently after a year long wait.

*

I have had as hard a time as any with my own books, which in part explains why I began *Panurge* in the first place. My first book *Samarkand* was turned down 25 times, then broadcast on Radio 3 immediately on publication. My third novel *Radio Activity* which received a good deal of critical acclaim, was rejected by 35 publishers. If I had my time over, I can assure you I wouldn't go through all that again. Here is what I would do if I were an unpublished writer who felt he had talent and could not get into print. I would save up a couple of thousand pounds by whatever possible means and I would have 500 copies privately printed. I would then go on a scenic coach trip of the whole of the country and disperse some 300 copies to selected libraries free of charge. The remaining 200 I would give away to friends or give to bookish-looking strangers passing through Brampton, possibly with a free bar of chocolate or tub of Cumberland Rum Butter, as a bribe for them to read the bloody thing. I mean this in perfect seriousness; I am not joking. All other orthodox routes are so weighted against

John Murray

you, that as I say you stand more chance of winning the Lottery. The old verities, the old certainties, however uncertain they were, simply no longer exist. There are no longer any Andre Deutschs or John Calders or Livia Gollanczes, willing to lose money in the cause of literary fiction by new British writers. The literary magazines are either full for three years ahead or are folding because of the deluge just like *Panurge* is now. The system is completely shot and the choice you have as an adult as opposed to a hopeless romantic is to walk away from it and start up your own. Whether it be self-publication, via the Internet, or reading your MSS aloud on a street corner on market day, you will have to find a new and lateral route. That is not defeatism. It really is the only way ahead.

*

A final and sincere thanks to all who have contributed to Panurge over its last three years. To Janet Bancroft for fine database and admin work; to Andy Williams for his covers; to Jessie Anderson for editorial work in 1995. A special word for the legendary typesetting of Henry Swan, (its excellence, speed and cheapness) at Union Lane, Brampton. Also to the brilliant printers, Peterson's. Also to our family breadwinner, my wife Annie. It was her job and her income much more than any grant aid or subscription money, that allowed me to spend most of my time on Panurge magazine. Lastly to all our readers, writers and subscribers, especially the ones who have been with us from the start.

John Murray, Brampton, Spring 1996

STOP PRESS - A NEW FICTION MAGAZINE?

There is a working chance that there may be a Northern Arts sponsored fiction magazine successor to Panurge magazine. **With a new editor, new name, new format etc.** Don't worry, all present and recent subscribers to Panurge will be circulated if such a magazine is to be launched.

Barèt Magarian

A Chance Encounter In The Café Royal

Every Wednesday I dine on my own in the Café Royal. I'm a wealthy man and I can afford it. I like it not because the food is outstanding but because the decor is. It speaks of another age, of a time that has been sealed off and distilled. The waiters all know me and always make great efforts to please me, they inquire after my health, and they know that I am not always in the best of health, they know too that I appreciate a little company as I'm an old man, old and a little disfigured by numerous deaths, divorces (two) and alienation. I sometimes feel that my money is the root of the problem. Who knows? If I have acquired a certain wisdom it must have been through the careful laundering of my dark money, my insistence on thrift and the regular keeping of accounts.

That Wednesday I was seated beside an attractive looking couple who were visibly involved with each other. The girl, like a rich Gypsy, had something serpentine about her gracefulness. She was at her ease amidst the silver plates and leather chairs. The boy wasn't. He looked so out of place, dressed oddly, wearing a badly knotted tie. It was a little bit comical. She was dressed very finely, in a black evening dress and her dark hair was tied behind her. Some strands of hair fell about her face, those that escaped her knot. Her face shone. A string of pearls was poised on her beautiful neck like a little garland of flowers and her dress was open to her breasts. I envied her beauty, the way that she moved, the ease with which she moved, the absence of deliberation. I envied the care with which she had dressed, the ready enjoyment that was signalled by such fastidiousness. The boy was much more like me. Sensing this, I chuckled to myself. I overheard him say something about wanting to become an actor. But he was a little clumsy and held his head in a peculiar manner. But he looked an amiable fellow. I thought briefly about their sex life, what it might have been like, if they would have let me watch them in exchange for a little cash. I dismissed the thought. The ghosts of pleasure, the desire for it still lingered. I had not managed to cleanse my life, like a Buddhist, of desire.

My main course arrived and I settled into it slowly. Tornadoes, the Café's speciality. It was very good. But alas I had no wine to do it real justice. My doctor had banned wine from my life some time ago as it had started to interfere more than usual with my digestion. Forgive this insistence on ill health but it is all that I have left to talk of. So I'm rather proud, in a way, of these various encumbrances that I carry around with me like luggage.

The couple had yet to order and they were milling over their menus. "Why don't we start with the dessert?" said the boy. I keep calling him a boy but he must have been about twenty-five. When I was twenty-five I got typhoid fever in Aleppo while working for an insurance company.

I beckoned to the wine waiter who approached almost immediately. He was a small man dressed rather elaborately and he had a golden medallion around his neck so that he might have been a cardinal. I looked up and said, "Can you fetch me a menu. I don't, or should I say, can't order for myself, but I should like to present this couple here" - I pointed in their direction - "with a gift." He wandered off and arrived a minute later with the menu which I examined for a few minutes. Meanwhile the lovers were silent, gazing into each other. I was touched by them and tried to imagine how they felt, what sensations were aroused by the sight of each other. It was no good, nothing came, I couldn't remember a similar encounter that I could unearth from the canopy of my past. I put the menu down and spoke some words in as light a tone as I could muster.

"Forgive me for interrupting but I have been watching you both from a distance and conclude that you must both be in love. I, as you've gathered, am an old old man. Such decrepitude, in my case, is an excuse for a frankness that I hope you will not misinterpret as anything other than honourable. Being decrepit it seems to me now that long ago I dropped the habit of loving and of being loved. And so I ask, as a friend of course, if you might share a little, some tantalising details, that is all, of how love feels. But please don't paint your picture in such a way that I might feel too keenly the presence of what is normally absent in my own life."

I coughed politely. The young woman was enchanted as I knew she would be. The young man was wary as I also knew he would be. There was a brief interlude while he shuffled about. Then she looked over to him as if to say, "You or me."

And then she broke into a smile and said with sudden confidence "My dear old gentleman, I find you and your request very charming but hardly feel that I can do justice to either. Our age, I feel, has forgotten how to love. Art has failed, God has deserted us and now it seems love has been shredded. But as to how we feel, or how I feel, for I can't speak for Paul, let me say only this: tonight I'm light, almost airborne. I feel indefatigable, ready to fall in love with three dozen men, my appetite for love scarcely to be satisfied by just the one, and I can feel a surge of its energy wash over me like waves over rocks."

I was truly captivated for a moment and sighed as she finished, then smiled broadly.

"That was nearly perfect. And now my friends I shall show you that I am not ungrateful. This readiness will be rewarded as I would like greatly to make you a present of some fine wine."

The waiter approached and I whispered to him as Paul made vague protestations, while the girl said nothing which delighted me even more. I looked away and watched the cardinal go about his business, then up at the ceiling and the chandeliers. I looked back at my little couple. The boy was staring hard at the menu. A minute passed. The girl looked over to me and said quietly, "Perhaps you'd like to sit with us?"

"Thank you, but no, I'm quite happy here on my little island."

"Are you sure?"

"Quite sure. It's a mistake to interfere in other people's affairs, I always find. One runs the risk of being considered poisonous and destructive."

There was a long pause. The girl looked hurt and shocked.

"Haven't you interfered already in our affairs" the boy asked, a little icily. I was annoyed.

"I should be honestly ashamed if that were the case. Correct me if I am wrong but I prefer to see mine as an innocent and harmless occupation. The only harm to be had is harm that I inflict on myself. But at least it proves that I am still alive. Now, there are other, less innocuous pursuits, I concede. But these are, at least in the realms of the interpersonal, practised almost entirely by women. Men are too stupid to truly become troublesome. I prefer the analogy that says a woman is like a cat and a man like a dog. I must go on a little more and add that

A Chance Encounter In The Café Royal

I would rather see a young couple basking in the sun and forgetting themselves. But I'm not claiming to be any saint. I'm a businessman, I make or rather made my living by feeding off other's weakness and naivety. But that, as they say, is another matter. I'm too tired to be interested in being truly intrusive. I regard this fact as tragic. Busybodies *are* quite charming if you think about it. I ask only that I be put in a hotel room somewhere, sealed off from the world and everything in it so that I can enjoy what is left me. Because, you see, people just don't listen, they don't use the ears that God has given them. So in future I shall be quiet, because when you are not quiet you are perceived either as wanting something or as... interfering in other people's... business."

I looked around me and cleared my throat. A party walked slowly into the Café. I guessed they were that dying breed: a large family. The father, tall, compassionate, formidable; the mother, tall, elegant, dressed in white; three young girls; one boy, the essence of inquisitive loneliness. They were bound to each other by invisible lines of harmony that stretched out to meet those who sat, like me, amidst silver plates and wine glasses. The sight of them made me ask myself what constituted interest and what interference. I was no longer sure of my own argument.

The girl looked toward me impatiently, trying to catch my attention.

"What if I were to tell you that I wanted you to interfere" she asked. "What then? Have you an answer? I am always meeting strangers, I seem to have a knack of chancing upon them. Perhaps I send out signals and I'm glad if I do. After all, people are important to me. If they weren't I should follow your example and book myself into that hotel room, but perhaps it wouldn't be such a gilded cage. I'm not so fussy, I prefer simplicity and ironing out the crudities and impurities. I try and make my life less, not more complicated. Paul likes complication though and he's always dying to know what's underneath the stone or the carpet or the pillow case. And he suspects that there *are* fairies at the bottom of the garden but he can't be sure. But I'm not really saying what I want to say. To go back to the first point, perhaps you'd care to join us, sit with us, not interfere in our affairs, nor preach, nor feel misunderstood. You don't have to be fit for human company, you only have to recognise that it's there, I suppose. I would like you to sit with us, please."

She finished and folded her arms slowly. I looked into her face, quite moved by her words. Her face looked different now. Her full lips were tight and anxious and a line appeared on her forehead that I had not noticed before. Her eyes were still and quiet. She had an oval face, her skin was slightly dark but unblemished and youthful. I sipped at my water and as I raised my glass the light of the chandeliers was caught in its delicate patterns. This brought my attention back to the bright surroundings of the Café. The couple at my side seemed to disappear. My gaze wandered slowly round in an arc of casual evaluation. Everybody was busy, preparing to order, tasting the wine, ordering, tasting the food, talking animatedly, talking. I felt happy, away from the messiness of everything, but yet I sensed that it was a droll cabaret, a carnival that was turning and spinning in front of my eyes, after all. I had the girl to thank for that. I sensed her peering at me, pressing for my answer. But I was too busy enjoying the view, it was a panoramic one and the scene before me glittered.

Julia Darling   BLOODLINES

Funny, poignant, abrasive, bizarre...Julia Darling's stories are **absolute dynamite**, and they're yours for only **£6.99 post free!**

BBC Radio 4 Kaleidoscope

'angry, ironic and self-assured...wonderful, very funny'

The Independent

'a razor-sharp edge...a consistently absorbing collection. Panurge can congratulate itself on a sound investment'

Please send me Julia Darling's book BLOODLINES for only £6.99 post free. I enclose a cheque for:

☐ £6.99 UK   ☐ £8 overseas   ☐ £10 Air Mail

Return to Panurge Publishing, Crooked Holme Farm Cottage, Brampton, Cumbria CA8 2AT UK. Tel.016977 - 41087

Name _ _ _ _ _ _ _ _ _ _ _

Address _ _ _ _ _ _ _ _ _ _
_ _ _ _ _ _ _ _ _ _ _
_ _ _ _ _ _ _ _ _ _ _
_ _ _ _ _ _ _ _ _ _ _

Julia Darling

The Bone Cafe

They were always drilling and digging around that windy limb of the coast.
The council were supposed to be making it into a car park, so that people could sit silently under tartan rugs looking out to sea, but however much they tried to flatten the earth it seemed to defeat the diggers. At that time there were still a few insecure buildings clinging to the cliff side, and an unsteady sign saying DANGER. LOOSE LAND.

I first came up here after my operation. If I stayed at home too long I found that I lived inside myself too much. I mentally picked at the stitches across my lower belly, folded back the flesh as if it was a curtain, and stepped into what I can only describe as an imaginary opencast mine.

So I started to walk, as far as I could, up to where the sea clung to the crooked coast as if it was a hand, pulling it further and further into its waters.

One day I was complaining to an indifferent seagull about a great hole in the middle of a public path, when a piece of grit landed in my eye and I found I couldn't see anything. I lurched about, my arms flailing, and fell sideways into the doorway of The Bone Cafe, and Slavenka said "Cappucino?" and a roar of steam cleaned the grit from my eye, and I found myself looking straight into the face of a glittering Russian woman with no teeth.

I like to think it was meant.

You could take off your face at the Bone Cafe. The Bone Cafe itself had no face. The word HERRING dropped from its forehead long ago. From the outside it was quite blank. The wind had blown away its facade, leaving an expressionless yellow wall, with two shining windows that were as perceptive as sailors' eyes.

Inside the floor was red, and the walls were hung with irregular pieces of driftwood, and ancient fish bones.

It had very few customers, but everyone there had lost something.

There was Ruth, who was recently bereaved and who sometimes clutched at an invisible hand. She wore long tear-stained scarves that got tangled up in her finger tips, and Martha, with her dappled face and cropped red hair, who sat shaking her head over and over again, looking into an empty tea cup as if it was telling her something challenging yet advantageous. Ruth told me that Martha had lost her innocence. She would not look up. At another table Henry, a crinkled Jamaican, sat wearing a top hat, spooning Russian ice cream into his delicate mouth. Henry told us that he was first black man to appear in the North of England , and grown men screamed for their mothers when they saw him. Now his skin was turning mysteriously white.

I often wanted to ask Slavenka about herself. Once I saw her polishing a samovar with her salty tears. She looked over all of us as if we were part of her powerful Russian body.

I wanted to stay forever in The Bone Cafe.

That's why I didn't mind when it happened.

It was nearly closing time, and already there were stars in an azure blue sky. I was pulling on my overcoat.

Outside the diggers and cranes were in a frenzy, battling with the uneven coast. The floor rumbled beneath us.

"Oh la!" said Ruth unsteadily.

Men, King's Cross, 1990

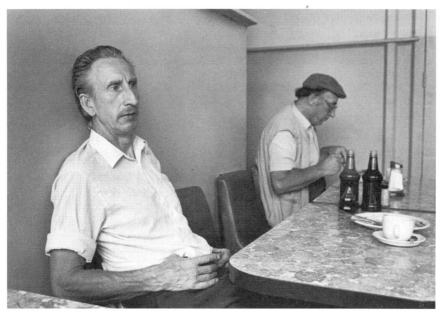

Philip Wolmuth

There was a sound like a branch breaking from a tree. I clutched at my stitches.
Then there was a wrenching crack and all the tables were thrown to one side. Henry's hat rolled into a corner. Martha clasped her teacup as if it was a buoy.
"Hey!!" shouted a man angrily from outside.
Slavenka got down on her knees and started to sing, and Ruth struggled to the steamy window and looked out.
"Lawks," she said.
Henry shut his eyes as if he was listening to an internal message
"Water," he whispered melodiously.
It was suddenly beautifully quiet. I hadn't noticed how noisy the world had become.
We rocked slightly.
"Good," said Martha and put her teacup down.

*

We were on our way. Severed from the world, in our unevenness. Riding up and down on a clod of earth amongst the walls of waves, while a row of Council workmen waved helplessly from the broken shore.

Subscriptions

As the magazine is folding there are no resubscriptions due obviously. This special issue you are reading is a **double issue Panurge 24/25 and contains all the fiction(about l00,000 words) that would have gone in the two 1996 issues.** Thus we have managed all our subscription obligations at this difficult time. We have got in twice as much fiction by the simple expedient of halving the typesize!

Patrick Cunningham

The Haven

Each summer of my childhood, in the month of August, I was sent on loan to the home of my Aunt Josephine and my Uncle Russell, the well-known lobotomist. They were a childless couple and it was considered only right that my parents, whom God had blessed with three other sons besides myself, should afford them a temporary taste of the joys of parenthood. And who could blame my parents if they hoped that Uncle Russell, when the time came, might see to my launching into the world, might perhaps even invite me to follow his footsteps into the lucrative world of lobotomy.

My uncle's driver, Sylvester, came in the Daimler to pick me up. My brothers and I called him Silly; my mother smacked my hand when she overheard me, but I had meant no disrespect. Sylvester was never referred to as a chauffeur - my aunt and uncle were not show-off types in spite of their wealth - but he had all the mannerisms of that profession, leaping out to open the door of the Daimler, standing to attention as I clambered in. He had a peculiarity of saying everything twice. "It's a nice day; I say it's a nice day. I'll put the luggage in the boot; I say I'll put the luggage in the boot," he would say, all in one breath. He had been a patient of my uncle.

Sylvester liked to tell me stories of accidents and disasters as we drove along. Aunt Josephine knew of this habit and had advised me to pay no attention. She said that Sylvester imagined things. "Dangerous cars these are if they're not driven properly," he said. "I say, they're dangerous cars. Queen Mary turned over in one of these."

"There's no such person," I said. "The Queen's name is Queen Elizabeth."

"Down Putney way, I say; turned right over. Queen Mary did," Sylvester said.

My aunt and uncle had a big old house on the slopes below Wimbledon Common. From the top windows you could see the factory roofs of Wandsworth, but lower down the trees shielded them from this intrusion. The house was called The Haven, and when I first read the name on the gatepost I thought the letters spelt The Heaven, for I had never come across the word 'haven'. And 'heaven' seemed appropriate, for it was a house where pleasures were plentiful, where no petty economies needed to be made and where I was never required to dry the dishes or take vegetable peelings out to the dustbin.

In front was a lawn, with a huge cedar of Lebanon in the centre under which the deckchairs and rugs were moved in the afternoons when the sun became too hot. The croquet hoops were set out between the hydrangeas, and Cassie, the youngest of the servants, brought lemonade in glasses frosted with sugar. Cassie jumped if anyone called her name too loudly and often dropped things. Uncle Russell had brought her from a hospital in Caernarvonshire. She had been one of his patients. "Cassie can black a grate as well as anyone can," Aunt Josephine said of her.

Mostly I loved the attention lavished on me by Uncle Russell and Aunt Josephine. At home I was used to being one of a group, the third child, enjoying neither the status of the eldest nor the lenience shown to the youngest, but here I was the centre of attention.

Aunt Josephine and Uncle Russell were sitting under the cedar tree when I

The Haven

arrived. They hugged and patted and squeezed me almost more than I wanted, but not quite.
"Take the boy's bag up to his room," Uncle Russell told Sylvester.
"I'll take the bag up to the room; I say, I'll take the bag up to the room," Sylvester said.
"Well, get on with it!" Uncle Russell said.
"Honestly!" Aunt Josephine said.
My bedroom was the second best in the house, looking on to the lawn and only lacking the bay window that my aunt and uncle's room had.
"What had Sylvester to say for himself?" my aunt asked, checking as she usually did.
"He said the Queen's car turned over in Putney."
"Pay no heed," Aunt Josephine said, "Sylvester always gets things mixed up. Your uncle should have cut off a bigger slice when he was about it."
I didn't need to ask her what she was talking about. Uncle Russell had explained to me what needed to be done when people had untidy bits in their brains that they didn't know what to do with.
"It's like having too many cupboards in your bedroom," my uncle had told me. "You fill them up with things you don't need and rubbish that's best thrown away. The same with the brain. It can get clogged up with memories and fancies and ideas that a person's best without. So I go in with my scalpel and with a snip here and a snip there I make everything tidy and manageable. People are the better for it afterwards, less trouble to themselves and others. Believe me, they are."
I believed him. Anyone would have believed Uncle Russell. But I wondered how he knew which bits of the brain held the things people wanted, the good memories and the good ideas, and which bits were clogged up with the rubbish that wasn't any good. And I thought I would have liked to have had a good root among the rubbish before it was thrown out because sometimes what one person thought was rubbish another person thought was a treasure, like in a jumble sale. And I wondered what Sylvester was like and what Cassie was like before Uncle Russell had given their brains a good spring cleaning.
The cook was Mrs Orora who had been married to a sailor from abroad. When Mr Orora had failed to return from a voyage, Mrs Orora, so my aunt said, had gone to pieces. "It was your Uncle Russell," she told me, "who helped her pull herself together." The consequence of this was that Mrs Orora had forgotten how to modulate her voice. Though she kept to the back parts of the house, her booming tones penetrated to the garden if a door or window was left open. "She's not a London person, you see," my aunt explained in excuse. "She comes originally from the turnip fields of Norfolk. The turnip folk are accustomed to shouting to one another across the fields. All our people here are from outside of London. We have opened our doors to provide a haven for them all."
Mrs Orora was sometimes an embarrassment, for things that were better whispered or that should have remained within her head as random thoughts were boomed out over the kitchen, the scullery and the back yard One day I asked Uncle Russell why she shouted all the time. "You can't win 'em all," Uncle Russell said.
It was unfortunate for Cassie, who had a nervous disposition, that she had to

Patrick Cunningham

work with Mrs Orora and this may have accounted for the amount of crockery she broke. "Servants!" my Aunt Josephine often exclaimed. "I could write a book!"

Mrs Orora was the same size and shape as Aunt Josephine and so she received my aunt's plentiful cast-offs. These clothes were the joy of Mrs Orora's life. She always kept her newest acquisition hanging on a satin-padded hanger on a hook on the back of the kitchen door. She would invite me to inspect them if I happened to go in. "Read this," she would shout at me, opening the skirt of a coat and pointing to the label.

"Marshall and Snelgrove, Oxford Street, London West One," I would read, or: "Derry and Toms, Kensington High Street, London West Eight."

"There now!" she would shout. "Marshall and Snelgrove London West One. Who would believe it! I don't read," she would add, as if it were a bad habit from which she had kept aloof.

"Mrs Orora is best on the far side of a sturdy door," my aunt said.

Cody was the last member of staff. He was kitchen boy, garden boy and houseboy and did a lot of the carrying, for there was a lot of carrying to be done at The Haven. Aunt Josephine was always on the move, like a royal court of old, from one room to another, from one corner of the garden to another, following the sun. Cody was called upon to carry the cushions, the footstool, the card-table for her games of Patience, the wind-up gramophone, her magazines and books. Cassie brought the little coach-table and the tray with the refreshments of the hour.

Cody rarely spoke: he rarely met one's eye. He performed each task with the same steady movements. It was mostly his back one saw, bent over a flowerbed or intent on some task. "Cody likes to be left alone," my aunt said. "He is reliable when you tell him precisely what to do." She did not tell me his history.

On Saturdays Cassie had her evening out. She walked down Wimbledon Hill and went to the pictures at the Odeon. On Mondays, in the steamy laundry room, she passed on to Mrs Orora and me the story of the film. Mrs Orora did not attend the cinema. She did not like crowds and she could not bear sitting still for two hours, but she liked to hear the plots and she loved to explain to Cassie and me the mistakes and follies of the characters. She was especially harsh in her judgements of the female characters. "That was her big mistake," she would say. "No good expecting a man to put up with that kind of carry-on."

She was always dubious about the happy endings of the films. "That girl could as easily have ended up in the gutter," she would say. "Take it as a warning, Cassie. It don't do to take chances with a man."

Cassie could never believe that there might have been an alternative outcome to the drama, and sometimes an argument ensued. Mrs Orora's voice became louder and louder until eventually Cassie began to cry or Aunt Josephine came from the front of the house to see what was the matter and to hunt me out into the garden.

It was on the first Saturday of my holiday that Mrs Orora's brother arrived. Aunt Josephine, Uncle Russell and I were sitting under the cedar tree, shaded from the sun. Cassie brought us the news. We had seen the small, wiry man in the blue serge suit come up the avenue and go round to the back door. We knew that whatever business brought him to The Haven would be attended to there.

The Haven

"It's Eugene," Cassie said. "Mrs Orora's brother. He come on a Green Line bus."

It was too hot for this news to be of interest. We waited to see Eugene go again. But he did not go. It was late afternoon when he came around the side of the house and across the lawn to us, followed by Mrs Orora. He halted in front of us, Mrs Orora standing several paces behind her brother.

"Eugene has something to say," Mrs Orora shouted.

What Eugene had to say was that his wife had passed away and that he had come to take Mrs Orora back with him to Norfolk. There was a home for her with him, he said. There was paid work in the turnip fields. I seem to remember that he emphasised the word 'paid'.

My uncle got up from his deckchair to reply to this proposal. He was a tall man. He towered over Mrs Orora's brother.

"You want your sister to go with you to Norfolk, do you?" he asked.

"I come on a Green Line bus," Eugene said. "I come to take her back."

Uncle Russell gazed down at him. "Such a move would seem singularly inappropriate, would it not?"

Eugene made no reply.

"I asked you a question," Uncle Russell said.

"Depends how you look at it," Eugene said.

"There is only one way to look at it," Uncle Russell said.

There was a long silence. Mrs Orora and Eugene seemed to be examining the lawn for signs of weeds.

"That will be all," Aunt Josephine said then. Mrs Orora said: "Yes'm," in a tone much lower than her usual shout and she turned and went back around the side of the house to the kitchen. Eugene waited for a few moments longer under the gaze of Uncle Russell and Aunt Josephine, then he, too, turned and followed Mrs Orora and we settled back in our deckchairs.

"The very idea!" Aunt Josephine exclaimed. "Those good clothes I gave her would look quite out of place in the turnip fields."

Mrs Orora was in low spirits for a few days. She did not shout. She showed no interest in Cassie's account of the Saturday night film. The kitchen was quiet.

She perked up when Aunt Josephine presented her with the previous year's winter coat, a sturdy tweed.

"It's a Windsmoor," Aunt Josephine told her. "You cannot buy better. The buttons alone would cost a fortune."

Mrs Orora tried it on. She walked up and down the kitchen.

"It could have been made for you," Aunt Josephine said.

*

I thought I was the only one to see Eugene waiting to take Cassie out on the following Saturday. It had been dull and showery and we had not sat in the garden. I was in my bedroom doing a jigsaw puzzle of Windsor Castle. When I looked through the window and saw Eugene in the drive, standing between two yew trees, I guessed he had come to take Mrs Orora away in secret to the turnip fields. I thought it wrong of her, when she had just accepted the gift of the Windsmoor coat, to run away from The Haven where everything was nice.

And then I saw Cassie hurrying down the pathway that divided the rose garden into two. She had on her pink dress and a white cardigan and she carried

Patrick Cunningham

a little bag made from raffia that Aunt Josephine had brought back from Portugal for her. Eugene met her at the corner and without stopping they walked quickly down the drive and out of sight.

The next morning, while we were at breakfast, there was shouting in the kitchen and the sound of a dish crashing on to the tiled floor. My aunt turned her eyes to heaven. She said: "Is it worth it? I ask you, is it worth it?"

Uncle Russell offered no reply and because I was not sure what she meant I said nothing either. She rose from the table and went to quell the disturbance. When she came back she said: "Mrs Orora says her brother has a notion for Cassie. It seems he came all the way from Norfolk to take her to the pictures on Saturday."

"I saw him," I said. "I saw him waiting in the avenue."

"The nerve!" Aunt Josephine said.

"See that Cody keeps him off the place," my uncle said.

"It's my opinion that Cody himself has a notion for Cassie - if my eyes don't deceive me," Aunt Josephine said.

"They're here to work, not to have notions about one another," Uncle Russell said.

All that day the kitchen was quiet and when I went in to the laundry room to hear Cassie's account of Saturday's film she and Mrs Orora were working together in silence.

"Did you enjoy yourself at the cinema, Cassie?" I enquired.

"Well you may ask!" Mrs Orora said.

This was too much for Cassie. She began to cry. She let go of the handle of the old wooden mangle and turned and went out of the room, banging the door behind her.

"See!" Mrs Orora said. "What good would a girl like that be to a working man on his own?"

"Do you mean Eugene?" I asked.

"Well, I don't mean Clark Gable," she said. "I blame those Hollywood pictures she goes to. Fill her mind with notions."

"Maybe Cody has a notion for her," I suggested.

"Cody!" she said. "Cody has no more sense in his head than a ball of string. Now be off about your business and leave me to mine."

I turned to go but she called me back.

"What makes you think Cody has a notion for Cassie?" she asked.

"Aunt Josephine said so," I told her. "Aunt Josephine said if her eyes don't deceive her Cody has a notion for Cassie."

"Is there no end to men's foolishness?" Mrs Orora asked.

"I don't know," I said.

"They'd be two of a kind at any rate," she said.

On the next Saturday afternoon I happened to be at my bedroom window again, whether by accident or design I can't remember, but probably by design, since I'd completed the jigsaw of Windsor Castle. This time it was Cody who waited by the yew tree. He was smoking a cigarette and his shovel stood against one of the trees. When Eugene appeared at the turn of the avenue Cody put out his cigarette with his fingers and stowed it away in a pocket of his waistcoat.

He stepped out from the trees and stood in the centre of the avenue, leaning

The Haven

on the shovel. Eugene stopped for a moment and then came forward again. I pulled back the net curtains, the better to see. Eugene halted in front of Cody and they spoke for a few moments. I could see their lips move. Then Cody pushed Eugene on the shoulder and Eugene staggered back. He steadied himself and tried to circle round Cody but Cody pushed him again. I knew what they were feeling, because that was the kind of fight I often had with my classmates in the schoolyard, pushing each other and making threats. But then the struggle took a more serious turn. Cody lifted his shovel, swung it, and hit Eugene in the middle of the back. Eugene stumbled, fell and lay face down, not moving. In fright I let the curtain fall back into place, then pulled it up again. Eugene was still lying prone; Cody stood looking down at him.

I ran from the room. I ran downstairs to the drawing-room where Aunt Josephine sat listening to a play on the wireless. "Cody's killed Eugene," I shouted.

"What did you say?" Aunt Josephine said, her mind still occupied with the drama on the Home Service.

"Cody's killed Eugene - out on the avenue!"

"Heaven help us!" Aunt Josephine exclaimed, pulling herself up from the depths of the armchair. "I told him just to tell Eugene to be off about his business if he came again. Go tell your uncle, child. No, don't - he's having his nap. Are you sure you're not mistaken? Show me where it happened, child. We can't have this kind of thing going on. Your uncle must put a stop to it. Perhaps you'd better call him after all."

She followed me out to the hall. "Mrs Orora! Mrs Orora!" she shouted. "Come at once. Your brother's had an accident."

There was a shriek from the back quarters and as we went out the front door Mrs Orora's heavy footsteps followed us along the parquet. Once outside, we could see that Eugene had not been murdered after all. He was being helped to his feet by Cody. He looked dazed and his nose was bleeding.

"He must have tripped," Aunt Josephine said to Mrs Orora.

Mrs Orora ran ahead of us down the avenue. "What happened to you, Eugene?" she shouted. "What happened to you?"

"He knocked me down with the bloody shovel," Eugene said.

Mrs Orora turned to Cody and hit him across the side of his head with her open hand. "You need locking up," she shouted. "I told you to keep him away from Cassie, not to half murder him."

We all turned at the sound of an upstairs window being pushed open. Uncle Russell, in his dressing-gown, stuck his head out. "What in hell's name is going on?" he called out.

"You'd better come down," Aunt Josephine said. "There's murder and mayhem going on here. It's all too much for me."

At that moment the side door of the house opened and closed and Cassie stood there, dressed in her pink dress and white cardigan and carrying her raffia handbag. When she saw us all standing in the avenue she stopped, uncertain what to do. Then she seemed to pull herself together and advanced towards us. I could see her face getting red as she came abreast of us. "Afternoon," she said politely, looking straight ahead. She walked on by, gathering speed as she got to the turn in the avenue.

Patrick Cunningham

"Well, I like that!" Mrs Orora exclaimed as Cassie disappeared from sight.

Eugene was pressing the back of his hand to his nose in an effort to stop the bleeding. Cody had moved into the shadow of the trees, still holding the shovel. Mrs Orora produced a tiny handkerchief and attempted to minister to Eugene, but he shook her off. Then Uncle Russell appeared. He had put on his tie and jacket.

"Cody - back to your work!" he ordered. He did not enquire what had happened. "Mrs Orora, take your brother inside, clean him up and give him a cup of tea. I want no more disturbance - is that understood?"

"Don't want no cup of tea," Eugene said. "I'm going to fetch a constable."

"No need for that," Uncle Russell said.

"Every need," Eugene said.

Mrs Orora tried to cajole Eugene but he shook her off and walked away, his hand still up to his nose, his head inclined backwards to help stop the flow of blood.

"Let him go," Uncle Russell said. "The police will keep him in the cells for the night, like as not. I don't want to see him here again, Mrs Orora, is that clear?"

"I had no hand, act nor part in his coming here," Mrs Orora protested.

"Well, see that he stays away," Uncle Russell said. "Poor Cassie is not safe with him around."

"And bring some tea to the drawing-room," Aunt Josephine said. "I feel quite faint."

Uncle Russell went back upstairs to continue his nap and Aunt Josephine asked me to stay with her in the drawing-room. She opened a new box of chocolates and tried to catch up with the play on the wireless, but it was too late. She could make no sense of it.

"Our afternoon is quite ruined," she said. "Can you understand people behaving like that?"

"No," I said. But I was trying hard to understand. I was trying to work out who had ordered Cody to hit Eugene with the shovel, for Cody always did as he was ordered and never did anything unless he was ordered. He was like a toy that had to be wound up with a key.

Next morning two policemen called. Uncle Russell saw them in his study. Afterwards he walked with them out into the garden and stood there chatting to them. They seemed shy, I thought. He pointed out the strawberry tree and the other rare shrubs. He put his hand on the shoulder of one of them in friendly fashion and walked all the way down to the gate to see them off. He looked angry when he returned and went to his study and did not reappear until lunch-time.

Cassie served lunch. She was even more nervous than usual and allowed the soup to overflow on to the lip of each of our plates, a return to an old habit of which Aunt Josephine had cured her only after long perseverance. My aunt did not reproach her on this occasion and indeed little was said during the meal. Afterwards my aunt and uncle went in to the drawing-room together and shut the door.

Later, Uncle Russell came out to me in the garden. He put his hand on my shoulder and I remembered him doing the same thing with the policeman earlier

The Haven

that day. "Your aunt's not feeling all that well, old chap," he said, "so I'm packing her off to bed for a few days. Not much fun for you here on your own, so Sylvester will drive you home in the morning. I've telephoned your mother to explain. And it's best to say nothing about what happened yesterday. We wouldn't want your parents to think badly of poor Cody. So mum's the word, eh?"

In the Daimler next morning Sylvester said: "Cody says he knocked that Eugene's block off, Saturday. Knocked his block off, Cody did."

"Cody has a notion for Cassie," I suggested.

"That's right, that's right, that's right," Sylvester said.

I did not tell my parents about the happenings of Saturday, not because Uncle Russell had told me not to, but perhaps because I was reaching the age when one does not tell one's parents everything or perhaps because I had not quite worked out exactly what there was to tell.

In any case they heard about it when Aunt Josephine phoned some weeks later to tell them that Cody had been bound over to keep the peace. Mrs Orora's brother had persisted in his ridiculous complaints, she told them, and there had been a lot of most unpleasant publicity in the local paper. Insinuations had been made about Uncle Russell's employing his former patients - as if, Aunt Josephine said, anyone else would have dreamt of employing them. The matter had been blown up out of all proportion and Russell was very annoyed. It was the ingratitude, Aunt Josephine said, that hurt the most.

It was my last holiday at The Haven. That winter Uncle Russell decided to retire early and settle in a warmer climate - for the sake of my aunt's health, we were told. They bought a villa in Antibes, living in a more modest style than before, but enjoying the mild winters. We did not hear a great deal of them; a note added to their Christmas card, a postcard once or twice a year. The sense that my family might have had expectations from them, great or small, faded away, if indeed it ever existed outside my imagination. It became understood that we would rise or fall by our own efforts, and we mostly rose, even if to no spectacular heights.

Eventually The Haven was knocked down and a block of flats was built in its place - thirty-five Havens instead of one. I sometimes drive by on my way to London. The cedar tree and the strawberry tree have gone. Cassie and Cody, Mrs Orora and Sylvester have gone. I sometimes wonder what became of them. Mrs Orora and Sylvester would be old now, if they are still alive. Did Cassie choose Cody or Eugene, or neither? Did she end up in an institution or in a hostel, cared for by the community, or in a shop doorway, cared for by nobody? Or might she be found working alongside Eugene in the turnip fields of Norfolk, if indeed there are still turnip fields in Norfolk?

Julie Charalambides

Mrs Corallo

Four floors above the elegant shoppers on Via Monte Napoleone was my four o'clock lesson, and my first student, Mrs Corallo. The penthouse suite was reached via a dark mirrored lift which swished breathlessly upward and whose dull gold doors slid open into a domed vestibule of honey-coloured marble. There was one door opposite the lift and that too was of dull gold metal, there was no handle on it, no lock and no bell, not any that I could discern anyway. I thought of beating on it, then of going away, but noticed a small gold box on the wall to the left of the door. When I raised the lid I found a row of numbered squares and one with 'prema' which I pushed. Simultaneously a light grew bright above me; no doubt I was on camera somewhere but the lens was well concealed. The door moved silently inward to reveal the most unlikely and unexpected keeper of such - a huge woman with a heap of dark hair knotted on her huge head who smiled broadly and bade me enter.

Conchetta was Mrs Corallo's maid and had a heart as big as her arse. She also had a bosom like a shelf on which she would balance gilt trays of freshly-squeezed orange juice or home-made lemonade in tall misty glasses clinking with ice. In her large hard hands she brought plates of biscuits, dusty with icing sugar and airy cakes, weighted down with real vanilla custard. She was a maid in heaven, but although Mrs Corallo lived so near to the clouds her home had an air of lubricity more appropriate to a bordello.

That first day I followed Conchetta's generous behind through the extraordinary apartment in a state of enchantment, like an astonished gawping fish. The front door opened immediately into a great round lounge, lit by a glass dome which rendered the room an aquarium, an effect further enhanced by the huge fleshy plants that thrust glossy leaves and curly fronds upward to the light. Shiny cushions of turquoise and crimson and purple and blue were scattered across the curved white newbuck sofa like tropical jewels and my feet sank into the plush white carpet, as soft and deep as desert sand.

There were several archways leading off this room; I only ever went through one. This was the entrance to a long corridor whose lemon walls were strung with beads, small citrine beads that formed a curtain down either side of the tunnel, hanging from a silver rail concealing the source of the soft uplighting. Overhead the curved lemon ceiling was refreshingly clear, and it was in this cool corridor that I would oxygenate my senses before succumbing to the opium den of Mrs Corallo's bedroom.

One entered through an invisible but palpable wall of tuberose and patchouli; indeed her perfume was so heavy it remained stagnant in the room. It bludgeoned all other senses into submission, even Conchetta's cakes tasted of flowers. Once in an effort to make conversation that wasn't about the vagaries of English grammar, I queried the origin of this olfactory sin. She leaned back in her chair, narrowed her large dark eyes and smiled - the effect was intended to be enigmatic.

"Ma cara mia, questo é il mio secreto."

I hope she guarded it well.

A more inappropriate setting for the begetting of anything other than carnal knowledge I could never imagine, but Mrs C insisted on taking her lessons in the boudoir.

Mrs Corallo

The room was surprisingly small, or maybe it was just the clutter that made it appear so. These walls too were well hung, but here red ribbons fell from cornice to floor, and to every ribbon was tied every piece of bric-à-brac imaginable, and some that weren't. Beads of every kind, colour, shape and size; paper putti, tiny concertinas of fans, miniature carnival masks, silk and lace and paper flowers. These covered three walls; the fourth was all of glass and opened onto a balcony festooned with foliage. On either side of the glass were draped gold curtains, caught up with red cords. There was in fact very little furniture in the room; a large bed, a small white wood table with suitably ornate legs, and a white chair with a red velvet seat that looked as if it had been carved and painted by Capodimonte.

One chair, two sitters. I was ordered onto the bed and Mrs C sat on the chair opposite, the table between us. Whether this was power play or some fantasy setting I never ascertained; it was however, extremely uncomfortable. First, I was always seated on the side of the bed that faced the balcony, so the glorious afternoon sun was invariably full in my face. This meant that I often left the boudoir with streaks of mascara on my cheeks where the brightness made my eyes water. Secondly, the bed was covered with the same heavy cloth as the curtains, a shiny gold lamé.

Although the season was officially Spring I was already in Summer mode; light, bright strappy dresses with little bolero jackets in silky fabrics that were impossible to place on the lamé. I would slide down like a slick and then slide myself back, the heels of my hands pushed hard against the mattress in an attempt to impede the inevitable progression of my bum to bed's edge. When I needed my hands to turn pages, gesticulate or eat and drink, I perched birdlike on the balls of my feet, the rest of my body only glancing off the gold.

My attention to Mrs C was therefore minimal, distracted as I was by the light, the lamé and the dog. He was the major distraction, lolling against the wall opposite the end of the bed, I was always aware of the massive Alsatian that shared Mrs C's boudoir. He lay still for the most part and Mrs C assured me that he was absolutely harmless and far too lazy to move let alone leap on me. In fact he spent almost every lesson masturbating. I had never seen a dog's prick before and when I first noticed from the corner of my watering eye the dog licking at its belly I thought that, like a cat, it was cleaning itself. When Mrs C realised the direction of my attention she laughed. She had a laugh that rang high and sweet like a child's and which always surprised me; I felt a throaty chuckle would have been more in keeping with her demeanour and her age, all of thirty six,

"*Guarda pure, che palanca di cazzo!*"

I did exactly as she bade me, I looked and saw the monstrous appendage and was instantly as petrified.

"*Molto grande no? Gli uomini non hanno una cosa cosi, non possono dare cosi tanto gioia alle donne come Kurt...*"

She looked at me wholly unabashed, willing me to meet her eyes, willing some reaction from me other than acute embarrassment at the shameful images in my young head. Was I supposed to get down on the floor beside Kurt and proffer him my arse? Was I supposed to ask Mrs Corallo to show me how and how much Kurt gave her pleasure? While I was trying desperately to find an appropriate response the hours of teaching finally paid off,

Julie Charalambides

"Do you know the English word for *cazzo* Mrs C?"
Mrs C did what she always did at my discomfort, she laughed, *"No cara dimmi, dimmi."*
"Prick, or if you wish to use the biological or medical term, penis. Prick however, is a verb - please look it up in your dictionary while I go to the washroom."

Mrs C continued to smile her knowing smile while I excused myself and hid until my flaming red cheeks had paled to the pink of the washroom walls. I could have stayed there the full hour, but the colour scheme was utterly nauseating and every minute away was a victory for Mrs C. I had very nearly lost my ground as her tutor, she had nearly become mine, and if truth be told I knew even then that her lessons would be far more interesting and useful.

Mrs C was one of my more able students. Already fluent in French and German as well as her native Italian, she wished to add English to her many social skills, and apparently fill several afternoons with my company. Married to a wealthy scion of an old Lombardian family, she was a legendary hostess and guest, and would entertain me with tales of outrageous dinner parties and weekends away. She was at ease and often in charge of any situation, any environment, and I was deeply ignorant of so many things, but I resolved that the acquisition of sophistication should not necessitate the begetting of dogs. I walked purposefully across the corridor and back into the bedroom, took up my pencil and demanded the meaning of 'prick'. To put it in context I told her the story of the Sleeping Beauty, pausing every now and then to note the new vocabulary - spinning wheel, spool, brambles, fairy and witch were all entered in the red leather-bound book she kept for our lessons.

The telling of the tale was a spell in itself. Perrault's analogy of sexual awakening so enthralled both of us, that the coarseness of our earlier mutual fantasy was smoothed into a pleasant hour, ended only by Conchetta's announcement of a waiting guest, by which time the thoroughly sated dog had fallen asleep.

The sexual power Mrs C exercised over me was far greater than that attempted by any man. First, I had no defences against a woman, I had never had any need either emotionally or sexually. I had never even guarded against my own attraction to my own sex. It was merely the logical result of an artistic education reinforcing the obvious assumption of the female form as the zenith of beauty, and consequently desire. In my convent school the only naked men we beheld were nailed to crosses; had their chests torn open to reveal flaming bleeding hearts; their heads on platters; or at their most benign, old and of necessity for God's purpose, impotent. A veritable pit of imagery for those of a sadomasochistic bent, but I was always drawn to the soft-faced Madonnas, muted Murillos and languid Leonardos.

Mrs C had the wide dusky face of a Pre-Raphaelite muse, heavy-lidded eyes, a full pouting mouth always coated in red, and a mane of black hair that she left free, unlike the well-coiffeured ladies in whose salons I enunciated my perfect English. She was not a typical Milanese, she had the dark sensuality of a southern Italian, shapely and short. The only truly elegant thing about her was her shoes, and even they were just a little too well heeled to be *di moda*. As a hobby she owned one of the most exclusive shoe shops in Milan, in which I taught two members of her staff. I always entered it with feet of clay, and wanted instantly to be barefoot and pedicured, ready to slip into the soft leather, to be strapped, clasped and buckled in one of those fetishistic dreams. Mrs C took great interest in my footwear, patronising me with appraising glances at my market goods with their counterfeit Gs and Vs; and when I left Italy she gave me a pair of the softest, smoothest tan coloured riding boots, so high they had to be mounted.

No, Mrs C was not like the other Milanese woman; she ate the cakes and biscuits that Conchetta brought, and was unfashionably voluptuous. Her clothes were unusually comfortable-looking. They seemed to caress rather than constrain her; figure-hugging and breast-enhancing - she had a magnificent bosom of which she displayed a great deal. She was always interested in what I wore, telling me to turn around, feeling the fabric, feeling the fit. No doubt her interest in my clothes and the body on which they hung would have seemed suspect to one more worldly. But I was quite literally under her spell, from the moment I entered her boudoir, I was in her thrall. Any superior stance I took as her teacher was illusory, I could ask to see her homework, interrogate her as to sentence construction, tense and meaning, but she always made me feel as if she were indulging me and that we were just playing at teachers and pets. It was all very improper and after only a month of lessons all pretence at learning was swept aside when she revealed herself to me as my sexual Svengali.

When assessing my appearance her hands sometimes lingered over my hips which she would grasp and sway to observe the flare of the skirt. To gauge the length she would kneel before me and smooth the seams against my thighs, and tell me *"Troppo corto"*, or *"Troppo lungo"*, then suggest I bring it back next time for Conchetta to fix.

But on this occasion, when she reached the hem her hand slid up and under my dress. She ran her manicured nails along the inside of my left thigh, naked and damp in the Italian heat. When she reached the top she rubbed the satin of my knickers with all five fingers, then she slipped one of them under the lace-edged elastic.

I do not know if I was faint with terror - lack of oxygen because I had been holding my breath from the moment of her hand's ascent - or from an amazed desire. I thought I would fall but Mrs C's other hand clasped my right leg behind the knee. At the same instant her finger was inside my cunt. I was stood at the end of the bed and with the utmost tact Mrs C manoeuvred me back onto it, her finger ever deeper in me. I sat and stared in wonder at Mrs C's smiling face - I had no voice and would not have used it to bid her stop if I could find it. The wonderful languor that was spreading throughout my body was emanating from her fingertips - those pressing into my thigh and my cunt. She removed her finger and wiped it slowly across her lipsticked lips. She rose from between my thighs and brought her face up to mine.

It all seemed to be happening so slowly - I knew her kiss before I felt it; such softness and strangeness. The intelligent horror at her act abated at the gentleness of her mouth - I did not taste myself, only the glossy pigment. So close her perfume had a narcotic effect, and I was utterly entranced. Her hands rose to my face and pushed aside the long hair clinging damply to my neck, which she kissed and licked as if it were delicious. She then removed my bolero and slipped down the ribbon straps of my dress.

Julie Charalambides

My breasts were young and small enough to go unbound, and her hands covered their nakedness. When her caresses became almost painful, she kissed them - tiny kisses around each aureole until I was sure my nipples were spurting pleasure - and then she sucked them, suckled me in her hot mouth. I felt fluid, and my cunt was flowing.

Until now I had been absolutely submissive, quite literally in her hands, but my need intervened. I pushed her away from my breast and while she knelt there before me I pulled up my dress over my head so I was sat on the gold in only my black knickers. I swear Mrs C had never stopped smiling and she continued to do so as she pulled them down. She didn't remove my shoe but raised one leg to free it of the elastic which she then left garlanded around the other.

I lay back against the usually uncomfortable coverlet - now cool and silky and friendly - and watched as Mrs C brought her fingers and her mouth to my cunt. I was so wet and wide that I could not tell how many fingers she had inside me, or at what point they were joined by her tongue. She knew where to lick and where to suck and I came quickly. As the tension eased out of me I became fearful of the consequences - would she now speak to me - break the silence and the spell?

She said nothing but was soon lying beside me. She wrapped her arms around me like a cape - the combination of her skin and the fabric of her dress against me so erotic, I thought I would debauch myself with obscene words and requests, but Mrs C took my hand and placed it on her breast. I could feel the nipple through the fabric, and with a calm curiosity sought to expose her beauty by unbuttoning the soft cotton shift she was wearing. The little gold buttons ran its whole length but my fingers did not tremble as I undid every one. I was not surprised to find underneath a veritable confection of lingerie. The brassiere was all of the palest, finest pink lace, through which the dark aureoles showed like the hearts of roses, and obviously served no structural purpose. Nor did it need to - her bosom was pneumatic. I lifted the filigree straps off her shoulders, and drew the lace down under her breasts, which had the effect of increasing their amplitude. I had never felt such skin before so rich and full. The nipples rose between my curious fingers and I bent my head to kiss them.

I had sometimes looked down on my own breasts and wanted to put them in my mouth, but I could not have imagined the actual sensation. When caressing my breasts I was always confused by the double experience of touching and being touched. Similarly when slipping my fingers in my cunt the delight at its silkiness was lessened by the intellectual gap between giving and receiving the pleasure. Now the gap was closed, the circle was complete - I could revel wholly in the feel of a woman's body, knowing that in following my own needs I was fulfilling hers. In her body I saw the mirror of my own desire - I saw myself beneath the body of the man who had loved me, and those that were yet to take their pleasure in me. Mrs C's body was a fuller version of my own - I could not feel the bones beneath her skin, as she could mine, but we both had small waists which slipped into generous hips. I had always admired that curve and the slope from hip to knee and now I could run my hands up and down and around. I felt like Pygmalion fashioning his Galatea, or was it Narcissus falling in love with his own image?

It was Mrs C's turn to disentangle herself from my embrace, and she did so to remove the undone dress which she shrugged to the floor. She then bent her arms

back behind her back, and I saw the loveliness of a gesture that must have delighted so many men as she deftly unhooked the bra, drew the straps down her arms, and flung it laughing onto the white chair. Her knickers were of the same pink lace and just as elegantly removed. For a few moments she stood naked before me - a vision of Venus with a froth of lace at her feet. Then she lay down upon the bed and pulled me on top of her. Our breasts crushed into one and I felt the burr of her pubic hair against mine. She drew my face to hers to kiss, then smoothed her hands down my back and ran her fingers between my buttocks. All the while she had been moving gently beneath me, pushing against my pubis; now she dug her fingers hard into my arse, so hard it almost hurt, but the softness of her labia was glorious, and she came with a shudder and a sigh that echoed in my head. I lay back upon the bed and became aware of a shape in the doorway - it was Conchetta and she too was smiling at me,
"*Ma carissimia Giulia, dovresti mangiare ancora torte fatte da me.*"
Conchetta was from the South and did not believe in thinness - fashionable or otherwise - and was concerned at my recent loss of weight. The dog had not moved - a seasoned voyeur he had observed us from his vantage point opposite.
I should have been ashamed but I was delighted. I was so light with delight I wanted to laugh, so I did. Mrs C raised herself up on her elbow and looked down on me,
"You are happy now teacher, your student is also happy, happy to have taught her teacher so much."
She turned to Conchetta,
"*Tutto é pronto?*"
Conchetta nodded and Mrs C stood and took my hand to pull me from the bed,
"Enough lessons, now let us bathe and dress."
Still laughing and naked, we followed Conchetta's well-covered buttocks further down the lemon corridor and into a room I had never entered before. I had always used the absurdly baroque washroom opposite Mrs C's bedroom, so was amazed to find myself in a cool white room with a skylight, through which the fading day was falling into a huge white marble tub, raised on golden claws, upon a black marble platform in the middle of the white marbled floor. There were no mirrors and no sinks. In the corners of the room were the same fleshy green fronds that filled the domed lounge. And along the walls were marble benches on golden clawed legs, some piled high with thick black towels, others covered in exquisite glass bottles in brilliant colours, no doubt full of the heady perfumes and oils that filled the air and floated in the blue water in the tub.
"This is my husband's bathroom. Do get in, the water will be just right."
I walked to the altar of our ablutions, and looked down on the shrine of my body that Mrs C had so recently worshipped. I don't know if it was the light overhead, the voice bidding me enter the water, the fragrant steam rising like incense, or the almost holy nature of the experience, but I was suddenly in another place before another bath, between another two women.
I remembered a Summer in Lourdes, and the time I went to bathe in the blessed waters, more out of curiosity than faith, of which I had very little even then. A stout old woman told me to remove all but my bra, and put on a dark blue cotton cape. I asked for a towel but was assured I would not need one - the water

Julie Charalambides

was so cold it would evaporate off my skin. Then I was led to a pair of blue and white striped curtains which miraculously parted, and a thin nun and a busty young girl, both with their sleeves rolled up, were smiling in front of a concrete horse trough. One of them whisked off the cape, the other my bra, and a damp pink camisole was slapped over my offending breasts. They led me down the steps into the icy water. I had to kiss a plastic statue of the Virgin at the far end of the trough while they chanted a few Hail Marys.

"We are going to lower you into the water, relax, you'll be safe."

I remember a strange dullness in the air, my body was numb. I did not feel the water on my skin but was aware of it tightening. In fact for several hours after the bath it was as if my skin had shrunk.

I looked down on my now adult form, seeming to bloom with the moisture in the air. I looked down on my adored breasts with the blue veins marbling the white and the dark pink aureoles. I thought of the thin, small-breasted, unknowing and untried virgin, not quite believing but so hopeful, in the icy bath in Lourdes, and felt the tears brimming at the edges of my eyes. Was it sadness or nostalgia or relief at her passing? The old shames rose like a shroud from my past to cover my present glory. I drew my arm across my breast and my hand over my pudenda.

"You are my Venus, *cara*. Botticelli imagined you - I have *la realta* here with me."

She was before me now and cupped my face in her hands.

"Look at me *cara*, why are you sad? You were so happy - you must not be sad, smile for me, *mia bella Venere*."

She raised my chin on her fingertips, as delicately as if my head had been a butterfly balancing there. I looked into her lovely dark eyes and saw myself reflected, a goddess of her desire, and the pale young thing I was formed a tear on my cheek which Mrs C kissed away.

"Vieni, cara."

She stepped into the bath and turned to take my hand to help me in. The water on my skin was bliss. We sat at either end of the vast tub and a magician, Conchetta, produced two crystal stems bubbling with champagne from out of the moist air. I poured the stinging golden liquid down my parched throat, any remnant of regret dispersing with the bubbles, and felt as rich and lovely as a fairytale princess. I had wandered not into a bathroom but another world. Mrs C raised the champagne bottle from the floor beside the bath and moved towards me with a wicked smile.

"I will wash my Julia, Conchetta, leave us alone."

Conchetta took the empty champagne glass from my hand, turned on her low shabby heels and walked out of the room. Mrs C slid towards me, the soapy water lapping around her buoyant breasts. She lifted the bottle to my lips and ran the champagne into my mouth. I swallowed but the champagne was coursing down my chin. Mrs C licked it off then poured what remained in the bottle over my breasts. My skin was so shocked at the coldness I did not immediately sense Mrs C's tongue slipping around and over my nipples. She raised her head to kiss me as she lowered the bottle onto the floor, but her lips still tasted of champagne. She kissed me so long and so hard I drew back for breath, Mrs C laughed and told me to stand, which I did, the water around my knees and running down my

Mrs Corallo

body. She remained kneeling in the tub looking up at me, and parted her lips, pushing the tip of her tongue between her smile, and applied its coolness to the bud of my clitoris now visible in the midst of my wet pubic hair. As she licked she slid her hands up my thighs, then into me, up to my cervix, and I came, the walls of my vagina closing around her long fingers. I felt them leave my cunt and the cold air on my clitoris, as Mrs C lay back in the tub, spreading her legs.

I knelt down in the water between her knees, and ran my hands up and down her soapy thighs while she pleasured herself. Her head was thrown back over the white curve of the bath edge, and her breasts rose and fell impossibly full in time to the rhythm of her fingers. Her nipples were so perfectly round I wanted to bite them off and roll them in my mouth. As I leant forward to suck them Mrs C came, and her whole body shuddered and the breath caught in her throat. Lost in herself, I watched her unwatched, and realised I wanted so much to be her, under her skin, inside her body. I wished more than anything to have a hard penis to put in her soft body, to spurt inside her like champagne, to wrap my arms around her as she wrapped her legs around me. She raised her head and opened her eyes.

"*Basta, cara.* Enough love making for today."

We conducted an almost ritual soaping of each other's body in wondering silence, then Mrs C called for Conchetta. She brought towels from the benches to wrap around us. She helped us both from the bath, then devoted herself to me, while Mrs C pulled on a huge black towelling robe. At some point Mrs C must have left the room, but I did not notice, I was too immersed in Conchetta's attentions to my toilette. She rubbed me briskly with the fluffy towel, drying every part of my body, even between my toes. She then took a pot of cream from the nearest bench and smoothed the white lotion all over me. I recognised the heady aroma of Mrs C's scent and for once succumbed to its intoxication. I was too stunned by the recent welcome assault on my senses to fight off another. In fact the perfume hung around me for days and permeated every piece of clothing I wore. She dusted me with silky powder and sat back upon her heels to admire her handiwork, smiling proudly as if she had just dressed me for my first communion. But I was of course naked and my clothes were damp and abandoned in a far room. As if on cue, Mrs C appeared in the arched doorway, her arms full of bright colours.

"Here Julia, now I will dress you as you should be dressed. I chose these for you after our first lesson. I know now how you feel, but I always knew how you should look - and it isn't like me, though you think you want to. No, you will be Julia, my beloved, our beloved."

She threw the confusion of colours and textures on a bench and from it pulled first a haze of lingerie in pale green. The near-transparent bra served only to accentuate my breasts and when she pulled an apricot camisole over my head, my nipples could clearly be seen pointing through the silk. Conchetta knelt again at my feet, and lifted first one foot then the other into her lap, to slip on the sheerest ivory stockings which needed no suspenders to hold them up. A sliver of elastic and lace circled each thigh and further heightened my divided sense of cloth and nakedness. I had to step into a peppermint green skirt, so short it barely covered the lace tops of the stockings, and a pair of ivory-coloured shoes with low gold heels. Mrs C then handed Conchetta a tailored jacket with narrow lapels. It was the same colour and silk as the skirt, but lined in the apricot of the camisole. As

Julie Charalambides

Conchetta slid it up my arms and onto my shoulders, I felt as if I were donning the soft water of the bath from which I had just risen. Conchetta stood back smiling and Mrs C came towards me with her hands full of pearls. She clasped a pair of baroque drops on my earlobes and a long rope of milky globes around my neck.

"We are almost done, come."

She took my hand and led me back along the corridor, Conchetta waddling behind, and into her familiar washroom. She sat me down upon the velvet-covered stool and took a silver-backed brush from the vanity unit. She stroked it through my damp and tangled hair which she swept up into a pleat and fastened with a myriad of hairpins which Conchetta passed to her over my head. She brushed apricot powder along my cheekbones and painted my mouth with coral. I gathered she had finished with me when she blotted my lips with her own - as her tongue slipped between them I grew immediately wet and my heart began to race.

"No *cara*, enough love for today. I do not want to spoil our handiwork. Look how beautiful you are."

I turned to the mirror at my side and saw that I was indeed beautiful. The fragile colours of my clothes contrasted strongly with the honeyed richness of my skin, which felt as if it were straining at the fabric in its eagerness to be once again naked under Mrs C's admiring eyes. I was as elegant and sexually self-assured as any Milanese and to the reflection of my lover I said:

"It is you who have made me beautiful by making love to me and now your clothes are making love to me."

She smiled with her whole radiant face.

"And I have made you happy, no more sad Julia. But now you must go, my husband will be here soon."

I must have experienced a second's jealousy and several moments' curiosity, as I thought of the man who shared Mrs C's bed and body, her past and her future. In fact he filled my thoughts as I sped down in the lift, and his imagined face was so strongly impressed upon my mind's eye, that the reality did not immediately register as the lift doors swished open and there he was before me.

"Buona sera signorina."

I blushed furiously and fled silently past him into the darkening evening over his shoulder. It must have been him, that lift only went to the penthouse. I hurried out into Via Monte Napoleone and was half-amazed to find it still there. Nothing changed, apart from the light, apart from me.

David Whitfield

Plane Sailing

It is two in the morning, and I have been awake for just over an hour. The sound which awoke me was the chiming of the grandfather clock on the landing outside our bedroom; a single chime, which I assumed signalled one o'clock, until I realised that it could have been the tail-end of two chimes, or three, or even the signalling of a quarter-hour, and so I have stayed awake out of some obscure desire to discover the truth without resorting to looking at my watch. It has taken me until now to decide that I was right all along.

The body next to me is breathing deeply, but quietly. Every time she exhales the sheet rises two inches or more, but there is no noise to be heard from her quarter-open mouth. About twenty minutes ago I wiped a thin trail of saliva from the corners of her mouth, but she did not stir. I turn to face her now, and I hope, for my sake, that she is not dreaming.

*

The body belongs to Lucy, and I have now reached the stage where I am convinced that it is quite the nicest thing about her. She has a dancer's legs, a swimmer's back, a diva's front, and the long, slender arms and hands of the hairdresser at the salon you used to visit too often when you were thirteen. She is, however, involved in none of these professions; she is an actress, and not just of the 'resting' variety, either. She does work. And the feel of this body of hers is such that, for a while, I truly believed that whenever the two of us were irritable or frustrated or even just sad, all we had to do was to immerse ourselves in our two bodies and we would then emerge - however long later - at a point where we both felt cleansed and calmed and happier.

It worked, too, for a short period; but a long time ago our hearts and our brains began to come up with more problems than our bodies could ever hope to solve. And now we're content just to let our bodies go their own way; and if they do just happen to meet, and if neither of them have got anything better to do, then we might just let them have their moment of fun.

As I watch her now, she quickly turns from her back onto her side, so that she is facing me. Her arms fold protectively around her breasts, and her knees rise slowly - foetally - up the bed, until they are level with her childlike hips. At least one of us feels protected.

*

We met at a blood donor session just over two years ago. I have had four noteworthy relationships with women so far in my life; and three of them have been with women I met at the blood bank. I don't know why - it's not as if I use the place as a deliberate pick-up joint, it must simply be that the women you meet there make certain assumptions about you (that you have a small degree of thoughtfulness, of altruism, and so on) which give you a colossal advantage when it comes to getting to know them. You may be a perverted monster, but at least there's *one* good side to you. And in any case, when you're lying down for your obligatory ten minutes after the needle comes out, there's really nothing else to do *except* have a chat to the person next to you.

So I first started talking to Lucy when we'd both grown bored of looking at the two posters the authorities had deigned to put on the ceiling of the rest room; and before I knew it four weeks had passed and we were spending more nights

David Whitfield

together than apart. If I sound plaintive or indifferent about this then I owe Lucy an apology, because I did genuinely miss her on the occasions we were apart; but I did have a problem with the way we were developing. There was a definite *predictability* to the progression of our relationship; a metronomic regularity to the way in which we passed from the cosiness of the first date to the entirely balanced exchange of subsequent phone calls, then through the traditional period of late-night coffee and medium petting to the start of our sex-life proper and the depositing of spare clothes in the other's flat. It was all too normal, as if there was an obligation placed upon us to take it in turns to suggest the next move forward. And the process was neither slow enough to make us believe we were worth waiting for, nor quick enough to indicate that we couldn't hold back and were onto something special.

But underpinning all of this was a genuine fondness. On her part I think she had found someone she could trust, after a succession of men she could neither trust nor - at times - feel safe with; and on mine I was grateful to be with someone whose perspective on life was at odds with my own. Lucy had been born a decade too late, but she made up for it with all the hippie accoutrements you could dream of - tasselled skirts, a roomful of Marilyn, candles, joss sticks, even the 'Why?' war poster on the back of her bedroom door. Her Sixties 'retro' thang coupled with her somewhat over-earnest approach to her acting could have sat uneasily with my own hard-nosed career sense; but they rarely came into real conflict. What others saw in her as being ostentatious, I somehow put down as being endearing.

*

The clock strikes the half-hour, and I lift my head away from the pillow in order to listen for noises from the outside world. I want to know that there's something out there, but I can hear nothing; it's the lowest ebb of the night, with the pubs all emptied and even the slowest curry-house dawdler safe in bed, but still too early for anyone to be thinking about the next day's work. I look at her face. I used to think she was beautiful when she slept, but now I'm not so sure; there seems to be an arrogance to her features which I've never noticed when she's awake. I turn away and decide that I'll try and stay awake through the night.

*

After a year of inconvenience living overlapping lives, we decided to rent together; but before we could do so Lucy was offered a part in a play. Not a big part and not a new play - a touring production of 'Blithe Spirit' - but enticing enough for there never to be any doubt as to whether she would take it and put our housing plans on ice. There was a month of pre-tour rehearsals followed by the start of the tour in the North, so that by the time I actually got to visit her and see the play we hadn't seen each other for nearly six weeks.

I knew from phone calls, of course, that she was throwing herself into it and loving every minute. But I have never been in love with telephones (they exaggerate my vocal limitations, whilst obliterating all the shrugs, glances and other features which actually enable people to understand what on earth I'm on about) and so our calls had been few, certainly on my side. So I was wholly unprepared for the change in her when we met, in a small Scarborough pub, at the end of the evening show of which I thought she had been the most professional part.

Plane Sailing

She was the same on the outside. But inside she had become, in the space of a few weeks, a terrible hybrid of raw Sixties sentimentality (which had been there before) and of Nineties new age pseudo-philosophy (which certainly hadn't). She spent the first hour bouncing acting theories off me and then, when we had returned to the extended burrow of bedsits she lived in with some of the other actors, she bounced off theories about everything else. Holistic, spiritualistic, masochistic - I'm guessing at what they all were because I simply can't remember. She was over-laden with jewellery (copper to repel arthritis, crystals for her spirit, moodstones for her moods) and, I soon discovered, she was taking more drugs; not hard ones, but still more than either of us were used to.

And this was no avant-garde company she was with; it was an everyday working group. But it seemed that she must have taken on board everything anybody may casually have mentioned to her over the previous six weeks. Drugs, seances, colonic irrigation were all the same to her. Because they were all different to what had gone before.

*

We are lying in her bed in the house of actors, right now; I think I heard one of them go downstairs to the kitchen a few moments ago. They are a normal, friendly group of people, and I can imagine Lucy and her all-embracing enthusiasm getting on their nerves a little. I know how they feel. I have seen Lucy three times since Scarborough, and the last time, when she came to visit me on her day off, was the first time that I have ever found myself looking forward to her departure rather than her arrival. Which is a terrible thing to say. But however much she sees her adoption of new ideas, beliefs and mottos as a sign of receptiveness, I can only see it as a sign of weakness. And I would have said as much, except that it was then that she came up with her idea.

*

She was lying across me as I sat on the sofa, listening to Springsteen. Her head rested in my lap, her eyes were gazing at the ceiling.

"You know," she said, "we hardly ever speak on the phone."

"I know - but it's difficult."

"How?"

"You're always working in the evening. And you know I can't ring in the day."

"But you never write, you pig," she continued. "I'd like to get a letter every now and then."

"But what's the point of writing?" I protested. "I spend two hours writing a letter and then it's all old hat because you've called me up."

She seemed to accept this, and for a few minutes we were silent. The track on the CD faded away, and in came 'Drive All Night', the finest moment on 'The River'. I settled back in the sofa, let the music take me away for half a song, and was about to prepare myself for the sweeping entrance of Clarence's sax solo when Lucy pushed herself up on her elbows, turned to face me and said,

"Now, don't dismiss this without even thinking about it."

"What?" I said irritably, having missed the crucial moment.

"I know you're not very open about these sort of things. But how would you feel if we could see each other every single night?"

"How do you mean?"

David Whitfield

"Don't jump down my throat now. But what if we could meet every night in" - she hesitated - "our dreams?"
"Our dreams? Oh, for God's -"
"No!" she almost shouted. "Look, just don't dismiss it until you've heard me out! Have you ever heard of lucid dreaming?"
"No," I admitted.
"Then listen. When you dream, don't you find that sometimes you can actually control what's happening to you - you *can* run away from that monster behind you, or you *can* jump out of that car before it goes over the edge? Well, that's really the start of lucid dreaming; the only difference is that in real lucid dreaming you could actually, say, escape from the monster and then decide to go to Rio in your dream, and off you'd go. There aren't any limits.
"Now some people can lucid dream naturally; but we can all *learn* to do it. All you have to do is to get to know the way you dream, by remembering what you were thinking about before you went to sleep, and then writing down everything you recall when you wake up, and soon you can control the type of things you dream about. After that it's just a question of practice, spending time sleeping and waking and getting better at doing certain things inside your dream. That's about the stage I'm at now.
"Now the thing is this - when you get two people who can lucid dream, they can actually *meet in their dreams*. You just arrange before you sleep that you're going to meet in Trafalgar Square, or wherever, and then when you're in your dream you've both got the control to go there and meet - and I know what you're going to say, that it's not as if we're *really* meeting, but that's just it, it *is*. How do we know that dreams aren't any more real than us sitting here now? People who believe in reincarnation believe that there are seven different planes of consciousness that we have to go through eventually, and that when we dream it's just a glimpse of a plane that's one higher than the one we're on at the moment. So what's wrong with us trying to get to a higher plane? Just imagine! We could go to the States for the night, or fly over to India - fly ourselves that is, these are dreams - or just stay and be here with each other. Come on, let's give it a try - what have we got to lose after all? What do you think?"

The room was silent. The CD had finished about halfway into her speech. I paused for a moment, collecting my thoughts and filing them away neatly in the appropriate recesses of my mind.

"I think," I said, easing my legs out from under her head and preparing to stand, "it's the biggest load of bollocks I've ever heard in my life."

*

All this was two weeks ago today. And since then, in each of the fourteen nights that have passed, she has featured in every one of my dreams. Or at least in every dream that I can remember, which may or may not be the same thing; I don't know enough about dreams to tell. I dream that I am at a party; and she is the host. I am taking an exam at school; she is sitting at the desk behind me, rubbing her big toe against the outside of my thigh. I am naked in the heart of the Amazonian rainforest surrounded by a plethora of divinely beautiful native girls, all of whom I am about to deflower; she emerges from one of the huts, wagging her finger and admonishing all of the lust from within me.

Of course I do dream about Lucy quite often, especially in the days directly

Plane Sailing

before or after a visit. But never as frequently as I have in the past two weeks, and never with such awful clarity; when I wake up I'm always shocked that she isn't actually there in the room with me.

And so, naturally, I have begun to think about what she said. I was sceptical at the time, and still am, but after the ninth or tenth time there was little else to turn to. If she *is* doing strange things in her sleep, then she's gone beyond what we ever even discussed, because I'm not a part of the plan and she's - presumably - having to go to sleep, lucid dream her way over to my flat, wait for me to fall asleep and then latch onto me as soon as I start dreaming. All without my knowledge. Which scares me; I might be ambivalent about being with her in my waking hours, but I know damn well I need some respite from her during the night.

The clock strikes four. I'm feeling drowsy. I had decided, when I came here, that the best thing to do would be to try and catch her in the act; to wake up from a dream in which she'd just made an appearance, shake her awake and ask her what the hell she thought she was doing. I should be able to tell if she's actually doing it from the look on her face. But now I don't know if I can really be bothered. I might just stay awake for another hour or two, get dressed, and then slip quietly out of the house.

*

I'm riding a motorbike, slowly climbing a steep hill on a hot Greek island. I'm not wearing a helmet, so I can feel the sun gently burning the top of my head; and there's no breeze because I'm climbing too slowly. It's beautiful. The small road is twisting through a parched landscape of olive trees, wizened bushes and earth which has been whitened by the sun; if I turn my head and look behind me I can see the sharp blue of the bay below and a flotilla of yachts silhouetted against the blurred horizon beyond.

And there's something else, when I turn my head; another motorbike, about twenty metres behind me. It's coming out of the corner from which I'm still myself recovering, the rider behind me struggling to change gear mid-corner without losing any momentum. I see her foot searching for the right gear and then hear, more than see, the bike kick into action as it pulls away. She grins a huge grin at me and I wave back.

We love each other, obviously; but it's more than that. As she draws along beside me and we pull the top of the mountain ever nearer, I have a feeling that this moment - this day - is the culmination of months or years of effort; I don't know what it is exactly, but we've been through something hard together, perhaps been kept apart by outside forces, and this is the first time we've really been together. It's the first time on a bike for either of us too, I'm sure, and I'm intoxicated by the mixture of the feel of the sun, the smell of the air, the power of the bike and the knowledge that this person next to me, with her dark hair flying out behind her, is with me for good.

We're coming to the brow of the hill now, and we don't know what's on the other side. We seem to slow as we approach the top, as if to savour the moment and increase the anticipation, and by the time the front wheels of the bikes flatten out at the top we've almost stopped and the heat of the sun is bearing down on us. I lift my hand to my face to wipe away a droplet of sweat which has already formed now the bikes have halted; and when I take it away I see for the first

David Whitfield

the vista before us. No-one can have been here before. We'd know if they had. In the distance, the road - our road - sweeps majestically down to a tiny, empty, perfect beach, a thin strip of warm sand waiting for our toes and our heels and our flurrying steps. And beyond the first stretch of clear, shallow water, within easy swimming distance, is a small island, immaculately formed and ready to be lived on, loved on, whatever. We've arrived. I turn to her to give her the look that means everything. Except it's not her, it's Lucy.

*

We awake brutally at the same time; me from shock, Lucy because I think I kicked her bike over and sent her toppling in the final desperate moments of my dream. I'm halfway out of bed before she thinks to look over towards me, and there, straightaway, I know that she was on the island; I half expect her to be clutching a towel or a bottle of sun lotion.

"No," I say softly, as I move to the end of the bed to pick up my clothes, "I don't want to know. Just stay there and I'll go."

She doesn't know what to say. She looks hurt and confused and powerful all at the same time, and she just lies there, her head and shoulders raised from the pillow, and stares at me.

"I'm going now," I whisper, "but I don't want you to follow me. And I don't want you to ring me - okay?"

I'm struggling with my trousers; it's hard to find the legs when I have to keep looking at her. Then I find one, and then the other, and with my shirt in my arms I open the door and step out of the room. I glance at the grandfather clock on the landing, then run quickly down the stairs, which are carpeted but still feel cold against my bare feet.

At the front door I feel safe. I push my shoes on quickly, and pull my shirt over my head, then open the door. There's a noise behind me, but I don't stop to look. I hurl the door open and run out into the street and carry on running. But I'm not quick enough. I try not to, but I can't stop myself hearing her cheery, throwaway, farewell shout.

She says that she'll see me tonight.

Chris d'Lacey
Routine Stuff

I was standing at a urinal when the sniffer dog came in. Ninety-something pounds of German black and tan; the sort of education that can dry a man up - but I was getting to the point of shaking off, anyway. So I took my time, I didn't get rash. I stood there, shaking, watching this dog going in and out the cubicles. Sniffing in the empty pans. Sniffing around. The handler stood in the doorway, silent. He wore a blue-ribbed sweater, ill-fitting trousers, some sort of crest on his black-peaked cap.

"What's up?" I said out the corner of my mouth.

His polished shoes squeaked. He bounced a few times. "We got a call just now. We're checking it out."

"Call?" I muttered. I was staring at the porcelain, waiting for drips. "A bomb, are you saying? You mean there's a bomb?"

I looked over my shoulder at the handler's face. He was a plain-looking man with surly, grey eyes. He held me a moment then his gaze flicked down. "Stand still," he said, "and you won't get hurt." I looked down where he was staring. The dog was sniffing at the seat of my pants, at the base of the urinal, at the flesh in my hands. The handler waited till the dog was sure, then he snapped his fingers and the dog pulled back. He opened the door and the dog slipped past him. It went out into the foyer. There was movement there.

I zipped myself up. I was trembling. I said, "What's it all about? Is it gonna go up?"

The handler sniffed. He pulled down his cap. He crossed his arms tight and said, "You tell me."

I shrugged. I told him, "I don't understand."

His pallid features dissolved to a smile. "You'd better get out into the foyer," he said. "We're clearing the building; it's just a precaution." He paused as he turned. "Oh yeah, you might like to know that Tasker found nothing explosive in your trousers." He pulled a false grin and went after the dog.

I stood a few seconds after he'd gone. Then I turned and stared at myself in the mirrors. I looked pale, unhealthy, thinner than usual. I told myself I should comb my hair; maybe I looked like I might plant bombs. So I took the comb from the pocket of my jeans, wet the teeth beneath the cold water tap. I groomed myself to go back outside. I thought about Alsatians slavering at the mouth. When I pushed the comb back into my pocket a dribble of urine ran along my thigh.

*

There were three of them out there, hanging round the foyer at the Medical School entrance. Security men: two in sweaters with black and tan dogs; one in a pale cream, knee-length mackintosh. The crackle of their short wave radios broke the air. The mackintosh man was speaking quietly, giving orders into his set. His eyes picked me up as I exited the gents.

"You," he said, pointing. "Wait there, please." He meant by the lift. I half-shook my head. I didn't want to be ordered around.

"I've work to do," I said, but I squeaked it out. I sounded nervous; I could have looked the same. So I decided to wait. It was better not to push it. One of the sweater men was tugging at his dog.

Chris d'Lacey

"You work here, do you?"

The mackintosh man was talking to me now. He looked like a man I'd seen in films: hard, smooth features; greased white hair. He showed me a card. Mr Douglas was his name.

I nodded. I told him, "Fourteen years."

"Department?" he said.

"This floor, Anatomy."

He dragged one finger across his bottom lip. "Good," he nodded. "Your ID, please."

I lifted my shoulders. We never carry cards - not on a Sunday afternoon in November. We have cards, yes, but we don't know where to clip them. It's stuck away somewhere, in a drawer, in my room. "I'm on the computer, the Mainframe," I said. I offered to show him. Then I took out my keys, my front door pass, my cheque card, cash card, library card - the lot.

Mr Douglas smiled. He accepted my keys. He peeled through the bunch and handed them back. "These rooms," he said, taking something from his pocket.

"Rooms?" I said.

"Where the bodies are," he said. He held up a plan of the floor below us.

I was silent then. I nodded in silence. I looked at the dogs. They were sitting to heel with their tongues lolling out. I knew then. I knew that they needed a guide.

"You want me to take you through the D.R.?"

"The whole lower ground," Mr Douglas confirmed. "You open the rooms and the dog goes in. The dog does it all. You wait by the door. You can lock up again when the dog has been round. Do you think you can help us out, Mr... Wilson?"

I gaped at the ground, ran my hands through my hair. I put the sole of my shoe up flat against the lift. I said, "Look, I came in to do some work: I didn't expect to get my ass blown off." I wanted to say, 'That's your job, pal'. One of the handlers looked at me and yawned.

Mr Douglas took a slow breath in through his nose. He drew back his cuff and adjusted his watch. "I don't know what you mean. What do you mean by that?"

I grimaced slightly and nodded at the handler who had been in the gents. "This guy here, he said you got a call. Someone's planted a bomb in the building."

Mr Douglas smiled and shifted his feet. He touched one finger to the bridge of his nose. He thought for a moment then leaned in close like he wanted to kiss. "David, don't go jumping to conclusions. It's true, we've received a threatening call. But we have the caller, we know who it is. He's out in the car. We're talking to him now. We've met this particular turkey before. It likes to run around with its head off at times. It's nothing serious, but we have to check it out. We have to go round. It's just routine."

Mr Douglas stood away. He opened his hands in a 'help me' gesture. His radio crackled. He let it speak. They were on the third floor, inspecting the labs. The animal unit was clear, they said.

"Jesus," I whispered. There was sweat on my face. I heard Mr Douglas speak into his set. They had access to Area 1, he confirmed. He was sending

Routine Stuff

Moorcock down there now. Then I felt a hand on the middle of my arm - a hand like a choke chain, tugging at my elbow. I locked onto a pair of steel grey eyes. Moorcock. It was stitched in white on his blue-ribbed sweater.
"You lead on, Mr Wilson," he said.

*

I took him first to the reading rooms at the western end of the lower ground floor. The students have to have somewhere quiet, somewhere to read; they fall asleep mostly. I was telling Moorcock this as we watched the dog. It was trotting round the desks, sniffing in the waste bins. Moorcock stood with his hands in his pockets. He jingled coins and rocked on his heels. In one of the rooms he pointed to a poster of resting lions and read the scriptural legend aloud. "Students," he muttered, "they're wankers, aren't they?"
"I was a student once," I said.
Moorcock sniffed. He looked pleased with himself. "Lock up," he said, and whistled to the dog to follow him down the corridor.

*

At the lockers outside the dissecting room entrance I decided to ask, "Is he a student - the guy in the car?"
Moorcock was frisking the empty labcoats. He pulled a pair of rubber gloves out of a pocket, put them to the dog then stuffed them back.
"What's this?" he said, ignoring the question. He was reading the sign on the embalming room door: No Unauthorised Persons To Enter.
I said, "No one's gonna stick a bomb in there."
Moorcock gave me a sideways glance.
I laughed. I asked him, "What's the point? Anything in there is already dead."
"You've got the key, Mr Wilson," he said.
So I stood in the doorway while Tasker went in. Moorcock followed him, peering around. There was a stiff on the table, a bloated male. A formalin drip was slashed into its thigh.
"Satisfied?" I said, when the dog had done its work.
Moorcock was picking up surgical instruments. He flicked his thumb across the blade of a scalpel then put it neatly back on the tray.
"This yours?" he said, meaning the cadaver.
I shook my head, half-laughing at the thought. I like to have something I can take home at nights. So I explained the way the department worked: the split between research and the teaching of anatomy to would-be medics. "Microscopes are more my area," I said, "image analysis, computer work. I've nothing to do with the clinical side."
Moorcock jabbed a finger in the dead man's gut. It left a dent that was slow to recover. "You can get in, though, you can get into the rooms."
I sighed and looked away, read the temperature gauge on the top of the fridges. "I've only got the keys because my boss is on leave. I wouldn't normally come down here."
Moorcock smiled, but he wasn't amused. He pursed his lips and his eyes traversed the body. "Look at this," he said suddenly. He lifted the shrivelled penis off the testicles. "Look what pickling does to your dick."
"I think we should go," I responded flatly. "I said you wouldn't find anything

Chris d'Lacey

here."
"You don't like bodies, do you?" said Moorcock.
I crossed my arms and tried not to frown. "I prefer them warm, if that's what you mean."
Moorcock grinned and rubbed his huge palms together. Without moving his eyes off the body he said, "I've seen bigger rooms than this, filled to overflowing. Lots of dead meat - mostly in bits."
To Moorcock's surprise I stepped into the room. "Then you won't mind going next door," I warned him, "see the sort of mess the students can make." I looked down at the body, lifted the penis and moved it to the opposite side of the groin. "I think he was hanging to the left," I said.

*

In the long dissecting room I kept an eye on the dog. I didn't want to see it picking at a bone. Its trained nose recognised meat on the trolleys, beneath the blue sheets. Dog food galore. It thought about its chances in the first of the eight bays the room splits into, but it didn't make a fool of itself all the same. It did its job and it came to heel. A professional dog. A veteran sniffer. Maybe the formalin turned its head.
Without waiting for Moorcock to give me the order I began to unlock the doors to the ante-rooms: the technical office, the bone store - the lot. I turned the keys and let the doors swing back. Moorcock was standing in the D.R. proper, talking to Douglas (I guessed) on the radio. He didn't take his eyes off me for a moment. But as I walked back from one of the seminar rooms he turned at an angle and seemed to hide the radio behind his hand. I felt uneasy about that movement. I began to imagine what covered words mean. I imagined a dog on the floor above us, its back arched up, its tail held stiff, barking at a package that didn't smell right. And I was fearful then of a sudden explosion, of walls imploding, of a breeze block rain. I could picture in my head where that bomb might be planted - not in a closed off area like this, not in an office or a reading room. If it was me, I would target a lab; a lab in the corner of the building, I decided. Anywhere we might keep inflammatory chemicals, cylinders of gas, high-powered electrics. I would tape a device in the ceiling panels, to the back of one of the removable squares - somewhere high, where the dogs couldn't sniff.
Maximum damage.
A good loud bang.
I'd put it in my old laboratory, perhaps...
I was thinking it through at the potting room door when Moorcock came and tapped me on the shoulder. I leapt at the contact, whipped right around. The sniffer dog growled and pricked up its ears.
"Douglas wants you," the handler said, absently stroking his best friend's neck.
I tried to look away, to collect my thoughts. I focused on the nearest, unoccupied trolley, at the bucket underneath where the smaller pieces fall.
"What about these rooms?" I must have sounded shaken. But Moorcock wasn't really paying attention. He was glancing beyond me, into the store. I looked over my shoulder at the shelves of pots; embryos, half-heads, organs, limbs; preserved and mounted in gelatin, in jars. I felt like saying, 'Stick three cards and you win any jar'. But Moorcock didn't have a sense of humour; he had

Routine Stuff

muscles, a radio and a black and tan dog.
"Forget it," he said, eyes rastering the shelves, "you can come back and play with your toys a bit later. Douglas wants the code to a digital lock. He's down here now, this end of the building."
I pictured the labs along the lower east corridor. There was only one with a digital lock. "I know it," I said, "I know the lock he means."
I knew the order too, the order of the numbers.
21-05-19-88.
How else would I remember my wedding anniversary?
*
In the Electron Microscope Unit Mr Douglas said, "What happens here, David?"
He was walking away from me, looking around, drumming his fingers on the smooth grey benchtops. He paused to inspect a shelf of reagents. Moorcock had taken the dog for a walk, to sniff out the darkrooms at the end of the suite.
I shrugged. I told him, "It's a lab, that's all. We have some high-powered microscopes here. It's a service facility. Everyone uses it."
Mr Douglas said, "Your name's on the door."
"Well, yes," I replied, slightly hesitant. "I was ten years here before I moved upstairs. A junior technician looks after it now. I only come down if there's any sort of problem."
Mr Douglas nodded. He was over by the windows. He stroked the leaf of an under-watered *Coleus* then turned and walked back to me, head lowered in thought. "What about the office?" he said as he passed.
I spoke to his back. "I don't know. What about it?"
Mr Douglas said, "Who works in there?"
I turned to look at the small corner office. "No one," I told him, "no one really. There's a store inside where we keep consumables. It's basically a room that nobody uses."
Mr Douglas was standing at the window of a fume hood. He had his hands behind his back, clapping gently. His radio crackled briefly into life. He listened to the message but didn't reply. "From the outside," he said, "I thought I saw posters - animal pictures, that kind of thing."
"Maybe," I said with a shrug of indifference. "A few posters brighten up the mushroom effect."
Mr Douglas glanced at the grey laboratory walls. "In a room that nobody uses, David?"
It was a couple of seconds before I replied. "There never seemed any point in taking them down."
Mr Douglas put his finger on a blemish in the glass. "Why don't we go and take a look," he said.
*
He sat me by the door like I'd come for an interview, perched himself on the corner of the desk. He had one foot on the floor, the other swinging freely. He wore smart black shoes, neat bows in his laces. There was a diamond pattern on his light grey socks.
I said, "Look, Mr Douglas, what's this all about? I've helped you out with the rooms and everything. I'm still not sure I should be in this building. What if there really is a bomb down here? What if this guy was telling you the truth?"

43

Chris d'Lacey

Outside in the lab I heard a noise. I glanced through the crack of the opened door. Moorcock was out there, opening cupboards. A plastic beaker bounced across the floor.

Mr Douglas said, "I've been meaning to ask."

"What?" I said irritably. "Ask me? What?"

"Could I make an outside call from this office?" He lifted the receiver of the set on the desk. It burred in his hands like an artificial cat.

I focused on the phone and let out a sigh. "Be my guest, we consider it a perk."

"Later perhaps," Mr Douglas said, and he placed the receiver back on the cradle. He tapped it lightly with the tips of his fingers.

He got up then and paced across the floor, stopping by a montage of pictures on a pinboard; newspaper clippings, articles and stuff; Desert Orchid winning the Cheltenham Gold Cup. "How often do you come down here?" he asked.

"Why?" I insisted. "What does it matter?" Mr Douglas read a clipping while he waited for an answer. My ribs went tight. I abandoned the argument. "Tea breaks," I said, "I come for my tea. It's quiet in here. I come down to write."

"Right," said Mr Douglas. It could have been a pun. It seemed to amuse him, whatever he meant. He dug a spare pin into the corner of the board. "I heard an interesting quote about writers once." His white hair brushed against his upturned collar. I looked down at the floor and kept my mouth shut. "To be a writer of fiction, I understand you have to be a natural liar. You have to be able to make things up. What sort of things are you making up, David?"

So I told him I was working on a book about squirrels - a big kids' book, not really for children.

He moved back around the desk and opened a drawer, poking the contents with the end of a ruler. "Squirrels," he said; "vermin, aren't they?"

"Not in my book." I was hard-nosed about it. I picked at my fingernails and didn't look up.

Mr Douglas laughed quietly and pushed the drawer shut. "That's what I don't understand," he said. He waited for my gaze to pan over the desk. "Seals, dolphins, polar bears, squirrels..." he was looking at the posters just above my head, "...it must get painful for you here at times."

I glanced away into the corner of the room, at the waste bin full of polystyrene chips. "What exactly are you getting at, Mr Douglas?"

"It must hurt," he continued, "knowing what goes on. How do you feel about what goes on?" He picked up a book of laboratory procedures and opened it like he was about to read a lesson.

So I told him some of what I'd told to Moorcock; that I worked on computers, a special kind of microscope; I didn't get involved with animal experiments.

"But you were here," he said, in a patronising tone, "you had this office, you've seen it happen. What would be the worst thing you've seen in this lab?"

I told him: "I don't want to talk about this."

He lifted the radio from the clip on his belt, strolled a few paces just fingering the set. "You're not making this very easy, David."

That was when my nails curled into my palms. I tried to look away, to make sense of the moment, but I couldn't take my eyes off his neatly-turned lapels. Out in the lab I heard Tasker bark. "Look-" I began, but Mr Douglas hadn't finished:

44

Routine Stuff

"I've seen literature," he said, "pamphlets, handouts. Some of what they print is hard to believe. Do you really break the legs of baby ferrets just to see how quickly they heal?"

"For the last time," I said, "I don't get involved."

"Perhaps not," he said, turning, "but that doesn't mean you wouldn't like to see it stopped."

He broke eye contact and opened up a channel. I began to reply but again he went on:

"How do they get their information, David?"

"What?" I said, straining. The radio was booming in reply to his call.

"How do they make their contacts, here?"

"Who?" I said. I almost spat it on the floor. "Who the hell are 'they'? Who are we talking about?"

Mr Douglas held the radio near to his mouth. He was telling them to close down Area 1. I started up again but he cut in fast: "You have a lot of stickers in the window, I noticed."

I looked at the window. It was starting to rain. "Everyone here puts stickers in the window."

"Not like these."

"Like what?" I said.

Mr Douglas turned. "You support these people?"

"What *people!*" I shouted.

"You know what I mean. These animal people."

Then I understood.

"Fuck you," I said, and got to my feet. Mr Douglas stood still. He didn't try to stop me. He was wanting to hear me blow my top. I crashed out of the office, into the lab. Moorcock was there. The place was gutted, stuff tipped out all over the floor.

"What the *fuck* is going on!" I screamed at Moorcock, but Moorcock was waiting for orders from Douglas.

Mr Douglas said quietly, "You know what's going on." He looked over at Moorcock. Moorcock shook his head.

"You're crazy," I said. "You're out of your mind." I kicked an empty tissue box across the lab floor.

Mr Douglas said, "David, we know about the call."

That jerked me. I asked them, "What about the call?"

"It came from inside the building, didn't it?"

I saw Moorcock take a pull on Tasker's chain, his thumb idling on the quick-release catch. I flashed a look back at the small corner office, remembering the game we'd had with the phone.

"Bollocks," I said, from one man to the other. Moorcock looked blank. Mr Douglas had his arms crossed, patting his biceps. "You haven't got a clue about the source of that call. You don't even have a suspect waiting, do you? You're fishing, the pair of you, hoping for a catch. You've got nothing but dog hairs in the back of that car."

Mr Douglas brought his steepled fingers together. His gaze dipped to Moorcock, then full beam at me.

"I'm going," I said. "I'm finished with this shit. I've done nothing wrong and you damn well know it. I should have been out of here ages ago. You bastards are putting my life at risk."

Then I did something dumb: I looked at the clock on the window wall, just above the cylinders of argon gas.

I saw Mr Douglas flash a glance there too.

The time was wrong, an hour in front.

Then we were all playing musical glances.

"Clock?" said the handler. Douglas nodded. I started to move. Moorcock let the dog go.

It pinned me up against the poisons cabinet. I climbed onto the cabinet. I didn't climb down. On the far side of the lab I saw Moorcock on a stool. He stepped onto the bench, just under the clock.

With a gentleness his hands hadn't seemed to possess, he raised the clock vertically, took it off the screw. He adjusted his hands to get a positive grip. Then, with precision, he turned the clock around.

Halfway through the turn his shoulders slumped. He looked over at Douglas, raised a disappointed eyebrow. Mr Douglas clicked his radio off.

Moorcock set the hour hand back a revolution. I reminded myself to bollock my junior. He never could get to grips with British Summer Time.

*

They let me stroke Tasker before they let me go. Mr Douglas told Moorcock: 'David likes animals.' I asked them, Why had they centred on this lab? Mr Douglas said, "It's all right, we'll tidy up the mess." He laid a paternal hand on my shoulder and walked me over to the laboratory door.

I said, "Look, Mr Douglas, what's it all about? You can't just go around accusing people. All right I like animals and I don't like them hurt, that doesn't make me a closet terrorist."

"Go home, David," Mr Douglas said. "The computer will still be here tomorrow."

He pulled the door open and I stepped into the corridor. As I turned I told him, "We have a code here, y'know."

"Code?" he said.

"We have an understanding - that life is precious."

Mr Douglas smiled and let the door go. It idled to a close and sealed the space between us.

For a moment, I watched him through the narrow band of glass. He waved at Moorcock to refill the cupboards, then pushed his hands into the pockets of his mackintosh and paced across the lab to stand by Tasker.

Tasker was pawing at something on the floor. It looked like a spider, but from where I was standing I couldn't be sure. Mr Douglas was closer. His view was the best.

He told the dog to sit.

The dog was looking up at him as he lifted his heel and rubbed the spider out.

Sally St. Clair
Concerning The Kindness Of Aunts

Until I was seventeen I lived with my four aunts in a tall grey house by the sea. Each of my aunts was as fat and round as a barrel but I was as thin as my mother, who had died before I was born. My father was a sea captain and my mother had come from far away across the sea. He had brought her home in his ship and his sisters had looked at her and sighed. They had fed her with soup and apples but the air was too cold and the sea too wild. My birth was due the day after Martinmas, but on All Hallows Eve, as my father lit a candle for the pumpkin, my mother gave a small cry and threw her hands up to her face. She slipped to the floor and died. My father took the knife he had used for the pumpkin face and he sliced open my mother so I came tumbling out. He scooped me into his arms and I wailed in the cold air and he wept for my mother. With all this noise my three eldest aunts entered the room and stood watching my father and me.

All this I know because when I was old enough my aunts told me. They buried my mother beside the house and her headstone looked out across the sea. My father came home each October with gifts for my birthday, and each time he laid his head on my mother's grave and wept. I never knew my mother. She was a stranger to my aunts and so she was to me. But my father grew familiar as the years passed by and my aunts, little by little, told me the tales of his childhood. He was the fourth child, born long before my youngest aunt. She was so young sometimes it seemed we were sisters. My father brought her strange and fantastic gifts as if she was always a child. She wore red silk dresses and painted her nails to match. Her hair was as dark as my own and in the evening light in summer red light sparkled from her dress onto her hair. She'd take me down on the rocks by the sea and tell me stories of places I could only dream of.

The eldest of my four aunts lived by herself near the top of the house. She had one large room with two sets of windows, one overlooking the sea and one overlooking the garden and my mother's grave. Her walls were lined with books which she arranged, not in any order of content, but in order of the coloured spines of the books. When I was very little I believed my aunt was trying to make a rainbow fly between her windows. The floor was covered in a patchwork of worn rugs and at the windows hung heavy curtains. Across one corner of the room my aunt had hung another curtain which hid a basin, and a table on which she kept a gas ring and a tin of biscuits. We sat at the sea window and drank hot sweet tea the days we waited for my father's ship to come home.

My eldest aunt was called Harriet and she called my father Harry, though his name was Henry. She'd been four when he was born and her sisters Alma and Jane, my two middle aunts, were still only babies. He was different, being a boy, and she'd kept her anxious eye on him all his childhood, believing somehow in the inherent weakness of the male. My grandfather had been a sea traveller, like my father, but he came home each year with an illness from abroad, not gifts. I barely remembered him, only a narrow yellowed face bending over me and his foetid breath whispering in my ear. I never got used to him and then he was dead, quite suddenly, but quite expected, of some fever. The shock of it killed my grandmother immediately. At the time my youngest aunt was only nineteen and had been away at boarding school for six years. I was four and each time she came home I'd forgotten who she was. But now she came back for good and

Sally St. Clair

filled the house up with her noisy weeping. She slammed doors and screamed at her sisters, who were shocked by her grief, and put aside their own mourning to care for her. After the double funeral, she wept more quietly, but I saw the tears make spots in her red silk dress even at breakfast. By the time I was five my youngest aunt never spoke of her parents. That last time she'd come back, she'd brought a new name with her and we all learnt it and learnt not to use the old name. Her new name was 'Stevie' and it suited her, despite it being a boy's name. She embroidered it on her night dress case and wrote it inside her wellington boots in ink.

My two middle aunts, Alma and Jane, lived on the floor below my Aunt Harriet. They were very alike, neither old and serious as Harriet, nor young and wild as Stevie. They shared two rooms, one a bedroom with high twin beds, and one a sitting room. In the sitting room, either side of the fireplace, were two armchairs in skirted covers and embroidered antimacassars. Here each evening Alma and Jane would wedge down amongst the cushions and pick up their knitting and knit vests for the poor. Alma's vests were always small and tightly woven and had a ribbon at the neck. But Jane's vests were loose and baggy and she laughed as she knitted. Between them, with a mug of cocoa, I would sit on a low stool whose legs twisted like barley sugar sticks. I would stare at their fire and listen to their chat above my head and, above it all, Aunt Harriet's heavy step as she paced in her room from window to window. Sometimes Aunt Harriet did not walk about, and then Jane and Alma would grow quiet and serious. Harriet had an illness that came and went, which was all I knew about it, and when it came she would lie in her bed in the centre of her room, and shut her eyes and go to sleep early. Those evenings I missed her because, although she was old and serious, she knew exactly how I liked to go to bed. Jane and Alma could never remember what to do. Even in October when my father was home, Aunt Harriet would put me to bed. My room was up above hers, right in the attic, and my window looked out only into the sky. I had a small bed and a chest of drawers which had belonged to my mother. It was made of some dark heavy wood and pressed into it all over was a swirling pattern made of pieces of mother of pearl. The walls of my room were white and the bed spread was white and on the floor was a white rug which Aunt Alma had made for me the year before my grandparents died. I kept all my clothes and all my toys in my mother's chest and each evening, Aunt Harriet helped me to pick up anything which had been left out. Then she'd wash me carefully with a bowl of hot water brought up from the basin in her room, and I would put on my nightdress. Except sometimes in the hottest summer nights, when I'd sleep bare. Aunt Harriet said it was to let the air freshen my skin. Then I would jump into bed, under the covers, and move over quickly for Harriet who warmed the bed as she lay beside me with her great arms around me. I would grow sleepy and relaxed as she told me, each night, long stories about the whole of the world, till by the time I was twelve I thought I knew everything.

At about that time there was a crisis in our house. It involved Aunt Stevie who began to scream and cry again as she had done eight years before when my grandparents died. I had no idea what had happened and took to hiding in corners to listen to my other aunts discussing it. Stevie's room was in the basement of our house and her moans drifted up to the rest of us. After a

Concerning The Kindness Of Aunts

fortnight of all this noise growing louder and more upsetting, it was October and my father came home. My routine of watching and waiting with Aunt Harriet had been interrupted, and father arrived unexpectedly, his bed un-aired and un-made up, his room still shrouded in dust sheets. He sat in Jane and Alma's room and they and Harriet whispered to him about Stevie's upset. His face grew serious, and he even forgot to give us our presents which stayed in trunks in the hall till I became impatient and asked for them. From all my listening in corners I understood that Stevie had been in love with a man who had been living in the town, and who had promised he would marry her when they had saved up enough money for a small house. After many months of saving money and of meeting the man for walks out, my Aunt Stevie had discovered that he was already married. I heard her angry wailing to my father as she told him that her heart was broken. Somehow, my other aunts and my father managed to comfort Stevie and she quietened down, though for a month the corners of her eyes were as red as her dress. Then Stevie found out somehow that the man's wife had divorced him and this news, which I'd overheard Harriet conveying to my father just before he left again, sparked Stevie back to life. Her misery had seemed to shrink her for a while but soon her red silk dresses were covering the roundness of her body as tight as ever. My other aunts relaxed again and the pattern of our life resumed, except that Aunt Harriet seemed tireder somehow. That Christmas, Harriet had to rest a lot, and the gaiety of our celebrations wore her out. Her hair, which had been the colour of walnut shells, began to turn silvery grey until I forgot the brown underneath. She stopped putting me to bed in the same old way, and instead, when I was ready for sleep I would go and say goodnight to her and she would hold me for a moment in her arms and kiss me. In the mornings I would knock on her door and go in to say hallo, and one day, when I knocked, I found her sitting quite naked at her dressing table, staring at herself in the mirror. Her hair hung down to the cleft in her buttocks, half way silver, half way brown, and the folds of her body lay one on the other. I could see in the mirror her breasts, and they too, like her hair, had changed and grown old. In her hands she was holding her hairpins and comb. When she saw me watching her in the mirror she started, as if she had been dreaming. It was only then that I knew my aunt was growing old. I began to fear her death, remembering the time of my grandparents' death, and feeling the death of my own mother always in the background of my life. But it was the first time I'd experienced the natural slowing down of age and as the years went on I grew used to it. After a while Jane and Alma too began to grow old. They stopped flirting with men who came to the house and I saw their hair also begin to grey. But my Aunt Stevie was years younger and it seemed to me she'd never grow old. She'd taken to going out dancing every Saturday night, and the sound that now drifted up from the basement was the sound of Stevie singing as she brushed her hair till it stood out around her face like shiny black petals. I rarely went into Stevie's part of the house, preferring to be higher up. She had three little rooms, each one with a small window near the ceiling, looking out to the edges of our garden.

The October I was seventeen, my father came home as usual for my birthday with gifts for me and for my aunts, and this time he was carrying a small bundle wrapped in sacking. He carefully unrolled it while we silently watched, not knowing what to expect. Inside was a bundle of twigs and earth. He carried it

Sally St. Clair

outside as gently as if it were a baby and, kneeling down on my mother's grave, he scooped out a shallow hole with his hands and pressed it in. It looked to me as if it were nothing but a dead plant, but when the spring came, I saw tiny pale buds on each twig. I took to going out each morning very early, before my breakfast, to see them swell and spread. By the time April came, my mother's grave was covered with pale green leaves, and small waxen flowers which smelt as sweet as honey. My aunts did not know what it was and my Aunt Alma said it must be from another country. Aunt Jane said it was a miracle to see it grow and blossom here, so cold, and so near the sea.

Since my father's last visit, I had been filled with an unfamiliar dissatisfaction. I felt as if my blood was itching at me from inside. I began to wonder if I would spend my whole life living in the grey house with my aunts and if I did, what should become of me when they had all grown old and died. I had rarely left the house in my seventeen years, only to visit the town occasionally with one of them for soap or other necessities. They had taught me at home everything I needed to know. I could cook and sew and raise vegetables. I knew how to mend my shoes and get milk from a goat. I knew the pattern and movement of the stars and the shape of the world. But now my own world seemed to be shrinking and becoming tighter and tighter till I felt as if I was wearing one of Aunt Alma's little vests. At night I could no longer sleep and sometimes I had to creep out of my room and around the house and hear my aunts snoring lightly before I felt the day was truly over.

Some time in July, I saw my Aunt Harriet open a letter and immediately I knew it was something to do with myself. I had recognised my father's neat thick handwriting on the envelope. I looked at Harriet reading my father's letter and saw in her eyes the brightness of tears. She looked at me and told me that my father had decided that I had grown enough to leave my aunt's house and go to the city. He would send money which would pay for me to find a place to live and then I was to go to the college in the city where I would meet friends of my own age and learn what I wanted to do for the rest of my life. As Harriet spoke to me I suddenly felt quite sure that I did not want to do any of this, that I was quite happy and content being at home and that I should stay with my aunts forever and look after them as they had looked after me. But it seemed that my father had made the decision for me and that when he came back in October for my eighteenth birthday I should no longer be living at home with my aunts, but instead I would be living in the city, and he would visit me there.

So now a new part of my life began. Sometimes it felt as if it was a beginning, and sometimes it felt as if it was an ending. Aunts Jane and Alma took me to town and we bought a large trunk, made of some kind of stiff board covered in green material. The trunk sat in Jane and Alma's sitting room and each day we filled it up a bit more. Aunt Harriet helped me to mend and clean all my clothes and we made a list of things I would need. Jane gave me a writing case and a new pen so that I could write to them as often as I had time, and Alma stopped knitting vests long enough to make me a matching set of gloves and scarf and hat. We had chosen the wool together and I was pleased with the result, knowing the bright colour suited me and went well with my coat.

All the time these preparations were going on, Aunt Stevie sat in her basement and clattered away on an ancient sewing machine, humming loudly to

Concerning The Kindness Of Aunts

herself. I looked in on her once and saw her mouth clamped tight on a row of pins. Something shiny lay in the sewing machine. At the sound of my step, Stevie looked up and frowned. She opened her mouth to shoo me away and the pins fell out. I laughed and ran up the stairs to where Harriet and Alma were arguing about whether I should need more new underwear.

One week later the trunk was ready and Jane and Alma sat down on each end of the lid, and Harriet and I fastened it down. Now I was ready to face the world. My father had sent money for my journey and instructions for travelling. An old friend of his was to meet me in the city. My journey would take all day. My aunts took great care to make my last moments with them special. They told me I was to be good, and strong, and to remember to write. I was to keep cool in the sun, and wear a vest in the winter, and not to speak to strange men. As I left the house with my trunk, Aunt Stevie pressed a parcel into my hands and kissed me goodbye. I kissed my other aunts and waved to them all. The journey was long and tiring and I sat still, holding Stevie's parcel on my lap. Hours later, I arrived in the city and was met as arranged by my father's oldest friend, who took me first to his own house to stay the night with his family. I was tearful and exhausted by bedtime, worn out by the journey and by the many new faces I'd seen. In my room I opened a window but all I could see were a thousand little lights crowding in on me. I thought of my aunts and wondered how I would ever manage without them.

Then I remembered the parcel and knelt down on the floor to open it. Carefully, I unknotted the string and wound it into a ball. Then I unfolded the brown paper. Inside was something wrapped in tissue. I lifted it out and it unravelled in my hands. Then I saw what my Aunt Stevie had been making. A beautiful red silk dancing dress. I stood up and held it against me and looked at myself in the long mirror on the wall. I saw a young girl with black curls and white skin, and a red silk dress lighting up her eyes and hair. I felt my feet begin to dance and my arms wrapped the dress about me. I shut my eyes and spun around and around and listened to the sound the city made. That night I slept so peaceful and dreamless and when I awoke in the pale early morning, there, at the end of my bed waiting for me, lay my red silk dress.

Ron Berry

That Old Black Pasture

1.

He dealt the pay clerk a fast, wristy backhander across the mouth. There were witnesses too, standing behind him in the queue.

The clerk yelped, anguished as a girl.

Inside the office, the tubby cashier strutted like an April bantam cock. "Lloyd, what on earth are you doing?"

Pushing his head through the hatch, "Gabe," he said. "Gabe Lloyd. None of your Lloyd to me. Shut up a minute, you crabby minded bugger. This isn't the first time I've been swindled. My water allowance, five bob a day, so dish it out or I'll be right in there with you."

The cashier exploded authority. "You can't treat my staff like this! If it's trouble you want, rest assured you'll get it, oh yes, I'll warrant that!"

"Not before I bust you one," he said.

"Leave off, Gabe," warned a greyed old miner. "You'll cop the worst end of it."

Way back in the queue they were yelling, "What we waiting for?"

"Keep moving, boys!"

And, "Same every bloody Friday! Dried-up gravy on my dinner!"

The clerk dabbed blood off his lip. He had overlooked the water allowance. Simple matter to put right. Next Friday, two water allowance payments. The cashier tutted confirmation, having survived twenty years of pay-day tantrums before nationalisation. Precedence, truth, ironed his brow as he paraded, quick white fingers tap-tapping his waistcoat buttons.

Gabe lunged through the hatch, grunting as he missed the clerk. Colliers hauled him away, sympathising, pacifying him at the same time. He shook free, glaring at the cashier. They made a triangle. Cashier, clerk and Gabe, his cheekbones shining baby pink beneath coal dust, tight grey eyes menacing above the meaty splodge of his nose. He snorted, coughed abruptly, alerting his wits, then held out his hand. "My money, I want it," blunt chin outslung, oddly offset by the puffy innocence of his mouth.

The cashier saying, "I shall rectify the error," plucking out his fountain pen, bottle-rounded figure leaning over the red-spined ledger. "Petty cash." The clerk sniffed, sorted twenty-five shillings in half crowns and slid the money across the hatch counter, and from the cashier, "You haven't heard the last of this matter, Lloyd."

"Very good of you." He was cocky now, grinning triumph. "Perhaps it'll teach him a lesson. He isn't the first been slapped in the teeth. You sods fiddling in this office, you'd raise the bile in any man. What d'you know about what it's like down under? Bloody experts you are, on the Consultative Committee an' all! Big laugh. You pair, you couldn't fill enough coal to boil a bloody egg." He jigged on the balls of his feet, haranguing the queue, "Harmony between workers and management? Load of ballox! Only management can afford to renege. Don't take my word for it though, just remember my old man." He shook his fist. "Mansel Lloyd did more than his whack to improve conditions in Black Rand! What for? I'll tell you. Bloody wreath from the NUM when we

That Old Black Pasture

put him in Tymawr cemetery." Gabe punched the stack of half-crowns into the palm of his other hand. "These slashers in the office, they never cleared a top hole, never filled a dram, couldn't pack a gob wall, never cut up a rib face, they'd be smothered in yellow working a low seam with the top pouncing like bloody Guy Fawkes' night. How can they think like us, ah? They don't *feel* like underground men. Same things, thinking and feeling." He let the half-crowns fall in a clacking, flashing current before dropping them into his pocket. "Never trust 'em," he said.

They bantered, "You like stirring it up."
"Lloydie know-all."
"Not a patch on his old man."
"Amateur," they said. "Three rounder."

He walked away. I'm different from my father and grandfather. They believed in the rank and file. I say, bugger the rank and file. It's all mouth, always was, always will be. This life is for Gabe Lloyd, to do as I want with it, mine from the beginning. Some men are born slaves. Not this kid. Never. It'll take more than religion or politics to alter things too, for definite. All I've heard is jaw-jaw. Bosses and workers, jaw-jaw. Good people, bad people, all yapping like costive poodles. I'm different from my old man and my grandfather. They broke Mansel's spirit, but he kicked the bucket sitting up in bed not flat on his back like those who spend a life-time squashing their arses in offices. As for Grancha Tommy, he worked on sinking Black Rand in the first place. They repaid him by breaking his leg in the '21 strike. Lovely people, great, these stupid sons of workers coming here to Golau Nos, bashing hell out of the strikers. Marvellous, the rank and file, wonderful they are. Shove them into uniform, give them orders, then they'll make Holy Christ out of some government creep. Next minute they'll hammer him to pieces. Following orders. That clerk I flipped across the puss, by tomorrow he'll have two shiners and teeth missing. There'll be more rumours floating 'round than bum paper. His name's lousy in Black Rand. They all detest the stingy bastard. Rumours and a bit of glory for Mansel Lloyd's son. Course you know him. Fists up before you can say boo. He's like a match. Aye, working a stent off Lower North heading. Decent enough if you catch him in a good mood, except you rarely find him in a good mood. Gabe Lloyd, he isn't just a mug either. There's that chip on his shoulder all the time. Got it from Mansel. Give the boy another ten years, let him settle down with a wife and kids, that'll tutor him. Sure to, aye, always does. Women, they cure rebels.

Chinking the half-crowns in his pocket, he vowed, Gabe Lloyd comes first, second and last.

July sunshine from naked blue sky, glittered the compact saucer-cambered town. Slanted windowpanes dazzled, denied staring at, and slate rooftops on the far slope shone like the flanks of battleships, TV aerials sprouting from every chimney stack. He passed two punters faithfully posed outside a betting shop, heads lowered, the shabby street invaded by the hard suavity of a Peter O'Sullivan commentary. Everywhere the same 3.30 race from Goodwood, accurate, factual as Gospel, the hullaballoo crowding down to a laconic summary. And Gabe was thinking; another week wrapped up, shan't see coal till Monday morning. Too warm for fires this weekend. Short week of short shifts. *Man's* job so the adverts reckon. You'd think all the bints and pansies in the world had dabbled in the face and cried off But it's worth sticking for the short week. Anyhow, blokes down under are better men, better for me. True, there's a fair quota of *trychs* in Black Rand. Where won't you find a *trych* here and there along the faces? Some bladder-brain who'd graft the heart out his young butty. They tried that on me, the fascist bastards. If you can't check your wages, too bad. You'll get robbed, diddled, up, down and sideways. The N.C.B."ll never pay us enough, but the job's worth sticking for the short week. You won't dodge a wet shirt anywhere off Lower North, water cold as lollipops melting down the back of your neck. Some shifts you're wetter than others. Sheer luck. Useless making a song and dance. By grubtime you're sweating from eyebrows to ankles. But it's a good pit, no doubt at all. Decent pit, decent blokes ... as he entered the house of his only sister.

She placed his dinner on the table. Arms folded, she looked down at him.

"What's up, girl?"

"Silly bugger you, Gabe. Why'd you go and bump that chap in the office? Her from next door came on the run to tell me."

"Sharp off the mark, Sue."

"Her two sons are in Black Rand Colliery premises, you couldn't have picked a worse place to lose your head. Time you used some brains for a change."

Sue Preece served lamp chop and vegetables for herself, clipping the oven door shut with her knee. She was thirty-four, severe from adjustment, her straight black hair cut for utility, the same principle affecting her clothes. She refused to primp herself as female. Her husband lived with another woman in a caravan sited with a dozen others behind Golau Nos cricket pavilion. Sue despised him. She always had, reconciled deep in her insular spirit. She practised loyalty by deed towards Gabe or anyone who sought it from her.

"Makes no odds," he said. "They won't do anything, not for a little smack across the mouth. I was twenty-five bob down on my money."

"There's the Lodge, you pay dues every week. Let them sort it out instead of taking the law into your own hands, specially with your record."

"Our committee's a right shower," he said.

"Point is, boy, you can't go 'round hitting people. You're not a snobby nosed *crwtyn* any more."

He glanced at the travelling clock tilted up in its plush lined leather case on the middle shelf of the dresser.

Below the clock, framed photographs of their parents, each quarter-turned inwards to a larger photograph of Sue and himself. Twice his size then, she had one arm around his shoulders, his hair boy-rough while hers surrounded her head in a stiff aura of permed waves. He wore a willing grin. Sue and their mother showed the same expression, humourless.

"Fetching that clock home don't give you the right to take a poke at the least one who upsets you."

"I must have been pretty handy, Sue, couple of years ago."

She jeered bleakly, "Bull-headed, and you wanted to turn professional. By now you wouldn't know if you was coming or going."

"I can still do a bundle."

"Ach, act your age."

"I beat everyone in the area for that clock."
"Novices. Be quiet and eat your dinner."
"I'm going out for a swim afterwards," he said. "Listen, lots of girls come out to the Lake, all you do is mooch around indoors as if there's nothing left till cowing doomsday."
Passively regarding him, "Never you mind about me."

*

From a crystal stream Melyn Lake ballooned to smooth, straight sausage shape. Vandalised trees and brambles wound in and out by pickers' footpaths covered the far bank. He approached aslant down a steeply turfed hillock, moving up the shoreline to level ground where sunbathers gossiped among romping kiddies. He stripped off, taking his time, the comfort of his dinner heavy on his stomach. Gabe's toe-nails were black, and dull blue scars hung like tattoo streaks behind his left shoulder, ending in a pink crinkled indent over his floating ribs. He wiped his armpits, draped his towel and looked around for company. Nearest were boys and girls, all gush and giggles. He returned a straight-armed salute to some young colliers entering the water, pushing and tugging at each other.
"See you later."
Then he sat down, elbows on widespread knees. Flat as glass Melyn Lake, ripples catching his eye in fits and starts, dwindling to flatness again. He dreamed himself behind the wheel of a brand new Standard Eleven car, Sue sitting beside him. Nearby ripples - a frog sculling close to the bank before circling back to cover. Gabe's tongue tipped out his lower lip while he groped for a pebble to lob at the spot where it disappeared. Spiky turf on bare clay, so he flipped his cigarette butt, heedless now, then laid back on his towel. He felt supreme, prepared to luxuriate while the weight of his meal subsided.
Twenty minutes later he walked slightly knock-kneed into the water and plunged his mountain stroke (half trudgen, half breast-stroke) to join the gang of young colliers.
"Here he is, best clouter in Black Rand," they said.
"Gabe's al'right."
"How's it going, Gabe-boy?"
"I had my money," he said. "Anybody been across to the other side yet?"
"Let's all have a go!"
"For a pint!" shouted the fastest man, foaming into crawl-stroke.
But forty yards winded them. They milled around, treading water, saying, "Nob it."
"Too much like graft."
"Leave it there."
Hard muscled face workers, they gleamed white skinned from daily scrubbing under the pithead showers.
"Hey, know what, Gabe, they might give you your cards on account of this afternoon."
"Aye, and I might bang a one-two on Monte Leyshon for a so-long present," he said.
"Only once you'll do that, *brawd*. They'll rush you inside, your feet won't touch the ground."
He relished foolish bragging, saying, "Fair enough, once will do me."

"They'll shove you down Cox's for months, man!"

The crawl swimmer said, "I heard they called a doctor to the office. What you bash him with, your bloody water jack?"

"Up your jacksi!" he said.

"You'll hear more about it. They'll get a certificate off the fucken doctor, see!"

Grunting, he rolled over for a relaxed float back to his clothes. The sun was hot, the water mellow. He floated. Forget about Black Rand. Why worry? Ruination of a man, worry.

*

Rumours ceased, verified by reality two weeks later when a police sergeant came to the house with a summons.

He said, "Seems like I got to attend the ceremony then."

"Plead guilty, say you're sorry," advised the sergeant. "Understand this, fella, you've assaulted a person while he was under the protection of his employer, namely the National Coal Board. It's worse than pub fighting in the eyes of the law. Not that I blame you personally; worked in the pits myself years ago. Say you're sorry, lost your temper, won't happen again, and hope for the best."

"What about the times I been booked in the past?"

Grave, furrow-faced, the sergeant hooked his thumb in his breast pocket. "They'll go down against you. How many times, fella?"

"Once for scrapping outside the Workmen's, one for foul language, once for pissing in a *gwli*, once for obstruction as they called it, and there was the time you blokes locked me up."

"Drunk?"

"More or less, aye, suppose I was."

The sergeant offered, "Good luck, fella."

"Same to you, Sarg."

Due to appear in Dove Street Court at 10 a.m. on a thundery morning. Sue was harshly critical while they were having breakfast, softening at the last moment, fussily adjusting his tie and smoothing his hair. She sent him off with a stroke of her palm on his chest, tenderly, like a blessing.

After Black Rand's cashier's evidence, judgement came within five minutes. Gabe was fascinated by the magistrate. Monkey Lips whispering to colleagues on the bench. They nodded together, at each other, dumb as marionettes.

"Lloyd, stand upright." The flat, dead-sure God Almighty legal voice.

He slid his elbow off the ledge of the dock, removed his other hand from his pocket and held his fists to his thighs.

Monkey Lips glanced from the cashier to the police inspector. "Young man, we have sufficient evidence of your lack of discipline." He paused to extend, slide down his upper lip, concealing the lower one. "You have appeared in this Court before but obviously you aren't prepared to learn from experience. The National Coal Board is determined to protect its staff from brutality and insults." Incurable neurosis writhed his lips again. "We fine you thirty pounds, and you shall remain on probation for a period of two years."

Thought Gabe, bloody old chimpanzee.

The clerk of the Court bawled out, "Will you pay now?"

Leaning over the dock, "Give me a few days, sir?" - *Sir* granted as part of

That Old Black Pasture

Dove Street rigmarole.

"Seven days to pay," announced Monkey Lips.

Chin tucked aside, he smirked to himself as he climbed down. That old stuff-pig, him telling me I'm short on discipline. Discipline's for goofies who can't think for themselves. Shitten-ringed old bastard, he scraped his way to where he is. They're all scrapers. Justice, by the Jesus, more justice in the weather.

The probation officer beckoned him into a room below the Court. A scrawny man, thin hair flighting off a centre parting along his flaky sunburned head. Gravestone teeth in his mouth, and, "Cigarette?" pleasant as a visiting uncle.

"Ta very much," he said.

"Did you enjoy hitting that chap?"

"What d'you mean enjoy?"

"Were you infuriated or simply using the incident to hurt someone?"

"I don't get you, mister," he said. "Look, why not leave it there? See, they paid my water allowance, so I'm satisfied."

The probation officer led him to a side door exit. "Gabriel, I would like you to appreciate my position. The less we see of each other the better I shall be pleased. That's best for both of us. All you have to do, stay out of trouble."

There's loads of luck in it, he thought. For two years I'll have to watch my step. They can pick me up for *twp* things like crossing the railway line or fiddling a bus ticket. Any-fucken-thing. When I buy my Standard Eleven next Spring I'll have to learn the Highway Code backwards. Soon they'll pinch us for not pulling the chain in the lav. LAW? Double rupture the law and every chimp-brained magistrate since the one who played crafty with the Jews. They're still chopsing about him and all, every Sunday in chapel.

He dry-spat on his palms. Anyone with a black cap in his pocket or a black staff dangling against his leg, he's a menace to society. My kind of society, when I find it.

*

Four days after the court hearing, a Lower North fireman came up the conveyor face. Gabe knew he was coming, word having passed from collier to collier.

"How old are you now?" says Iago Eynon, resting on his kneepads and aiming a chameleon's tongue of tobacco juice at a roller carrying the rubber belt.

He hunkered closer to Iago, his caplamp killing the glare of the fireman's at half-way. "Why then, any bother?"

"No-no, boy. They're inquiring in the office."

"I'll be twenty-three next October."

Iago poled slowly to his feet on his safety stick. "Manager wants to see you in the top pit cabin, near enough ha'- past two." He jabbed at the coal, "Lovely face slip that. Hole under a few inches and she'll spill out like a bag. You can't beat Lower North coal. S'clean!" Iago gently toed the seam. "Righto, boy, don't forget, ha'- past two in the cabin."

He watched the fireman crabbing up the face. Another brilliant N.C.B. official, he thought. Otherwise ignorant. Streamers from the roof glinted ahead of Iago's lamp but he ploughed on, hooped forward, trailing his safety stick. The buggers are up to something. They'll be waiting in the cabin. Gog-eyed Monte and his clique. Brainy Monte, his missis no thicker than a tee-head rail. Poor dab always looks flummoxed. She's in a worse state than Sue. But Monte Gog-

Ron Berry

eye, what he doesn't know about production isn't worth knowing. I expect he'll warn me to keep my hands quiet. No choice, Monte, I'm on probation.

He stepped out of the cage seconds after the 2.30 p.m. hooter skirled from the roof of the winding house; echoes were still pounding around the gullied mountain above Black Rand as he crossed directly to the officials' cabin.

Iago Eynon and two other firemen stood behind the colliery manager. Gabe grinned amiably. They were like a photo from COAL magazine. As if they went grouse shooting together. Monte, you clever sod, something's hatching behind that shiny snake-eye.

The manager removed his white pit helmet, decorous as an undertaker doffing at a funeral. He placed it on the table, folded his hands upon it, friendly, smiling. The off-centre pupil of his left eye swole behind his spectacles. "*Shwmae* there, Gabe. I suppose you're wondering why I wanted to see you?"

Iago rubbed the underside of his chin. "Don't jump to conclusions now, boy. Mr. Leyshon don't intend victimising you at all."

He licked coaldust off his lower lip. "Aye, right, okay, no messing about, ah, let's hear the news."

The manager accentuated some downright nodding as if saying *Here we are, man to man.* Then, "Gabe, I'd like you to drive the cutter in Lower North. As you know, Billy Holly drives the cutter by night. I want you to help him behind the Longwall until you get the hang of it."

"Behind the cutter, Mr. Leyshon?"

"Exactly, until you can drive the machine. In due course you'll be more or less your own boss. That's important, Gabe, surely? It's a damn good job anyhow, one of the most skilled jobs in the pit."

He said, "I'm happy filling out coal."

"Colliers are two a penny in a conveyor face. I want a reliable cutter operator."

"Find someone else, Mr. Leyshon."

"Now listen, Gabe, I won't have you dictating to me..."

"Nights! Bugger night-shift." He felt the eyes of the firemen ganged behind the manager: Keep your dagger looks to yourselves.

"I'm afternoons regular," complained a wizened official.

Gabe shrugged. This little short-arse with about nine kids, afternoon shift was good enough for him. "Your problem, man. Maybe it suits your missis." He regretted the insult, but when you speak out of turn you either back down or bash on regardless, so he jerked a reverse vee sign at the fireman: Up your pipe.

The little fireman ranted, "I know what I'd do if I was Mr. Leyshon!"

The manager waved his hands for peace. "Look here, I'm afraid you'll have to go on night-shift until I find another man."

He said, "For how long?"

Monte Leyshon returned superior irony, dry brown hair puffed across his forehead, his strange eye starred behind his glasses. "Until I find another man."

"I'll see our Lodge sec." he said.

Iago rolled his chew to his jaw teeth. "What kind of talk's this? Don't sound a bit like the Lloyds, boy. Lodge can't do nothing for the simple reason Mr. Leyshon isn't down-grading you at all. My own son, he spent a few years behind the cutter. More's the pity he smashed his elbow that time, put paid to him

That Old Black Pasture

proper. By now he'd be on cross shifts with Billy Holly, cutter-man himself."

He hardened his stomach against rebellion. They had him back-pedalling. Troublemakers never lasted on day-shift, not without blessing from the Lodge. Committee-men carried *constitution* on their tongues. Before nationalisation trouble-makers were sent up the road. Principle older than the N.C.B. These officials were a breed, connivers from their socks up. They had him where they wanted him. Reading the situation as true, nevertheless, "You can stuff the job," he said.

"Fortnight's notice, that's the alternative," confirmed the manager.

Old Iago Eynon cluck-clucked. "It's a bad thing to sack a man, Gabe-boy. Means they'll stop your dole for six weeks. Paid up your fine yet? If not, how you going to? Use a bit of common, that's all I'm saying."

"Well?" from Monte Leyshon.

Gog-eyed bastard, he thought, he isn't bothered either way. Me neither. There'll be a Standard Eleven outside our house next Spring. "Right, I'm on for a quid a week extra," he said, "on account of the night-shift."

"Ten shillings. Consider yourself lucky."

"Make it a quid, Mr. Leyshon."

"Ten shillings."

The puny afternoon shift fireman protested again, "Bloody big-head, I wouldn't have him in my district."

And, "Thinks he's chocolate since he boxed for the Coal Board," said another official, confident beyond need of malice.

The manager rose from the table. "I don't expect the cutter to run up and down the faces like clockwork. There are sure to be snags occasionally, resulting in overtime. You'll make a pound a week over and above the rate."

He conceded, "Fair enough."

"Good, start Monday night."

Soaping himself under the shower, he thought, Christ, I must be easily led. It's the bloody probation. By the time I buy my car I'll be down on my knees every night. Ah, by the loving Jesus...

Still carping at himself, he met Iago Eynon on the steps outside the baths.

"I'm on night-shift reg'lar myself next week," says Iago. "Getting on a bit now for rushing about the place. My legs it is, aye, bloody rheums." Wry self-regard crossed Iago's blue scarred face. "See, boy, I'll be overman by night."

"Give us a fag then, Iago. Might be I'll do you some favours once I'm on the cutter job."

The fireman upended a solitary kinked Woodbine. "Genuine now, Gabe, you and Billy Holly will make a go of it al'right. Like Monte Leyshon said, Billy's his own boss, y'know, give and take now and agen."

He grinned his teeth, "Come off it, you fucken old hypocrite. Why didn't you tell me when you came up the face this afternoon?"

"Not my place to, boy. Mr. Leyshon says where and when in this pit. He's paid for doing it." Iago unstrapped his knee-pads. "Fair do's Gabe, you took it better than I expected."

He pressed a derisive thumb lightly on the old fireman's nose. "See you Monday night on top pit."

Ron Berry

2

Nationalisation brought new washery plant, pit-head baths, canteen, ambulance centre, and a crescent of brick buildings, the kind of neat, spartan administration compound attached to light engineering factories. Situated at the upper left corner of a quincunx of pitshafts, Black Rand held favour for wages and generally safer conditions. All five collieries bore the stamp of a power industry planned for the millennium. At Black Rand, mown sward bordered a tarmacadamed road out to the motorway, the grass perhaps symbolizing greater permanence than red ash footpaths to the canteen and pithead baths.

Airgun slugs had pocked the large green and white sign:

NATIONAL COAL BOARD
BLACK RAND COLLIERY
NUMBER THREE EASTERN AREA

The designation irritated Gabe. His first shift on nights and he felt readier for bed than changing into pit clothes. Eastern Area be buggered. They've organised everything, these N.C.B. experts. Whole country's floating on paperwork. You could paddle Wales across to Europe on a raft of pulp. Call it democracy, more expensive than pee-tee actresses standing in a queue from Golau Nos to Scotland. Dent somebody's teeth for trying to swindle your earnings, then you cop two years probation plus £30. Plus you're shoved on nights. All paperwork for the blue-eyed cuthberts. More mistakes are made on paper than with bombs. Me, I'll make plenty. *Twti* mistakes though. We're ruled by paperwork. Words and figures, out and out killers. They finish off kings, popes, politicians, millions of ordinary people, aye, even God up there. Some day I'll have my cut price quota in Tymawr cemetery, along with Tommy Lloyd's and Mansel's and Martha Lloyd's.

Number Three Eastern Area: Rubbish. As if the pit got lost somehow, until the N.C.B. went popping along to find it again.

He met Billy Holly in the lamp room. A lean man, pale auburn haired, Billy had deformed feet and dire righteousness, the kind of spleen which succumbs to raging temper. Billy was respected for his outbursts. He drove the Longwall coal cutter. He could 'make it talk' they said, but, handicapped from birth, Billy was merely concerned to spare his frailty. When conditions were bad he served colliers a skimped undercut which had the appearance of a good clean cut to the full extent of the jib. After a couple of feet, colliers were hand-cutting, cursing Billy Holly, but dispassionately, because a 4' 6" undercut might have collapsed the roof. Puncher, mandrel and shovel work with a chance to make money was better than day-wage clearing and packing roof muck. And safer.

"Howbe, Cochyn" he said. "I'm supposed to learn about the cutter from you."

"I heard Cochyn enough when I was a kid."

"Doesn't mean a thing, man."

Billy explained, rocking thoughtfully on the heels of his stumped feet, "Point is, if you're going to be bloody chopsy, well, see, I can shake you up good and proper if I've a mind to, only we got to work together."

"No argument, I'm on your side." He lifted the sack of sharpened cutter picks

off Billy's shoulder. "I'll lug these."
Billy's neat pursey mouth exuded complacent grunts. "Been hoping you'd offer, though I wasn't going to ask, not first shift."
The top pit banksman opened the gate. They stepped into the cage behind Iago Eynon and a group of repairers.
"Last bon down as usual," from the banksman as if talking to himself.
Billy told him politely, the way of rebuking a pest, "Mind your own poxy business."
The banksman passed it off, having no authority bar the safe, standby grumbling of his job.
Then a fireman came running from the officials' cabin. The banksman grimaced false teeth. He swung the gate open again.
Angry, wheezing short, scrapy breathing, the fireman shouldered around to Billy Holly, accusing him of negligence - the cutter was in the fireman's district, buried under a fall. No spare labourers to clear the machine.
"How much muck is there?" asked Iago.
Billy's forbearing gesture with womanish, claw-fingered hands, "Wait, listen, before carrying on any more, let's find out who shifted the cutter since last Saturday morning."
"Bloody cutter's where you left it up near the gate road. Who's going to drive it? No bugger, not till young Gabe here takes over on afternoons."
"Ah, now I think I can explain ..." began Billy.
"Fucken dead loss you are," said the fireman.
He saw Billy's eyes retreat, glitter inside slits. The bones seemed to contract under his brow and cheeks. Billy's steel tipped boots went *Tap-tap-tap tap-tap-tap* like the disregarded menace of metallic beetles. Proud Cochyn, he thought, bending his knees, tightening his legs as the cage slowed to a ear-filling pause then glided delicately to pit bottom.
They stepped out, the fireman rowing Iago, demanding to know who was going to clear the fall. Iago chewed tobacco, waiting for his colleague to finish. Meanwhile the pit bottom hitcher hand-pushed a full tram of debris into the cage, clanged the gate shut, pressed the green button and the thick heavily greased guide ropes squelched as the cage lifted into darkness. Suddenly the sack of cutter picks was snatched off Gabe's shoulder; Billy Holly held it dangling at arm's length, the weight of it canting him as he hobbled around the two officials.
"Watch out," warned Iago, stepping aside.
Snorting from his small hooked nose, Billy advanced, crouched over, wild to land a swinger with the sack of picks on the fireman's head. The fireman backed away, between the guide ropes and beyond, to the brink of the pit bottom sump.
"Stop him!" ordered Iago. He pushed Gabe. "You! Get on, boy, quick!"
He yelled. "What am I supposed to do, crack him on the chin? Do your own dirty work, Iago!"
Iago appealed, "Just stop him."
Taking for granted that he wasn't personally involved, entitled to dramatise, he charged past Billy, then a sharp about-turn, "I'll take care of him!" and he grabbed the fireman's lapel. "Move! Out on the main or you'll be in that sump and you won't come up again."
The fireman blustered, "This all you're good for, hitting a man old enough to

Ron Berry

be your father? Carry on, you'll land in worse trouble!"
He realised the man feared Billy more than himself. Sample of guts, at least for a Black Rand official.
Billy was screaming, "Lemme gerrat him! I'll show him who's a dead loss!" He dodged the loaded sack, but Billy missed anyway. The fireman wriggled free, running around to the wide, traffic side of pit bottom. Billy almost fell into the sump with the momentum of his attack. He lost grip on the sack of picks. They leaned over, watching it bubbling to the bottom of the sump. Sixty sharp picks in four feet of black water. It took them an hour to hook the sack out with a length of wire, guaranteeing the event as legend in all five Golau Nos pits.

Iago Eynon brought labourers from another district to help clear the fall. Three o'clock when Billy started the Longwall cutter, Gabe behind the machine, scooping away hot, fine gumming as it churned out from the jib, thinking, we'll never get 'round to a bust up, me and old Cochyn. One thing, this is slightly cushier than filling out coal. Unless I cop pneumo. Or bloody deafness. What if a paratrooper worried about diseases? He wouldn't learn to live rough and kill without warning. Similar down here. You can't have coal and pure spit. You can have the House of Lords, you can have the House of Commons, two loads of crap for sure, so why respect? Why respect any system? I'm a Lloyd, therefore I'm against respectfulness. Definitely too. Us Lloyds are entitled.

He shovelled, musing, dreaming, squaring his manhood.

In front of the cutter, shuffling backwards, bent kneed, bent backed, Billy Holly kept his right hand on the bull-nosed machine, near the control chipper. He watched the roof, overhanging coal slips, timbering, and he dragged the heavy electric cable ahead as the cutter crept forward, steel tow rope lapping on its drum housed in the nearside of the Longwall. Billy would listen, chipper raised, stalling the machine, listen for wrong sounding creaks from the roof, the jib clearing itself under the seam, its snarling roar diminishing as the picks spun free, chaining around at constant speed like rattling bracelets above the heavy drone of the electric motor.

Coming up behind, watching, listening, he hung poised over his round nosed shovel. By knocking off time they were established butties, but it took him a few shifts to orient himself to the Longwall. It was something to cope with. Nightshift soured him. He slept poorly by day, split in two parts, morning and late afternoon. Grouchy at home, "Like a bear to live with," in Sue's opinion, her dourness tormenting him. There was no yielding in her. Home had always nourished his morale. Outside the house he made his own way, following the only rule: Fight to have and hold what's yours.

He learned how to doze while standing, hanging forward over his shovel, a wafer of consciousness sensing the roof and crackling, sagging coal. Sometimes the cutter crept on and on, leaving him drooped, duff spreading out in a thick level carpet behind the jib. Six inches deep and deepening, the Longwall ploughing slower, groaning, burning the picks. Unless conditions were suspect, Billy left him alone. He'd chip hauling speed to zero until the jib cleared itself. Gabe repaid by taking on heavy work. He dragged the cable when they moved to another face, he heaved, levering the crowbar when they flitted out of the seam onto the cutter trolley.

No question of guilt regarding bouts of dozing. He awoke easily, muttering,

That Old Black Pasture

"Night-shift be buggered, I'll never acclimatise myself. It's only good for owls and fucken grave robbers."

Most shifts they cat-napped for a few minutes at grub-time. Billy nominated dry sections of conveyor face.

After sandwiches and mouthfuls of water they settled down for a little sleep, breaking mining law, liable to prosecution. Billy's alibi: "It takes a sneaky bastard to spy on a man when he's at his grub."

Comfortable on warm, powdery gumming, he agreed. The waster deserved a running kick.

"What I mean to say, once a bloke's on top of his job, see?" insisted Billy.

"Right, let's take five."

He relied on Billy to rouse him. Billy prolonged groaning yawns, or clanged the lid on his tommy box or raised his water jack for loud echoing gargles. Or related dirty jokes to spurt his consciousness. Cruel at four o'clock in the morning, wrenched between conscience and the flesh. Billy affirmed *duty* with rectitude, while ever concentrating on making it as light as possible.

One night they were in D face off the main heading. Broken roof had fallen behind them as they were cutting down. One of those bondage shifts when everything went hellish. The tow-post pulled loose three times, the picks blunted from chewing through a rising roll of slag inside the coal, and Billy Holly swore he was in the throes of tonsilitis. Sweat streaked his haunted face, coalescing with icy streamers from the roof. Damp globules highlighting his pal gingery eyebrows, dripped off the tip of his small, beaky nose. This hard, grubbing shift, aggravated by visits from Iago Eynon who preached responsibility. Fevered Billy lost his cutterman's caution. He took risks. Iago squatted with them at grubtime, shooting tobacco juice and quoting estimates per man hour, per length of stent if day shift colliers had no ready-cut coal waiting for them in the morning.

He felt harassed behind the cutter, the onus on himself to keep the jib clear. The Longwall ripped quickly under dangerous sections of roof. He crouched from one steel prop to the next, his fears eased by cold metal against his ribs. Often he shovelled one-handed at full reach of his arm. On ahead of the cutter, two repairers were chopping and fixing extra timber props. Behind them the whole face pounded, coal crashed down, grinding roof fissures fractured, buckling timber flats above the props. Time after time he scurried to safety in front of the machine.

It was a normal conveyor face squeeze, temporary, worsened by the Longwall coal-cutter. Self protection hinged on experience gambled by chance.

Worn by fever and strain at the end of the shift, Billy tottered back to pit bottom. The following night however, saw him riding down in the last bon, thick-speaking from his inflamed glottis, yet steadfast, saying, "We'll change the picks first thing. Won't take us long."

"Righto," he said. "Didn't think you'd be here tonight, Coch. Missis boot you out of the house?"

"Mine's a good un, don't you fret. Seen Iago?"

"Went down earlier."

"Hear the way he carried on last night? Notice how he gets his pound of flesh out of the daft likes of you and me? Crafty bugger, Iago is, on the quiet."

"We won't see much of him this shift. They're re-laying the double-parting

Ron Berry

on Gomer's heading."

"Better not, or I'll be fast into him." Billy rocked promissory *Tap-taps* on his heels.

"You're a bloody hog for punishment," he said.

They found Iago waiting for them, dollops of his tobacco juice glistening on the flat, steel clad Longwall.

"News for you, Gabe. Monte says you're ready to cross Billy on afternoons. I told him you could handle this cutter."

He dropped the sack of sharpened picks. "Leyshon reckoned I'd only be on this job till he found another man."

Sliding his backside off the machine, Iago crawled on hands and knees until he was able to stand up in the roadway. "Gabie-boy, you're in the same position as five weeks ago, as I understand it. Either drive the cutter or take fourteen days notice as from tonight."

"Al'right, al'right, on your fucken way then, don't rub it in," he said. And he realised, here's the discipline. Old Monkey Lips in Dove Street, he put the jinx on me when he yapped about discipline. Monkey Lips should have been with us when we cut down through D face last night. Born and bred bloody chimp, he'd cry for mercy.

Billy shouted after the retreating cap lamp, "Switch the power on, Iago!" and, "Now then, boy, told you he was a proper bastard. Him and Monte, they make a cowin' pair."

"No rush, take our time changing the picks," he said.

"Course! We got a pretty dry run in front of us tonight too, thank Christ."

3

After unlocking the jib he signalled Billy to haul forward a few yards until the jib straightened itself out from under the seam. Billy linked the tow-rope to the jib, ready to chip it back at right angle to the machine. He trilled a pigeon fancier's whistle for Gabe to start changing the picks.

Reaching for the sack, he dabbed his hand on Iago's tobacco juice. Minutes later Billy did the same thing. From shared animus they cursed the official and his family. Straining wits, blaspheming him almost respectfully in the manner of miners, sailors, soldiers, prisoners, slaves. Language alien to domesticity, inane to the eye, the ruination of dialectic, gross heaped on dross, idiom of tongues obeying harmless, subtle phantasmagoria. He changed the picks one at a time. Short stubby picks locked in the chain by a single nut-headed grubscrew. Simple, just a tug on the spanner, remove the blunt pick from its socket, tighten in the sharp pick. Blunt picks were bagged ready for the blacksmith next morning. Billy hunkered at the controls. Heeding the word from Gabe, he chipped the chain around the jib. Between times he oiled the machine. He sloshed half a pint on Iago's Eynon's trade marks, covered them with duff and scraped it all off with a shovel. And Billy sang a doleful *O more and more, I adore you, Gianina mia* in thoughtless bath-tub tenor.

Cochyn kidding himself as the great lover, he thought. Him hopping on his bad feet, crooning from that little mouth under that hook of a nose, hair the colour of apricot jam sprouting over his lugholes. He's like a bloody tropical

That Old Black Pasture

parrot. God Almighty, you'll only find his kind here in Golau Nos or some similar place where the spunk of every man's ancestors has taken a lambasting from trying to prove himself stronger in the goolies than in gumption. I bet Coch's a sticker on the nest. He's the goods all right. Found himself a woman, which is more than I can say. After I buy my Standard Eleven I'll be on the look-out. Bloody chronic, not having a regular girl. I'll end up like our Sue. Least she gave it a try before chucking the towel in. First buy the car. Afternoon shift... by Jesus, best shift invented for saving a few quid a week.

He moved away from the jib. "Right, Coch" - there weren't many picks left to renew.

Billy tipped the chipper, inching the chain around.

"That'll do, butty." The chain stopped. He shuffled in close again on his left knee, right leg outstretched, dragging the spanner and sack of picks with his left hand.

Then it happened. Perhaps a lump of coal fell on the controls, or a flake of roof. Later, Billy pledged on the lives of his children that he hadn't touched the chipper. The chain roared around, the tow-rope began hauling the jib into the coal, and a cutter pick jabbed through Gabe's right boot, thinly slicing skin where the arch curves under. The leather held. His boot rammed against the coal and the cutter *stalled*, power to mince granite whining, raging from the motor. But the chain stopped dead. Miracle, luck, anything beyond reason.

Billy cut the motor, he unlocked the pick and loosened Gabe's bootlace.

His foot pulsed fire on Billy lap. "My jack, Cochyn, pour some water over the fucken thing."

Billy fingered the reddened underside of his sock, "Bleeding, man, best take a look at it." Removing the sock, "Ah, good Christ," said Billy.

He brought his foot up high across his left thigh. It felt worse than it looked. "Bruised and that bit of a cut. Fetch my jack."

"Bones all right, Gabe?"

Flexing toes and ankle, "Aye, bound to be."

"We ought to keep it warm. Can you hang on here while I fetch Iago Eynon?"

"No option. Gimme my jack before you go."

At this point, handing him the tin jack, Billy again vowed he hadn't touched the controls. How could he while lodging the empty oil can on the gob wall? "Jonnack now, I didn't touch the chipper. Honest, boy, honest!"

He ignored him, saying as if to himself, "I could use a cuppa tea and a drag."

"Hold on, Gabe, I won't be long." Billy set off at his odd rickety trot out to the main heading where he telephoned the overman.

Gabe journeyed back to pit bottom in an empty tram. He felt comfortable, his foot undramatically numb, wrapped around with his pullover. Two labourers rode up in the cage with him. They shoulder-armed his weight to the ambulance centre, where the attendant cleaned and bandaged his foot. Near two o'clock in the morning, showered and changed into day clothes, he knocked on the kitchen door.

Hushed with dread, Sue let him in. "By God, you've had an accident."

"Don't panic, love, s'only a tap, that's all it is." He walked unaided to a chair.

Ron Berry

"Come in for a cup of tea," she invited the two men, not even glancing at them.

They called, "Goodnight," hobnailed boots clacking out to the N.C.B. van taking them back to Black Rand. They were young fellows, conscious of pit dirt grained in their clothes. Their fathers would have sat at her table and discussed Gabe's 'bump' over tea and Woodbines.

The frayed hem of her brown dressing gown swished the hearth rug. "How much is it, boy?"

"Bruised. Should be okay in a couple of days."

"See the doctor this morning."

"Nuh, I don't expect so."

"Want anything to eat?"

"Not for me, Sue. Run off back to bed. I shan't be far behind you."

"I'll take a look at it," she said.

Unwrapping the bandage, he insisted, "Bruised, just bruised."

Stroking all over his foot, she gazed up into his eyes, "Thank God."

Her hair was bedraggled. "G'night, Sue," he said, thinking, she looks like a golliwog.

In two days he felt fit enough to work. His instep carried a browning patch of purple flesh. Sue advised him to take the week off, shrugging indifference when he mentioned buying a car.

"Fool of a man. What's a pay packet between your foot and the price of a car?"

"I'll be able to drive you out in the country on weekends."

"Why?"

"For the fun of it! We're stuck in Golau Nos all year round."

"Grow up," she snapped meanly.

He left the house then. In the Workman's Hall he won a game of skittles and strolled home in time for early supper.

"Cheese and tomato sandwiches in my box, Sue. I'm not losing another shift."

"Greediness, like every other bugger in this place. See 'em in the shops, all dissatisfied, wanting this, wanting that."

He brooded about her while walking to the pit. Miserable Sue, downright sour. If she had any kids there'd be slaughter in our house. Christ, the way she's turned since Sid Preece packed his hand in. Sid looks on top of the world. No signs of night starvation. Sid's like a boy with a new toy. Lucky sod. For a man to pick and choose when he's well into his thirties, he must be a right bloody dog. Hard headed Sid. Sue, she had the lot ten years ago. Lovely shape on her. Now she won't put decent shoes on her feet, slopping about in things fit for the ashbin. She's over the hill, and I haven't started yet. Not properly. Few months time I will, aye, Whitsun with any luck.

Idealising himself behind the wheel of a grey Standard Eleven as the dark blue Popular pulled up beside him. Black Rand's canteen manageress: "Want a lift?"

"I'm almost there, Mrs. Passmore, thanks all the same."

"Third class ride is better than a first class walk. Foot better?"

He sat in the car, tommy box and water jack in a gas mask satchel tucked

Waitress, King's Cross, 1990

Philip Wolmuth

under his arm. She drove past the N.C.B. signpost, turned left, rounding the stores compound to park behind the canteen.

"You have plenty of time for a cup of tea, Gabe."

"As I intended, Mrs. Passmore."

She climbed out, neatly buxom, a blonde woman with small hands and feet. Mrs. Passmore put on the grand manner when dealing with rowdy bull-ragging colliers. There was an ageless glow about her, sustained by gestures of intimacy. She had charm, wayward in effect, the evidence being her husband. Smiler Passmore neither smiled nor worked, spending his days between Hebron chapel, the council library, two cafes and sick-man plodding along the river bank with a black and tan mongrel. Due to religious convictions and a 'bad chest' he looked anciently forty-four, nineteen years married on the rebound from his boyhood sweetheart, who escaped with a married, backslider deacon. The Passmores had no children to muddle their lives. Smiler prepared economic meals three times a day, tended the kitchen fire, hoovered, and made up their single beds. Mrs. Passmore was wildly fancied, literally subterranean fantasy of collier boys who went down the pit with her Cornish pasties and syrupy tea in their bellies. Miners' wives sneered, especially when annual pregnancies sagged their shoulders and varicosed their legs.

"I've come to collect my accounts book," she confided. "Awful nuisance this time of night." The shy, elderly woman behind the counter, twisted and thinned her mouth off and on like trick photography. "Gabe wants a mug of tea. Hasn't gone stale, has it, Gillian?"

Gillian's indignation crowed faint, "Wetted a minute ago for them blokes over by there."

Mrs. Passmore spun around, nimble, lifting the counter flap, smiling at Gabe as if measuring him for glory. "Be careful in future, boy. After all, when you find that special girl, she won't want a cripple for a husband." The smile faded on a slow thrown away lift of her hand, replaced by compassion, frank brown eyes evoking the misery of broken love. In brave upsurge she regained her allure, leaning towards him on the counter flap, her white hands maidenly cupped. "We are only young once in this life."

He passed fourpence across to Gillian, then waited absorbed, patient, the heat of the mug tingling his pick and shovel-hardened fingers. Mrs. Passmore unlocked a cupboard, her skirt tightening as she bent down to reach the accounts ledger.

He said, "What d'you think, Mrs. Passmore, I'm being sent afternoons next week. Cutter operator, afternoons regular."

She creamed a smile over her shoulder. "Oh, shame. Bed to work, that's all it will be. Of course it doesn't matter as much for the older men."

"Anyhow, I'm saving for a car," he said.

Bible-patting the ledger, "Very nice too. Please excuse me." She raised the flap, came out in a rush to follow Gillian who was disappearing into the canteen stores. "Don't forget to lock up!"

He crossed over to a table near the door. Mrs. Passmore paraded jauntily down the long aisle. Instinct prickling his senses, he felt humble towards her. Nothing he could hope for. This blonde didn't want him, not the secret whoring part of it. Yet she promised quietly, "Tomorrow night I'll pick you up outside the Great Western Arms. Look out for me. *Nos da*, Gabe."

Narrow-eyed for a moment, he tried to read her mysterious face.

Billy Holly came in as she drove away. "Bitch of a woman she is," said Billy. "Smiler Passmore's worn the same suit on his back s'far as I can remember, and there she is togged up like a bookie's tart. Beats me how she runs that car. Can't be done, see, not on the wages she's gettin' here."

Tomorrow night with Mrs. Blondie. *Saturday*! What time? He dropped a cigarette on Billy's tommy box. "You were bad the night we brought the cutter down through D face."

"Swollen bloody tonsils, aye."

"I've seen you kipping in a wet face with braddish wrapped round your bum."

Casually contemptuous, "Bright fucker to talk you are," said Billy.

"D'you know her first name, Mrs. Passmore's?"

"Mildred, and if she was my Millie I'd show her the four corners of the room." Billy slurped quick pulls at his tea like a small, alert mammal.

He mimed punching. "That's what I like about you, Coch, you're such a nice gentleman."

"How's the foot?"

"Nigh on perfect," he said.

"C'mon then. I've had a real dopey kid for a coupla nights."

"They are about, Coch. Wonder who they'll put with me when I'm driving the cutter."

"S'all bloody luck," said Billy.

They went down in the crowded last bon, every man chuckling, hooting at Billy Holly making mock of the night he flung a sack of cutter picks into the sump.

4

With an hour to go before knocking off time, Iago Eynon asked them to help a heading miner. The man was single-handed, his butty at home with a broken finger. Cutter jibbed out from the coal, wedged on its trolley ready for the haulier, they were going through the motions when Iago's cap lamp appeared.

Inquired Billy, "What's it worth?"

"Double time," guaranteed the overman.

Helping out in emergencies on off-shifts was inevitable. Top grade men dickered for allowances, especially under abnormal conditions.

They walked back and turned left off the main haulage road. It was a worked-out district, just this single heading driving on through old Number Two to new coal.

He said, "Don't be so fucken cynical, Coch."

"Why's Stan bothering if his butty's not in? I reckon he's making about four quid a yard."

Iago carried his safety stick under his arm like a sergeant major. "Wait till you see the place. It's not safe. I'm only asking you to give Stan Evans a hand with this last pair of rings. From now till ha'past six I'll be busy with traffic. There's a journey of muck to be sent up before the dayshift comes in. So-long now, boys. Do your best."

Billy said to Gabe, "Leave the picks by here. Collect 'em on the way out."

Ron Berry

He whistled *Blue Moon* as they walked on, Stan Evans's lamp flickering ahead like a glow-worm.

"Listen," he warned. "Hear that? Going to be rough. Wouldn't mind gambling it's a proper shambles in there." He tightened his right arm around Billy's shoulders. "Got your sky-hooks handy? You're bolting the fishplates."

Billy tilted his head, gazing up at old twelve foot rings arching the heading. Some were twisted, the fishplates skewed. Thin squirts of dust came down through cracks in the lagging, mildewed timber lapping from ring to ring. They heard their own breathing and the persistent whispering of moving earth. "Pinching a bit," said Billy.

"Hold still a minute, Coch, plenty of time."

Tiny rivulets of crushed shale sifted down behind the stone walled sides of the heading. They dribbled and suddenly stopped like scatterings from the claws of rats. High up in the roof a persistent booming, echoes nagging distant as far away thunder. Billy stumbled backwards, impelled by the tension of his neck muscles, upflung chin exposing his Adam's apple.

A fist-sized piece of rock plumped hollowly on the over-head canvas airbag ventilating the heading. Dust shone innocently, swirling away to nothing. Billy had tucked himself close to the side, one foot resting on a 2" blastpipeline clipped low on the rings.

"Aye, long way off yet though," said Billy.

"Pretty far off," he agreed.

They went on another twenty yards, paused again, listening to hissy squeal-creak grinding of timber like crossed branches strained by winds. Ordinary too, common enough the way it creaked slow and steady.

Billy tished judgement, "Long way away. She'll settle by and by."

He said, "Let's get this ring up and clear off out."

The heading man grumbled, "I asked Iago for help two hours ago. Where the hell you been?" Stan Evans was big, middle-aged, wearing a half-sleeved woollen vest. Badgerly hairs bushed on his chest, and his cud of Ringer's seldom left his front teeth. Brown stain crystallised, riming the edge of his lower lip. Removing his helmet, Stan wiped his baldness with a hairy forearm.

Pushing past him, he said, "Never mind about Iago. We came straight off the cutter."

Billy offered genially, "So this is where your butty broke his finger."

Stan argued, "Some youngsters these days, they don't know they're born."

"Goes double for miserable sods like you," he said, laughing. "Righto, Stanley-boy, let's shove this bloody ring up."

"Go easy," warned the heading man.

They stepped over a stack of four and a half foot posts, new timber ready for lagging, and on to a tramful of debris with sprags locking the front wheels. Both halves of the new ring were propped sloping against the sides of the tram. Beyond the tram, patches of slurry at the base of shattered rock blown down by shot firing. Inches wide, a glistening seam of rider coal slanted some nine feet above the tramtrack.

Stan pointed at the rider. "When she runs out we'll be into four foot of clean coal. Cause of all the trouble, that dirty little rashing of *mum-glo*. Nothing solid up above."

That Old Black Pasture

Back in the heading, broken rockstones bounced, echoing on the lagging. "Coming nearer," Billy said.

Stan tossed a pair of fishplates with nuts and bolts on the full tram. "Which of you?"

Billy clambered up off the hitching plate, monkeyishly skinny, dexterous, slipping the nuts and bolts into his jacket pockets. "Spanner, Stan?"

"On my toolbar. I'll fetch it when we're ready."

Stan and Gabe raised one half of the twelve foot ring, then raised the other half. Billy drew the heads flush together. They held quite still while Billy slotted the fishplates into position. He sent the bolts through, turned the nuts a few times, saying, "Ready".

Stan whoofed satisfaction, jerked around as timber groaned, tearing across the grain, followed by sibilous roaring of soft shale pouring from a break in the stone walling between rings. "Couple of drams of muck back there," complained Stan. "I'll get my spanner."

Billy looked down, Gabe still humped against his half of the rings. Teetering uneasily on his heels, Billy said, "Slacken off, she won't fall now."

He was muttering, "I don't fucken like this, Coch."

"Me neither. Where's Stan going to, for Christ sake?"

The heading man was twenty yards away by the spilled-out shale, his cap lamp beam roving as he looked up at the old lagging and bulging sidewalls. When the next fall rumbled, rising dust obliterated his lamp. Stan's shout was incoherent.

Perched on top of the tram, Billy saw it again, the light low down, moving away. Stan's bellowing rose to screaming, "Come on out!"

He urged, "Let's move," offering his shoulder for Billy to jump down. Billy landed on all fours like a thrown bundle. Unhurt, he began running out.

Snatching his jacket hanging on a corner of the tram, he saw Billy halt suddenly, heard heavy stuff crashing farther out on the heading, lags cracking, and Stan's light disappeared. Billy came backing away, soft-stepping as if hunted.

"Keep going!" he yelled, glimpsing the heading man's light shining like a blurry star in blackness.

"For Jesus' sake!" protested Billy.

"We gotto make it, Coch! Keep moving!"

They were a few yards beyond Stan's toolbar - two sets of tools, the other belonging to Stan's cross-shift mates on afternoons. Whining echoes resounded the heading. Hardwood sills split beneath the steel rings. Rings plunged askew as the lagging buckled. Stones crackled like fireworks inside the sidewalls.

"We're right under it!" cried Billy. "Back to the dram!"

Forearm hooked under Billy's armpit, he lugged him forward. They ran together, Gabe lifting him along. Another fall spewed out from the left side of the road. They waited, cursing, praying for it to stop. A fishplate bolt snapped, the bolthead pinging away like a bullet.

He thought, we must get out. There's a bloody big *cwmp* on the way.

"Back to the dram," pleaded Billy, his misshapen foot scuffing dust.

"We'll soon be on the main," he said, heaving him over the fall. But there were more falls. Sidewalls burst open. Half a century of compressed slag poured out, broken roof cramming down on the rings, smashing the lagging, ragged stones pounding in the roadway, and no sign of Stan Evans's cap lamp. They were alone in ground roiling like ocean.

A small stone struck Billy's shoulder up near his neck. As he keeled sideways another stone skidded off his left buttock. Billy screamed, trying to roll himself over.

He grabbed Billy's jacket, dragged him closer to the base of the rings, but his grip was shattered by chutting stones deflecting off his arm and wrist. While he crouched low, tight to the rings, the rubble flood continued, dislodging Billy's helmet, burying his head and shoulders. Hugging his bleeding hand between his thighs, unaware, he watched Billy dying, heard the sickening knock of stone on bone. The bones of his butty's skull.

Frenzy annulled dread, gave him the blind power of heroes and desperate cowards. He seized Billy's boots one in each hand, dragging him clear, the cap lamp trailing on its flex from the battery clipped to Billy's belt. Unbuckling the belt he hitched it over his own, abandoned the helmet and pushed the cap lamp into his pocket. Then with Billy in his arms, he weaved stumbling back to the tram. Seconds into minutes later came the worst fall in memories of Black Rand. Thirty yards of heading thundered down, hundreds of tons blanket crashing, leaving half a dozen pairs of new rings strained but upright directly behind the tram.

Breathing shallow in the pall of dust, he sat on the hitching plate with Billy laid across his thighs. "Man, you were right, Coch, you were right."

Stinging pain from his dangling forearm. Running blood blackened on his knuckles. Lacerations rawed his wrist. He clenched his fist, the forearm muscles, beguiled by relief, a sense of wonder. His arm was okay, sound.

"Coch," he whispered, "hey, Billy Cochyn, you hear me?" He widened the spread of his thighs, bending over to lift Billy's head. A bubble of blood swole out, bursting from the small mouth, the lips motionless. "Billy!" - sitting him upright, seeing the pulped flesh of his ear, the bone crunched inwards, all of it wet black, minute glints fading, shrinking to matt black. And he grieved, "Ah, Christ, Billy," lowering him across his thighs, careless now, letting the head loll down.

Desolated, wrung bankrupt, he didn't know what to do. Sitting on the hitching plate, he listened to the roof sounding off, high away air pockets exploding in rock laid down, molten and sealed for 250 million years. Tension emptied, interred by unstoppable memories: Sue on her wedding day, Sid Preece shouting the odds in the front room, half drunk, confetti prinking his curly hair. Flabbergasted Sue But she managed Sidney. How though? Stopped cock on him? His father Mansel fixing stair carpet with tintacks. The big surprise his mother was supposed to have when she came home from hospital after her gallstones operation, only the old lady created ructions. Carpet clashed with the wallpaper. Last round against Nobby Graham, two hard lefts smack on the point, then Nobby fetched up a right-hander from nowhere, so they wobbled back to wrong corners like a couple of punchies. Crumped-up old Tommy Lloyd showing cuttings of his letters to the *Cadwallader Clarion* when pit officials refused to send food down to men on stay-in strike. Grancha Tommy's clay pipe rapping the teapot, his voice gone husky: "Cruel buggers, they'd leave men to die." The winter of twenty foot snowdrifts, everything altered, hedges vanished, bank manager's bungalow just a white tump with two red chimney pots sticking out. Mrs. Passmore up there in the canteen, blondie hair tressed like Goldilocks. Lovely piece she was, that Mildred Passmore.

His breathing dried at the idea of himself stranded in the dark. Levering to his feet, he lifted Billy over the rim of the tram, laid him out on the rubble. He ignored Billy's bloodstained clothes. Didn't matter any more. The cuts on his left hand were sore, fingers stiff as he unclipped his cap lamp. He switched on the low pilot bulb. The sparse glow made him turn, stare pop-eyed at the glare of Billy's lamp. He switched Billy's off, looked around, protesting, "Not enough light to give a bloody rabbit nystagmus."

Afterwards he drained his water jack, the last half cupful chilling his throat. He settled down on his heels, pondering, tired but sure of his strength. He thought about the dead cutter-man. What a bloke, Billy, tongue like a whip defending his corner, his rights... Air. AIR! Christ, the fall must have smashed the big air-bag to smithereens.

He went to the edge of the fall, searching for the 2" blast pipe, the compressed air which powered Stan's boring machine. It was buried.

5

Hunkered in the middle of the tramroad, Gabe talked to himself the way conscientious miners discussed work during grubtime: "Pipe column finishes way this side of Stan's tools. By the boring machine. Blast bag's connected to the column. Stop valve's turned off. So I reckon about five yards between me and that bloody valve. Say eight drams if I can post up as I clear away. Twenty drams if the big stuff starts shifting again. It won't move though, not if I go careful with the timbering." Climbing to his feet, "Hell, any case it's shit or bust."

And he returned to the tram for Stan's shovel, mandrel and hatchet. He tested the cutting edge with his thumb. In three journeys he carried all the four-and-a-half-foot props to the fall. Sweating now, sniffing for air. Not much circulating this side. Perhaps none at all. The canvas airbag was about fifteen yards out from the tram. Sure to be in ribbons.

Before starting he filled his water jack under a thin streamer jetting below the narrow seam of *mum-glo*. He never once looked at Billy Holly. Useless worrying about a corpse. First things first. Dig through to the valve and bang like hell on the blast pipe column, prove to those at the other side that I'm still alive and kicking. Time to worry about Billy when they bring in a stretcher for him.

He worked fiercely, careless of his strength, following the left hand tramrail, excavating a man-sized burrow between the rail and the line of buckled rings. Every shovelful had to be thrown well back. Eventually the muck would have to be handled twice, three times as he drove into the fall. He cleared mashed, sliding rubble for the first hour. No alternative to reaching the solid rock-stone packed fall.

He counted his posts: Thirteen, one extra for luck. Flats, I'm short on flats. Without flats I'll have the stuff tamping off my helmet. Can't risk holding up big stones with these thin Norway posts. Flats? Sleepers! Well-aye, rip the

Ron Berry

bloody lot up, from under the dram and all!

Taking the mandrel, he prised out rail cramps from the last sleeper, then pushed the tram forward over slack rails and removed another three sleepers. Pleased with himself, he said, "Now for some more bloody graft."

Massive slant-locked stones were enemies. He tackled them warily, hooking away loose rubble, his head always protected by a length of sleeper flatted across two short props. He chopped one foot six inches off each 4° foot post (the height of his burrow), using the off-cuts for wedges. The sleepers were cut in half. Small tunnel, less timbering and less muck.

After a couple of yards he met a great steeply-pitched slabstone. Crouched on his knees, he touched smoothly indented fern-shape trackings in the stone, but he didn't *see* them inches from his eyes. They weren't a novelty. He crawled out, squatted in safety, trying to think his way around or under the big stone. Instead he wondered if day-shift men were out there, digging into the fall from the other end. Lucky bastards, plenty of timber, steel flats, lagging. A few six-and-a-half foot posts would do me. I'd hold that stone up for evermore. Four six-and-a-halves, that's all I want. Hundreds rotting away in sidings all over Wales. What would Mansel and Tommy Lloyd do if they were stuck fast in a crib like this? Aye, that's the no-answer question. Probation? Nice way to spend probation. Monkey Lips ought to be here. Up on that dram of muck instead of Billy Cochyn.

Then, straightening out his legs, he whaowed insight, the scrape of his bootstuds on the nearside rail shocking him alert. "Just the job!" He knew he'd found a method to work under the big stone. Rake a couple of two yard rails against it, with heavy fox wedges.

But hard graft wearied him. A prolonged, desperate struggle to fix the rails, poking out fistfuls of rubble from inside the rings, clearing back to a firm base on which to rake two rails against the stone, the great sloping stone carrying unknown weight of broken ground.

His voice croaked, "So far, so good," crawling out for a drink of water. Tired, bone weary, the gristle of his bones aching. Take a spell, he decided, falling asleep in the dark with his arm beneath his head, his damaged hand holding the precious cap lamp to his stomach.

He awoke fearfully, conscious of time wasted. How long? Inhaling, slowly exhaling, he tasted the air. It was like being in an airway before knocking through to a properly ventilated face. He fingered his lamp switch. It's not too bad. I can stick a lot of this. Besides, doesn't seem to be any gas in here, thank the holy bloody Jesus.

He averted his head from Billy Holly on top of the tram.

Gabe plodded at his task until late Saturday evening. His hand throbbed. The longer he stayed in the burrow, the worse he felt. He shortened his shovelthrow, fiddled with the mandrel instead of hacking debris loose enough to shovel. Crawling out, sheer peace, sitting, body all slack for a while, then he shovelled the excavated muck further back, making space for the next heap from his burrow. Sometimes he crawled out simply to listen. Surely to Christ they were working on the fall from the other side, colliers fresh from the table, rescue teams from all over bloody Number Three Eastern Area. They could work side by side under new rings, slash into it, change and change about every half hour. Dim

That Old Black Pasture

witted bastards, why didn't they bang on the pipe-line? Let a man know they were getting stuck into it.

*

Clear sterile water dripped, spun into tiny streamers from the narrow layer of impure coal, accumulating as slushy puddles around the base of grey rubble. It crept back under the tram along the furrow grooved by the right hand tramrail, spreading damp in the dust. Surface coiling pencil currents seeped beneath the fall.

Thank God it isn't travelling out this side, otherwise I'd be soaked up past my knees in that dug-out of mine. I've cleared about seven, eight drams. Another hour should put me by the stop valve, near as damn it I hope, *hope* so 'cause I'll be just about beaten by then. There's comrade Cochyn, he's out of it, finished, poor bugger. His Missis, she'll scream off her tump when she hears about him. As Tommy Lloyd used to say, here's what you pay for the old black diamonds. Mansel and Tommy Lloyd were never stuck in a crack like this. This place is exactly right for testing out the office boyos, all the mob from Robens down, who treat filling out coal as if it's like making parts for Standard Eleven motor cars.

Head between his hands, he blew dry chuckles; I'll have a Standard next Whitsun for certain, aye, too bloody true.

His mind drifted to Mrs. Passmore, hazily for lack of imagination. He swallowed tasteless water from his jack and crawled into the hole.

"Anyone back there?" his reckless bellowing rage promising to protect him. But again he slaved until fatigue and stale air flagged his strength and spirit. He threw the muck twice and dragged in his last two posts. When they were sledgehammered into position, he came out and fell asleep again, fitfully, cap lamp in his hand, consciousness trickling as if through a clogged filter, repeating: The stop valve. Get on to the pipe column or you'll wind up a goner like Billy Cochyn. *Never*, he vowed, defiant, his body fallen languid, unfeeling.

He dug slowly at the rubble, levering out larger stones, rolling them aside behind his boots, using the tramrail as a base for shovelling, lifting, screwing sideways, turning every shovelful over his left thigh. Suddenly, like divine impact, he saw the dull black streak low down in the debris. He scrabbled with his fingers, freeing the length of rubber hose - the blast bag connected to the compressed air pipe column. Confidence gave him a bright spell of coordination. Scratching up through rubble he uncoiled the tough hose until he found the smooth iron pipe. He turned the wheeled stop valve, clung to it with a searing wrench of fear, terrified as compressed air came howling from a leak at the hose clip connection, purging the burrow with prickling dust and grit. Sobbing for breath he turned down the wheel. Air purred out, gently consistent, like soft draught drawing a kitchen fire. He tied his muffler around the leaking clip. Nodding victory to himself, he went back to the tram, convinced now that all he had to do was rest until the rescue gang worked through the fall. Sprawled outstretched in the roadway, cap lamp and helmet held on his chest, the flowing air reminded him of his fight training days. He was preparing himself to enter the hole, start banging on the pipeline.

He switched on his cap lamp as he rolled up to his knees. Go careful. Save light. Battery's almost finished. The weak glimmer focused on Billy's bootsoles, a stubby vee of studded leather above the rim of the tram.

"Poor old Cochyn," he said, futile as godless prayer.

Chill had numbed his bones so he pulled on his jacket. Faint human-breath air whispered out from the black rubber hose: he patted it as he crawled into the burrow. This time he carried the hammer-headed hatchet, held it against the pipe and knocked six solid bangs. Eyes closed, his mouth gaped. Six far-off signals replied, resounded faintly through the metal. He hammered again, aggressive to fearful, realising he might dislodge stones above the pipe column. Answers came as before.

"Bloody miles away." Amazement shedding to dismay, "Christ, Christ, it'll take ages to drive through."

He huddled in the burrow, signals dully whanging on and on, on and on. All the time far off. He couldn't estimate how far. Head wrapped in his arms he lapsed into misery. Worse than a physical beating, worse than the death of his parents. He felt reduced, flawed in the secret core of his faith.

He crawled from the burrow a frightened man, skulking near the tram, peering at Billy Holly's stiff-set, shrivelled face. Mawkishly superior, "Billy Coch, know what, Billy, we're trapped in here behind a bloody big dose of it, heading's blocked right out by the way they're knocking on the blast pipe." He reached over and buttoned Billy's jacket, tidily the way Sue straightened his tie the morning he appeared in Dove Street Court. "But you're safe, lucky man you, Cochyn."

He walked once around the tram, pausing to listen. Automatic peckings from the burrow. He touched Billy's boots, "They've put a bloke on the job, bashing the pipe column. Monte Leyshon's back there. The gog-eyed wonder, he's in charge of operations. Better be, for Christ's sake. If anyone can get me out of here, it's Monte."

Silence invaded him when the knocking ceased. Abruptly, with the surety of instinct, he leaned over the tram and rifled Billy's waistcoat pockets - jacket pockets never carried anything but water jack and tommy box. A thick muffled WHUMP froze him in the act. Shot firing on big stuff. Guiltily relieved, he watched whiffs of dust floating down.

Crouching into the burrow, he examined Billy's things. Three sixpences, piece of lump chalk, broken hacksaw blade attached to a wrist loop of baling string, small pair of pliers, box spanner for the nuts on the cable pommel in the Longwall cutter, and two dirty, boiled sweets. He lowered his mouth to the sweets, crunched them, collecting fragments to his upper palate, sucking the sweetness. He resisted swallowing the fragments. Over an hour later he returned the articles to Billy's waistcoat pockets.

He licked butter and breadcrumbs off the greaseproof paper which had wrapped Billy's sandwiches. Like a robot he folded the paper and stuffed it in his own pocket. Ideas came: Catch up on my sleep. Best thing I can do for the time being. Sue's heard the news by now. Ten to one she's up on top pit, blinding at the officials. Sue and Cochyn's wife. That hulking woman. Where's she from? Lizzie Holly isn't local. Funny piece, like out of a comic. Lizzie Flop.

Checking the ground both sides of the tram: Not much choice for a place to kip. I'll freeze unless I turn that blast off. Give them a knock first.

He clanged the pipe six times with the hatchet before curling up with his coat

That Old Black Pasture

around his head. Seven hours later he awoke like a raw nerved alcoholic - a third mines rescue team had begun working on the fall.

Gabe drank a lot of water, felt its colicky binding in his stomach. I'm starved. Starving. By Christ, I could eat now. I could put away five eggs and a stack of rashers. Forearms clutching at his stomach, he see-sawed from the waist, defending himself against the gnawing cold of his insides. Gripe. It's bound to go. I'll have to lay off the water. Go easy. Just a sip now and again. All I've got to do is keep myself warm. At a pinch I'll borrow some of Billy's clothes. Won't be any grub. Set my mind on that. God help me if I can't go without grub for a couple of shifts.

He went into the hole and banged on the pipe. "C'mon, knock through, you tired bastards."

The same flat rapping came unchanged along the pipeline.

"Slash into it, slash into it!"

Exactly the same dumb answer meagrely plangent inside his burrow.

Idle buggers, they're not putting their backs into it. Every man in the pit should be out there in the heading, all the timber and flats coming up right behind their arses. Everything for the asking. Everything.

He listened, fear punishing his senses, eyes clenched against weeping, but as he crawled out tears dried stickily alongside his nostrils.

Threatening himself, "Must hang on to my nerve. Once my nerve goes I'll be hopeless. I won't lose my nerve. Won't. I'll stick it. Aye, I'll hang on. Stick it out. Might take them a few shifts to work through the fall. Nerve, hang on till the first lamp comes up the heading."

He unfolded the greaseproof wrapping from Billy's tommy box, chewed it, swallowed bits of slimy pulp. Chewing the greaseproof, spitting out residue in pellets, thinking, some feed. Sue should see me eating this lot. She'd curse flashes. Little she knows, little she knows.

His shout broke like nightmare, "Cochyn, how you doing, old tiger? Aah, poor old Cochyn."

On in front of the tram, waxily black against the grey rock face, the thin seam of inferior coal wheezed airily, a few handfuls tumbling down on the rubble. He didn't lift his head. He was trying and failing to calculate how long he'd been cut off in this heading driving through old Number Two district. This bloody death trap.

6

Boots treading, circling like a dog, he made a resting place in soft shale and laid himself flat out on his back. Tactics, he thought, staring in darkness, his cap lamp clipped to the front of his belt. More I sleep, less I'll worry. What's important, I'll keep my strength. I'm a long way from licked yet, hell of a long way. Guaranteed, aye, if Mrs. Passmore was here. I could use a good woman, put some life into my guts. She, the blonde, she knows the game. I had the green light off her last night. But since the fall? We'd finished cutting when Iago came around six o'clock Saturday morning. After, I worked at least till Sunday digging through to the stop valve. Slept then. Slept twice. Must be Sunday evening. Maybe Sunday night. Aye Sunday night, getting on for Sunday night.

Ron Berry

He languished, aching, spent from hunger, cuddling his privates, the only wistful comfort in his body. Subsequently within his drowse, the amorphous female visited Gabe, a concubine of dream brought succour, dissolved benevolence through his bones. He slept peacefully, forgetting her instantly and gone forever in the barren time of his wakening.

His cap lamp glowed eerie, marking the outline of its filament. Staring at it, his hand reached for Billy's lamp on top of the tram. Ready now, Billy's lamp between his knees, he gazed, waiting for the slender curves of red wire to die. He counted off seconds. The glow ceased when he was already blind from staring at it.

What am I doing? Why don't I work on the fall? He sniggered feebly. No timber, nothing, nothing left but waiting. "I'm not a fucken mole," he whispered. Just Gabe Lloyd, aye, N.C.B. Eastern Area welterweight champion two years ago.

He switched Billy's lamp on, gazed sidelong at it for a while, complaining, "Billy's dead in here. I can't take this much longer."

Water trickled under the far side of the tram, spreading outwards to his bed of soft shale. He focused the lamp on Billy Holly. Unclipping his expended lamp and battery, he placed them beside Billy's boots. "Swap mine for yours, Coch. You don't need light no more."

The corpse stank, black tartared teeth exposed inside spread-away lips. Like a man drugged Gabe picked up the end of the rubber hose and fanned the weak, purring air over Billy's face, explaining reasonably, "Bugger all else I can do." Excusing himself, "Pointless burying you, even if I could same it would be, the stink. I'm taking a real bloody homing, Billy, I'm that weak, man, my guts turned to cat's piss."

He dropped the hose, muttering, "Christ knows how long I've been in here."

One knock on the blast pipe brought instant reply, nearer, urgent, like hard slaps on a domestic pipeline a few rooms away. Too weak to lift the hatchet, he clanged the column with the blade of his shovel. Someone outside the fall hammered furious drum rolls, the mad syncopation stupefying him, so he crawled out of the burrow. He kept moving, hands and knees each side of the tramrail. Lying down on the soft shale, light switched off, he held his lacerated hand up close to his mouth. Gradually from inner wreckage the idea persisted, ugly as oracle.

"Never," he mumbled. "Sooner be dead."

Everybody goes sometime, Gabe. This isn't your turn yet.

"Sooner be dead."

Jibber, you're jibbing.

"Naah," and cataleptic sleep engulfed him.

But the world-old edict came again and again, to the seventh day. Curled in blackness, he feebly chewed pieces of leather bootlace. He gnawed as if disinterested, the dead lamp between his ankles. Pitch dark no longer worried him. There weren't any terrors. Nine short pieces of bootlace clustered inside his stomach, and Billy's hacksaw blade hanging from his wrist. He heeled the lamp away, began licking the dried cuts on the back of his hand, cold skin against scant warmth of his mouth. After a while his tongue pushed out the pieces of bootlace. Groping upright against the tram, whispering, "Either you or me,"

That Old Black Pasture

laboriously sawing a lengthwise slit down the thigh of Billy's trousers with the hacksaw blade. Struggling sightless, he puckered flesh between his fingers, tried to saw, cut himself and mangled shreds of trousers. Defeated, he collapsed. Defeated, he recovered awareness, less of remorse than acceptance. The blade tinkled, glanced off the cap lamp as he sighed into the coma which sustained him on ebb until Sunday night, when the first rescue miner found him.

The man came bundling out from Gabe's burrow, anxiously fast, swinging himself forward on hands and feet like a grounded ape. He paused, hand over his nostrils, his lamp beam striking Gabe lying on the shale. He shouted into the hole, "Come on in! They've had it! We're too late!"

There were men gathered around the tram, all busy, covering Billy Holly's body on a Stoke's stretcher. Monte Leyshon held Gabe's head while the ambulance man trickled diluted brandy down his throat. He twitched, jack-knifing from the groins like a baby, and they swaddled him in blankets.

"Carry the body out to the main," ordered the brigade leader. He spoke quietly to the ambulance man, "Will he make it?"

"Should, unless there's something busted inside. No signs of anything. We'll try him with some warm milk."

"The doctor's on top pit," cautioned Monte Leyshon.

Scowling disregard, "Open the flask, Mr. Leyshon."

Minutes later he regained consciousness. He blinked infantile. Blazing cap lamps flashed grinning teeth. His tongue felt wooden, huge inside his mouth.

"Gabe, listen, you're all right. Take it easy, boy, there's nothing to worry about. Right, Gabe? Here, have some more of this. Slow now, slowly does it." The ambulance man fed him patiently. "He's ours," he said. "Bloody marvellous."

Monte Leyshon blew his nose and cleared his throat. "Iago! Where's Iago Eynon?"

One of the team said, "He's back on the main. Old Iago's knackered, been working too many doublers."

The manager crawled into the burrow. "Bring him back to pit bottom when you're ready. Iago will have to let Mrs. Holly know..." His voice clouded to monotone as he scrambled away.

"Sooner Iago than me," said the ambulance man.

Striving through groany whines, "I was finished... it was all over."

The ambulance man wiped Gabe's lips with cotton wool. "Let's get him out from here. Four of you now; head, feet and middle. Gently on the stretcher. Gabe-lad, you'll soon be under the bedclothes. We're taking you home."

He yammered moans as they hoisted and slowly man-handled him through the burrow. "I was all in. Oh Christ, I was dead beat."

"Don't talk so bloody daft," laughed the miner at his feet.

They took a breather out on the main, Stan Evans bending over him, frantic, pleading, "I didn't expect it to come in like that, indeed to God I didn't. See, Gabe, I couldn't do anything, the whole bloody place fell in, I couldn't warn you in time."

The sweating stretcher bearers pushed him away. "Lay off, Stan. Waste of time. He's been in there all fucken week. No call for you to take it on yourself."

They lifted him into an empty tram, two men squatting each side of the stretcher, easing jolts as they journeyed back to pit bottom. A doctor examined him in the ambulance centre, chatting familiarly while the attendant spooned chicken soup into Gabe's mouth. Then the door opened for Sue, just in time for him to grin, warmly befuddled before he slept, hooked jawbones pressing his lips together, and Sue, unknown to herself, feared Gabe would never again wear his loose mouthed arrogance.

7

At the end of November, dry night-time chill and moonglow on Golau Nos, he stepped out to the curb as Mrs. Passmore's car approached the Great Western Arms. She lowered the window, "You look wonderful, Gabe! Where are you going? I'll drop you off."

He thought, speak blunt, "Hey, nice to see you. How's things? Our date, is it still on? What I mean, you dropped me the hint in the canteen. Ever since I've been thinking about you."

Gaiety shivered her blonde hair. "Good gracious!" She opened the door, pressed herself back in the driving seat, arms locked, gulps of delight whooping from her.

"Great coincidence this," he said, "but we're on the right road. Ah'm, turn left once we're over the bridge then left again and we're in Gyppo Lane."

She sang, "You devil!" cutting the engine, coasting down Gypsy Lane to a gravelled lay-by outside a derelict orchard.

He unbuttoned his shirt collar. "Get out shall we?"

"Of course not." She exulted joy. "Think of my reputation!"

"Well, if it's okay with you."

Her hand curved to his nape. "Want *cwtching* do you, love? Come to Mildred."

Their mouths clung.

She mistressed him on the cramped rear seats, murmured directives cogging his senses, "Wait, love... don't rush, boy... there, Gabie, there,": comely Mrs. Passmore freeing his blind rut as their lives centred.

The sequel surprised him. Saying, "Excuse me," she left the car, hid from moonlight behind tumbling mounds of bramble.

Time loitered meaningless inside his head.

Returning, she lit two cigarettes.

"Ta," he said.

Mrs. Passmore Eskimo-rubbed noses. She slantwise crossed her legs and puffed away, glow- "puhh," glow- "puhh," perfectly contented until suddenly her cigarette lighter flamed again and she was peering down at her stockings. "Dear God, they cost me a fortune these days."

"What?" he said.

Her cigarette end arced through the window. "Second pair of stockings this week!"

He waited inert, distant until her plaint registered. Stockings! "Look, Mildred, don't worry, here's a quid for you to buy some odds and ends," insisting quickly, "If you refuse I'll be offended. True now, cmon, take it please."

Charming as a birthday girl, Mrs. Passmore accepted the money. They arranged to meet the following night. Same place. Same time.

She picked him up four nights in succession, warmly affectionate always in

That Old Black Pasture

the Gypsy Lane lay-by. Sometimes they exchanged quite friendly mercenary quibbles.

Late on Saturday morning, Sue came upstairs. She stood at the foot of the bed. "Move yourself, Gabe."

"Be right down. Don't get ratty."

"When you starting back to work?"

"Monday. Nights again until there's a place for me on the coal by day."

"About time and all. Wake up, Gabe, you bloody loafer!"

"Al'right, al'right!"

After breakfast he went walking up the river. East wind stripped shrivelled alder leaves and bankside boulders were drying darkly grey above water level. His first long jaunt since they carried him out from Black Rand. Scornful towards sloth, loss of muscle tone in his body, he kangaroo-jumped across ditches, made short sprints and finally settled down to a homeward saunter. Alongside the football field on the outskirts of Golau Nos, he met Mr. Passmore.

Rugous-faced from emphysema, Smiler Passmore stamped his walking stick in greeting. "Glad to see you out and about again. Must have been a terr-rrible ordeal for you down below. Reminds me of the proverb: The finest blades are tempered in the fiercest fires. Tell me, brother, no doubt you prayed when you were alone in the bowels of the earth?"

Gabe scratched the unmoving mongrel.

Smiler made high, feverish baton motions with his stick. "There isn't a man alive who can afford to ignore the Almighty in his hour of need. Every day Christian lives are being saved by prayer." Climbing to pulpit gusto, Passmore's walking stick hovered near Gabe's shoulder. "Without prayer our sins mount up higher and higher! Without the power of prayer there cannot be salvation!"

He caught the end of the stick. "Do me a favour, pick on somebody else, ah, if you don't mind."

"How can you be so brazen, so wicked?" demanded Passmore.

"Doesn't matter about that, man," ready to appease in allegiance to blonde Mildred. He resented this holy jumper. Scratching the dog's ear, he said, "Well, so-long. My dinner's waiting for me in the house."

"No, wait. Wait for the word of the Lord!" cried Smiler Passmore, victimising him again, the brass ferrule of the stick trembling above his shoulder.

"Don't bloody-well do that," he snarled, attack glinting his eyes. He clipped a fast, barely touching blow on Smiler's elbow. "Listen, you drippy bugger, best thing you can do is buy a pair of working boots and get your Missis to fill your tommy box. Leave me be, right? You go your way, I'll go mine."

"God bless, God bless," urged Passmore meekly, arms twitching, seeking to propel motion into his legs.

Nodding truculence, "No offence, Smiler, it's just, well, listen a minute!" And it blurted out, "For Christ's sake do something about your Mildred! She's like a bitch on heat about the place!"

Mr. Passmore's head planed forward, vulture hanging.

Gabe turned away, jog-trotting, cursing himself for a damn fool. Typical, no better and no worse than Sue. Another Lloyd. Good for what? What the hell am I any good for?

81

Sarah Currie

Astronomy

Everything here is hard. He sometimes makes me walk over hot coals. At other times he lays out carefully a path of broken glass; the blood lubricates my progress and there's a satisfying crunch. My wardrobe is all stilettos, dog collars and pointy bras. He wears leather and leopard-skin print. I've screamed at him about his hair but in my heart of hearts I know shoulder-length suits him. He's thin and boyish, and girlish too. He's generously pierced. He has tattoos of wild animals, marine motifs, creeping tendrils and MOTHERs. On his upper arms are green serpents with red eyes. He boasts that if you stare at them hard, for a long time, you can catch them writhing. He gets charmingly annoyed that I never see it. Fortunately it seems to work on others with malleable minds, who can't resist his entrancing ways. I'm paler and less voluptuous than I used to be. We drink a lot. Some would say it rules our lives. For me it's a bulwark against the abyss.

When we met it was divinely glamorous. I was ecstatic and frankly, there was nobody else on the horizon. I had been left on the shelf and he promised me the heavens. My elevation was complete. It was uncannily like the Human League song, he tells me, : "I picked you up, I turned you round, I made you a star, changed you into something new."

In my new life I miss things which yield and bruise and give, over-ripe figs and oozing honey, goat's kid meat and barley-porridge, cow's hides, lamb's wool and baby-flesh. We had children, an entire bunch of them, but they drifted away. Sometimes I think I catch a hint of their intoxicating smell or a glimpse of their taut, cloudy skins. I never intended to be such a cold mother. I melted once but I'm icy now, through and through. My mother was monstrous in a different way, unnerving, and hopelessly passionate. But I forgot. We're not allowed to talk about her.

The penthouse is colourless. There are none of the browns and greens to which I was so partial, only black and white, and the light is aggressive. The new white is a contrast with the old which was wet, warm and fathomless. This white is dried milk. The wallpaper is imitation Bridget Riley. The ceilings are mirrored and there are black and white stacking-units everywhere, with sharp corners and edges. One houses our clumsy stereo with its gargantuan speakers. There's no carpeting, just dark tiles. My bed is made of granite. I fall asleep thinking of the rocky bed I abandoned. Nothing grows here either, which is strange because he has a reputation for green fingers.

My bullish moods have become less frequent. I endure. My hands often itch to do something. I think that's why I started injecting. I'm not allowed Diana Ross any more, only synthesizers and Richard Strauss, and on vinyl of course. I admit I watch satellite. I scan the ether for the erotic and the heroic, for tales of the errant and aberrant, slaughters and transformations. I see him rarely. That's the downside of being placed on a pedestal. I know he has a girl in every port. He's understandably interested in the accessible, earthier types, though some he picks up are real crazies. A psychologist would doubtless say he possesses a deep-seated insecurity that drives him to seek out adoration. I think it's something to do with his father. I've seen it a thousand times; a wayward child struggling with the burden of an austerely powerful family. Sometimes, when I'm very lonely, I pretend I have a brother. We're twins and we turn this awful, styleless and

Astronomy

soulless place into our playground. We scamper and hide and pounce on each other. Our games include blind man's buff and still blindfolded, we take turns to guide each other. I tickle him behind his furry ears, the way he likes. He slays my captors and helps me find my way out of the cold tunnel.

I haven't forgotten my old fiancé. He was terra firma by comparison, like Robert Palmer. He was muscular, sturdier, though not without animal emotions and cunning. He was on a therapy-binge. He wanted to open me up and explore inside. It seems he didn't like what he found and he kicked and screamed to get out. I heard he pulled it all together and became a top manager.

My man spends all his time with a loud, exotic crowd. At first I was invited to their party which appears never to begin or end. Now he prefers me to be reserved and aloof. He's old-fashioned that way. It's difficult to describe his friends. They're devoted to him. I hate that fat old codger who's been hanging around forever but I know he'll never give him up. The rest are sexual and pharmaceutical experimenters and bizarre to look at, neither fish nor fowl. They're musicians, artists and wanderers, shapers of the counter-culture and giants of the avant-garde.

Any intimacy between us takes the form of bondage-sessions sustained by stimulants. I've taught him to be gentler and more proficient with the rope so it doesn't cut into me so much. I'm beginning to get the point, the theatricality of it all. Afterwards, when I'm untied, he starts crying about his mother. He's so moody and changeable. A tempest will blow up out of nowhere and then we're safely in harbour again. Some of it is certainly pretence. He loves to make an impression, to cut loose emotions and watch the reaction. This has no effect on me. I'm as tough and immutable as diamond. He has phases. I hated his eastern craze, when he accompanied some hippy caravan to meet the Maharishi. There are limits to how much Ravi Shankar and sitting cross-legged anyone can take. Others are terrified of him. It's true he likes to mind-fuck people, confuse them about where he stands and who they are. But that's his baby side, his enchanting sense of mischief. I can see the fiery sweetness in his eyes. He's just gentle to those who give him his due and ferociously brutal to his enemies.

Then off he goes to first-nights, openings and galas for more carousing and adulation. I believe these orgies of consumption are creative not destructive. The partings have become unbearable to me. I watch until long after he's disappeared, convincing myself that I can still see a smudge which is him. Then at length I have to admit the train has left the station, the ship has sailed. My nights are tedious. I tend to pace up and down the corridors for hours until I'm dizzy. Sometimes I'm scared to turn the corner. I think I must be scared of myself, of a secret bit of me I have to keep hidden. We must all have our savage under-side, our barbaric nooks and crannies. He always said it was my innocence which made me queen of his heart. But I'm no longer sure that my pleasures and pains are so different from my mother's. Forgive me. It just slipped out.

There used to be white sand and blue sea. The sea's bigger and colder now and it's black. The view from my air-conditioned eyrie is disappointing. I can see the other islands twinkling in the distance, but I can't orientate myself like I used to. No-one visits, though I'm not difficult to find. I had my favourite dream again last night, the one in which I sink slowly into a mountain of turkish delight. I have other soft dreams of flax and jelly-fishes, feta cheese and yoghurt, and

Sarah Currie

tiger's fur. Then I awake to see the same black leather sofas, glass coffee-tables and steel chairs.
Our romance was widely reported. We made the perfect couple, a magnetic union of purity and excess. And although I was on the rebound, our love was shiny and new. We had the happy ending and many envied my luck. Yet few can have guessed what the life of a star would be like, how fixed and unrelenting it would be. The sacrifice was too great for me. He still pulls on my heart-strings. Yet, if you will pardon the impudence, my crown now jabs me like a crown of thorns. I was once whole. But it's as if I've been torn to pieces and my remains scattered madly about. I know this must sound ungrateful - and of course I always wanted to be a star - but won't someone rescue me ?

Which magazine of new writing

...guarantees each subscriber a full-page editorial critique of all work submitted for publication?
...is seen by agents, editors and critics both here and in the USA?
...pays contributors promptly on publication?
...publishes six times a year?

the **source**
M A G A Z I N E

Six issues £16. Please make cheque payable to Lemaitre-Kelly
Publishing and send to
The Source, 19 Cumberland Street, Edinburgh EH3 6RT.
Call 0131 556 8673 for brochure and submission guidelines.

David Almond
Jonadab

Jonadab was our grandfather's place, a place more impossible and distant than Timbuctoo. Where you going? we'd ask him. Jonadab. Where you been? Timbuctoo. Where is she? Jonadab. Where's Jonadab? Timbuctoo.

I'd seen Timbuctoo on the map, in Geography. There it was in the African desert, tiny and exotic, a week's camel ride through the blazing heat from the nearest town. But Jonadab wasn't in the index of the atlas. It was nowhere. It was an invented place. It was a place to tease us, to halt our questioning, to silence us.

At school we moved lesson by lesson through the world. We coloured in the remnants of the Empire. We traced the routes of great explorers, we followed the missionaries and saints, we marked the places of conquest and conversion. We studied the longest rivers and the highest mountains. We learned the populations of major cities, the names of the seas and the plains. We studied the way of life of the Eskimo, the Pygmy, the Arab, the Red Indian. We were shown the fringes of civilisation, the wildernesses of heat and ice and savagery beyond.

And then one term Miss Lynch arrived and our studies came home. She was a small woman who drove a small white Fiat and who had teardrops of silver dangling from her ears. We watched her in assembly and saw how she didn't say the prayers. We leaned over in our steel-hinged benches and looked at her legs. She told us that we were the centre of all geography and the focus of all history. She said we were growing at the most privileged of times. We'd have been crawling through Felling Pit less than a century ago. We had a duty to understand our place in time, to keep History moving forward.

She spread maps on her desk and invited us to stand around her. We gasped to see the names of our streets in print. We stabbed our fingers onto our own houses and gardens, we traced familiar pathways through familiar streets and parks and playing fields. We located the places of great fights and football matches. We followed bus and train routes through Gateshead and over the bridges into Newcastle. She showed the shafts going down into the coalfield and the places where ships were built. We saw the great curves of the river as it made its way to the North Sea, and I caught my breath and halted, for there, in tiny letters just beyond Felling's boundary, was Jonadab Lane and then Jonadab itself: a small empty space on the banks of the Tyne.

*

When she pinned the map to the wall I sat below it and drew my route. I carefully named the familiar streets I must take: Rectory Road, Chilside Road, The Drive, Sunderland Road. I sketched the graveyard and Memorial Gardens at Heworth. I marked the places where I would cross the railway and the by-pass and go beyond Felling into Pelaw and then into the unknown fields below, until at the foot of my page by the crayoned blue river, I came to my map's most distant and exotic point whose name I went over time and again. Jonadab. Jonadab. Jonadab.

Miss Lynch came to me and smiled.
"You do this very well."
"Thank you, miss."
Her eyelashes were dark and curved. There was pale lipstick on her lips.
"You come from a Felling family."

"Yes, miss."

I showed her our house in Coldwell Park, then the other places we'd lived: Felling Square, Thirlmere, Felling Square again. I showed her our grandparents' homes in Ell Dene Crescent and Rectory Road.

"And where were the family before?"

"Don't know, miss."

She smiled again.

"You should ask about these things," she said. "You should write down everything you find. Or the memory will be gone."

She moved among us. She kept returning to me. She watched me drawing, the pencil following the shapes my finger made as it moved across the map.

"You won't understand this," she said. "When you travel through the place in which you were born, you travel through yourself."

*

I set off that Saturday morning. I put bread, cheese, fruit in a haversack. I put in my map and a notebook. I told our parents that Miss Lynch said it was my duty to understand my home, and that I was going to explore for a few hours.

"Just in Felling," I said.

They laughed and said I'd hardly be lost, then.

As I walked from the garden through the gate, Catherine called after me.

"Where you going?"

I grinned and looked back at her.

"Jonadab," I said.

*

On Rectory Road our grandfather was watching from his window. He beckoned me over. I waved and walked on. I called that I was going to Jonadab and knew that he couldn't hear. It was early spring and crocuses were growing in the verges beneath the trees on Chilside Road. The sun was drying the pools on the pavements left by last night's showers. The distant river was gleaming between banks crammed with cranes and warehouses. The sea on the horizon was dark as ink. As I turned down onto The Drive I heard a voice calling me. I turned and waved again, to one of our aunts, from this distance indefinable, one of the identical twins. I crossed the by-pass at Heworth and paused on the high steel footbridge that trembled as the traffic roared beneath. I looked down across the graveyard and tried to distinguish our sister Barbara's grave and tried to recall how she had been in life. I paused again in Pelaw, in the shadow of the huge CWS buildings that lined the road there. The clash of printing machines came from inside. I nibbled some cheese and looked at the unfamiliar faces passing by. I consulted my map, walked on, turned left at Bill Quay Park into a street that suddenly steepened in descending to the Tyne. There were a few rows of terraced houses, an area of waste ground before a pub, the wide expanse of the river, shipyards filling the opposite bank, ships as tall as St Patrick's church resting there. I found the small white name plate with Jonadab Lane written in black, fixed to the wall of a low warehouse or workshop. The lane was uncared-for: broken tarmac, cobbles showing through, potholes filled with black rainwater. A slope of weeds and broken buildings hung over it. I followed it and it opened out into an empty area, a small rough field sloping to a six foot drop to the water. Then there were factories and workplaces and houses stretching all the way to the

Jonadab

city with its arched bridge.
Three ponies were tethered to stakes, with their heads lowered to the grass. A boy and a girl sat on a pile of stones facing the river. A small fire burned beside them, its smoke rising languidly through the clear air. A bony mongrel was tied to the stones by a rope around its neck. It growled, and the children turned to me. They leaned closer together and muttered and laughed.
"Who this?" the boy called.
They laughed again and turned to face me.
"Who this?" he repeated.
They had long sticks in their fists like spears, the tips pointed and scorched. They had sheath knives in their belts.
The boy jabbed his spear at me.
"Ungowa!" he said. "Speak!"
The girl stared. The dog growled again.
"Is this Jonadab?" I said.
"Not understand!"
They laughed.
The boy shouted, "Piss off home!"
I stood there.
The girl took her knife from its sheath, ran her thumb over the blade. The boy lifted his pullover, pointed to a scar that slanted through the right side of his stomach to his waist.
"She do this with she knife." He glared. "Understand?"
I nodded. "Yes."
"She mighty wild. You touch her and you finished. Where you come from?"
I pointed back up the hill towards Felling.
"Where your people?"
I pointed again.
They grinned at each other.
"Him all all alone."
The girl ran her thumb on the blade of her knife.
We watched each other.
They were blond, blue-eyed, a little older than me. Tangled hair. Filthy faces. They wore jeans, broken shoes, ripped pullovers. A cooking pot and a kettle were on the blackened earth around their fire. Stuffed rucksacks and rolled-up blankets rested on the stones. Beyond them, sparks cascaded over the hull of a half-built ship. The crackle of welding rods and the voices of workmen calling to each other echoed on the water. Beneath everything was the endless low din of engines and machines, the sour scent of the river.
I stood there and felt no fear.
"Is this Jonadab?" I said again.
I took the cheese from my pocket and nibbled it.
"Him bring food," said the boy. He beckoned me with his spear. "Ungowa! Ungowa!"
I pulled the haversack from my shoulders and moved towards them. I showed them the bread, the cheese, the fruit. I squatted in front of them.
"You live here?" I said.
They laughed. The boy stamped on the earth.

87

David Almond

"This sacred ground," he said, and he stuck his spear into it.

He reached out and took some of the food. He broke some cheese and gave it to the girl. He pointed to me, to the food, invited me to join them. The girl giggled.

"Mighty good," he said. He pointed to a rock. "You sit, boy."

I ate the bread and the cheese. I opened a pomegranate with my penknife and gave each of them a section.

"You're brother and sister," I said.

She giggled again.

"Last of our people," he said. "Why you come here?"

I shrugged.

"Just to look."

"This sacred ground."

"And you live here?"

"Many suns. Many moons. She and me. She mighty wild. Beware."

He turned his face away. The girl delicately picked out the pomegranate seeds with her fingertips. She raised her eyes and stuck her tongue out at me.

"Mighty danger here," he said. "Bad people come. At night we see ghosts that dance on water. Sometimes the dog kids come and watch us in the dark."

"Dog kids?"

"Children got from woman and dog together. Paws for hands and feet and hair on backs and howls like babies crying. Fire keep them away from us. And the spirits of our people come watch over us." He lifted his spear. "This dangerous place for you, boy. Mebbe time go home."

She raised her eyes. She nodded. I looked at my map.

"It is Jonadab," I said.

I sketched the place in my notebook: the field, the stones, the broken buildings. I copied the graffiti that was carved into the stones around me: names and dates going back centuries. I thought of Miss Lynch and I built a settlement in my head: houses, a mill, a farm, stone walls enclosing a field of sheep, a little jetty joining Jonadab to the water.

"Where do you come from?" I said.

He contemplated.

"Too many questions," he said. He swept his arm towards the horizon. "Far far way, boy."

"Have you been here long?"

He scowled, took a crumpled cigarette end from behind his ear, lit it in the fire and smoked. He passed it to the girl.

"Bad people come, want to take her way from me. We leave in the night. We bring horses. We ride many days to this holy place."

He turned his face away. They laughed.

"We kill many," he said. "Much blood has run from our knives. We mighty wild."

I was about to ask more, when he raised his shirt again, showed me the scar again.

"Appendicitis," I whispered.

He stood over me with his knife in his fist.

"So what you got, boy? What blood you had? What pain you had?"

Jonadab

I contemplated my body, the meagre grazes on its knees, the lack of scars. My easy breath. The easy beating of my heart. I shrugged.
"Nothing."
His face was scornful.
"Ungowa," he said.
He turned to the girl.
"Show him," he said.
She pulled her hair back, showed a healed gash across her temple. She lifted her pullover, showed where an area of her lower back was distorted and discoloured after burning. There were other burns, smaller, more recent, scattered on her skin.
She glared with her blue eyes.
"See," he said.
"What happened?" I said.
He thrust his knife at me.
"Too many questions. Touch," he said.
I laid my fingertip on the blade, felt the sharpness, how it would cut so easily.
"See," he said.
"Yes."
"Much danger, boy. You think you safe, but always danger coming. Why you come?"
"To look. To see."
"Ha. Ha."
He unfastened one of the rucksacks by the rocks. He took out a book, *The Boy's Big Book of Indians*. On its cardboard cover was a young bare-chested brave on a galloping pony. The pages inside were brittle and bleached. The faded print told of the tribes, the great plains, the freedom before the white man came. There were pictures of more braves. There were herds of buffalo, villages of tepees, ferocious chiefs, beautiful squaws with babies.
"Our people," he said.
I looked at the girl. She stuck out her tongue. He thrust the knife at me. I nodded.
"You come look see here, boy."
He stood up, tugged my arm, took me to the final drop to the river. We squatted at the edge. Below us was the dark slowly moving water, its slimy surface, the waste it carried. The mud above the water line was slick and shining, rainbows of oil shimmering upon it. The exposed earth higher up was cracked and crazed. He leaned over and tugged at the earth, lifted a thin splintered bone from it.
"These the bones of our people. We keep watch on them. This holy place."
He stood up and held his hands towards the earth of Jonadab.
"The bones of our people. Somewhere here our father, somewhere here our mother." The girl on the stones sniggered, giggled. He held the bone in his palm. "Mebbe this a bit of mother, a bit of father. Mebbe from an older time. Mebbe from time way way back, boy." He went to the fire, raised the bone over his head. He grunted several times, stamped his feet, muttered and wailed. His voice intensified. He howled and howled. Then was silent, sat by his sister. She stuck her tongue out.

David Almond

"Now you piss off back, boy," he said.
She nodded, formed the words with her lips: piss off back.
He dropped the bone. The dog crawled to it, started to lick.
The boy and the girl leaned on each other. They faced away from me. He lit another cigarette stub and they smoked together.
I sketched them. I stared towards the city, saw the huge construction cranes turning so slowly across the rooftops, saw the glint of traffic in the sunlight as it moved across the bridge, saw the world moment by moment being created on what was gone.
"I knew somebody who died," I said.
They were lost in themselves. I imagined following them, entering their silence, moving through it step by step. Another little journey, another Jonadab.
"I knew somebody that's in the ground," I said.
The girl turned.
"Where that?" said the boy.
I pointed back up the hill. "There. Up there."
"Ha. Up there."
I moved to them. I sat on a stone at their side.
"There's ground up there filled with people, too," I said.
The boy nodded.
"Places everywhere built on bones."
The girl held the cigarette to me. I smoked it and my head began to reel and I smoked again.
I stood above the fire and stamped my feet and grunted. I muttered and wailed and the girl giggled. I put my hand flat to my mouth and hooted. The dog growled. The boy came to my side and stamped and hooted too. Then the girl at last. She circled the fire and held her face up to the sky. We circled the fire together and squealed and screamed.
When it was over we sat on the stones again. The girl was at my side. I wrote in my book, *I went to Jonadab today.* I closed my eyes and moved into the silence. After a long time, she whispered, "Yes. This is Jonadab." And then another long time, and she whispered, "We bring the ponies for the grass."
She leaned on me.
"We sleep out in fine weather," she whispered. "Our home is not far away."
Her body rose and rested on her breath.
"Your people are good," she said.
"Yes."
"Write your people."
I wrote their names: my father, my mother, my sisters, my brother.
"Write the one that's gone."
I wrote her name.
"Write us."
"Who are you?"
"John and Jane."
I wrote their names.
"Who are your people?" I asked.
"Our father died and then our mother died. We live with another, who is bad."

The boy was silent, until he knelt before us with his knife. He took our thumbs and cut into their soft flesh and squeezed out the blood. He cut his own thumb. We pressed our wounds against each other's wounds.

"Now we brothers and sister," he said. "We joined in blood."

We meditated on this.

"One day much blood will run from our knives," said the girl. "We will go off on the horses."

I asked no questions. We sat there. The field by the river was quiet and still. The men in the shipyards called to each other. Sparks cascaded into the water.

"One day I thought I was going to die," she said.

She turned. We looked together towards Jonadab Lane, saw the dark figure waiting below the broken buildings.

"It's nothing," she whispered. "Don't look. Don't ask."

After a time she kissed my cheek.

I thought of Miss Lynch and of my duty to move forward. I thought of my sister in the ground at Heworth. I thought of the stone with her name on it, the space beneath waiting for other names. I thought of passing her, of climbing home again through familiar streets, passing familiar faces, and there came a great ache of desire to stay in Jonadab this day, and then to disappear, to ride into the unknown places with these gentle children and their beasts.

Dick McBride THE ASTONISHED I

First-hand memories of Kerouac, Ginsberg, etc.

In *Panurge 22* I wrote: "If I could find £1,000 over and above the amount necessary to keep alive I'd show you kids how to do it." In *Panurge 23* Nicholas Royle answered my "withering scorn", by saying it was "absolute nonsense, clearly". Maybe... Anyway I've found the little bit extra and brought out a book called THE ASTONISHED I. It's about San Francisco and City Lights in the 50s and 60s. It's nostalgic and probably absolute nonsense - the part left out by eminent historians and prominent poets, in other words - true, unvarnished lies. It's published by -

> McBride's Books
> 1 Evendine Cottage
> Evendine Lane
> Colwall, Worcs WR13 6DR

It costs **£5.99** including postage and packing.

Thanks, Dick McBride

Charles Wilkinson

Treasure

It was usually winter when they left me. I'm not quite sure why. Perhaps they found the flat cramped at weekends; or maybe they didn't like the central heating turned down so low, a legacy, I'm afraid, of my upbringing: I've always been used to cold houses. Anyway, for whatever reason, they would be gone by February; most didn't make it to Christmas. Their departures were arranged to coincide with the times that I was in. I would wake up - so many of these flights back to mother or a previous boyfriend took place when I was half asleep - to hear them jangling coathangers and hurling framed photographs into suitcases. A terrible noise: it was as if they wanted me to listen to them opening and closing every single drawer in the place. But I'd pay no attention; I'd just go off to the kitchen and make myself a cup of tea. Then, usually about eight fifteen, would come the final clump down the corridor, complete with bulging suitcase banging against the wall, and the ritual slamming of the door. After that there would be silence for a bit. That was the moment they expected me to come to the window. Once they were safely in their cars, their luggage tucked up in the boot, their stereo equipment stacked beside them, they wanted to be able to see me standing there all by myself, alone amongst the potted plants. I'd stay exactly where I was, sipping my tea and reading a newspaper, and after a while I'd hear the car choking and stuttering in the drive. Once or twice the engine died altogether, and then I half-expected them to bang on the door and ask for assistance or the use of the telephone. But somehow they always managed to get going. I'd hear them accelerate down the road, brake at the junction, and then the sound would fade away, merge into the hum of the traffic. I tell myself that I never missed them, any of them. But it is true that at such times I would become a little introspective, and just not notice the things that would normally have bothered me. The only real problem was that I'd forget to water the plants, and then one evening I'd come home from work, and there they'd be, brown and curling. I'd have to throw them out, and that was always, I'll admit, a melancholy task.

*

Why have I started with them? I think it was because Colin and Steve told me to. Ever since I've been in this place, they've been encouraging me to write about my past. I'm not sure it's a plan that I like: there's always the possibility that someone may read what I've written before I've finished with it. In fact, that is what happened yesterday. When I went down for lunch, Colin found a draft of the piece he'd told me to work on and read it without my permission. I don't think he liked it very much. He said it wasn't even very clear. What sex were 'they' for a start? I had to laugh at that.

I suppose I've been here for several months. It's hard to be certain. Colin and Steve assure me that I'm making progress, but I sense a growing impatience. Colin keeps on running his fingers through his hair and has developed an irritating habit of saying 'right' the whole time. The other week in one of our sessions, as soon as he saw that I was beginning to stray away from the subject they'd asked me to talk about, he sprang to his feet, said 'right' in a very firm voice, and simultaneously raised his hands as though he were telling a small child on a tricycle to brake immediately. Steve had stopped taking notes and was just staring out of the window. I asked them what the trouble was. They said that

Treasure

they just felt that they simply didn't have enough to go on. They needed something more, something definite. It was then that Steve suggested I should write it all down. "Let's have it on paper," he said. Well, frankly I'm not at all sure that this strategy has been a success. For the first three days I didn't write anything at all; I just sat there staring out of the window. As I told them later, they were asking me to write about things I didn't want to discuss; things that I didn't even want to think about! I became a little upset after that, and they had some difficulty in calming me down. Nevertheless, it was later that evening that I wrote what Colin read yesterday.

*

The house where I am living is a narrow, wooden building that has recently been painted white. There's a veranda at the back that overlooks the bay. You can't see the rocks that lie far beneath, but if it gets rough the air is scratched with Pacific spray. I've yet to learn the names of all the seabirds that wheel ceaselessly above us. When the wind is in the right direction, you can hear the soft deep honk of a distant ferry. To the east of us lies a city built around glimmering lakes and bridges. With the aid of a telescope, I can see the light glancing off buildings of steel and glass - grey, silver, iron-blue. And, far beyond, the faint white outline of mountains brings memories of pinewoods and the smell of snow in high places.

My bedroom is at the back of the house. When the weather is very bad, I can hear the waves crashing against the rocks. Sometimes I can't sleep, and I lie there for hours, listening to the howl of a storm. One night I got up and went over to the window. Although I couldn't see a single star, the moon was out, suffusing the sky with an eerie purple glow; the ocean was ribbed with foam as far as the eye could see. I climbed back into bed and pulled the sheets up to my chin. I told myself that somewhere beneath the angry white surface everything would be dark and calm. I tried to imagine how silent it would be on the seabed; and there would be no rocks, just invisible sand and blind fish, motionless as stone. And as I lay there, hardly breathing, I remembered the octopus. Although I'm not exactly sure when I first saw it, I must have been about six or seven at the time. It was not a real octopus, but a drawing of one, rather crudely executed, a cartoon, or, more probably, part of a comic strip. The octopus is sitting on a treasure chest, and the expression on his face is both ignorant and implacable. He has no idea what is in the chest, but nothing will ever induce him to leave it. He will remain there forever. Behind him lies the wreck's ruined geometry; in front, a cutlass half-buried in the sand. And yet the scene as I remember it is not unchanging. The octopus may always be on top of the treasure chest, the grip of his tentacles unfailingly secure, but sometimes a shoal of fish swims into view; fronds bend first one way, then the other. A crab scuttles across a trail of coins. In one scene, the octopus lies heavily on the chest; his tentacles appear incapable of movement. A solitary diver, limbs alight with avarice, glides towards him - but the octopus has one eye open. In another scene, there are two divers; they stop swimming and tread water. About them streams of tiny bubbles rise upwards. Their bodies are turning towards each other in dismay, and through their masks I can just make out their disappointed faces.

*

Colin and Steve have announced that at the end of the week they will be giving a

Charles Wilkinson

party. I suggested to the group that it should be held on the veranda, overlooking the sea. Unfortunately, this idea was not taken up, and now it seems likely that we shall gather on the lawn at the front of the house. Somehow I can't prevent myself from thinking that this will make the event more English, and that's not at all what I want. I made a little speech asking that we should all be allowed to vote on the matter, but this appeal to the democratic instincts of the average American proved unsuccessful. However much I resent this, I am forced to admit that the fact that two of our number - Sharon Nordstrom and Gunther-Bryan Patel - refuse either to speak or gesticulate is hardly conducive to an atmosphere of rational discussion.

Whether there was some official displeasure at my intervention, I cannot say, but at lunch both Colin and Steve were uncharacteristically laconic. Afterwards, they asked to see everything that I've written in the last few days. We went up to a small room at the top of the house that contains nothing apart from a few chairs, box files and some back issues of academic journals. They both read the manuscripts carefully; and Steve, I noticed, read the passage about the octopus twice. For a long time they said nothing and then Colin began to speak. I was not, he said, going about things in the right way. Neither he nor Steve were interested in an unusual choice of verbs and adjectives; I had not been set a High School creative writing assignment. What they wanted was for me to write down simply and sincerely exactly how I felt. Only if I did this would it be possible for them to help me. Simplicity and sincerity were what was needed. And clarity, added Steve; he was still not, he maintained, at all sure what sex 'they' were. Even the term 'boyfriend' was ambiguous in the context.

It will not be easy for one who has been taught the value of insincerity to obey these instructions.

*

I betray no one when I assert that from the age of seven, my father being dead and my mother abroad, I was sent to boarding schools. The holidays were passed in the company of my Uncle Gustavus, a widower. His home, a rambling, half-timbered farmhouse with uneven floors and crumbling red-brick chimneys that threatened to fall through the roof whenever the rains became too heavy, was in Herefordshire, a county then even more remote than it is now. Uncle Gustavus was a very tall, lean man with a thin, heavily lined face that was, perhaps because he never wore a hat, tanned throughout the year. The darkness of his skin was accentuated by his startlingly white hair, which he always wore cropped close to his skull. When I was a child he was so much taller than I was that I hardly ever met his eyes. I think they were hazel. It is easier for me to remember his open-necked shirt and the mass of wiry grey hair that sprouted from a chest the colour of teak. I never saw him wear a tie. If it had not been for his masterful bearing, he might easily have been mistaken for a labourer. After my aunt's death he sold many of his fields and let others to tenant farmers, but he kept a few acres, and these, he always claimed, he could manage quite easily on his own.

Uncle Gustavus was not a talkative man, and I must have spent weeks of my school holiday without speaking to anyone. I often walked the narrow lanes, picking blackberries from the overgrown hedges or swiping at verges rife with cow parsley. If the loneliness became unbearable, I would cut across the fields to the village shop where there were comics to look through, and, behind the

Treasure

counter, tall glass jars filled with boiled sweets. Once, I bought myself some fresh bread, cheese and salted Welsh butter - the ingredients of a simple feast that I consumed in the woods above our farm.

My new home was at the end of a long road that in winter degenerated into a track so muddy that it was almost inaccessible to any vehicle more elegant than a Land Rover. There were also three or four quite unnecessary gates. Uncle Gustavus had erected these himself and kept them in a state of good repair accorded to no other structures on his land. The road led onto a filthy courtyard where geese, cats and pigs had to pick their way through mud and straw. Some bantams had been permitted to colonize a wheelless black Zodiac. Although there were no sheep on the farm, Uncle Gustavus kennelled a few dogs close to the front gate. I think their function was to act as an early warning system. At the first tentative growl, Uncle Gustavus would stop whatever he was doing and listen. Once the yapping started in earnest he would turn to me and say "Let's take cover." And then he would move unhurriedly to some vantage point where visitors could safely be inspected without their knowledge. Only if he decided to greet them would he then emerge from byre or barn, his face crinkling with careless affability.

*

What will they remember, those companions who shared the winter months with me in the flat they said was too cold, and which I always found too warm? The prints by Mondrian; the houseplants and the anglepoise lamp on my desk; the white walls and the furniture from Malmo. "Everything looks so new," they always said, "the place looks as if you just went out and bought the whole lot yesterday. Then they'd move in with their guitars and brightly painted pots; their stereos and rugs woven in Peru. One wanted rough red wine and great peasanty meals served from huge orange casserole dishes. When they'd gone, taking all their noise and colour with them, all the little sounds would come creeping back: a door brushing the carpet; the faint hum of the central heating; the creak of the floorboards, a neighbour's key in the lock.

On the evenings after a departure, I'd stay in, letting the silence gather around me. And as it grew dark, I'd remember Uncle Gustavus standing by the front door of the farmhouse. It was a hot afternoon and our guests were leaving. I'd helped to carry their suitcases to the car. Uncle Gustavus was smiling. He'd shaken several hands and kissed a woman on both cheeks. As the engine started, I ran to open the gate. Uncle Gustavus walked up behind me, and we stood and waved as the car disappeared up the drive in a cloud of exhaust and dust. Uncle Gustavus remained there for a long time after we had both stopped waving, and it was not until the sun sparkled on a metal bar, and we both knew that the last gate was being closed, that he turned towards the house and said, "Thank God they've gone."

*

This morning I was sitting behind the french windows that led out onto the veranda. For once the wicker chairs next to me were empty. Buffeted by the wind, gulls rose and fell soundlessly; there were white scars on the ocean.

I didn't hear Steve until he was almost beside me. He was wearing jeans and a T-shirt emblazoned with the crest of a university he did not attend. After fiddling with a clipboard, he began to talk in a soft, sincere monotone. At first I could hardly bring myself to concentrate on what he was saying; only a few phrases like 'up front' and 'telling it like it is' detached themselves from the general verbiage. Then he mentioned the flat. It was easy to understand, he said softly, that there were certain things that happened there that I wasn't yet ready to talk about, but frankly at the moment I was giving so little away, and writing in such vague and general terms, that we as a team were getting absolutely nowhere. Couldn't I at the very least be more gender specific? Without warning a white flash of anger ran through me: "There are days," I told him, "when I cannot help but wish for greater formality. I cannot see why you and Colin have reduced yourselves to your Christian names and wear clothes that give no hint of your chosen profession. Oh . . . and I do not wish to call Mr Patel, Gunther-Bryan."

After Steve had gone I opened the french windows and stepped out onto the veranda. The seabirds had vanished, and it was oppressively close, as though a thunderstorm were imminent. It was on a not dissimilar day that Uncle Gustavus had driven me through the Herefordshire countryside for my first term at boarding school. For weeks beforehand I had pestered him with questions: Had he been to boarding school? What was it like? Would the food really be inedible? Apart from confirming that he had attended a boarding school, he said little. Eventually, and I felt in lieu of answers, he took me off to his workshop, and I was allowed to watch while he made me a wooden tuck box. Later I helped him to paint my initials and number on it in black. "Name, rank and number boy; that's all you'll need," he said when we had finished it.

The day of departure was grey and hot. After breakfast, I went for a last walk round the lanes; the boredom and the silence seemed infinitely valuable at that moment.

After lunch we went to the attic and took down an old trunk that had once belonged to my father; his initials had faded and the lock was broken. But that was nothing, said Uncle Gustavus, that a bit of paint and some rope wouldn't put it right. The school had sent a list of things that I would need, all of which had to be clearly marked, even my hairbrush and the three tubes of toothpaste that were expected to last until Half-Term. The name tapes had been sewn onto my clothes by a woman from the village. My initials looked so unfamiliar that I could hardly believe they were mine.

Uncle Gustavus helped me to pack. Standing in my bedroom, with its pink and green curtains inherited from my aunt, he seemed utterly bewildered to find himself performing such a task, and held my white shirts in his hands as if fearful of staining them for ever. We ticked off the items on the list: two rugby shirts, one striped, one plain; one dressing gown with cord; one sleeveless pullover; the three shirts that could only be grey, and the ones that must be white for Sundays; the soft animal that was permitted to boys who were not yet ten . . .

When it was time, I changed into the grey flannel suit that could only be bought from Daniel Neal. The material felt too thick and tickled slightly. I picked up my cap and saw my name stitched in gothic red, the initials so much brighter than my father's.

*

Apparently the party that Steve and Colin have ordered us to attend is to be some sort of grotesque parody of an English village fete. There will be croquet,

Treasure

cucumber sandwiches, a tombola, a raffle, and a bouncy castle for the nurses' children. We are all to be encouraged to dress up as squires, vicars and cricketers. Denise Schneiderpecker has said that she will be attending in hunting pink. I hope all this is not for my benefit. When I tackled Colin on the subject this morning, I did not find his answers entirely persuasive. He mumbled something about 'a project aimed at encouraging social interaction' and then became so evasive that I decided against pursuing the matter any further. None of the group is able to shed any light on Colin and Steve's motives, and, to my irritation, most of them appear to be looking forward to the event.

My relations with the group leaders have degenerated to the point where little remains but mutual antipathy, At the last meeting, Steve took exception to my account of our discussion on the veranda, describing it, if I remember correctly, as 'wilfully one-sided and deliberately biased'. I retorted that I was pleased to see that his talent for tautology had not deserted him. Colin then weighed in with fifteen minutes of bumbling oratory, the burden of which was that I was on no account to mention the group leaders or any member or associate member of the group in my writings. If I did not agree to this stipulation, my right of audience at the next meeting would be suspended, and I would be accorded 'observer status' only.

I offered my apologies, and, these being accepted, proceeded to read my account of Uncle Gustavus's treasure hunt, all copies of which have since been destroyed. I told how, in order to celebrate my eleventh birthday, Uncle Gustavus had invited a number of children from the village to participate in a treasure hunt. He had devoted the whole morning to creating suitably ingenious clues; these he had concealed under flowerpots, beneath drainpipes, in the boot of the rusty Zodiac and fifty other hiding places, all in the vicinity of the farmhouse. Uncle Gustavus then retreated to his study, from where the cries of anticipation, the feverish scurrying and scampering, and the delighted hoots of discovery were all clearly audible. As the afternoon progressed, a curious silence descended, punctuated only by the occasional moan of disappointment or ragged sob of frustration. Clue after clue had been found, but no treasure unearthed. At five o'clock the children departed empty-handed.

Widespread condemnation of Uncle Gustavus's behaviour followed. Even Sharon Nordstrom made a brief but passionate speech, thus breaking three weeks' silence. I let them continue for several minutes and then, just when I could see that Steve was about to ask a question, I told them I had made the whole thing up. Either that or it was a story I'd stolen from an author whose name I had forgotten. I wasn't sure which. They were aghast, What about Uncle Gustavus? Did he exist or had I made him up too? I said that I would tell them nothing: it was up to them to decide. The meeting broke up acrimoniously.

Twenty minutes ago Colin came up to my room. He was still very angry, The work the group was doing was based on openness and honesty. My fictions were a violation of the trust that had been placed in me. I'd lost the respect of everyone. When *Dr* Neuberg returned from Chicago, my case would be referred to him. "Oh it's Dr Neuberg now, is it," I said. "Not *Aaron!*"
See how at the first signs of a challenge they come rushing towards me, whitecoated and waving diplomas.

Charles Wilkinson

*

Once they heard I was out of danger, the hotel sent my clothes along in a plastic bag. My wallet and credit cards were still in the back pocket of my trousers, but I had lost the keys to my flat. At first I was sure that they had been stolen, and then I realised that I would hardly have bothered to take them with me. After all, I couldn't possibly have believed I would be needing them again. I suppose they're sitting on the hall table next to the bowl I have always kept filled with apples. Apples . . .I wonder what colour they are by now.

At the hotel, although my lack of luggage made them wary, clean clothes and a willingness to pay in advance - it had not seemed likely that I would be able to settle up afterwards - were enough to allay their suspicions. When it was all over and I had to come to terms with my failure, I wondered what had made me choose a hotel in the first place. Colin told me that it was because I didn't really want to die; in the hotel, the chances of someone discovering me before it was too late were much greater. He was wrong. I did want to die, but I knew that it might be weeks, even months, before they found my body in the flat. You see they had all stopped coming round. The summer was almost over, and I would be there alone. Somehow, I just couldn't convince myself that I ought to be glad.

What did they wrap me in when they carried me out of the hotel? I used to believe that they used the towels in the bathroom; now I feel certain that the ambulance men would have bought blankets. For weeks I've been trying to visualise every detail of the scene, trying to get it all exactly right. I told myself that I couldn't have been there for very long. If the people in the hotel hadn't found me so quickly, I'd never have survived. They must have been upset, though - seeing me naked and unconscious in the bath. At least there wouldn't have been any mess. Just a little water on the floor - that's all.

I've been imagining the expression on the face of the girl at reception desk when they carried me out. She must - I was so certain of this - have been upset that she didn't question me more closely; I know that she sensed something was wrong. But perhaps by then she wasn't even on duty. She could easily have been at home, asleep in some quiet suburb, at the very moment they brought me down. I'll never be certain of this, of course. Yet I have convinced myself that if I can come up with an account that is completely plausible, one in which event succeeds event with perfect inevitability, then I will never again have to think of what I did to myself in that place.

It was almost the same when I was in the mountains. Alone in a cabin with nothing but snow for company, I'd somehow imagined that I could start again, but all I'd been able to think about was the flat. I'd imagine it room by room: a hand on my hand as we sat at the breakfast table; a grey shape behind the shower curtain, a pinkish leg emerging from the steam; an arm round my waist as we stood at the window, watching the birds in the garden; laughter in the dining-room.

I don't think she would have seen me, the receptionist. They'd have brought me out the back way, discreetly, so as not to upset the other guests.

*

It is to be my first night at boarding school and we are late, lost in a tangle of Herefordshire lanes. Sunday afternoon has gone. *Sing Something Simple* has been on the radio. The clouds part for a moment and weak September sunlight falls on

Treasure

the fields, turning them from grey to sodden gold. Baffled and angry, Uncle Gustavus peers at the signposts and changes gear far too often. Later I will realise that he had lived in that county all his life, and think of us circling aimlessly, as though lost in central Poland. But now I just feel small inside my suit. The soles of my shoes are too shiny. When we get out of the car, I shall go skidding towards my new life.

We are an hour late. A church with a wooden tower stands alone in a sea of corn. I want to know why there are no houses nearby - nothing but a clump of elms, turning from blue to black as evening comes. But I cannot bring myself to speak. The cows are lucky in their fields, I tell myself. And then, almost as if by accident, we are there, bumping up the long drive. At its end I can see a dark house with turrets and lights in its pointed windows.

"I won't come in if you don't mind, dear boy. Not good on these occasions, I'm afraid." There are tears in my eyes. He is all that I have of familiarity. A figure in white, whom I will come to know as Matron, is scurrying towards us across the drive. I lean towards Uncle Gustavus and he shakes my hand. "Remember," he hisses, "tell them nothing. Let them work it out for themselves."

*

I have told Colin that I shall be taking no further part in the group discussions. He accuses me of pre-empting the verdict that Dr Neuberg is sure to give on his return from Chicago, and, whilst I have certainly done that, the truth of the matter is that my motives have once again been misunderstood. I would have faced my expulsion with indifference. No, the real cause for satisfaction lies elsewhere. By resigning prematurely I have succeeded in irritating Colin and Steve to such an extent that they have refused to read the latest instalment of my life with Uncle Gustavus. This is just as well because it is the present tense. I was told the act of writing would control the past. To discover a narrative is to create order and meaning, they said. Do this with us and - how did they put it? Your pain will become no more than a book you have read and understood. No, the memories come back, flooding the brightest day with sorrow.

*

I have been on the veranda for almost an hour. It is the only part of the house where the preparations for the party are not clearly audible. Although I shall not be boycotting the proceedings, if only because I am perfectly sure that is what they expect me to do, I shall, on this occasion, risk compromising my reputation for punctuality.

Since the storms there has been a dangerous lucidity in the air: outlines have become too clear, colours too clean. A fishing boat sails across the bay, leaving lines that might have been scraped on glass. The gulls are no longer distant or plaintive; each cry rings above them on the hard blue stone. A promontory that was once a blurred grey finger has moved closer, so that I can see a headland fringed with rocks and a bay of scalding sand. Although I have abandoned all attempts to express my thoughts on paper, I believe I have in spite of the culpable stupidity of Colin and Steve - gained something from the project after all. I am no longer, as I told Dr Neuberg this morning, prepared to be the passive object of my experiences - a sponge soaked in acid. The practice of writing has given me a capacity for articulating my thoughts and converting the chaos of sensation into the order of grammar. Whilst I shall no longer be writing anything down, I shall

Charles Wilkinson

comprehend my experiences - sentence by sentence. I do not think I could bear what I am seeing - the boat, the rocks, the sand - if it were not for the words I give these things.

"Hi."

It is Denise Schneiderpecker. She is dressed in jodhpurs, riding boots and a tweed hacking jacket.

"What happened to the hunting pink?" I hear myself inquire.

"The what?"

"The . . . never mind."

"Say," she says, "you look great. Are you coming to the party?"

I am wearing white trousers and a striped blazer indicative of membership of a club or university.

"In a minute. I've got to see Dr Neuberg first."

As soon as she has gone, I step back through the french windows and walk purposefully in the direction of his office. There are several matters that I mean to take up with him. I cannot, for example, imagine what good could possibly come from my rejoining Steve and Colin's group. I shall ask him to show a more personal interest in my affairs.

Dr Neuberg's door is open, and he is seated behind a large desk, his head bowed over some papers. Yesterday, the room was light and airy, but I notice that he has since had fake Edwardian panelling installed. A few silver trophies gleam fitfully in a glass cabinet. He looks up.

"Come in, dear boy," he says.

For some reason I feel utterly miserable. I advance a few steps and look down at the frayed green carpet. To the right of his desk is what may either be a very bumpy yellow rug or a partially stuffed golden labrador. A couple of spent cartridges lie in the wastepaper basket.

"Do you know what the cure for all your problems is?"

"No," I reply.

I raise my eyes and he gets up and goes over to the window. He is wearing a thick brown tweed jacket that may well have been serviceable in Scotland but seems ill-suited to the present climatic conditions. Outside, ropes creak as a marquee billows into the air.

"A small glass of medium dry sherry."

I cannot tell whether this is a question or a statement until he lifts the decanter and pours. He is so very much taller than I had remembered, and his hands are white and strong. "Shall we join the others," he says, "they have gone to so much trouble."

America is vanishing fast. I walk into a garden party fixed in the sunlit nightmare of a beautiful day. The church spire, the wellingtonia, the dark green shadows in the lawn and the sky that is so exactly blue have all developed a terrible permanence.

"So you went there to find yourself?"

I turn towards the smile frozen on her face. Her unblinking eyes and brittle hair have locked themselves in front of him somehow. I know her name is Mrs Kilterkerdine.

"It's not," I reply, "a question of finding oneself; more, I think, of losing oneself. Ever since I was a boy I've been trying to get rid of my personality."

"But you are still a boy."
"At heart, at heart."
"Now my Angus was always a man at heart."
"Always?"
"Yes, he was a man at heart even when he was a boy."

A cloud crosses the sun. The light flies away from the weathercock and the shadows escape into the grass.

"Excuse me," I say; "I really must find Dr Neuberg."

Her smile thaws, and I disengage myself with a nod. I can see no sign of Denise Schneiderpecker and the others as I make my way through the farmers and the solicitors.

"Punch?"

It is Dr Neuberg. He is standing behind a table covered in a gingham cloth and on which rests an aluminium bowl. He has dispensed with his tweeds and is wearing a suit of white linen and a Panama hat.

"Thank you," I reply.

As he dips the ladle into the fruity red liquid, I observe that his arms are unnaturally long in comparison to the rest of his body. At last I understand who he is.

"Uncle Gustavus?"
"Yes, dear boy"
"But you're dead."
"That," he replies, "is as may be."
"And you don't like parties."

He drops the ladle and fixes a monocle in his left eye.

"We'll talk," he says, moving away from the table.
"Talk?"

He wraps an arm round me and steers me through the lawyers and their wives, past the estate agents and the metal brokers. I nod at the man who made his money by opening a chain of launderettes and smile reassuringly at a doctor. We turn left by a rather small accountant, cross a path between two retired naval officers, accelerate up the slope towards the gentlemen farmers and move away into open country.

"Tell me," he says, putting another arm around me. "Try to tell me everything."

"Man to man."
"Man to man, heart to heart."
"Eyeball to eyeball."
"Man to man, heart to heart, eyeball to eyeball, you to me, me to you, person to person, uncle to nephew, nephew to uncle, boy to boy, what happened?"

In front of us there are no fences, no gates, no hedges, no trees, no cows, no sheep - only the hills and the sky.

"I told them nothing."

The earth ripples as he puts his third arm around me.

"Nothing?"
"Absolutely nothing."

His hat and monocle are floating away like planets.

"Just name rank and number eh?"

Charles Wilkinson

The sun bronzes the surface of the sea.
"That's right."
"Well done, old boy; well done!"
As we sink through flickering designs of light, my breath rises in delicate hoops of air. His clothes are gone, his moustache drifts behind him, like seaweed. His arms enfold me and he squeezes me, so painfully, so tenderly. Far below lie the white sea bed, the forgotten guns, the broken ships of war. And now it is just me and his round mouth and his round eyes and his curious propensity to defend treasure. We will rest amongst the bone-smooth rocks, where no light catches the coins and only the blind fish stir the sand. With his eight arms, he will caress me. So grateful am I to be in his arms. He will protect me inkily forever.

Patience Mackarness

Mushroom Soup

The leaflet was a triptych and its outer panels were crammed with colour. There was a photograph of the house itself, ancient red-brick warm in evening sunlight; an eye-straining view across Dorsetshire farmland; a high-beamed dining-room with twinkling cutlery; and a kidney-shaped swimming-pool in and by which large, healthy young people frolicked. Your first impression was that the leaflet was selling weekend breaks at a country hotel.

Most of the text inside was highly practical: lists of guest speakers, weekly and weekend rates, special discounts for school parties. But here too was reproduced the small print of human shabbiness, a lot of dismal stuff about greed and cruelty and war and everybody being alienated from everybody else. It was perhaps designed to cast you down, in order that you might subsequently be uplifted by the message which was located dead-centre on the middle panel: a joyous congregation of capital letters.

> JESUS IS ALIVE AND LIVING AT BEECHWOODS.
> COME AND MEET HIM!

FRIDAY

They came to Beechwoods at the end of a damp autumn, when the pool was empty and dark with dead leaves; the views were as pictured, but greyer. They were four schoolkid stereotypes: the weedy swot (male), the morose fatty (female), the thoughtful poet (male again) and the sultry siren (obviously). They are arranged here, as they were in their own piercing adolescent self-awareness, according to their degree of attractiveness to the opposite sex. Moreover, they formed a neat chain of lust, longing and disappointment, for the weed fancied the fatty who fancied the poet who fancied the siren. Whose own desires were elsewhere, and higher.

There was a teacher with them, a young church-going man called Mr. Rowland, to whom the siren was a secret test and temptation. He was officially the leader of the party. In the eyes of the four teenagers he was merely an adult, well away from his own scholastic territory, and therefore irrelevant both to themselves and to the stormy bewildering things that were going on inside them.

From the wrought-iron gates across gravel to the huge oak front door, it was rather like arriving for a late-Edwardian houseparty at which several guests can expect to be murdered. But entering, they found that the house's original cavernous spaces had been subdued by division, brightened with new windows and muffled with thick carpeting. They stared about them, forgetting briefly to be cool, and fat Cath murmured to skinny Aiden that Jesus seemed to have expensive tastes. Aiden replied, under his breath, that there must still be big money in the God business, despite the Dissolution of the Monasteries.

Mr. Rowland signed the school party in at Reception - a brisk and secular little office - and then they went, following directions, to leave their bags in the dormitories before lunch. The dormitories reminded of upmarket youth-hostel accommodation with light pine bunk-beds and duvets in pastel shades. The two girls and two boys would be sharing with others whom they had not yet met; Mr. Rowland seemed to have managed a room to himself. There and back, along pile-carpeted corridors with tasteful abstract paintings on their walls, Cath examined the other guests that they passed, and found, with a twinge of annoyance, that they were not as she had expected them to be. That is, most of them did not look sad or downtrodden, the sort who would be forced to turn to Jesus for consolation. In fact many of them seemed embarrassingly - uncoolly - happy.

Outside the dining-room a young man in a scarlet pullover strode up to them and thrust his hand towards Cath, saying one word in a strong and warming voice: "Benedict."

Cath thought for a second that the young man was trying to bestow a blessing on her. She recovered enough to surrender her hand nervously to his warm, firm grasp while whispering her own name, and then watched admiringly as he shook hands with the others. He was rather plump and extremely wholesome, with a gleaming helmet of blond hair like an aura of joyful optimism about his head. Showing them into the dining room with an air of mine host - he seemed to be some kind of director or team-leader - he turned to Cath again and asked in a friendly conversational way:

"And how long have *you* known Jesus?"

Cath went deep red and after a couple of false starts was able to say jerkily that she wasn't really - um - sure; she was saved from further inquiries by Minnie interjecting:

"*I've* known him since I was about ten." This was said in a thoughtful, faintly wondering tone, as though Minnie were trying to come to terms with the number of years that had rolled by since then. Benedict nodded gravely, but Cath thought she saw just a glimmer of disturbance in his guiltless blue eyes. Minnie was very well-developed for seventeen, and was especially vain of her legs, which would have looked well, in season, beside the kidney-shaped pool.

The conference room, to which their schedule of events directed them immediately after lunch, was a glassed-in terrace overlooking the pool. It was full of low easy-chairs and had strong sunny overhead-lighting to supplement the pasty grey of the afternoon.

'... And in the fourth watch of the night,' read Benedict to his Bible study group, 'he came to them walking on the sea.'

Cath and Minnie listened not to Matthew's words but to Benedict's glorious voice. Aiden, who was sitting next to Cath as he usually did at school, looked bored and cynical as though this were A level History again. Tim had got into a different study group by mistake and Cath saw, over Benedict's scarlet-clad shoulder, that he was not even pretending to listen to the reading. He was scribbling something on a piece of paper, probably a new poem.

"'...Jesus immediately reached out his hand and caught him, saying to him: 'O man of little faith, why did you doubt?'"

A reverent silence; one of many at Beechwoods.

"Now," said Benedict, "does anybody have any thoughts about what this story might mean for us today?"

Minnie said brightly and without hesitating: "I think the sea symbolises the stormy confusion of our souls, until Jesus comes to rescue us."

Everyone in the group looked at Minnie, who had her head on one side and her eyes on Benedict, very humble and earnest.

"And what's *your* name again?" asked Benedict.

Mushroom Soup

"Minnie," Cath said.

"Actually my name is Melinda," said Minnie sweetly.

"Melinda," said Benedict smiling, and looking her for just a shade too long. "Well, Melinda, that's a very good thought indeed. Jesus as our lifeboatman on the raging sea of doubt."

Cath said truculently: "And Jesus didn't *have* to save Peter. It was Peter's own fault, Jesus could have let him stew in his own juice."

"Right!" said Benedict on an encouraging note. "Good point, ...?"

"Catherine."

"Catherine," repeated Benedict, but he looked around at the rest of the group instead of at her. "So that shows us ..."

"That Jesus loves and saves us even when we don't deserve it?" asked someone else diffidently.

"Of course," said Aiden in the slow sarcastic voice that was very much more impressive than his too-thin body, "there's the possibility that the whole story was based on a misunderstanding or a fabrication. Possibly Peter fell out of the boat and Jesus pulled him back in again, and some bright spark on the shore saw the whole thing from a distance and started crying 'Miracle!'"

"I don't think ..." began Benedict, but Aiden went on steadily, "... and by the time the disciples got back to land, the story was half-way across Galilee and they decided it would be too much trouble to set the record straight."

Benedict's tone became less soothing and more severe. "Well now - Adrian, is it? - you have to understand that we're not here to discuss the historical *truth* of the Gospels," - Aiden's eyebrows went ostentatiously up - "but that people come here to Beechwoods to *build* on the faith within them, to strengthen it, asking for Jesus' help in understanding the messages that the Bible holds for us..."

Cath saw that Aiden was ready, even eager, for a ruthless debate, but Benedict forestalled him by getting up and asking the other groups for their comments on the text. Fisherman Peter's nasty moment on the waves was pulled to pieces in more ways than Cath could have imagined, and finally Benedict said:

"In the group I was leading, someone made a very useful comparison between that turbulent sea and the doubt in our own souls - which only the Lord Jesus can save us from."

Minnie flushed with pleasure at being quoted. Benedict did not look at her directly, but gave a great benign smile that embraced everyone in the room.

"Well," said Cath to Tim softly, as they left the conference room with one-and-a-half hours free before supper, "what do you think of it so far?"

"The food is acceptable," answered Tim. "Infinitely better than school dinners. But as for the rest of it, I can confidently say that the people are tosspots and their beliefs are bullshit."

'Timothy,' said Cath, "you are subversive." They had only met the word recently, in History, and she was pleased to be able to use it so soon.

"If you want to see something really subversive," said Tim, "read this."

It was a not very clean piece of file paper, three times folded. The poem was written in pencil, with multiple crossings-out.

> 'God,
> If you are what they say

> The men in purple, the men in black...
> (Are you that one who slung out of Eden
> a pair of dumb kids who asked too many questions?
> Drowned all the world but a family of Noahs?
> Set up young Cain cause you hated his smell?
> Like to hear people pray, like to see people kneeling
> and got an odd kick out of seeing your son
> strung up for some deal that makes no sense to me?
> - No sense to him either, when he choked out his last)
> ...If that's what you are, and I'm just a germ
> a microbe, a nothing, this nothing still says
> You're not my God
> You can't be.'

"You'd better keep that well hidden," said Cath uneasily.

"Actually I thought I might read it out at the next Bible study session," said Tim. "You know, ask people for their reactions."

"I hope you're joking," said Cath. "I never know."

Tim looked back towards the conference room. Minnie was standing with Benedict and Mr. Rowland, and looked as if she was asking intelligent questions. "Cath?" said Tim suddenly.

"Yes?"

"What about Melinda and me?"

Cath's stomach went into free-fall and she felt sick, but she could not say no to Tim; she stepped fast into the too-familiar role of confessor and oracle.

"You mean, do I think you have a chance with her?"

"Sort of, yes."

"She likes you," said Cath hesitatingly.

"Does she? Really?"

"Yes. But Minnie - you see, Minnie ..." Cath found that she was tired of being loyal to Minnie. "Minnie has a thing about males in authority. There's Mr. Rowland when we're at school, and now there's Benedict. And I think she may be getting ready to have a pash on Jesus as well."

Tim had begun to look hurt, but now he laughed. "You're taking the mick." Cath shrugged, irritably.

"Seriously, Cath. Why did Melinda come to this place? I mean, you and I are here because we're agnostics, right? We want to see if Benedict and his lot can come up with anything to convince us. And Aiden's here because he likes stirring things and giving self-satisfied gits like Benedict a hard time. But Melinda ... well, she seems to have everything already. What does *she* need?"

When Tim asked that question - which Cath did not answer, since it was not the one she wanted to hear - it was like hearing the voice of their school. At school it was assumed that those whom the opposite sex desired had everything. If the school pronounced at all on the disastrously uncool subject of religion, it would declare that only rejects went in for it, those who could never aspire to the real prize.

In which case people at Beechwoods should be showing more humility. Surely the most you could say of God's love was that it was better than nothing; yet here, some of the guests glowed, actually looked *blissful*, as though borne along by the most triumphantly satisfying form of love. Even people who, judging by their physical appeal, should have had nothing whatever to glow about.

Benedict went off to his administrative duties until suppertime and Minnie, losing interest in the conference room, went upstairs and read her Bible, arranging herself on the bunkbed like a languid Victorian miss on a chaise-longue. Cath went outside alone and mooched along a formal avenue of naked trees. The ground underfoot was soggy with a dark papier-maché of wet leaves and knobbly with fallen conkers, and the air was grey and very damp. It seemed a suitable place to brood in, but she was not alone there for long; Tim came running after her.

He was breathless, not from running, and his tawny-brown eyes burned. He held out his hand; in the palm lay two small, spindly, fawn-coloured mushrooms. Cath stared at them, and asked in a whisper: "Are those the ones?"

Tim nodded. "This white bit on top shows they're not poisonous. I checked against the photo in my book."

"Where did you find them?"

"Round the back, a sort of boggy meadow. There are lots of these all dotted about."

"Let's go there now."

"Not now, it's too visible," said Tim. "Anyone looking out from the second-floor windows can see you."

"We could get up very early tomorrow," Cath said thoughtfully, "just as it's starting to get light. While everyone else is still asleep."

SATURDAY

In pre-dawn twilight they climbed out of the picturesquely-mullioned library window and combed the wet squelching field that was bisected by a peaty trickle of stream and spotted with the little, pale mushrooms. By the time it was properly light their plastic bags were nearly full.

"Looks like about a hundred here. We should both get a good high from this lot," said Tim knowledgeably. "Maybe as good as mescalin."

It was right to be doing this in the company of a poet, Cath thought; poets were worldly-wise and decadent. Like Coleridge and the opium.

"What did Castaneda call that cactus-creature that he saw when he was high?" she asked.

"Mescalito. An Indian god, I think."

"Perhaps we'll see him."

"Perhaps we'll see Jesus. According to Benedict and Co, he's lurking around here somewhere."

"I think Mescalito would be more interesting."

The other girls in the dormitory were still asleep when Cath got back. She stood looking at Minnie for a few moments. Minnie had kicked off most of her duvet, and her skimpy nightie had ridden up and bared the amazing legs in their entirety. Her bottom stuck out. Her lips pouted fatly, sleep-sheened. Her sleeping attitude, the smug unconsciousness of her, made Cath want to push her off the bed. She was glad neither Tim nor Benedict was standing here now.

Patience Mackarness

The morning session was Bible study again, but the afternoon one was billed as a 'talk'. In obedience to the Beechwoods schedule, all the guests were seated sharp at 2.30 and the conference room was quiet and expectant; so Benedict's entrance at 2.34, haloed and guitar-bearing, was rather effective. Aiden, at Cath's side, muttered: "That prat thinks he's God's bloody Anointed". Minnie sat up sharply and glued her eyes to the golden Benedict. Cath was determined not to be so obvious.

Instead of saying an opening prayer, Benedict sang and played. All the guests had been given songsheets and instructions to join in after the first verse.

'Jesus, Lord, you fill my breast with sweetest ecstasy,
Asking ever: When, dear Lord, when will I come to thee?'

Cath saw, out of the corner of her eye, that Minnie had gone a little pink in the cheeks at Benedict's use of the word 'breast'. Cath had seen Minnie examining hers, luxuriously, in the mirror last night. Cath herself had undressed quickly as usual, trying not to look at the stretch-marks round her nipples and the repellent convexities of her belly.

Benedict read:

'"My beloved is all radiant and ruddy,
distinguished among ten thousand.
His head is the finest gold;
....O that his left hand were under my head,
and that his right hand embraced me!'

"These beautiful words are from the Song of Solomon. It was written thousands of years ago, yet it still has a very real message for all of us," Benedict told the guests. "It gives us some idea of the tremendous attraction that exists between the Lord Jesus and those he loves. St. Paul tells us that the relationship between us and our Lord mirrors that between husband and wife."

Tim had managed to sit next to Minnie on this occasion, but Minnie's eyes never left Benedict. Cath was on Tim's other side, and it was to her that he whispered: "This stuff's pornographic." He pointed out an earlier passage in the Bible lying open in Cath's lap.

'Oh, may your breasts be like clusters of the vine,
and the scent of your breath like apples,
and your kisses like the best wine
that goes down smoothly, gliding over lips and teeth.'

"I didn't think the Church allowed that sort of thing," Tim added, and Cath giggled.

Mild Mr. Rowland was glaring at them both, and they shut up.

Benedict did not sing in the evening. Instead he came into the conference room with someone they had not seen before, a young woman with a pale freckled face, and ginger hair that was somewhere between knotty and frizzy. Her jeans were a size too large and she had a button missing from her crinkly cheesecloth blouse. The four teenagers noted these details while examining the young woman as though she were a new teacher; certain that if she had been, they could never have taken her seriously. Scruffiness was only cool if you were young. Even Mr. Rowland, though drippy, was never unkempt.

Benedict sat down quietly, without even speaking ("for once," hissed Aiden). The young woman stood there alone in front of the big glass panels now made mirrors by early dark; the swimming pool, the far views, already gone. Then she spoke. And the voice that came out of her was unexpected: deeper, slower, more carrying than any of them had thought. "My name is Shirley. Tonight I'm going to tell you a love story." The younger guests became very attentive, and one person giggled. Cath saw that Mr. Rowland, on the contrary, was calm and smiling; he was perhaps too old for love stories, or else he had known in advance what Shirley's address was going to be about.

The story was long in the telling; but whether because of Shirley's voice or because of its fairytale elements, it was altogether enthralling to the audience. It began with Shirley the child prodigy, the brilliant mathematician, who had gained her PhD at twenty-two and believed she had everything in the world she wanted; moved on to Shirley's brother, an unpleasant young man with a contempt for religion, who had been crippled in a car accident and then miraculously healed; and ended with Shirley, in tears, falling on her knees in front of a congregation of strangers with her brother beside her.

"My dear friends," said Shirley softly, looking around the room, "I have never regretted that first step. I am loved - I feel his love surrounding me every day. It is a love so strong and so deep that I can't even comprehend it fully. Deeper than the ocean, higher than the stars, as a Christian poet has said. I have never been so happy, or so fulfilled. I can hardly believe now in the emptiness, the loneliness of my life before the Lord Jesus came into it... such a dark, miserable time. But now that's all past. And I wanted so much to share my story with you."

To Cath the air in the room, and especially that around Shirley, seemed to glitter and tingle; she found that her mouth had fallen open. But now Shirley turned her eyes directly on her audience, searching out the faces lined up in front of her. This, for Cath, was suddenly much less comfortable. She only now realised what was coming.

"Jesus is in this room with us, *now*," said Shirley. "Some of you here tonight know it already, feel it within yourselves. You *know* that the time has come for you to take that first step towards him, to ask him into your heart. He is here. He loves you more than you can imagine. And he is calling you to come to him. Stand up now, as I once did, even if you are afraid. Stand up, walk to the front and kneel. Only you can take that first step; but afterwards Jesus will be by your side for ever."

Shirley took up a guitar that had been resting against a chair behind her and began to play, very soft chords at first. Still the air in the room seemed charged with sparks like electricity; and Shirley sang:

"Take up your cross and follow me..."

People in the audience were standing up and walking forward, some firmly, some jerking woodenly upright as though their strings had been pulled. Cath was on the edge of the chair. She was being pulled too; the desire to stand up was strong and sweet and also frightening, and out of Shirley's song there came to her mind's sight a great straggling procession of people, bare-footed and moving slowly, but every eye resting in longing on one figure, far distant at the head of

Patience Mackarness

the column, a man nearly naked and bowed beneath the rough crossbar he was dragging over the stony sand, and Cath wanted to follow him too. To keep him in her sight, whatever desert or hell he was struggling through.

Minnie was on her feet and moving forwards, staring glassily ahead of her. Then, astonishingly, Aiden got up too. His face was frowning, absorbed, as though trying to work out a mathematical problem. And yet the steps he took were longer and firmer than anyone else's; he arrived at the front of the room before Minnie, and went down on his knees with a quick, bony movement like a skeleton collapsing.

The song ended, its last notes vibrated in the absolutely silent room, and Cath was still sitting in her low chair. She knew that in a moment Shirley would look straight at her, and she would no longer be able to hide.

But Shirley didn't. She spoke to the kneeling ones instead.

"Don't go back to your seats, not yet. Go out by the side door. Someone will be waiting for you there."

They got up slowly from their knees, ten of them perhaps, mostly teenagers, and filed out by the side door in silence. Now the others in the room turned to each other and spoke, and with the hum of their soft speech the spell began, gradually, to dissolve.

Tim had been watching Minnie's back until the second it disappeared, but now gave Cath a conspirator's grin that said: Well, *we* didn't fall for that, did we? Cath drew a breath that shuddered only a tiny bit, smiled back at him and nonchalantly slung her legs over the arm of Aiden's empty chair.

The evening session seemed to be over. Tim said quietly to Cath: "I'm off to bed now. I'll wake you at two," and left. Looking around the emptying room, Cath saw that Aiden, alone, had come back in through the side door. He walked slowly towards her.

"Why aren't you looking happy?" she asked him spitefully.

"I can't see that *happiness* has anything to do with it," said Aiden.

"That's not what Shirley said."

"I can only speak from my own experience," said Aiden dryly. "Personally, I simply found that I no longer had a choice. I was cornered, so I gave in." He turned and left the room. Cath was well used to Aiden's manner, but oddly (oddly, because Aiden had always been the one who wanted her and not the other way round), she now felt hurt and shut out.

She went up to the dormitory to wait for Minnie, and cross-examine her instead. A virgin questioning the new bride, dying to know what it felt like. Minnie's eyes were dreamy and still disbelieving, and she seemed to be on the edge of tears. She was very beautiful.

"What happened when you went outside?" Cath demanded. Hoping desperately that Minnie would not go all lofty and say "You wouldn't understand, you're not one of us." But it was not in Minnie to be secretive.

"Laura was waiting," she said. "You know, one of the Bible study leaders, the one with long black hair. She kissed me and said 'Welcome, sister'."

"And?" asked Cath sharply.

"We had a long talk. She said this was only the beginning. She said I've just been reborn and like a newborn baby I need ... what was it? ... special nourishment. That means the Bible. I have to read it every night and morning to

Mushroom Soup

help my soul grow strong. Oh, and I mustn't expect to go on feeling like I did tonight. She said tonight was the honeymoon, but I've given myself to Jesus for life."

Cath wanted very much to know if Minnie could be made to regret what she had done and said facetiously: "You'll have to behave yourself now, you know. You do realise you won't be able to read Jackie any more? Teen mags are *very* unholy."

Tearful giggles from the convert; relieved laughter from her friend and tempter. At least Minnie was still with her, not unreachable.

SUNDAY

"Mushroom soup," said Tim's voice in Cath's left ear.

She sat up in the darkness; followed him out into the dim corridor and down the stairs, carrying clothes and shoes that she had left stuffed under the bunkbed, ready.

The library was a tiny room with only two armchairs and one desk besides its many shelves of books. The long heavy curtains, floor to ceiling, were drawn and one small desk lamp switched on. Beside the lamp stood two full mugs, steaming.

"But how did you ..." Cath asked, still in a whisper.

"One of those little doo-dahs for heating water in the cup," said Tim with pride, and not bothering to lower his voice. "I brought it with me, and a packet of Cup-a-Soup in case the food turned out to be crap. The mugs I nicked from the kitchen."

The liquid in the mugs was brown and scummy, dense with limp, boiled, black mushrooms. Cath felt queasy looking at it.

"The boiling is sure to have killed all the maggots," said Tim cheerfully.

"I don't think I can do this."

"You'd better. I'm not going on my first trip all alone."

They held their noses and drank; Cath closed her throat tightly on a reflexive retch. Then they stood looking at the empty mugs, each with its puddle of muddy dregs and little black specks that they preferred not to examine.

"How long do you think it takes to work?" asked Cath.

"Haven't a clue."

They sat down and waited. A clock on one of the bookshelves ticked with theatrical loudness.

"You're shivering," said Tim after a while.

"I'm scared shitless. Suppose Benedict comes in and finds us?"

"Benedict," said Tim sourly, "is fast asleep and dreaming of knickerless angels."

"More like knickerless Minnie," said Cath unwisely.

"Minnie is anybody's wet dream. Even an angel's."

Cath said nothing. She felt sick already, and hoped Tim would not make it worse by going on about Minnie.

"I knew a boy once who had a bad trip on these," said Tim after several more minutes of silence.

"You never told me that."

"He said he thought the trees had faces, and the faces were horrible. He started screaming and sweating and smashing things up. His friends wanted to take him to hospital, but they were too scared of getting caught."

"Oh, *God.* Now I *am* scared."

"I think he took too many," said Tim easily. "A hundred and fifty, maybe more. Loads more than we have."

"Look, seriously," said Cath, turning to Tim and finding that her words were coming out too slowly, "I mean, seriously, Tim, if we...we...start...making a noise, or something ... someway ... somehow ... and someone should, you know, hear us..."

"We could go outside."

"Yes. Yes, yes, yesyesyes. Muchmuchmuchmuch safer."

"You're talking funny," said Tim. "I think you're high."

Cath said nothing because she was not sure what her voice might do next. Tim got up out of his chair, held out a hand to her, pulled her up; they both collapsed onto the floor. Cath banged her head on the leg of an armchair but it did not hurt, or perhaps the pain was happening somewhere else. They lay side by side, crumpled where they had fallen, and stared upwards.

"Bright," said Cath suddenly.

"Hmmm?"

"Light. Brightbright light."

"You're right," said Tim, lurching up. "The light's brighter. And the colours on the curtains. Look at those patterns! And hey, Cath, your eyes!"

"What about them?"

"Dilated pupils. Gigantic. Come on, let's try again. I want to see what outside looks like."

Cath got up cautiously, holding onto the armchair and then the desk. Tim got the window open and they both climbed out, slowly and with immense concentration, without falling again or knocking anything over.

Of course there was nothing to see outside; they had both forgotten it would be dark for hours yet. They stood together on the lawn, breathing the cold dampness.

"I think I can hear better too," said Cath. "There's rustling..."

"..and wind.."

"..and a car. But that's miles away. And some sort of bird away in the trees..."

"It's cold," said Tim softly.

"But that's nothing to do with us." Cath took his hand without thinking about it, moved slowly across the lawn. A big dark tree, perhaps a cedar, stood alone in the middle. Cath knelt down in the long wet grass at its base and spread her arms, reaching halfway round the trunk, pressing her palms and face against its roughness. She thought that if she waited long enough the tree would speak, or perhaps send secret impulses through its bark to her fingertips.

"Has it got a face?" asked Tim behind her.

Cath did not answer, but she let go of the tree and turned back to Tim. His hand when she held it again was warm; that warmth transferred to her, though the cold of the night air did not.

They wandered over to a little summer house by the edge of the lawn; went in; sat down facing one another on the bare dusty wooden floor. Cath looked up through the window towards a faint light. The moon was partly there, partly

Mushroom Soup

behind a dark cloud; and one star.

Tim leant over towards her. His pupils were huge, he looked like himself and yet different. The look on his face was like Shirley when she had called on them to take the first step.

"Cath," he said, "I think we should fuck. To complete the experience. It would be amazing."

"All right then." She experienced no surprise at his using the F- word. Nor did she think about what her body looked like as they both undressed slowly. Tim's body fascinated her though; bare and goose-pimpled; she guessed that it would be all tawny, like his eyes and his hair. His penis looked dusky-smooth; it was not quite straight, but Cath was impressed. It was so different from the small hanging things that statues had, it looked as though it must have a bone in it. She was not absolutely sure where it was supposed to go, but Tim seemed to know.

Cath had thought that people sweated a lot when they did this; and she seemed to remember, too, from some novel, that they made 'animal sounds'. (What sort? Grunts? Purrs?) But Tim was making no noise at all, and his movements had a soothing slowed-up quality. He was a slender boy, not heavy, and his body was agreeably warm against her in the chilly air. The sensation was really very pleasant, very relaxing. Cath fell asleep.

Although it was daylight by then, they were not seen climbing back into the house again just before breakfast. Clearly nobody had been into the library yet, which was lucky because the desk lamp was still on, the empty mugs beside it, and Cath's clothes and shoes were lying on one of the armchairs. She had gone outside in pyjamas and bare feet, but neither she nor Tim had realised it. Climbing back into the library, her feet were so numb she could not feel desk or carpet against the soles, and her head hurt where she had hit it.

Minnie and the other girls in the dormitory were awake and packing when Cath came in.

"*There* you are! Where *have* you been?" cried Minnie with grown-up reproachfulness.

"Walking," said Cath, who felt tingly and fragile.

"I bet you had a tryst with Aiden," said Minnie archly. Cath said nothing.

Out on the gravel driveway, Benedict had a manly handshake for Cath, Tim and Mr. Rowland. To Aiden, holding his hand a little longer, Benedict said: "You've made a hard choice this weekend. Be strong in the Lord."

Aiden muttered: "OK," and Cath could see he still loathed Benedict.

Then Benedict took Minnie's hand in both his, looked into her eyes and said: "Be strong, dear sister. Feel his love surrounding you each day, and trust him always."

Minnie was speechless, her eyes began to fill up. She dropped sorrowfully, but prettily, into the front seat of the car beside Mr. Rowland. Tim, after hesitating for a second, climbed into the back next to Cath.

"Well!" said Mr. Rowland, feeling it was his duty as leader to provide an apposite concluding remark. "A weekend of powerful experiences, for some of us."

Not even Minnie answered him; she was sniffling quietly and clasping the Bible to her bosom.

Patience Mackarness

Scrunching gravel, then soundless tarmac; the car swung out through the iron gates and accelerated away.
"Who's for I Spy?" asked Mr. Rowland.

LETTERS

Love and Lancaster
The Lancaster comp. results are an eye-opener. I enjoyed the 3rd and 2nd prize stories but not the First prize 'Fighting For It'. If that represents the height of a student's ambition when attending Creative Writing Classes at Lancaster University, I would prefer my offspring to be educated elsewhere. A department trapped in the ethos of loveless carnality is as dangerous as the Charles Manson cult. It sure says something about Lancaster U and its judges.

Literary stories revel in the F word, thrill to the C word, but never never face the L word. It simply isn't done. Well Derek Gregory did it with *Water Baby*. After reading it and recovering from shock, I rang my son 2000 miles away to tell him I loved him. It seemed the thing to do.

I think women are inclined to see the world through a self - induced haze of tenderness and romance and we wouldn't offer our stories to *Panurge* because it simply doesn't publish warm and tender stories, however beautifully written they might be.

As for Julia Darling, I find *Bloodlines* the best thing I have read for years. No F and C words, no menstrual blood after the title story(we have more than enough of that in real life). It deserves to be read.

**Jane Leigh,
Mitchelton,
Australia.**

Pro Lancaster
I thought the winners of the Lancaster Comp were well-deserved. Karen Stevens' First Prize and Siri Hansen's story were extremely powerful. Derek Gregory's story stood out as plain brilliant.

I do think most small press mags are male dominated, but not Panurge. But if male subscribers made a better response to *Bloodlines*, could it be they have more spending power?

**Susan Davis,
Craven Arms,
Shrops.**

Contra Maughfling
I think Daphne Maughfling's letter about women writers being discriminated against in *Panurge* is ridiculous There are so *many* outlets for them and you can't open anything these days without seeing Penelope this or Maureen that in huge capitals!

**B.M. Gould,
Norwich.**

Bleakness
The writing in Panurge 23 was of an extremely high quality but the vision of life seemed terribly sad and no-hoping. Even the love pieces *Untitled* and *Sealed Room* were forlorn. Peter Dorward's story was far and away the finest. I actually *saw* those people.

The Lancaster winner had a nauseous tone. I suppose that decadent brand of sexuality which gets no one anywhere is trendy. The four competition stories were I thought less good than the body of the magazine. I found the content a depressing read as a whole.

**Dorothy Schwarz,
Colchester.**

Wayne Dean-Richards

The Dead Man

I was born a year to the day after the stillbirth of my brother, Anthony. Mom has a picture of him, taken just after he was born, but she's never shown it to me. She did tell me about the funeral for him, though, where there was just her, Dad, a priest, and a tiny coffin. "Death marks people," she said when she'd finished the telling. She wanted me to think that was why Dad left us, but I knew it wasn't.

All this I say to him as we stand, pissing, in the GENTS. He's big and covered in warts, and began by asking me whether I supported Liverpool or Everton. He hears me out, shakes, then hits me. He shouts some abuse at me, but I don't hear it: I'm on the floor, my nostrils full of the stench of beery piss, my mouth full of blood. He wants me to scream, so he kicks me. But I won't scream. Not ever. Finally, panting, he gives up and I get up and wipe the blood from my face and return to the BAR.

Lynn, the barmaid, seeing my face, wants to help. But, as kindly as I can, I shrug off her attentions.

Outside, it's cold. I hate the winter. I was born in January, the dead of winter. I walk through the town centre. Dad used to work in the steel mill they knocked down to build that deserted bus station. Briefly, I wonder where he's working now. He could be dead for all I know. I hope he's not.

I take a shortcut along the canal towpath. Once, I saw a dead pig in the water. It was bloated, ready to burst. I saw it a year ago. Since then I've dreamed of it. In the dream, I was in the water with it and it was biting me. Its teeth were like razors, able to rip through flesh and bone.

Back at the flat I think again of Anthony, but not as a dead baby made monstrous by my imagination, as a grown man, at forty a year older than me, tall and thin, dressed in a smart blue suit, his hair slicked back. I see his lips moving, but I can't make out what he's saying.

*

The next day, perhaps inspired by the state of my face - the size of a football and sore looking as a cyst - Mrs. Evans, the lady who lives in the flat across the corridor, asks me to wreck her car. She introduced herself to me as Mrs. Evans, but I doubt she's ever been married. She has twin boys. When she moved in they were a year old and she used to stand in the lift holding one in each arm. "It's easy," she says. "I'll leave the keys in the ignition. You drive away, and wreck it. Then you phone me and I phone the police and the insurance company." Mrs. Evans is twenty-five. She wears clothes that are very tight, and masses of mascara. "I'll give you a hundred. Cash," she adds.

"Why d'you want to get rid of it?"

"It's had it," she says. "The body's rotten and Henry reckons the big end's on the way out."

Henry's her boyfriend. He lives on the top floor of the high rise opposite ours. He's on the dole, but he spends most of his time fixing people's cars. He describes himself as 'an MOT specialist.'

I shift my weight from one foot to the other while Mrs. Evans studies my face. "A hundred's all I can afford," she says. I nod. "You won't get caught," she says, but it's the possibility that I might, I think, that compels me to accept her

Wayne Dean-Richards

offer.

"Phone me when you're done," Mrs. Evans says. I tell her I will and I drive off. It feels good to be driving. It's a nice day for November. Bright, lemon sunlight, dissipated by dirty streaks, slants through the windscreen. Though it's cold, I roll down the window and let the air buffet my face.

I've decided to make a day of it so I fill up with petrol and get on the motorway, heading north. I stop once, for a fried egg sandwich. There's a radio in the car, but I hum instead. By the time I arrive, the cold wind coming in through the window has made the swelling on my face start to go down.

I drive to the seaside. It's been years since I've had a summer holiday. The last time I was here I was a kid and an old man bloodied my nose for pulling a face at the smell of his scampi and chips. When he saw the blood, he was sorry he'd done it, but he didn't apologise. He told me he'd got a steel plate in his head and insisted I take a chip before leaving him alone.

I park and walk along the seafront to the pier, making my mind up to wait until it's dark before driving the car onto the pier, setting it on fire then pushing it into the water ...

*

The last of the fishermen left hours ago. It's dark and bitterly cold. I drive onto the pier. It's quiet. There's nobody about. All the places along the seafront are boarded up.

Two feet from the end of the pier I stop the car, knock it out of gear and put on the handbrake. I sit staring at the rearview mirror, my heart thudding. I don't see anybody so I get out of the car. I stumble and almost fall. It's the rum I had to keep warm. And the excitement.

I take off my jacket and lie it on the floor. This pier is almost a hundred years old, made of wood and cast iron. Shivering slightly, I tear the sleeve off my shirt. It's an old shirt anyway. With the money I've got from Mrs. Evans I'm going to buy a new one, one of those lumberjack-style shirts.

The lights of the town seem miles away. I take off the petrol cap and feed my shirtsleeve into the tank. The smell of petrol makes me feel drunk. I'm smiling. On the second strike the lighter lights and I touch the flame to the shirtsleeve and step back. All I have to do now is take off the handbrake and shove the car into the sea.

*

But before I can get the car moving, the tank blows. The force of the explosion drives me backwards! My shirt catches fire. The hairs on my arms dance in the heat. I stagger...

... And fall. I never scream. Not ever. There isn't time anyway. The sea swallows me.

*

My throat is full of saltwater. A fire rages inside my chest. My arms and legs are numb and heavy. I'm sinking. Dying. I wait for the pig to come and finish me, like in the dream. When it doesn't I thrash against the weight of my limbs.

I break the surface a hundred yards from the pier. The sky and the sea are black. I gulp in air, and let the tide take me.

Shale scrapes the flesh from my shins. Exhausted, ecstatic, I haul myself out of the water. I'm naked, trembling with cold. Blind and dazed, I stagger a dozen

The Dead Man

paces before collapsing beside an upturned rowboat. When I mutter something to myself, the old lady laughs. I feel her breath on my face, and suck in the sickly sweet smell of sherry. "You're a sorry sight," she says. "Thought I was on my own," I mumble. She laughs again. "It's too cold to go swimming this time of year." I start laughing with her. I'm still laughing when I close my eyes.

*

When I open them again, it's daylight. I'm under the rowboat. I'm convinced the old lady was a dream until I see I have on an old pair of baggy blue trousers and a woollen pullover. There are even shoes on my feet: a pair of laceless brown brogues.

I crawl out from under the boat. It's still cool, but the sun is high. It must be nearly midday. The old lady has gone. The tide is out and I stare at it. I feel as if I've crossed the sea.

Watched by a cluster of people, a truck is busy towing Mrs. Evans' car from the end of the pier. I join them. "What happened?" I ask of a very short man in a faded denim jacket and jeans. "Bloke got killed last night," the man says. "Washed out to sea. They found his jacket." He points to a dot in the sky a mile from the shore. "Helicopter's looking for the body," he says. I've no money, I'm wearing someone else's clothes, there're no laces in my shoes, but I feel good for a dead man. "I'm Anthony," I say. The man in the denim jacket nods and we watch them haul the burnt out car off the pier.

Robert Stone

An Uncommon Error

It had been over in a moment, but it was a moment for which I had been preparing myself for all of my life. Anyone might have fallen into my error but perhaps no one with such a maladroit precision as I had. It is something, I think, for a man to make the mistake which calls to him personally and not simply to have his heart shovelled into the common grave of a general inaccuracy.

My father collected all stamps, every example of every issue. No used stamp that came into his hands ever left it again until he died. At home there are many fat manila envelopes full of worthless duplicates and gaudy foreign nonsense with which he would not have parted for the world. For my father, a staid and in many ways, and I say this with filial reluctance, really rather a dull man, stamps were the one example in his life of the principle of the revelation of loveliness in the close examination of simple things. He was irreligious, a materialist, a disinterested supporter of wealth and conventional beauty, but stamps had a magic for him. He recognized that they were unvalued but he valued them. They were transformed by his keen interest in them.

I can only speculate that this is why my father continued in the boyish pursuit of collecting stamps until the end of his long life; at any rate by the time I was old enough to take notice of such things he had a pleasing collection of inexpensive distinction. To my infant eyes, however, page after page of Victorian stamps were replete with the fascination which another person could not have felt for a display of the thumb-nails of all of the Roman emperors. My father would open for me his weighty, red, leather-bound albums interleaved with the ethereal mist of the thinnest tissue paper, like a veil of tears, and I would gaze at that dull spectrum of faded colours with the rapt awe of a monk for a stained-glass window. It would be lovely now to find it, when I arrive home, on the shelves where it had stood for more than half a century, and look upon it with the cold eye of philately, unimpeded by the cataracts of an over-egged nostalgia. But it is gone now. Gone to Stone House Court, where I can never go again, broken for its recyclable materials and sold on blocks in a public place. How many of these cherished stamps, a little dirty, cancelled clumsily, thin almost to transparency in one corner, will be plucked from my father's carefully made mounts and thrown in a pile to be sold by weight? I have a catalogue of all of the stamps, much of it in my father's hand, and although the stamps are anything but irreplaceable I have not at present the funds to purchase replacements, nor, moreover the heart to even think about it. Indeed, I believe my heart may be broken.

He had two disparate enthusiasms within philately; the first for the line-engraved definitives of Queen Victoria's reign and the Second World War. He collected over-prints from the occupied territories, stamps especially issued by the occupiers and propaganda stamps, not real stamps at all, issued by the enemy and dropped behind the lines by parachute. Splendid examples were the Nazi parodies of the 1935 Silver Jubilee half penny showing a hook-nosed Stalin in the place of George VI and 'THIS IS A JEWSH (sic) WAR' printed above and below him. Hammers and sickles and Stars of David replace coronets. I believe these were originally introduced into the Arab world. Another is a parody of the three-halfpence Coronation showing George VI and Stalin once more, this time in the place of the Queen Mother as she now is. This is dated 'Teheran 28.11.1943'. It

118

An Uncommon Error

is easier to be delighted and amused by these stamps than it is to explain the method by which they achieve these effects. I think it may be the deceptively subtle modulation between the slight and the extreme, so that the colour is right and the portrait of the King, but next to him, although His Majesty seems not to have noticed the exchange, is not his beloved wife, but President Stalin. I imagine that many Iranians must have used the stamps all innocent of the switch. And how they must have tested the patriotism of philatelists who retained in wallets or stashed away at the backs of drawers what they should have handed in or destroyed. It is just this difference which so characterizes the glamour of stamp-collecting, to stoop and retrieve the pre-historic arrow-head from the path along which a thousand men have walked. This metaphor, however, is altogether too suggestive of luck, whereas what I would like to stress as all-important, what I have striven to achieve, is a substantial scholarship, an incontrovertible expertise. I never really understood the modesty of my father's ambition which allowed him to be satisfied with his amateur collection and his dilettante grasp of its significance. To know more and to want more and better, even the best; these are the desires which lured me into the perilous waters in which I have so recently lost myself.

Mr. Hurst's stamp shop in Stone House Court off Houndsditch was the scene of many, largely humiliating, skirmishes between the proprietor and myself during many years, ending with my rout and utter destruction. My first visit there, one that I made alone, was a rite of passage and my first visit to any stamp shop. The chief anxiety, having travelled so far, was to see it open or closed. In those haphazard days, and very much in the character of the shop, it was by no means certain that it would be open at the advertised times, nor even on the advertised days. If Hurst took it into his head to sit at the back of the shop sorting and to glare out of his shop windows at any passer-by impertinent enough to propose himself as a customer, silently daring them to knock or try the door, even shooing them away with the back of his hand, then that is what he would do. Stamp-collectors as a class are deferential and timid and Hurst exploited their individual traits with a ruthless nicety matched only by the sheer pointlessness of his wicked endeavours. At least I once imagined them to be pointless; I see now that they may have been very lucrative indeed.

Of course, I made no great study of Hurst and knew nothing of him except as he appeared in his relations with me and in those too he was changeable to a baffling and even frightening extent. He evidently had a large collection of extraordinary headgear which he would wear in his shop with great aplomb and no apparent awareness of the remarkable figure he cut as a result, save that unspoken challenge in his eye which invited you to betray in any respect that you thought his hat at all unusual. Am I mistaken in thinking that he went so far as to risk the occasional fractional raising of both eye-brows as if to say,

- Well, what do you make of this one then?

I very much hope that his challenge was taken up by some of his visitors and that they laughed in his face as he deserved, but I never did. There was not only the self-confident and hostile blandness of Hurst which prevented me, nor only the manner in which his shop was fitted out so un-shop-like and so like the lair of the peculiar beast Hurst, but also a process which is endemic to the very practice of stamp-collecting. To go to a stamp shop and ask the proprietor for a

Robert Stone

stamp is to reveal something very private about oneself. The philatelist shows his collection to no one, its deficiencies are a profound secret, but what surer way of revealing them than to ask Hurst to supply them?

- Do you have a George VI ten shilling?
- Dark blue or ultramarine? Hurst's reply would be accompanied by an extravagant display of tried patience with the time-wasters who patronised the shop. He might now begin to do something else whilst dealing with this customer having ascertained that it was altogether unnecessary to give the matter his complete attention.
- Ultramarine.

This is roughly a third the price of the dark-blue but still not especially cheap at around fifteen pounds. Hurst would now pause indicating a lack of surprise at the alternative preferred and simply say,

- Yes. As if to a question provoked by abstract curiosity and not to a request.
- Do you think you could show me some?

Hurst would look up from beneath the brim of some preposterous hat and having decided on either making a sale or humiliating the poor man further he would say,

- Most certainly sir, and fetch a tray or an envelope.

Or,

- How many would you like to see? Six? Twenty-one?

Hurst escaped retaliation for this dreadful behaviour partly through the conditions I have already mentioned and partly because of his undeserved reputation as a dry humourist. His victims, of course, were anxious to find him merely amusing. Hurst would smile but only grimly and unexpectedly or late. After buying an inexpensive stamp in its grey, tissue-paper envelope the hapless customer might be asked.

- And would sir like a bag?

And then Hurst would grin disarmingly.

In the recollections of some writers people like Hurst are relished as eccentrics, but I was always afraid of him and I paid him the respect which I have paid to a number of men whom I have hated in my life; that of seeking his approval. We would have made a natural alliance of master and servant in another age and it is a sad reflection on this age that I should find myself in such a relation with a shop-keeper.

When I first approached Hurst's shop it was to stare enviously at the pages of stamps with which he decorated his windows; pages of lovely deep, rich two-penny blues which looked and even sounded like trays of butterflies in the drawers of a Victorian entomologist, the amazing million mark stamps of the German inflation, the strangely shocking portraits of Hitler, dozens of them in miniature, and the tiny turbanned figures of Indonesian boy-kings which seemed to belong to another world than Hitler's modern one, and to have been preserved in it, in shrunken form only, in the formaldehyde of philately. There was little enough to see on display inside Hurst's shop, however, and I was wary of entering without a very specific purpose. If asked what I had wanted I could only have given the anti-specialist dilettante's reply,

- Everything.

Fortunately I had a specific purpose to hand. Another of the eclectic

An Uncommon Error

ingredients of my father's collection was that it contained the complete philately of Singapore. Singapore has a tedious philately. Having collected it most people would have discontinued it and called it complete up to a certain date, but my father could not let it go. He insisted on buying each new issue of pretty birds or colourful fish and it was of such a latest set that I had to enquire of Mr. Hurst.

My first sight of him was in a cloth cap, his fingers drumming lightly on the many buttons of a plain, double-breasted waistcoat as if he were a very quiet, wheezy sort of accordion, indeed until the door closed behind me with a shudder and a click he may very well have been asleep. He raised a finger to his brim and said,

- Guv'nor, just as if he were selling china seconds from a market stall.

I stepped up boldly with my embarrassing request. He leaned over behind him, opened a shallow drawer marked 'Singapore' and put the stamps on the table before me.

- Tropical fish as usual. 75p.

Looking back on this a little later, having been the reluctant witness of a number of quite undeserved humiliations at the hands of Hurst I couldn't say why he was not scathing towards me, but it was as if he had a complete understanding of my situation.

- I know they're rubbish but if you have the complete Singapore then you have to buy them, don't you?

He certainly made me want to go back and to impress upon him that there was more to me than the latest Singapore. So he had already worked some sort of spell on me, he had already become one of those men in authority whose applause and respect I craved. If this was his game then he played upon me well; he kept me craving, wanting to do better, wanting to do more. He was cruel to me too, of course, part of the reason I had to go back was to show that the last time had been a mistake and that actually I was not like that at all. Perhaps this was the case with all of his regular customers; their humiliations may have been only one stage in the push and pull of the relationship, or Hurst may have been ridding his shop of unsympathetic subjects. Much may depend on my discovering what made me a suitable case. Most came back, I suppose, because Hurst was cheaper than the Strand and the belief, common to all stamp-collectors, that there is no fool like the fool who pays too much for a stamp.

I remember going to see Hurst half-conscious of the intention to make an impression on him. I had been examining some of the early numbers in my father's collection and had come across a most unexpected error. He had a stamp in the mount he had made for SG 12, the orange-brown 1841 penny red, but this stamp was surely SG 9, the pale red-brown 1841 penny red. Now these stamps are difficult to identify in that each colour description represents a range of colours within the given field, nonetheless here were two SG 9's and no SG 12. I resolved to buy one from Hurst; a good one would cost around £300. I had telephoned ahead to be sure that he had one in stock and he was ready for me when I arrived. He was wearing a stiff black bowler. Beneath this he wore not so much an ambiguous expression as two separate expressions quite different when viewed from different angles. With his head tilted downwards and to the side he looked the city gent, if rather a ruthless one, but with his head tilted upwards, the skin of his cheek taut and a staring eye illuminated by a gleam of

Robert Stone

madness he might have been a criminally wealthy proletarian, a promoter of illegal, bare-knuckle fist-fights.

He laid an A4-size piece of black card four-square on the counter before me, a single ferruginous stamp trapped beneath its cellophane, like an ancient insect drowned in amber. I placed a hand either side of the card and leaned over it; it had four good margins and was neatly cancelled with a crisp Maltese cross. No matter how well preserved these stamps are they never look new, they always look conspicuously old. They belong to a lost world of quite different textures where matter is other; it is brittle, not pliable, grainy, not smooth, where when things become soiled and get creased, they do not wipe clean and spring back into shape.

- £275. I sensed the ears of the other customers pricking up behind me; I had been disappointed not to have been invited into the back room.

I took cheque-book and fountain pen from my pocket as if they were a superior hand at cards only to have them trumped into oblivion by what happened next.

- One moment please. Hurst spoke in a voice of unprecedented astonishment and reproof. That looks a little too lake-red to me. I do believe that is SG 11. Do you know that that stamp is worth £600?

My jaw dropped in the manner of the shoplifter caught in the act. I was being accused of basely taking advantage of Hurst's innocent, careless mistake.

- Well, erm, yes, it does look rather lake.
- For goodness' sake, can't you tell? This in a stage whisper. You were about to spend £275 on a stamp, don't you know what it looks like?
- It isn't always easy to distinguish these shades without a comparison.
- Well perhaps we should compare it with this. And this. And this.

Three more black, cardboard leaves were dealt onto the counter. Hurst stared into my face, raised an eyebrow and stuck his tongue into his cheek.

This was not what I had anticipated. My cheeks burned. Even so, I felt some distant enjoyment of this puzzle. I looked closely at the four stamps; the possibility of my not being able to tell mine began to well up in me. I could remember the descriptions from the catalogue; red-brown, red-brown on very blue paper, pale red-brown, deep red-brown, lake-red, orange-brown. But here and now I could not tell SG 12. I had to guess. My philatelic knowledge being temporarily unavailable I based my guess on what I knew of Hurst. I recognized the stamp I had first seen from its post mark and pointed to it.

- I think this is orange-brown after all.

He turned the card over and let it fall. In one corner, was a white, circular sticker on which 'SG 12' was neatly written.

- Quite right. My mistake. So sorry. Tell you what, take the latest Singapore while you are here. Some nice lizards.

*

What could I have done? I was indignant, bur really more ashamed than angry. If through some unforeseen consequence of Hurst's strategy I had left the shop without making the purchase, then I think that I might never have gone back and, who knows, perhaps even discontinued my interest in philately, but this was no time for such a thought, having just paid nearly three hundred pounds for a stamp. I needed to return too to make everything alright. However, like a chess-

An Uncommon Error

player routed in a dozen moves, I was driven back to my books before I could set up the pieces again. My pretensions had been exposed; I was no match for Hurst in cunning or cruelty; if I was going to defeat him, then I must know more than him. Any of the self-effacement I might have inherited from my father had been shot away by Hurst; I must compete with distinction, or I would not wish to play. I did not realize at the time that this resolve to play better was my first really serious mistake.

I began a rearrangement of my collection, made some minor purchases through mail order, pored over my stock of magazines and compiled a note-book. Finally I was ready to announce a new interest to Hurst and to instruct him to look out for certain stamps for me. Modern errors. Amongst modern British stamps these are created accidentally in the printing process when, for instance, two sheets are pulled through the machine at once so that the lower sheet does not receive the colour being applied at that time. The results of such an accident can be spectacular. These errors are, of course, destroyed by the Post Office if they are noticed. Foreign post offices, driven to the use of less scrupulous printers often unwittingly issue contrived errors, a reserve stock of which is held by the printers for sale to collectors. One of these came to light recently in which a series of famous tennis players in action was printed with the tennis ball omitted on a dozen or so sheets. Even more remarkable mistakes are sometimes genuinely made. The most famous of these was produced by the US Postal Service, the 1918 Curtis Jenny; a twenty-four cents stamp in which a bi-plane is depicted flying upside down. A number of these were issued before the error came to the attention of the authorities who then decided to release millions more just like it to avoid creating a rarity. That the same authorities came to a different decision in 1994 has helped occasion my despair.

I have in my wallet at this moment a newspaper cutting which I will quote.

Red faces at US Postal Service

A stamp mistakenly released with the wrong portrait could become one of the most valuable ever because the US Postal Service has ordered it to be withdrawn.
The Postal Service said it will recall and destroy 250m stamps of 20 Western heroes because the designer used the wrong picture for black rodeo star Bill Pickett. The portrait used was of his brother, Bob.
The withdrawal came after a post office in Bend, Oregon, mistakenly sold three or four sheets of the stamps, not due to be issued until March, creating a potential rarity that could be worth hundreds of thousands of dollars.

My palms did not itch when I first read this story; I do not have hundreds of thousands of dollars; such stamps are owned only by the very rich, the very lucky, briefly, or, as I now know, by the very crooked. My chief reaction was amusement at a country which, in the cause of political correctness, could dig up a black Western hero from a history whose momentum was fuelled by genocide and race slavery and then get the portraits mixed up presumably because no one knows this 'Western hero' from a Harlem drug dealer and on the principle that

Robert Stone

all blacks look alike anyway. One wonders if 'mistake' is the right word for this phenomenon.

I was in Hurst's shop enquiring from Charlton, his very young, bald, etiolated assistant, of an extravagant blurring effect on the 1975 Turner anniversary stamps. Charlton had never heard of this, in fact Charlton's knowledge of and even interest in stamp collecting was clearly limited. Not only that, but in spite of years of service in Hurst's shop Charlton retained his layman's capacity to be flabbergasted at the amount of money his clients spent on stamps. You could see him laboriously calculating the difference between the price given for the stamp and its face value and blowing out his cheeks to prevent his good nature from pointing this out to the buyer. When asked by a courageous client why he kept Charlton in the shop Hurst replied,

- To liaise with the general public. He has the common touch.

I was getting pretty fed up with Charlton's common touch on this occasion, as I was having a great deal of difficulty in explaining to him that I wanted to buy badly disfigured stamps for a great deal of money and not the perfect, unused, mint version for hardly any money at all. I was surprised mid-negotiation by a summons from Hurst himself into the back room.

Naturally he was wearing a hat which I had never seen before, a sky-blue fez with a cream-gold tassel. The room was lined to the ceiling with drawers as shallow as trays like an old-fashioned chemist's shop. Each tray sported a brass frame holding a strip of card neatly inscribed with what looked like Arabic characters. It was so typical of Hurst that I should see this for the first time on the day he was wearing a fez for the first time. I almost remarked on it. There were no stamps anywhere in sight. On the one wall which had space for a picture hung a six year-old calendar decorated with photographs of a naked girl. We sat in the room's two arm-chairs and I was given a Turkish cigarette. Hurst did not smoke and occupied his hands in dipping a lollipop into a bag of coloured sugar and then licking this off. As ever he showed only a barely perceptible consciousness of the eccentricity of his behaviour. His head on one side so that the tassel of his fez rolled round lazily Hurst broke the silence,

- Banks, I would like to sell to you the rarest and perhaps the most expensive stamp that I have ever sold.

I mumbled over my reply like a toothless and generally underfed dog presented with an indigestibly large bone.

- That would be a very great compliment Mr. Hurst. It must be a very expensive stamp.

- Yes it is. About ten thousand pounds, but that does not matter. You see, it is the Pickett error and once I have given it to you I shall never see it again. It is the most desirable stamp in modern philately. Its value will rise forever.

- Ten thousand pounds ...

I began the sentence with the utmost reluctance, not wishing to break this chain of privilege. Hurst did not let me finish it.

- I don't need all of that in cash; I'll take your collection for half or two thirds of it depending on its worth. It'll be worth around that won't it, or won't it?

- Yes I imagine it will. It includes my father's too you know.

- Oh does it? Yes, well I knew him of course, poor man. That should do it

An Uncommon Error

then.

What was I thinking of at this time? Certainly I was not being so foolish as you may now consider me; I was not entering into any legally binding agreement, I was handing nothing over to Hurst at this point and I had time to pull out after turning it over in my mind and deciding what I really did want. Basking in this elevation of esteem and importance involved no immediate pecuniary loss.

- There is one thing; are we sure of the Postal Service's plans for the Pickett error? If they simply re-issue the two hundred and fifty million errors then the stamp will be worthless.

- They will not do that. It would embarrass them in front of too many of their uppity citizens. They are to re-issue the Western heroes in one week from today with a portrait of the right darkie, Bob or Bill whichever it is, in the place of the wrong one. The vendor, whom you will meet in a Dover hotel in two weeks, is an American. I will ask him to bring some of the re-issues for a comparison.

- Why Dover?

- He always stays in Dover. In case they close the airports.

Hurst's jokes always gave me an uncomfortable feeling. They weren't meant to be got. They weren't actually jokes. I suppose they were meant to produce an uncomfortable feeling.

He showed me back into the shop and before disappearing into his room once more he said,

- Charlton, just give him that Turner error will you? He is going to give it back in a week anyway.

As he closed the door he finished his sentence either with,

- ... and good day.

or

- ... for God's sake.

I would like to think that he was wearied by what he had achieved rather than that he exulted in it, but I don't know.

Over the following week I spent rather less time looking through my books to see if I could afford the four or five thousand pounds than I spent looking through the collection to see if I could bear to part with it. The quaint pageantry of Edwardian jubilees, the richly comical, poodle-like profiles of George V, the delicious lemon-yellow of Victorian higher values. All of this for a picture of the wrong black hillbilly? Whatever would my father have said? This was the deciding factor; my father was not one of those mysterious men whose esteem I cherished and posthumously and hypothetically I found it very easy to disagree with him. I removed the modern errors, including the spectacular Turner blur and decided to part with the rest of the collection. I took these errors to the negotiations should they have been necessary to have clinched the bargain, but they were not and Hurst did not refer to them. I do not wish to rehearse those negotiations; Hurst was the cunning and seductive bully of old, charming and menacing by turns. I think he gave me a fair price. He wore a straw boater but looked rather more like an old-fashioned butcher than an undergraduate in holiday mood. I felt much lighter on leaving the shop and really quite happy. I had delivered myself of the burden of love grown old and complicated and was young at heart and fancy-free once more. In celebration of this boyish humour I bought from the restaurant-takeaway place outside of the station a thick

Robert Stone

strawberry-flavoured milk shake which was much too sickly to drink and a flat little hamburger which I did not eat because it did not taste of anything.

And so to Dover. Among souvenir shops and ice-cream parlours and open counters stacked high with piles of boiled sugar, rock-hard and lurid in shape and colour I sought my American contact. I found him in a room above a cafe called 'The Cup o' Tea' outside of which stood revolving racks of post-cards scenic and bawdy. I was still in something of a careless mood, going through the motions of keeping my appointment without much thought about what might go on there. This mood changed to one of a dislocated anxiety as all four browsers at the towers of cards moved away upon my approach. They were not together which is what made their simultaneous departure the more unusual. One of them wore what looked from a distance like a skull-cap such as some Jewish men wear but they were otherwise unremarkable. The blatant illegality of the transaction in which I was engaged sprang up before me like a jack-in-the-box; the Pickett error should be worth much more than ten thousand pounds; had it been stolen? As I turned up the dirty alley-way next to the shop which soon became a flight of steps I collided with a nervous young man wearing a common little moustache of the sort that adolescents think makes them look distinguished and so much the air of a man exiting a private book shop that I almost went back to check the number above the cafe. What I chiefly noticed about him, however, was that as soon as we had exchanged the customary apologies after our collision he put his hand in a panic to his breast, obviously afraid that I might have picked his pocket. I only thought of this afterwards. There were several doors on the stairway and there is no reason even now to suppose that he had come from my destination. I was a little and quite unreasonably disconcerted by these matters.

The door ahead of me was open and a man stood in the doorway,

- Hey, come in, come in. I saw you from the street.

This was undoubtedly the man with my stamp. I immediately saw him as if he were a cartoon with a bold, black outline; he was at once a stereotypical American, a Westerner even, and a precisely calculated opposite of Hurst. He was burly and very tall; his hair was blond and shoulder-length and he had a blond Van Dyke beard and unshaven cheeks. He was dressed in denim. His name was Peters but I thought of Custer as soon as I saw him. He bowed me in, shook my hand and offered me a cup of coffee. Was this actually the lucky purchaser of Bend, Oregon I wondered?

- Well Mr. Banks, you'll be wanting to see that stamp. He had the lop-sided smile of the habitual kidder. Here was a man so different from Hurst and yet who evidently did business with him on a basis much more intimate than any I had ever contemplated. I had never seen anyone like Custer in Hurst's shop. Should I have behaved more like Custer to have got in with Hurst? Would I have done so if I had known him earlier?

The room was very dark, with the curtains drawn, illuminated only by a reading lamp at a desk before the window. Custer moved to the other side of this desk and so made it a counter. He opened an A4 ring binder which was on the desk containing a single piece of black card. Suspended on this in a plastic mount was my stamp.

- Take a good look; the once wholly insignificant brother of Bill Pickett now elevated to an undreamed of stardom.

An Uncommon Error

There it was, the Bill Pickett error, just as I had seen it and studied it in a magazine article all about it which I had in my pocket.
- A most uncommon stamp, he said.
- I understood that several sheets were bought.
- That is not my understanding.

I was wary of being indelicate or ingenuous in my questioning. I could see that it would not do to ask Custer whence he had got the stamp.
- Hurst said something about the possibility of your bringing some examples of the official issue.
- Surely.

From the desk drawer he produced an envelope from which he shook a few dozen stamps into the light. They were singles, pairs and strips some of which fell face up, some of which did not. Long used to never touching the most commonplace stamp without tweezers I bent over them and examined them carefully. This was certainly a different portrait, either of the same man, or of another.
- The wrong jigaboo, said Custer, generally.

The word was so wildly out of date that it had to be a quotation and it could only have come from one source. I smiled a conspirator's smile at him.
- I'll give you some to look at on the train.

He picked up a block of six or seven stamps, turned to pick up a small white envelope for them from a pile on the window-sill and dropped it onto the ring binder. I put the envelope into my inside pocket and closed the binder.
- You can take the binder if you prefer or I do have some wallets. These were pocket-size versions of the black card in the binder, such as those which hold new stamps one may buy from post offices. I took the binder. There was no embarrassment about my leaving immediately. We parted mutually much satisfied and I left for the station. Once out on the street I opened the binder for a quick look at the stamp. No conjuring trick had been performed; this was the stamp that I had chosen.

On the train I had four seats to myself although the carriage was quite crowded. With a childish impatience I opened the binder and looked carefully once more at my purchase. I shall not describe it. Millions of people with no interest in the subject are mindlessly familiar with its appearance. Delightedly I took the envelope from my inside pocket. It was unsealed. I shook its contents onto the page before me. To my blank surprise a strip of British first class stamps fell out. These were not the stamps which Custer had picked up from the table. I checked all of my pockets for more satisfactory envelopes although I recognized at once the catastrophe that had overtaken me; I had fallen amongst thieves. I took out the magazine article on the Pickett error and unfolded it. My lightness had become an emptiness. I compared the illustrations reproduced in monochrome in the article with my stamp and saw that, of course, I had bought, in the splendid isolation of its own ring binder the new official portrait of Bill Pickett of which there were hundreds of millions of examples currently on sale at wherever it is that you buy stamps throughout the United States. 'The wrong jigaboo.' The Pickett errors, the portraits of Bob, had been those stamps which Custer had thrown carelessly onto the desk from the envelope he had taken from the drawer, about seventy thousand pounds worth of which he had then picked up

Robert Stone

and not put into an envelope which he had taken from the window-sill behind him. As it was, the first class stamps he had given me were worth around fifteen times as much as the stamp for which I had given up my father's collection and a good deal of my personal savings.

I have done an extraordinary thing, have I not? An act of grotesque folly for which there is no redemption. I do not know where this humiliation will take me now; perhaps further than a collection of very rare stamps would have done. I do know that I now feel tremendously upset and rather ill. I have had to laugh (not altogether the right word) at the picture of myself self-importantly scurrying through the streets of Dover clutching a stamp worth twenty cents to my breast. This is a sign that I have already changed and that my old self is outside of me perhaps. I am beginning to collect my compensation. I tremble and am breathing rather queerly making what I had thought was a virtually inaudible keening noise until an evidently rather foolish and bad-tempered but kind-faced old gentleman at the table across the aisle leaned over to me a moment ago and said,

- If you are going to keep up that tuneless whistling all the way to London then I shall be forced to move to another carriage.

I am moved, forcibly, beyond money and stamps to other and smaller pleasures.

FIRST PERSON

Success

D.J.Taylor

Some years ago, on a crowded tube train heading from Victoria to Oxford Circus, I made the mistake of engaging Enoch Powell in conversation. To this day I don't know why I did it. There he was, dressed in a morning suit, Homburg hat and overcoat (it was a blistering July morning, I remember) hunched in a corner by the carriage door and being given a fairly wide berth by the other occupants of the train, and for some reason - perhaps the memory of my father's quaint assertion that famous people 'like to be recognised' - I advanced towards him and began to talk. It was an unmitigated disaster, whose details I can't even now bring myself to record, but at its end, when we were both standing on the platform at Victoria (he was off to the BBC to deliver a talk on Schopenhauer) Powell fixed me with a look that was not at all a benevolent look and remarked, with an absolutely awful gravity, "I regret that when we began this conversation I did not take the opportunity to enquire your name." I supplied it. "Mr Taylor," Powell hissed back - and I have an idea that he may even have raised the Homburg in valediction - "I wish you *success.*"

For some reason I thought about this brief encounter from Hell last week - I am writing this in December 1995 - when I sat down to conduct a little exercise that I conduct every year at about this time: compiling a list of 'Work done in 19-'. The 1995 list discloses that in the past 12 months I finished a novel *(English Settlement,* published January 1996), assembled a collection of short stories provisionally entitled *After Bathing at Baxter's,* to be published next Spring (this involved writing three extra stories, one of them 10,000 words long), wrote 30,000 words of the next novel, and worked desultorily on a biography of Thackeray which a supportive publisher is keen to know if he can bring out 'by the end of the century'. I also wrote eight feature articles, 55 book reviews (one of them Edgar Harden's *Supplement* to the collected letters of Thackeray which took me a month to read) and numbers of other occasional pieces for periodicals as various as the *Sunday Times, the Oldie,* the *Times Literary Supplement* and *Accountancy.* It seems hardly necessary to add that I also have a part-time job which takes me into the City three days a week. No, I am not joking, and no I am not proud of it, and no there is no immediate prospect of it changing.

There are several explanations for this frightful torrent of print, splashing out each year from a study in London SW15. Two are entirely non-literary. I have a wife, a four-bedroomed house in Putney with mortgage to match, and a child (two, God willing, by the time you read this) whom no amount of liberal sentiment will ever allow me to have educated at a London state school. I am also the child of a provincial middle-class home founded on the Protestant work ethic. The other, though, is a complete absorption and delight in what might be called the old-fashioned literary life - the review-writing, book-compiling end, rather than the screenplay-fixing, internet-crawling end.

D.J.Taylor

'Wanting to write' is a time-honoured English joke, of course, on about the level of mothers-in-law or kippers, and from an early age I was familiar with the intolerable young men in P.G. Wodehouse stories who wrote unpublishable poetry. When I was 17, I even devised a spoof Wodehouse piece of this sort for a school magazine which contained the line, 'The literary urge, once implanted, is, like haemophilia, practically ineradicable.' Certainly true in my case, and from such an early age that I don't really remember a time when I didn't want to write or foresee a destiny in which I didn't end up as a pixieish 80 year-old fondly regarding the shelf or so of volumes produced in the course of a hectic career. Inevitably this ambition took the form of highly imitative 'phases'. There was the children's historical phase (models Henry Treece and Rosemary Sutcliffe) which lasted from about ages nine to eleven and supplied a sixty-page version of Robin Hood and a bloodthirsty tale of Angevin derring-do called *My Master To Avenge*. There was the Tolkien phase (ages twelve to fifteen) which hatched two immensely derivative fantasies set in imaginary pseudo-Middle Earths and employing cargoes of elves, wizards and whatnot. Then, most injurious of all, there was the Orwell phase (sixteen to nineteen) which realised a dystopian 'political' novel written one school holidays and - painful to relate - a semi-autobiographical work whose composition occupied the whole of the nine months off between school and university entitled *Tomorrow Belongs To Me*. None of them, I should add, caused even the slightest quickening of pulse among the legions of publishers to whom I sent them, though in general people were very kind, and I still have somewhere the letter from Allen & Unwin informing me that 'Tolkien was very well established in this field.'

Even now I don't quite know where this impulse came from. My parents, while 'educated', were not remotely bookish people (my mother's idea of a 'good' book, repeatedly pressed on me when I was a teenager, and which in consequence I never read, was Arthur Grimble's *A Pattern of Islands*.) At bottom, though, I think I found something intensely romantic and comforting in the idea of 'being a writer', and Gordon Comstock in Orwell's *Keep The Aspidistra Flying* with his cynicism and his take-it-or-leave-it attitude to women (who, inexplicably, still seemed to find him attractive) remained my role model for longer than I care to remember. At the same time, despite the reveries about the old gentleman with his row of volumes, I still had hardly any idea of where this might lead. I elected to do History at Oxford, in deference to a very old ambition to be a university don, but I think I did so with the not quite conscious aim of leaving the thing that really mattered for later. Afterwards - there is nothing like a tutorial with Sir Keith (as he now is) Thomas for convincing you of your unfittedness for the academic life - I found myself in exactly the position that I'd always sworn to avoid - the bright young graduate who hasn't a clue what he wants to do except 'write'. Eventually, six months after graduation - times were hard for Arts graduates in 1982 - I ended up in London working for a small public relations agency.

Meanwhile, the 'phases' (most recent one a Simon Raven fixation which produced a drivelling Oxford novel called *The Garden Party*) were coming to an end. When not working for the PR agency - let's be honest, quite often while working for the PR agency - I wrote a novel called *Great Eastern Land*, which a literary agent called Toby Eady (who had offered to represent me as the result of

Success

an article of mine he'd seen in *The Spectator)* agreed to take on. After a certain amount of prevarication involving the firm or rather the person of Anthony Blond, still just about in business on the upper floors of a couple of houses knocked together in Great Ormond Street - Muller, Blond & White later failed for around £400,000 - he managed to sell it to an editor named Jane Wood, then of Secker & Warburg, subsequently of Century Hutchinson, and now a biggish cheese at Orion. The advance was £750. I can remember being quite literally overcome with emotion on hearing the news, and a day or so later - it was December 1984 - embarking on a huge, solitary walk around the streets of South London - Battersea, Vauxhall and Wandsworth - glowing with a sense of vindicated purpose. The future, that bright, consoling future crammed with books, seemed to stretch out ahead of me like a conveyor belt. Come the New Year I sat down and started writing another one. It had all the traditional faults of a second novel, being extraordinarily long and about subjects of which I knew nothing (in this case West Indian immigrants in Brixton) and Secker quite properly rejected it out of hand. *Great Eastern Land* had been published by this time, garnered a smattering of decent-ish notices, and one or two complete stinkers - some gallant ornament of *British Book News* remarked that it was a lot easier to get your stuff into print than he'd imagined ha ha - and been bought for paperbacking by Flamingo, an event that had coruscating personal consequences as it led to meeting and marrying my wife. While pursuing the worst day job I have ever had - the marketing department of Messrs. Coopers & Lybrand, Chartered Accountants - I wrote a third novel that was, if anything, even flakier than the second. Whereupon, as the historical romances of my childhood used to say, our hero's fortunes fell very low.

Help came from an unexpected quarter. Since leaving university I had done a certain amount of journalism. Alexander Chancellor, to whom I shall ever be grateful, had printed some occasional pieces in *The Spectator,* although it was galling to discover that he'd imagined the first, a description of the train journey from Liverpool Street to Norwich, to be the work of a 50 year-old. Later I moved on to the gratifying but time-consuming task of reviewing books for the *London Magazine* (six novels, say, in 1200 words, payment maybe £35). Reviewing, though, was hard to come by in the mid '80s: newspapers had less space available, what there was tended to be the resort of leathery oldsters. What changed all this was the advent of Rupert Murdoch, specifically the *Times* lock-out of 1985-6 which broke the power of the print unions and created the conditions for the late '80s newspaper revolution to take root.

Speaking as a concerned citizen I find Rupert Murdoch the epitome of ghastliness (which doesn't, I'm afraid, stop me writing for the *Sunday Times*). Speaking as a *writer* I salute him as the fairy godmother of my career. Post-strike, print journalism boomed. There were more newspapers; they had larger arts supplements, and they wanted younger people. I started reviewing for the *Independent,* then for the *Evening Standard* (recompense from an embarrassed literary editor who had noticed *Great Eastern Land* twice, favourably and unfavourably, in separate publications), then the *Sunday Times,* to which the *Standard's* man had conveniently moved. I started taking a line, too, about how feeble the novels I had to write about mostly were (something I believed at the time, and continue to believe.) Quite by chance a couple of these homilies on the

D.J.Taylor

death or extreme ill-health of the English novel appeared back to back in *The Spectator* and the *Sunday Times* in October 1988, and in so far as literary circles ever allow themselves to become truly disturbed, caused a ripple or two. *A Vain Conceit: British Fiction In The 1980s,* written in the course of a fortnight's holiday early in 1989 and which Bloomsbury published later that year, grew out of these pieces.

After which the pattern of my professional life has proceeded more or less unhindered. On the one hand more books - *Other People,* a collection of sketches written with Marcus Berkmann (1990), two novels, *Real Life* (1992) and *English Settlement,* whose reception I nervously await as I write this, and a bigger, fatter critical book, *After the War: The Novel and England Since 1945* (1993), the submerged nine-tenths of the iceberg first sighted in *A Vain Conceit.* On the other, more book reviews: for the *Independent,* the *Sunday Times* and the *Guardian,* for *The Spectator, New Statesman & Society* and the *Times Literary Supplement,* for the *European,* the *Oldie* and the *Literary Review...* Of the six books I've written the first made a small profit for its publishers (not difficult on an advance of £750), the second broke even, and the rest conspicuously didn't, largely owing to Carmen Callil's habit of paying over the odds for things she liked, something on which I can wax hugely satirical in articles about the state of publishing, but of course grudgingly accept with my own stuff.

Is this what you call success? What I call success? I have long discussions with my wife Rachel (an editorial director at a firm where they pay out six-figure advances and the books stack up on the airport shelves), sensible discussions about writing novels that are 'more commercial' and all the rest of it. The occasion, not long ago, when *You* magazine accepted a story of mine, makes a good illustration. Rachel was wholly (and rightly) approving, on the grounds that hundreds of thousands of people will read it. I was, well, pleased about the money (£600), and slightly cross about the kind of compromises you have to make in order to satisfy *You's* exacting editorial criteria. All ghastly elitist arrogance, no doubt, and what I really want, inevitably, is to have my cake and eat it too: write tricksy highbrow novels *and* get paid stunning amounts of money for them. Then I remember the ambitions I had when I set out, how little I would have settled for in comparison to what I have and the pure delight in spending a substantial part of my time doing something I enjoy. Even now, after nearly 15 years of frenzied book reviewing, it still strikes me as nothing short of remarkable that people are prepared to pay me as much as £250 for my opinion on that most redundant of cultural artefacts, a book. Like the Victorian critic George Saintsbury, whose septuagenarian fingers still twitched as he unwrapped the latest parcel from his literary editor, I hope I'll go on feeling this way.

Clayton Lister

Our Lady, The Virgin Lily

Should I be happy? I'm told I should be, always have been - in Heaven and this place even the whores call Hell. I am privileged after all, more precious than them, for they must serve while I may only be adored - as pure as the lilies that border my bower, I am above the lustful claims of men.

At my feet there is a sign that Denzil himself put up:

Our Lady, The Virgin Lily
Do Not Touch

And no one ever does. The men, they come, they inspect - as though I were some waxwork dummy - smiling; but then they must leave me; choose from the whores who lounge across the sofas - be led away.

So I should be happy - they tell me so, the whores: 'Girl, you have it easy,' they say, 'Sat there night and day.' But they're contemptuous with envy, and as they lead their men away, they cut their eyes at me which they shouldn't do.

Only once a man dared to touch me. When, being real, my breast wobbled, they laughed with him, the whores, at his surprise, and only stopped when Denzil appeared and did what he did to his face with his blade: he had him read the sign out loud first, down on his knees with everybody listening, and still he did that with his blade, for everyone to see. 'Girl,' they said when Denzil had gone and the blood been all mopped up, 'You one dangerous bitch!' But to each other - I've noticed this - they're very kind and caring.

How *could* I be happy, do they think? At least in Heaven I had Nina who was my friend.

It's just as Daddy said:

'Indeed, Lily, Hell is below, though not so far as you might think - not far away at all. Beneath the earth, you'd have it? It's on our doorstep - at the bottom of the stairs. Haven't I told you so before? Oh, of course, that's hard for you to understand. Of course you're curious - of course. That's the nature of Temptation. But I assure you, it's more wretched and lonely down below, my darling, than you could ever imagine. Do not be Tempted down there, please.'

But I was. I was Tempted. I was Tempted to Tempt Daddy as a means. Denzil the devil, as Nina might call him, Tempted me to Tempt Him, and through Heaven's own letter-box no less, when he came to visit.

*

'Wh'appen?' he said when I called to tell him not to ring the bell. He bent down double to see, then still bent double, breathing heavily, approached the door saying: 'Chile, yah Daddy keep you pris'ner 'ere! Hopen de door. Lyet me 'ave words wi' de man. 'ee 'ave no right!'

'No, Denzil, you don't understand. He only does because He loves me, and holds me so precious. But I must see you.'

'See me climb dem styairs dair! Hopen up an' gi' me refreshment! Show me yah Daddy t'ink 'ee's God! I give 'im God, myakin' me walk dem styairs!'

'He has the only key.'

'Den 'ow we s'pose do business, chile? Wha' you drop me notes out de sky for? Yah wyastin' mi time!'

'No, Denzil, I do want to see you.'

'Den fetch yah Daddy's key! Lyet me in.'

Clayton Lister

'Denzil I can't. He keeps it on Him.'
'Cha, man! When de man slyeep.'
'He'll wake.'
'So gi' de man some lovin' so 'ee dwon't wyake.'
'What?'
'Yah say 'ee love you all up - de man's a byeast! Love 'im back dis one night so 'ee slyeep good an' sound, an' tyake de key, chile.'
'I don't understand.'
'Girl, yah not spyeak de language! Go t'im in 'is bed an' myake 'im slyeep. I be wayitin' in de mornin' for yah at de bottom o' de styairs dair.'

*

At the bottom of the stairs... Daddy, you were right. Hell did begin right there. But its heart's here beneath the earth; this Godforsaken basement that's windowless completely, and always dimly lit but for my bower - focal niche in the lobby wall that's lit all mockingly celestial at the foot of, and facing, the steps across the way that wind on up to the only door out of here, that's guarded at all times. And hot, so hot it is under the lights - just like Hell's supposed to be; that they can't disguise - it's torrid. Me, they plaster with paste to hide the sweat and make me paler than I am already naturally. It's the other whores who do this, when they've time, when there are no men around - I can't be trusted to do it myself they say; they slap it on and smear it hard so it hurts, saying Shut up and It's a small price to pay for sitting on your arse all day, girl!

Here, Daddy, more than ever, being precious is my bane - more so than it was in Heaven. See here how my privileges redound against me.

Is it wrong then - tell me - to wish sometimes to be like them, these surly unloved whores who serve men but at least have one another? I know I can never be like them, adored so as I am - sometimes, though... I just can't help but wonder. There must be something more than simply being adored being precious is good for - some good I can do with the love I have to give. I gave my love to You, to my shame - why not some other man then, to the good if he be bad?

Daddy, why not Denzil?

After all, in his own way, you know, Denzil is special - like You. I mean, different of course, but - well, he loves me well enough.

Why else would he keep me here the way he does?

It's just the way of men - something Nina used to say: covetous, wanting, needing to possess what they love exclusively. Why else the sign at my feet reading Do Not Touch? If he didn't love me it would state a price.

They like to keep their true loves pure - something else she used to say. Of You keeping me: 'Dat wha' myake yah precious to yah Daddy, girl - yah purity an' hinnocence an' all.'

That's precisely how Denzil keeps me: precious; embowered in lilies. Our Lady, the Virgin Lily.

I know you men now - how you work: your love for us confines us because you fear so much our love returned. A woman's love is too great - it can't be borne: with love she gives life, the boy - giving love, she takes it.

You'd say in Heaven, Daddy, looking at Your photograph of mummy that You kept: 'There are but two things in this life, Lily my dear, love and death - for our own sakes we men should resist you women, sad but true. Mmm. Love!... in itself a Temptation. If only we did not succumb to that. Then we might never know the pain of loss. But we are fools and weak... and never can resist.'

I *think* I know now what You meant.

'Go t'im in 'is bed an' myake 'im slyeep,' Denzil said. He knows, too, how you can't resist - the danger we pose when loved.

*

Denzil said yesterday in passing: 'De boy, 'ee call me Daddy.'

He called him Daddy. He's speaking now. How old would that make him? I should know these things. If I did, I'd know how long I've been here. But since the boy's birth time's been a straight unvaried line for me that's hard to measure. It's only those whores wrapped in blankets and carried out limp over Denzil's men's shoulders I have to mark it -"... about two a month,' I once heard one whore tell another, but I'd long lost count by then how many had passed already, up the stairs and away to where I don't know - to be dumped. At least in Heaven from its east- and west-facing balconies I had the sun to watch rise and set, could count the passing of the days by that means when I had a mind to.

But this much I do know: if the boy's talking, he needs me now - for if he learns the ways of men like Daddy and Denzil, as of course he will with Denzil for a Daddy, then in time he himself will take a girl and make her precious, won't he; keep her pure - he'll have no way of knowing how dangerous that can be.

If I'm the boy's mummy, isn't it my duty to warn him; teach him the error of these ways? Who else will tell him if I don't? The whores won't. The safest, the only way to love: for goodness sake don't, my boy!; the whores, they can serve you well enough.

Of course.

This is how my love can best be put to use - save it for the boy.

Would Daddy approve do you think? I mean, it would be atonement of sorts for giving Him my love, wouldn't it? You never did like Denzil, did You, Daddy - though I don't think you ever thought he was quite the devil Nina did. Why, you didn't even believe in God was what she said:

'But Nina - Heaven and Hell! He talks all the time of Heaven and Hell. He must believe in *God!*'

'Chile, yah Daddy do much talkin' an' preachin' to suit 'isself an' assert 'is hown belief. 'eaven an' 'ell serve 'is purpose well. But God now, 'ee feel God gone done 'im wrong when 'ee tyake yah muhder haway - 'ee do a better job 'isself 'ee t'ink. So 'ee refute de Lord's hexistance an' put 'isself hin 'is place... Dat be honly mah hopinion, mind, so you be sure keep *shtum.*'

Yet You loved mummy precisely because she believed in God, I thought:

'Chile, yah muhder was de mose beautiful 'oly white woman I ever 'ave met, yah can be sure. She 'ad de mose 'eavenly glow habout 'er hanybody hever did see - I defy de Lord 'isself t' say udderwise. She like a hangel, she was so pure an' precious an' all. Yah Daddy might never 'ave believe' in de Lord like she done but 'ee love 'er for de devoutness dat she showed 'im, yah can be sure o' dat.'

I think she meant God when she said ''im' - not You, Daddy.

Strange, though, that not believing in God he'd so often ask for the Lord's prayer. 'How does it go?' he'd say.

Clayton Lister

I say it still today - though only to myself of course:

Our Father who art in Heaven
Hallowed be Thy Name;
Thy Kingdom come; Thy will be done
On earth as it is in Heaven;
Give us this day our daily bread;
And forgive us our trespasses,
As we forgive those who trespass against us;
And lead us not into Temptation,
But deliver us from evil...

It's for comfort, you think I do this? Because I'm sorry now I didn't do His will and was led into Temptation, that His constant greatest fear for me; because just as He predicted, it did bring me here to Hell, where they've taken my boy away - the only thing I have now, or don't?

He was always fretting so about my being Tempted. That night I gave my love to Him, I heard Him talking to Nina about it then.

*

He'd had her serve us our supper in the west-facing dining-chamber - we sat at the table now, between courses, He watching me closely I could feel, like I always could, His beard fanning out around and over the knuckled altar His clasped hands liked to make for His chin, and me gazing out the window, as I always did, the sun going down now all garnet-red and rueful.

I used to wonder what it was like beyond the buildings it slid behind... a hazy memory I'd sometimes call up of rolling soft-edged hills with trees on and long winding paths of damp earth through you could stroll along on Sundays - though in the memory I'm not; I'm running, running through the waist-high fern that's thick on either side, shocking up the fallen beaded rain into silver showers ahead of me; bespattering the backs of my hands it is, cheeks, lips - the startling freshness of it, the smell, its taste; and He and mummy - I can hear them, see them, every now and then somewhere along the path, laughing, watching for me; holding hands.

But they were way out of view now, these hills - even with my trusty bins... just a roughly crenellated skyline of concrete and metal in silhouette - so many fingers I'd think, needling the sun, bleeding it; ghoulishly staining great swaths of cloud - mauve, orange, purple... all sorts. Perhaps they were only a dream, then, these lush hills with their greens and woody browns, that I imagined had their own smells even, even their own sounds the wind helped to make? Something I'd got from those outlandish fairy-tales, I wondered, that Daddy so liked to read maybe - or maybe I should say so liked to read out loud to me. I just had no way of telling, Daddy - no way at all. They might as well have been a dream.

'Daddy, don't you ever wonder what it's like outside now?' I asked. The words just came tumbling out, but even when I'd said them I knew there were more to come: 'We haven't been for a long time, have we. It must be a long time because I've lost track. Is it years?'

I think I'd taken Him unawares, though still His face looked like it suddenly weighed a lot. He sighed deeply and sat back in His chair.

'I've told you before what it's like outside, Lily - you know what it is. How many more times are we going to have this conversation? It's dangerous down there, it's evil. I don't believe you can't remember for yourself. And really, anyway - is this a suitable discussion for the dinner-table?'

'Oh, I don't mean below,' I said. He'd folded His napkin and was dabbing His lips with it now. 'I know it isn't nice there - Nina tells me, and... well, I do remember for myself... a little,' which was true enough - just... I couldn't say that; couldn't tell Him I had good memories, too - Marcie, Nina's daughter. 'I mean where it's green. You used to live there, I thought. Didn't you? With grandad, when you were little?'

'You know very well I did,' he said, more curt now than before. 'Why are you asking these questions? This is our home - Heaven.'

I knew at the time I really shouldn't say it, but it was like I couldn't help myself - honest, I couldn't. Why, it didn't even bother me that He was working Himself up now - it was Denzil, his having been to Heaven just that morning: 'I just wonder sometimes what it's like, that's all... I was thinking. I was thinking of going to see for myself.'

He leaned forward again now, but this time He didn't make that altar with His hands for His chin - it was so he could better be disdainful. I'd not been very tactful.

'I've told you before,' He said with His eyebrows heavy, 'You're not to. There's nothing there, Lily. Nothing. Understand? It's bad, evil. I've told you. You're not to go downstairs. Even the stairs are dangerous. The stairs are very dangerous. You're not to.'

'I could take the lift,' I said.

I'd meant it to be funny: the lift's always broken - he wouldn't have it fixed. But He only said: 'Lily! The subject is closed!'

*

I've noticed that difference between Daddy and Denzil. Daddy used to get angry with me sometimes. Denzil never does. He only sometimes grows irritable with some of the whores, the ones who complain like I used to Daddy, that they're dissatisfied and bored - they're the ones I think who usually end up being carried out rolled up in blankets. But I don't do that anymore - I don't complain. I've learned my place. I just sit here in my bower and think - remembering and thinking; things Nina used to say when I'd ask about the past; those things Daddy never liked to talk about - for instance He and mummy:

'Well, girl,' she'd begin, maybe laying down her rolling-pin and dusting flour off her hands on to her apron. I knew how she liked to tell these stories - I'd have her talk for hours. 'Yah muhder hallways live 'ere. Hallways. She a little girl 'erself on dis hestate way before it 'come wha' dey call de ghetto - when dair was de white an' black folk all church goin' togedder. Sure, Sugar! I recall back so far when *hus* was hin de minhority, an' it be *we* 'oo too scared t' leave our 'omes for fear o' vi-olence! You hain't hallways been de honly white folk livin' 'ere, yah know. I holder dan yah Daddy, Sugar - an' 'ee holder dan yah muhder by years, too. I recall t'ings from way before she come hinto dis Godforsaken world! Yah ha'ntie Nina one wise hold woman, yah know, wi' hample busy livin' be'ind 'er.'

Clayton Lister

And now really settling into it, with her big brown eyes so wide and flour on her cheeks - the part I liked the best: 'Well any'ow, chile, yah muhder was dis *byoo*-tiful white girl, as I say, wi' many, many boys queuin' up t' walk hout wid 'er, but none successful see, 'cos boys be boys whadever an' want honly one t'in', an' yah muhder, as you know, a girl o' 'oliness an' virtue, wid an 'oly muhder of 'er own wid a watchful eye hall de boys in too much hawe of t' defy. Till one day dis holder white man 'oo's pwoor like hus but hova better hupbringin' has can be told by 'is haccent 'oo is yah Fahder come along an' sweep 'er off 'er feet wid 'is big broken spirit yet hexemplary good manners. 'ee not from roun' dese parts but 'as wandered far from 'ome hin search o' somet'in' more dan 'ee t'ought 'is hown fahder's hample wealt' could hoffer - 'ee fancy 'isself has a poet an' a hartist, an' be de black sheep o' de family hon account of it. Dishowned 'ee be. But 'ee no longer 'as fait' hin de dreams 'ee left dem with so many year ago.'

I'd think that a very great shame for Daddy but wouldn't say a thing. You could see in Nina's eyes it would be rude to interrupt.

'Neverdeless,' she's saying, ''is good breedin' an' honest love for yah muhder's 'oliness himpress yah muhder's muhder so much heven she like ''im.' That's good at least, I think - it's nice to think she liked him. 'Tyake ''im to 'er 'eart she do despite 'is bein' pwoor. Because wha' she see his dat dough 'ee be pwoor 'is love for yah muhder 'as hinspire' 'im to give hup completely 'is fanciful dreams hov hartistry - 'ee determine' now t' myake 'is fortune hin business jus' like 'is fahder before 'im has a means o' tyakin' care of 'er. Haltogedder more rehalistic hin 'is houtlook on life 'ee become she say. And she right, too, for heven as dey marry 'is wealt' startin' t' swell wi' de sound hentrepreneurial decisions 'ee been myakin' wi' de backin' o' de bank - which was somet'in' new t' folk round 'ere, Sugar, I can tell you!'

She'd be leaning forward now and whispering, like maybe it's a secret - she knew how to tell a story, Nina, even those I'd heard before. 'De rub be dis, dough,' she says, 'For dough she love ''im hample, yah muhder hon no account gonna move from de harea like 'ee want for dem - de hestate 'ere be 'er 'ome despite hit gettin' rougher hall de time wi' de white folk 'ereabouts movin' haway. She got 'er loyalties, chile. So wha' 'ee do, 'ee tyake de hunprec-hedented step o' hactuwally *buyin*' a flat off de cursed government - de very one hopposite yah ha'ntie Nina's, which 'ad been hempty for so long halready hon account of its bein' on de ground floor.' And here she'd pause, as if for thought. The ground floor - it's always that that does it. I've noticed. Not something that's ever said - something that's never said.

But then she's off again, thinking nicer things I'd think: 'Dough 'ee does it hup real real nice, 'ee do - I give 'im dat. Hit one good eye fo' hinterior decoratin' yah Daddy got, girl.' Then, though, looking around at the white tiled kitchen, floor to ceiling: 'Maybe dese days 'ee hoverdo it a bit wi' dis celestial hatmosphere t'ing.'

'But hanyway, dey fas' becomin' de bees knees o' de whole hestate, girl, I tellin' you! She so pure an' byootiful an' all, an' decked out hin de hendless stream of pearls an' whatnot 'ee buy 'er, an' ee so much holder an' wiser now it seem wi' dis newly discovered talent of 'is for myakin' mwoney. 'and hover fist hit seem it just keep rollin' hin. We can't keep track o' de mod-cons an' fine new furniture and sorts bein' delivered - barrin' hup de corridor houtside mi door

Our Lady, The Virgin Lily

when dey brought. An' before long hit not just dese dey gyot harrivin', Sugar, bu' a *byoo*-tiful baby da'hter 'oo his yahself, to complete de perfect picture.

'De honly t'ing...' leaning in again close, over the pastry between us, and looking mighty frightened, 'Folk startin' t' gyet hangered an' jealous now o' de mwoney 'ee earnin'. Wi' so many white folk lyeavin' de harea 'ee be haccumulatin' hall de property 'ee can wi' shrewd borrowin', an' puttin' hin de new black folk comin' in. But pretty soon, I tellin' you, dis mwoney 'ee be myakin' 'and hover fist do *not* seem right t' dem, girl. Not t' dem folk 'oo be *puttin*' it hin 'is fist it don't! But 'ee just keep keepin' on... decoratin' yah muhder so in pearls an' all sort - an' de bot' o' dem so hoblivious o' de bad feelin' it creyatin'. A fine state o' haffairs 'ee do creyate, a fine state - '

'Is Daddy really so rich, Nina?'

'Chile, how you t'ink 'ee hafford to creyate dis place 'ee call 'eaven for you! 'ee myake more mwoney dan de church hitself! Vast sums 'ee myake now, heven from dis very block halone! Hevery hapartment hin it 'ee do hown now - hincludin' yah ha'ntie Nina's. Halways de same dese men be. Halways wantin' t' control udders an' myake demselves so himportant an' grand wi' de false power dey to happropriate. Hit be a *hempire* 'ee control from way hup 'ere, girl - a *hempire* I tell you!'

'Really, Nina? Is He really that important? I've no way of knowing these things for myself. He never talks to me of serious matters.'

'Well, lyet me put hit dis way, Sugar. 'ee gyot hall de folk round 'erehabouts hin 'is pocket. Yenough for 'im to play hat bein' God wid hany'ow. Yah Fahder one mighty man more dan mose - more heven dan 'is hown fahder was hin 'is day.'

'He's special. That's why.'

'Oh, girl, 'ee be dat hall right - when dey made 'im, dey broke de mould yah can be sure.'

*

So you do see, Daddy, just why I say Denzil's special? He's got his empire, too - just like you had yours - as well as his keeping me so pure and precious, which I'm sorry to have to say for everybody's sake, though especially the boy's. Why, I think Denzil began to love me even before I first spoke to him, he considers me that precious. That's what made him climb the stairs to Heaven and Tempt me.

Early every morning from the balcony, with my breath white on the cold air, and all along the backs of my thighs and on my backside the concrete even colder, I used to watch for him through my trusty bins. He'd be bringing Marcie home - Nina's youngest; Marcie, who'd used to dress me up in her older-girl's clothes and play with me all that time ago after mummy died, when I lived with them for a while. They were nice memories, very nice. I liked Marcie. She was good to me. If Denzil was a friend of hers I was thinking, then he must be a good man - he must be.

She always sat in the front passenger seat of his open-top car when he brought her, dressed to the nines now and looking very proud just to have been with him the whole night-long wherever it was they'd go together. Heaven's so high up you could barely ever hear the traffic, just sometimes horns blaring one after the other for minutes on end, hours sometimes, but you could always hear Denzil's hi-fi pounding, up through the ether: *boom-caca boom-caca caca-caca*

Clayton Lister

boom-caca. So unlike any music I'd ever heard Daddy listen to - unlike anything I'd ever heard in fact; loud and deep enough to make the air quiver, it seemed - this that first got me out of bed that time, drew me to the balcony to look down and see him there. I had to ask Nina about him, I had to... Well, not him exactly - his car: Daddy was rich but He didn't own a car - Nina?

'Sure, Sugar - Denzil! De man know no hexpense. Why 'ee heven wear a diamond studded tooth.' - A diamond studded tooth, Nina! - 'Dat tooth was knocked hout long 'go by a man 'oo 'armed 'is girls hunjustly, den set habout Denzil, too - or tried. For Denzil fatally cut 'im wi' de knife 'ee halways carry, an' have de tooth capped wi' de gemstone hin so de girls might know dair wort'.'

Daddy would *never* have done such a thing with his money. As far as I could tell all His money went on shaping Heaven, his pride and joy. No diamond studded teeth for Him, or hi-fied cars - though it all sounded wonderfully exciting that someone, Denzil, might think to buy such things; different, at least - Tempting, I suppose.

'Does he really care for his girls as much as that?' I asked.

'Girl, 'ee love 'is girls like 'ee love 'is car!'

Well, that just did it - anyone could see how much he loved his car. You could have seen your reflection in its bonnet, it shined so I thought. Children queued for the honour every morning, waited for him along the pavement. And they'd never have dared take the hub-caps off or scratch or try to steal it - or any of those things they'd usually do. He'd peel them off crisp notes from rolls he kept in the pockets of his fur- or leather-coats he'd wear.

I knew. I'd seen it - through my bins. He *was* a nice man. Why not my friend if Marcie's?

*

'You what!' said Daddy.

Nina had served our dessert now, and it dripped from His spoon that trembled in His hand inches from His mouth. Of course I knew well enough He'd closed the subject, but it was just as if that Temptation He feared had been too long at work already - I couldn't keep my mouth shut. It was just this loneliness lately, and the boredom; my head filled only with my own thoughts ever - indeed brimming over with them it seemed these days; my sending them out from Heaven over the balconies for damp chilly hours on end - even after Denzil had long dropped Marcie off and gone; into that sometime drab swell of cloud beneath that might at least roll them slowly on and carry them away*, away, away...* I thought - some place where I might not have to be the only one to listen.

'I've made a friend.'

'How, Lily? How have you made a friend?' Just the way He looked at me, so angry I couldn't answer for the minute - I could barely believe I'd said it myself. Always like this He was, though... why so? *'Lily?'*... My mouth opening, but no sound coming out, just a little pool of saliva welling on my tongue. *'Lily for God's sake! How have you made a friend!'* It snapping shut at that, I bit my tongue and snorted, wincing - snorting, bit it again. And His fists, too: the cutlery bouncing loud and clattering - that didn't help; custard leaping out His bowl, off His spoon - Him not caring, though, not even seeing; His eyes too icy-blue and gimlet - and trained on me. Though, peculiarly, when I swallowed it, the blood oozing from my tongue gave me calm, I noticed.

Our Lady, The Virgin Lily

'I thought as You don't like to go outside,' I began, rather more measured than before - because, after all, I didn't have to meet His eye; and why should I be hurried? 'I might go with him instead. He has a car, you know. He could take me out of town to the hills where it's green, where we used to go with mummy - we might take a picnic. I wouldn't have to walk the streets alone or even down the stairs - I wouldn't want to, anyway. He could come and meet me and bring me home like he does Marcie.'

I glanced up at His silence to see the gimlets dulling a little as He weighed my words - He was thinking how there was a difference in me somehow.

'Marcie?' He said, 'Nina's Marcie? What's she to do with this?' Then, picking up again - a little more fiercely: 'Is this Nina's doing, Lily?' though I didn't mind really.

Blood's quite sweet, I was thinking, How funny - it felt nourishing somehow. 'Not Nina's exactly,' I said.

He didn't believe me, though - pulling His beard slowly through His fist and eyeing me till: 'Nina! Get in here!'

I was excused, but left quite leisurely. I thought: Oh, well, what'll be'll be. I even took my time to slide my feet in their cotton socks across the polished parquet. Then, outside in the hallway, squeezing little bubbles of blood out of my tongue, and quite liking the intimate sound it made squelching with saliva I found, I listened carefully, ear to oaken double-door.

'Nina! Has Lily been seeing Marcie I want to know?'

I could imagine how she'd be standing there before Him - heavy flattened heels in worn out mules and baggy tights; her cotton dress frayed at the hem. She'd be drying her hands on her apron across her belly - and that would be annoying Him.

'Since when Lily seen any livin' creature but you an' me?' she said and sounded so ingenuous I thought - knowing it would annoy Him.

'Don't be impertinent, woman! She's talking about some friend she's made - someone Marcie knows.'

'Man, I dwaunt heven know no friends o' Marcie's an' I de girl's muhder!'

Thank you, Nina, for always being here to help, but I'm a big girl now... don't cry at such things anymore - there isn't any point. Squelch, squelch - blood and saliva.

'Well, she's been seeing someone, Nina - and I don't know how, unless it be through you.'

He'd be using His eyes on her now, gimlet again and icy, to get out of her what He wanted. He could cow her these days far more easily than He'd used to, it seemed.

'De girl give me some letter for Marcie.'

'And you *gave* it to her?'

'Lard, no...' sadly, but then her rearing up - like she'd just thought of something: 'Dwaunt You t'ink it cos I t'ink she don't need no friends now, mind! A girl 'er hage cooped hup like dis - it hun*nat*yural, I tell you! I honly didn't give de t'ing t' Marcie cos -'' but she didn't finish.

I thought for a moment she might have taken poorly: her blood pressure - she was always saying that of late; pressing her fingertips against her temples and closing her eyes when I would go on so - though I never went on the way Daddy

Clayton Lister

was now.'
   But no - she must have been all right, because still He pressing on: 'Why, Nina? *Why?* Because she's a slut? Is that it? That's it, isn't it! You can't deny it, can you - her own mother! Ha!'
   And her now, rallying again, really raising her voice, much more like her old self - *when mi 'ave more henergy for it, girl*: 'Man, wha' you say t' me 'bout ma hown da'hter! Yah hain't got no *right* t' say dat kind o' t'ing I tell yah - an' me hin dis pwoor state o' healt', too!'
   'But it's true, isn't it, Nina! You know it is! You've a slut for a daughter and you know it! Well, I forbid it. Do you understand me? Forbid it! They shall not communicate. *Do-you-understand?*'
   And then an eerie silence - but then, with a tremble in her voice she couldn't help let rise:
   'Do I hunderstand? Do I hunderstand! Do I 'ave hany *choice* but to hunderstand! Dis Your 'ome! All our 'omes Your 'ome - from top t' bottom dis Yah Kingdom! Yahs be de power an' de glory! I hunderstand! I hunderstand!
   'But You listen hup, Mister, an' You listen good, cos Yah da'hter gonna be hout dat door de mwoment hit hopen one hitsy-bitsy crack whedder me carry correspondence or no before too long! All cos Yah wife be murdered an' so *broot*-hally rape downstair hon 'erown doorstep so many year ago - I know, I know dat why Yah keep Lily pris'ner 'ere! I know You know hit honly be honaccount o' de person *You* be dat Yah wife be vi-olated de way she was, an' still Yah feel guilty honly won't hadmit hit. But lyet dis wise hold woman tell Yah somet'in, Mister - Yah slowly murd'rin' *'er* wi' dis hisolation!'
   His voice was low now. I could barely hear it, it was that low - low and tight. I couldn't keep squelching if I wanted to hear this:
   'She will not be Tempted, Nina. She will not be. If you won't consider me, consider what's at stake for you - consider your job.'
*
So I went to the kitchen ahead of Nina to help her with the washing-up. She followed quickly though, and straight away took me by the shoulders.
   'Now, girl, yah listen to yah ha'ntie Nina. Yah been talkin' yah Daddy 'bout dis Denzil boy you seen - dwaun't t'ink I don't know. 'ave I not tell you one hun'red times hif once, dough, *forget* dat boy - 'ave I? I haskin' you - *'ave I?* 'ee yain't *no* good, I tell yah, girl! 'ee yain't no suit'ble boy for you - 'ee one big nasty 'ellish man you dwaun't *hever* wanna meet. 'ee de devil 'is*self*, I tell you.'
   I said quite truthfully I always thought Denzil looked a very nice man when I saw him through my bins - so smartly dressed, and he always had a smile for every passer-by. Why just this morning hadn't I seen his diamond-studded tooth shining through the letter-box even when he wasn't smiling? But I didn't tell her that. I ducked my shoulders out of her hands and about-turned to do the washing-up.
   ''ee gyot good ryeason t' smile, girl,' she said, like it was a warning, ''ee de honly man wid mwoney to 'is name round 'ere hexcept yah Daddy, dat's for sure... an' maybe 'ee honly myake dat de bad way 'ee do 'cos yah Daddy so do down folk dey gyot nowhere helse t' turn but sin in desperation - but, chile! Wha' yah gyot mi talkin' habout? Dat not de hissue. De man's de devil 'isself, I tell yah! De devil 'isself.'

Our Lady, The Virgin Lily

I thought maybe, after all, she was taking poorly. Poor Nina, I thought, Poor poor Nina. Didn't she think he treated Marcie well enough, I reminded her - 'Mmm?'

Her heavy shoulders shook, and no sound came out her mouth. She could have been laughing or she could have been crying - it was hard to tell. Poor Nina. She sat down at the kitchen-table and began to talk, though not so much to me I thought as to herself, or maybe someone she was imagining was there instead of me.

'Do 'ee tryeat Marcie well? Well now, dair be a question to contemplate. In she come a-drippin' an' a-glitt'rin' in 'er finery 'ee give 'er, an' hexclaimin' wha' a man 'ee be - 'ee buy 'er dis, 'ee buy 'er dat. But wha' de price she hexpected t' pay in return in time? Dat what I wanna know. Wha's de price hall 'is young girlfriend pay to be tryeated so?'

I didn't really know - but I comforted her with my hand on her shoulder: everything would be just fine. What did she mean though about Daddy doing down folk and turning them to sin? I had to ask that.

'Oh, chile, I been spyeakin' mi mind too much hagain has usual... but I guessin' yah's hold henough to know hif yah's hold henough t' hask. Sure, yah Daddy tyake our mwoney by wha' dey call legyitimate means but 'ee tyake so much now 'ee give no one hany better hoption in life but t' gyet dair t'rills cheap off de likes o' Denzil 'oo hunderstand dair susceptible, corruptible nyatures. 'ee tyake wha' little dey gyot left wid 'is women, 'ee tyake hit wid 'is drugs. Yah Daddy cryeate 'eaven for 'isself an' yah Denzil creyate 'ell for de rest.'

All this was most peculiar sounding. Poor Nina, I thought, confusing herself so; calling Daddy God the way she did - and now Denzil the devil.

As far as I could see: so few people ever came to Heaven, only her, and Daddy paid her to, to cook and clean and whatnot, but Denzil, he had hadn't he - he must be nice; I'd only had to ask and he'd come - like an answer to my prayers he'd been:

Denzil, I have watched you a long time from Heaven and would very much like to meet you. I want to ride in your car like Marcie does, and have you take care of me like you do her and all your other girls her mummy tells me about. I live on the top floor in the same tower block as her but in Heaven with my Father who won't let me out. Can you help? Just the odd afternoon when you have the time would be nice.

All my love and kisses,
Lily

*

I'd wrapped the note around a lily stem and secured it with a pin. Daddy always had lilies delivered to Heaven. It cost Him a small fortune to have it done all the year round I knew, but was worth it He said. 'Purity, Lily - that's what they represent.' In the summer, He'd fill my bedroom full of them - 'Lilies for my darling Lily' - now was autumn, though, when there were fewer around, so I'd had to choose one carefully from where He wouldn't notice - the kitchen.

I threw it with the note attached way up in the air over the balcony like you might a dove, but watched it tumble tumble ever downward till it disappeared from view - so *so so small...* I thought. Then I caught it in my bins, the last few

Clayton Lister

storeys and... Bingo!; straight into his lap as he parked the car. Guided by the hand of God! I thought, and let go my bins to clap my own together. I gave a little dance I was so happy.

He read it and I saw them talking now, he and Marcie, craning upward, the pair of them together - though of course I knew they couldn't see me. Then they both got out the car. I knew Marcie would - she always did; but Denzil didn't. I'd known it meant he was coming up to Heaven.

Could he be that bad? I thought. Of course not, of course he couldn't.

It was always the same: ever since mummy died, Daddy thought everyone was bad, and, more and more, Nina - well, she just told me whatever He told her to because she was scared of losing her job.

'Nobody gyot honest jobs round 'ere no more 'cept me. I work for de Lord 'isself!'

*

Now, in the brothel, Denzil's Lord - His will be done: that's the way of it. He keeps me here as Daddy did. Though he also has the whores to consider. They're not precious like me, but they still have to do what they're told, even when they're not on duty - which is stay put and quiet in their rooms mostly; even Marcie - she's a whore now, too. Where are all the fancy clothes she used to wear I wonder.

When we were children a long time ago she'd play with me, dress me up in her clothes for fun, have me speak in patois even, just like her. It was fun. It was. Here, though, she won't so much as look at me. A short while after Denzil brought her, a short while after me, she said I was nothing but trouble - if it wasn't for me, she said, she wouldn't be here. Then, when the child was born, he put her in charge of him, even though she didn't want to be - he said because *she* was responsible for bringing *me* here: we deserved each other. It's just his way of controlling things, like men always have to - like her mummy said they do. She doesn't understand that.

When she isn't working, she lives down the corridor the men aren't allowed down along with all the other whores. I do, too, of course, although precious and privileged, in a room of my own, and also because I used to cry a lot. I've stopped that now, but still I have to sleep on my own. If I had to share like the whores do, I wouldn't complain of cramped conditions - I'd be happy to share whatever. I wouldn't even moan about the smell like I know they do, like I've heard them do through the walls. I don't know how many rooms there are exactly down there - just lots; it's like a maze - but the boy, he's in one of them. I do know that much. I've heard him.

Why, sometimes, even now he's talking, I hear him crying, and sometimes Marcie and sometimes others, too, telling him Shut up for Chrissakes, Shut up! It doesn't do to cry in Hell at all. I'm sure, having learned how for myself, I could stop him crying more nicely than that - I wouldn't tell him Shut up. But Denzil, being Lord here, says he doesn't need me; being how I am, which is touched he says, I'd only complicate things - he's got more than enough mummies, he says, and he's his daddy now. He visits him when it's time to cash up and unlock me from my bower when it's time to eat and sleep.

It's then I must speak to him I think, when all the girls have retired - which is never for long, though; when he's alone and cashing up; when he's sneaking

Our Lady, The Virgin Lily

those looks at me the same as Daddy used to - those loving looks that men would rather resist but are helpless to if you're pure and precious to them like I am. His eyes aren't ever soft like Daddy's could be, and they're dark of course, not blue, but both are special, so I know - I'm sure - deep down they must share the same sort of love for me. I mean, I am precious after all.

When he's cashing up, when there's no one else around...

*

'Denzil?'

'Wh'appen?'

'Why don't you ever give your love to the whores?'

'Mi dwon't want no disease, girl!'

'Don't you ever need loving though?'

He stops his thumbing and counting of notes, and looks at me straight - and very hard. But that's not a problem. That kind of thing doesn't bother me anymore.

'I get so lonely, Denzil. No one ever speaks to me unless to jeer and call me names. No. No, I'm not complaining - I know you don't call me names - it's just... well, I don't have diseases, Denzil - do I?'

*

After we'd finished the washing-up, and Nina had gone home, I went back to Daddy in the dining-chamber.

He wasn't so gimlet-eyed now. Always - or more and more of late - after He'd been mad, this thoughtful, almost sad mood would come upon Him. I realised when I saw Him now, staring into space from where He was just sat there at the table still, I'd been expecting this new soft mood all along.

I wrapped my arms around His neck from behind and buried my face in the great hoary bush that sprouted out His head every which way. He'd used to like me doing this - He'd laugh and maybe wrestle me into His lap, tickle me or hug me to Him; of late though, He'd stopped.

'You know I love you, Lily,' He said.

'I know, Daddy - you old silly-billy, you.'

He pulled out his chair, his great big leather-backed dining-chair with wings for arm-rests there was ample room for me in despite me growing so big these days He said. He was readying to leave, retire to His room, without so much as a squeeze for me. But I stopped Him and made Him. I sat on His lap and curled myself around Him, nuzzled His neck. He wouldn't nuzzle back, but He said very softly:

'You must understand, Lily. We can't leave here now. It would be foolish, don't you see. I have My pride. This is our home now. I've built it especially - you know that: Heaven - where it's safe. Don't people look up to us here? What it's like below... it's dangerous, Lily. People are evil - do wicked wicked evil things you wouldn't understand. I don't want to lose you. What would I do without you - mmm, my little angel? You are so pure... so precious.' He was stroking my hair now and that was good: He was softening - still going on: 'They'd do you harm, you know. I know they would - they'd take you away and I wouldn't know where. Do you dislike it here so much?'

'No. Of course not,' I said back, looking deep into His sad eyes, 'It's just... I do get bored, Daddy, so bored - and lonely. It's as if sometimes time has stopped or gone on without me, or at any rate doesn't change things like I think it should - like it does for Nina and her children. They've all grown up, you know - did you know? Some of them have children of their own now. Oh, Daddy, You mustn't be mad with her. It's only talking we do.'

He said nothing, but His eyes, they were so soft now, so very very soft.

'Daddy,' I said, 'Let me sleep with You tonight, eh? Please?'

*

Denzil says nothing. He's deep in thought.

I know he loves me. He doesn't jeer at me like the whores do - or genuflect and laugh.

He just looks, resisting all the while.

'Denzil?' I say.

'Wh'appenin', girl?'

'Don't you need someone to love? Let me give my love to you. Please? Just this once... just the once, Denzil?'

*

I'd never felt Daddy tremble so.

He let me lead Him by the hand out of the dining-chamber, and along the passage, His free hand supporting Him the entire way - it was just as if he thought He needed that support, even though I was right there on His other side to support Him. So light and frail He felt, so light and frail - like I'd never known before, bless Him. He knew where we were heading - He just couldn't resist: it's white from floor to ceiling and vast - the most restful room in all of Heaven I used to think; so restful you felt you almost had to whisper in there - should only whisper; if you spoke too loud its surfaces threw your words back at you - just faintly, but enough to make you think hard about them, too hard ... Make Him sleep, Denzil had said.

He let me sit Him down on the edge of the bed - his great four-poster, with its pristine sheets changed every day; the scent of lilies at great expense. I slipped off His slippers and lifted His feet up, straightened His legs, and, shuffling lightly along, puffed up His pillow; whispered softly: 'You must relax now - you work yourself up so, Daddy.' The pads of my fingers around the whorls of His ears; His eyelids lowering, I kissed them.

'Lily. Oh, Lily, my dear. My darling daughter Lily... so pure, so precious. You know...'

My finger on His lips:

'Shh. Not now, Daddy. Not when I'm giving You my love. It's rude - don't you know... '

*

Denzil is Tempted. He unlocks my shackles and lifts me from my bower. He takes me by the hand, down the corridor to the left into my room. It's funny to be led so - but really, men are so fickle... so foolish. Didn't Nina always say as much.

They like us to be pure, not be stained by others. But the greatest Temptation for them is our love - even though they know the dangers. They never can resist - be it led or leading.

Nina never told me how when you let them stain you, when you give your love, it changes everything so drastically, throws you out of one time and place

Our Lady, The Virgin Lily

into another as it were, though only if they so love you it's unbearable to them. She must have known because she told me all her children had different Daddies and each of them was special in his own way and loved her, but none were ever around that I ever saw. She should have told me why this was exactly. If she had, then maybe I wouldn't have given my love to Daddy, and then I wouldn't have wound up in Hell where it's even more boring than Heaven. I wouldn't have been Tempted so easily - I wouldn't have Tempted Him.

Daddy,

You must forgive us our trespasses,
As we forgive those...

But Daddy had to give me a son - just like God gave The Virgin Mary hers. So in a way it was His will. And I can't be that bad really. I know it was Daddy who gave me the boy because the whores have told me so - and didn't God give The Virgin Mary a son to save other men with. That's what Nina said. My boy must be for saving other men, then. He must teach them not to try and keep their women so pure and precious as they do; it's dangerous - it's safer to love the whores. I must teach him that.

If I'm to teach him that:

'Denzil, don't talk...'

*

'Girl, wha' de hell shit you talkin'? Yah daddy kill *'isself* af'er fuckin' you! Yah t'ink me feel bad? Cha! See me swallow pills! Yah wish! Yah t'ink me feel bad? See 'ow bad I feel. *Feel* mah blade, girl - dat 'ow bad I feel!'

*

Oh, Daddy... Oh, Daddy... but it didn't hurt with You. You were so gentle... You let me make You sleep.

You let me give my love and afterwards You said: 'Lily, darling, put the pills under My tongue and go and get Me water... '

*

It hurts so much - and everywhere. I can't see for the blood. My face, Daddy, my hands...

'Marcie? Is that you? Help me Marcie if that's you... Help me. No, I'm not - I'm not so precious. I know it, I know it. He called me a whore, Marcie. But where's the boy? Where's the boy, Marcie...?'

Marcie...? Marcie...?

Daddy?

Neil Grimmett

A Christmas Gift

How, he wondered, could you eat so much and still feel such a deep and empty hunger? He knew that there was an answer and that it lay a long way from the simple act of feeding and yet was as basic and necessary. That somewhere between the spiritual event they were celebrating and what it had been turned into there was the human need to break bread together and accept each morsel as a gift that built and enforced love.

The children sat next to their mother hypnotized by the entertainment spilling from the TV set. Christmas was being dished out, as it had been for weeks, devoid of any meaning and still to be paid for. He looked at their faces: they knew the stuff so well their lips moved in sync. with the actors: "The Lord is my shepherd," he whispered.

He made several attempts to use the occasion to bring them together. Games, a ghost story, a walk through the frozen fields: all were dismissed with an electronic bleep as another form of life marched in an endless but essential sacrifice. Now even they were quiet and forgotten, along with all the other things.

Present after present they had wrapped. Christmas Eve spent like insomniac shop assistants. Everything in place, itemised and double-checked, free of any last minute arrivals stepping in from the fog to a glow of comfort and everyone's relief. Last night he had told them: "One year my father made us a model castle for Christmas. It was perfect with towers and a drawbridge; he had painted it all in grey with a rough stony type of finish. It must have taken him weeks; of course nobody was telling you what you had to have back then."

"Don't start Simon," Paula had warned. She and her best friend, Mary, who since her divorce had insisted on joining in on the 'magic' of preparing the children's surprises, were getting to the end of their labours. Simon watched as the pile of gifts mounted. Stockings had become bin-liners and each child had an armchair with their name-tag hanging from it.

The three of them were sat on the floor drinking a bottle of sherry. His sole contribution to the night was to keep their glasses topped up. In fact, it seemed as if everything had been managed without his involvement: He felt as if he had just woken up to find it all there, fallen like night snow but without the beauty or disguise. The slow, even flashes of the Christmas lights held and bathed each face in its best and worst colour, making them appear lovely or grotesque, honest or cunning. He found it appropriate to the mood.

"It's a time for children," Mary said, "that's all."

"He thinks we should go around like something out of Scrooge," said Paula.

"I just think we are losing all the magic," said Simon, wanting as always to appear calm and in control when Mary was around. "I can still sense and feel the power out there. A collective willingness to believe. It's just waiting to be tapped; only you have to shut out all the crap and take the time to listen."

For the briefest second there was silence.

"I have to go," said Mary: "I've got a date to keep."

"Another lucky man," said Paula.

Simon tried not to notice the look that passed between the two girls, friends since primary school and with so many shared experiences that he could never

A Christmas Gift

hope to understand. Also, he knew Paula told her about their rows and problems and that had found a place in the look.

They helped her carry her presents out to the car and then stood there as the fading sound of her car abandoned them.

"Look at all those stars," he said, gazing into a night where the universe seemed to have contracted and become young and fresh again. "When did you ever see so many stars?"

Paula looked up, trying to see what he saw. They were stood close together and he reached for her. She allowed herself to be held but turned her face as he tried to kiss. She made an exaggerated shivering and moved away.

"Do you know that most of those lights up there are left-overs from stars that died before this planet was even born," he said, as their back door opened and without waiting for him closed. For what felt like a long time he made himself stand there and search the heavens for that one bright spot that had once led the way to so much hope. He could find nothing except an unfathomable infinity that mocked his imprisonment.

*

Now dinner was gone, the wrapping paper was ripped and crushed and filled the bin-liners. His two pale, exhausted-looking daughters sat and mirrored their mother. He tried to gauge from their faces if they felt as he did and if it was still not too late to make something special happen.

"This is a great book," he said, holding his present open and pretending to read as he was dragged into the perfect resolutions of the movie: "It really makes everything clear."

Outside, and unnoticed, someone walked by their door. They lived in the first of a row of terraced cottages. Once they had been the tied homes of the labourers that worked the surrounding fields. The farmer and owner lived in the nearby house that still managed to tower above and overlook their lives though the work was done by tractors and they paid rent for the short-term lets.

Their next-door neighbours had lived there for thirty-seven years. Stanley had worked for the farmer as a boy and had moved from the village with his bride to the cottage on their wedding-day. Now they did the same as their new neighbours: trooping to the farmer's door each week with the rent and being allowed in every twelfth one to re-sign the contract.

"I can't imagine going anywhere else until I die," Stanley had told them a short while after their arrival.

"We'd like to stay for a long time," said Simon; and had noticed a look come into the man's eyes he did not care for.

Stanley still liked to help out on the farm. Every time the farmer came creeping around the cottages hoping to catch one of the men and ask for another little favour, Stanley would jump at the chance, even if he had just come in from a long day at the feed mill and Simon was already on his way. "That's all right," he would yell, "I'm here now." And then march off in front of them leaving the farmer to dismiss Simon.

On the few occasions when Simon had got to help on one of the jobs: usually driving sheep through pools of dip or helping load bags of grain ready for drilling - nothing that ever required anything but muscle or mind-numbing patience: Stanley would always get to hear about it. His first reaction was to ignore Simon's greeting. Then he would keep going in and out of his house making lots of noise hoping to attract attention. When he did, the job would quickly be mentioned.

Instantly there would be a story connected with it that implied more than familiarity. Stanley insisted on calling the farmer 'Boss'.

"Me and Boss did that job once in the year of the great snow. The snow was so deep we had to walk along the tops of the hedges in places to get out to the sheep. Carrying bales of hay for their feed on our backs. Can you imagine? Can you picture the two of us completely cut off and struggling through?"

Simon had asked the farmer, Mr Wills, one day when he was helping him to drive some sheep along the lanes: "Was Stanley a good worker?" Mr Wills had eyed the newcomer with his usual slow, market-day assessment before answering.

He was a small rushing man who always appeared to have an insight into the weaknesses of people and the exact reasons for their failures. He also liked to believe that he was a shrewd judge of humans as well as stock. "I knew as soon as you pulled up that I was going to let you rent the place. Do you know how? Clean car, tidy kids, no cigarettes in the ash-tray and both slim. What do some folk expect, coming out here with fags hanging out of their mouths and four stone overweight?"

It had been some months before Simon realised that fat probably meant you would not be able to stand a long session at the top of the hay barn and that it was hard work cleaning walls and ceilings after smokers. He sensed now that Mr Wills was beginning to doubt his decision.

"Stanley was strong enough," he answered; "but always had too much to say. We like to go about our work in silence and be alert to the sounds and messages all around."

The sheep bleated and stamped their desperate requests.

Simon knew the farmer was not telling. Somewhere behind the spotlessness of their house and garden there was the untidy truth. No one, he thought, works in a place for twenty odd years and then stays chained to the endless cycle of growth and harvest for free. Stanley's wife appeared even more bound by some force. She had spent every minute cleaning and polishing the dingy little cottage until its gleam had dazzled her into madness.

They had been amused at first to hear her vacuuming the carpets at four a.m. every morning; now it was disturbing and made him want to pound on the wall. It had been another joke to share when she had run about the garden threatening the starlings flying above her clean washing; or then out burying balloons in an attempt to scare away the farm cats scraping her ground.

"Filthy cats; dirty birds," would be the start, getting more and more obscene and hysterical until one of them could not stand any more and had to step outside and let her know they were home.

Sunday afternoon was the only time Stanley and his wife stopped. They would sit at the top of their garden on a crudely-built bench and stare at the gate. The only person Simon ever saw arrive was Mr Wills.

"Boss is here. Boss is here," Stanley would cry. His wife would rush in and return with a tray of tea and cakes. Then they liked to sit and gossip, resentful of any intrusion by Simon, Paula or the children.

Also, if any of them did go out, Mr Wills always said the same thing in his

A Christmas Gift

loudest and best voice: "And how do you like the new neighbours I've found for you Stanley - are they up to the mark?"

"We've seen so many," Stanley would say, "they come and go and you can't keep count," Then quickly lead him away with a: "Do you remember..." As his large, short wife dangled her legs above the path and shook the blue rinse out of her hair with the effort of keeping still.

Once, Simon hid behind his curtains trying to hear what was being said. Then endless lists of names and events were meaningless to him. They measured everything in years. He thought of how many times they had already moved and wished there was some calmness in sight. He looked at himself in the mirror hiding and trying to spy, he saw dust clinging to its surface and outside, weeds starting to go to seed in his garden. "One year's seed: seven years' weed," he thought he heard - or had heard before.

*

Mr Wills had gone off for the day. It was the first time in the year and a half they had been here that the farmer, his wife and son had all been away on the same day.

"Don't you dare go and buy us anything for Christmas," Mr Wills had instructed him a week earlier. He had been lingering in their garden when they returned from another Christmas shopping.

"We'll be going off for the day," he announced, "so if you are around perhaps you will keep an eye out. Stanley is going to feed and check on the lambing so everything should be fine." He had stared out towards the horizon as if some terrible fate were calling.

"I'll be here," Simon had reassured him. "Maybe I'll take the girls for a walk."

Mr Wills had looked even more horrified and left before anything else could be said. Simon remembered instantly why.

One day, he had asked Paula and the children if they would like to come and see the lambs. The farmer had suggested it to him on a bright crisp morning at the start of the lambing season when the newly born lambs had been frisking in the fresh straw and the whole scene was idyllic.

He had tried to pick a similar day. Paula held the two girls and followed him as he led them towards the pen. He had deliberately timed it so that the farmer and his son would be at breakfast, leaving him free to show off his bit of knowledge.

Cara, the youngest of his two daughters had started screaming first. A high pitched note that cut and then reverberated back off the barn's steel roof. Then Emma had joined in.

Paula had looked in the direction the girls were staring. "Oh my God," she had cried, looking at him in disgust as she began dragging the girls back towards their house. He had stood there unable to move as the screaming carried on and on swirling around the yard like the whirlwind he had once witnessed in the same place.

Next to the large open-ended barn that had been turned into a pen for the pregnant sheep there was another barn partly filled with bales of hay. Just inside its entrance lay the bodies. A tangle of five or six lambs all covered in a slime of blood and muck. Next to them was a dead ewe. She looked abnormally large and bloated, with milky white eyes glaring in frozen agony. Hanging out of her was the head and foot of a partly born lamb.

The farmer and his family had arrived at the run, looking shocked and guilty.

"What was all that screaming about?" demanded Mr Wills.

"We're not responsible if anyone gets injured on the farm," said Mrs Wills.

"It was a bad night," said their son as a way of explanation. Then adding as his mother and father turned on him: "Where you have livestock: you have deadstock."

*

The film had finished. Simon loosened his collar. He had got dressed up: best suit and shirt, patent leather shoes and a silk tie. They were not going anywhere and no one was expected. He had done it for the day and for them. Now, as the next programme rolled into view and he watched the three of them twitch into more comfortable positions, he wished he had not bothered.

He felt an anger and resentment as every slow word of the introduction spelt out its map to another great journey as they sat in their void.

He knew there would be another row and that his clumsy stilted sentences would carry nothing but a weak echo of what they considered drama. What was it she had told him last time? "This isn't a rehearsal: this is life."

"Paula," he began. And there was a loud, continual hammering on their door.

Stanley looked flustered and uncomfortable. "You have small hands," he said as Simon closed the door and stood outside with him. He placed his large, calloused palms towards Simon.

"Quite small for a man, I guess," said Simon, putting his own small hand between them.

"One of the ewes has a lamb stuck and I can't reach it. I've been trying for hours; she's getting pretty weak."

"What about the vet?" asked Simon. Mr Wills had told him to always call the vet if there were any problems.

"I can only get the bloody answering machine. I've phoned Boss but he's going to be an age getting back."

"How about your wife?" Simon knew she was the daughter of a farm worker. "She's got small hands I bet."

"My wife! You haven't got a clue have you. I've got to get back."

He moved off leaving Simon stood on the doorstep. "I'll come," Simon called after him. "Just let me tell my wife." He opened the door and listened for a few seconds before following.

The ewe lay on her side and appeared to be sleeping. A short way off the rest of the flock carried on eating or dozing oblivious to anything that might be happening. Two fluorescent lights hung from the girders were switched on and held the place in a weak yellow embrace. It made everything appear gentle and old. Like stepping into a photograph, Simon thought, as his feet sank into the straw.

Next to the sheep there was a galvanised bucket and a towel with a bar of soap lying on it. Stanley washed his hands and then pushed one inside the animal. She groaned slightly and tried to lift her head. "I can feel its head and a foot," he said, "but there isn't enough room to feel anything else. It might be a

A Christmas Gift

back leg and mean that the lamb is all twisted. I've tried pulling a bit but nothing moves. I might end up tearing it in half if I try any harder." He withdrew his hand and stood up. He suddenly appeared to notice what Simon was wearing. "You can't do anything dressed like that," he said.

"Yes I can," said Simon. "I've never done anything like it before but I'll try."

*

He takes off his jacket and rolls up his shirt sleeves. The water is full of mucus and wisps of blood. It is icy cold and for some strange reason the smell of the soap reminds him of his primary school.

The inside of the sheep is warm and soft. Simon is amazed at the strength of the suction that grips and draws his arm in. He can feel a hard lump that he realises is the lamb's head, and then a foot, then another.

"I can feel two feet," he said, "two."

"Grab them and pull, " said Stanley, "quickly."

He can hear the man's frustration and anger mixed with desperation. The sheep's contractions squeeze around his arm like a tourniquet and he is drawn further in. A stain of pink begins to seep into his shirt. He feels a dampness creeping through the crust of dry straw as he kneels behind her and his arm feels as if someone has scraped the skin from it.

"I think it is a back leg," he decides suddenly; "it doesn't bend right for a front one."

Stanley sucks in a slow deep sigh.

Then Simon feels something else.

"There are two lambs: I can feel another head."

"She's not a twin," said Stanley. "It's a single. They all get scanned so we know. This is no good."

Simon pulls his arm out and begins washing.

"I'm going to go and get the vet or she'll be dead," said Stanley. He left without looking at Simon. The metal gate shakes as Stanley jumps off it and the noise fills the air like a muffled drum roll. Simon looks down at the sheep, her eyes are becoming glazed and distant. He drops back onto his knees.

"Come on girl," he whispers.

Inside he can feel a head and legs. He can also feel the place where legs cross each other and form tight holds and a slight way behind what he knows is another head. He begins to untangle the legs and tries to ease the other head back. Also, and for the first time that he can recall, he begins to pray.

He does not ask for his life to get any better; or for hate to turn into love. He concentrates solely on the sheep and her need.

"Please," he asks, bringing two feet into line, "let me get this one thing right."

He gently eases them out, the head follows tightly and then with a rush the whole lamb comes out. A mass of dark blood and other liquids spill over his legs. He wipes the lamb with a handful of straw as it leans bleating against him.

The next one already has its head starting to come out. He thinks it will jam if he does not get the legs out first. He pushes the head back in and reaches for the legs. "Just this," he breathes, and brings it out with one easy pull.

He notices as he cleans it off that instead of being all white like the first one it is heavily marked in black like a badger. Before he has finished, the ewe is on her feet calling both of them to her.

He sits back against the side of the barn and watches them bumping and tugging as they begin to feed. Outside it is very dark and he knows exactly where that bright star would be. He hears voices and watches as Stanley arrives at the gate and stands there looking in with a shocked expression on his face. Then Mr and Mrs Wills arrive with their son, followed closely by Paula and the two girls.

They are all lined up along the gate looking in. He waits, daring any of them to make the slightest sound or movement at this moment and on this day.

William Palmer
Even In Dreams, He Thought, We Lie

He never knew how his father died. He only knew, because she moved in straight after the letter came, that Aunt V must have had something to do with it. For some time after his mother would say, "Your Dad would have liked this," or, "When Bob was here..." But she stopped speaking like that in front of Aunt V, and soon his father dwindled back into the photograph frame on the dining room sideboard.

The two women sat every night in the dining room and Aunt V talked about the neighbours: about the women who were tarts, the men who were idle, and the children who were noisy and dirty and whose rushing about had nearly knocked her over this morning and yesterday morning and would tomorrow morning unless a constable intervened and weren't there laws about footballs in the street and bicycles on the pavements as much as anyone cared nowadays?

His mother said only, "Oh, I'm sure they mean no harm..."

Colin was forbidden to play in the street.

His white face appeared at the front bedroom window for half an hour at a stretch. Up the street he could hear the children shouting.

In 1950, he marched lead soldiers across his crumpled bed. The soldiers were Guards in charge of the Empire, with short red coats and tall black busbies whose paint came off in tiny specks on his fingers. The soldiers were hollow, so that great rents could be made in their chests with the pointed steel shells that the little spring-loaded fieldgun fired. Sometimes he would get up and go round the bed to be the enemy commander. From there the hills were differently shaped; the soldiers lurched forward to the gun.

Evening faded the battles. Then, to terrify himself, he would stand at the window and look up as the vast, starred sky replaced the blue dome above the houses.

The area they lived in was not good. "Practically a slum," said Aunt V. She persuaded his mother that the local primary school was not at all suitable for Colin. So he was taken out of there and dressed in a green and white striped cap, a green blazer with white piped edges, grey shorts, grey socks, and black shoes.

This was the uniform of his new school, a mile away, on the edge of the suburbs. The school was run by a genuine BA from Oxford. Mr Cassell. Not Castle, he insisted, but Cas-sell. A board in the overgrown front garden announced The Bevis Preparatory School For Boys. A short gravel path led to the black wooden porch of a large red Victorian house. It had been a rectory; the church next door had been bombed and never rebuilt. "So, you see, we have no chapel facilities as such at the moment..." Mr Cassell explained to Aunt V at the interview.

Fortunately the school let out its pupils a quarter of an hour earlier than the state primary, so, by running all the way, Colin was able most times to avoid the jeers of the local children.

At home, his mother calling Hello from the kitchen, he went upstairs to put away his things.

He had to pass Aunt V's room.

Sometimes, if she had just come in, the door would be open. The curtains were always half-drawn on the sash window; two hats, like bowlers, one olive, one beige, both with black bands, sat on top of the wardrobe. And Aunt V, standing, or walking a few paces round the centre of the room under the one light shade, dressed in her brown outside coat, or with that folded across the end of the bed, would squint if she saw him, a cigarette between her fingers, then turn impatiently away.

The only time he ever went into that room was for his birthday. An inadequate florin was searched for in her purse; "You are eight, fancy," "You are nine, well, well," the words as cold and precise as the coin angled into his palm.

One Saturday afternoon in the long summer holiday, when his mother and Aunt V both were out, he went upstairs.

He didn't go on to his own room. As he stood in her doorway he became afraid that Aunt V would have the magic to still be here though he had seen her go talking and walking up the street with his mother. He pushed the door with his fingertips and it swung slowly inwards. He entered.

The afternoon sun fell through the dusty window onto the wall above the made-up double bed. He looked round. The room was very tall and narrow and empty. On the mantelshelf above the closed-in fireplace was a green, glass statuette of a naked woman.

He reached it down. It was heavy and cold. One of the woman's arms was raised, clutched round a fluted pillar. At the top was a candle socket. There was dust inside and under the dust a yellowy-grey resinous caking of dirt and used wax. The glass woman's hair was parted in the middle, curling in glass waves to her shoulders. His finger glided over the soft, square face, the surprisingly sharp pointed nose and lips, to the chest, between the breasts, over the belly, the channel of thighs and legs, to the heavy square glass rock and weed-entangled base.

He carried it to the dressing table. He sat on the stool and turned the statuette, watching the face travel slowly round in the tall mirror. He examined the rest of the table top.

A snake of blood red and sea blue beads veined to look like stones hung out from an over-full jewellery box. Its lid was inlaid with mother of pearl and sliced wood chess squares. His fingers fumbled in the box. Under the beads was a silver butterfly, thorax banded in green and black enamel, wings studded with points of blue with one missing - a concave lead-gold star. More beads, black, bright; a string of pearls; a chain of thick, dulled silver links.

He put the stone beads round his neck. His face looked back from the mirror. He opened and sniffed warily at a small bottle with a rubbed label, 'Eau de Toilette'. The yellow-tinged liquid had a thin, exotic smell. Behind him, in the mirror, the wardrobe door was closed on a corner of black cloth that stuck out like a tiny wing.

There were footsteps coming up the stairs. He was almost too late. As he came through the doorway and ran up the corridor to his own room he heard her round the stair-head and suck in her breath.

Through the wall, he heard her moving about, then she came out of the room and went downstairs again and he heard her voice raised. He came out on the landing, and listened.

"... my room... my room," Aunt V was saying. "Little enough privacy... do what I can... if I can't call that my own... boy? Baby, more like... oh, yes, baby... at nearly eleven." Her voice rose and fell like a siren.

His mother's answers were muffled and evasive.

"... a key... a bolt..."

"There's no lock - and how can I have a bolt when I am out of the room?"

The atmosphere had stilled and soured when he came down. Aunt V sat behind a magazine. Her lips were pressed so tight together that they had disappeared. When at last she got up and went out of the room, his mother leaned over and whispered.

"Don't go into Aunty's room again, will you Colin? Not without her permission. She was very upset when she found her things moved around. I don't know..."

Aunt V didn't speak to him directly for weeks.

Then Arthur came.

Money had become a problem it seemed. Whatever Aunt V had had was almost gone. The war pension wouldn't keep them. She didn't see how it could keep them. His mother had never worked. "Your Dad didn't want me to," she explained to Colin. "He said my job was to look after you. To be here when you came home. He hated an empty house."

Aunt V said, "Well, I hope you don't expect me to go to work. Not with my heart."

Mr Cassell was teaching them French. *"L'horloge sonne trois heures,"* he said. The exam for the grammar was that summer.

His mother had placed an advertisement for a lodger in the local shop. Aunt V only hoped it would be someone suitable. Arthur called on the afternoon she was at the library. He was large and smiling. He was to move in the next day. That afternoon his mother moved her things to Aunt V's room and made up the back bedroom.

"He works in a factory?" Aunt V wailed.

At the first evening meal, she maintained a tight reserve, not looking at the newcomer as he ate slowly and appreciatively. She got up halfway through and said, "Excuse me, I am going to my room." Arthur wished her a cheery good night.

Colin joined her in resisting the newcomer. Arthur tried to be friendly. He was a tall man with a hard body when Colin punched it once, in response at last to the friendly dabs and feints of Arthur's big, deeply stained hands.

By some reversal of what he expected from war, Colin learned that Arthur's wife had been killed at the beginning of '45. "One of the last," Arthur said, in his odd, cheerful way. "V-2. What can you do? It was all like some great bloody silly accident."

Aunt V pulled a face at the word.

The first night that Arthur took his mother to the pictures, Colin and Aunt V sat on either side of the living room fire. Aunt V pretended to read a book; Colin could tell because she kept beginning at the top of the same page. She sent him to bed early.

Il est neuf heures moins quatre, said Mr Cassell.

She woke him up.

"I never go out. I never go anywhere." Her voice came through as if she had

William Palmer

bored a hole in the wall.

"Well, you never want to," said his mother.

"Perhaps I was never asked," said Aunt V.

Arthur bought Aunt V a large box of chocolates with a red bow. She left it untouched on the sideboard. After a week, Arthur broke it open. "Shame to let them go to waste," he said.

On Colin's eleventh birthday, Arthur gave him a set of slender, mottled wooden fishing rods in a long green canvas bag. There was a wicker basket too, with reels, a folded keep net, and hooks and lines neatly packed in tobacco tins.

"They were mine, Col," said Arthur. "When I was a lad. I don't get the time now."

Colin didn't know what to do with the gift. He picked up the rods and they slithered under his fingers in the bag. "Thank you," he said.

His mother smiled across at him and said, "Aunt V wanted us to save them until after the exam. As a reward. But we thought you'd like them now."

The basket bumped against his legs as he carried the tackle upstairs.

A couple of weeks later the letter arrived. He had not won a scholarship to the grammar school. He had only been offered a fee-paying place.

The uniform had been bought already. The blazer hung in his wardrobe, scarlet, with a unicorned and gryphoned breast pocket badge shining gold, white and silver. Aunt V caught him in the hallway that afternoon. His mother and Arthur must be out.

L'horloge sonne.

"You are a stupid boy. After all we have done for you," she panted. Her right hand twisted his shoulder, her left plucked at his shirt. "You have wasted it all. Thrown it away. Now we have to make more money. Make sacrifices. Work because you were idle. Your mother will marry a common little factory worker. He will sleep in your father's bed. And I will be put out." Her face was huge and he could smell her cold soup breath.

He broke free and ran along the hall and out the front door. Only when he was halfway down the road did he slow to a walk, his tears drying like lead cooling.

That night he stood on the landing again, listening to the row downstairs.

"Canada?" said Aunt V.

"Canada," said Arthur.

"And what about the boy?" she demanded. "What is to become of the boy?"

"He'll come with us of course," said his mother.

"And what about me?"

There was a silence.

"If we do - then you come too," said Arthur.

The conversation bubbled on. His mother came into the hall. Colin retreated to his bed.

He lay awake for what seemed a long time, then fell asleep.

What woke him he did not know.

There was no sound in the house. The street lamp cast a lime green strip across the ceiling. He got out of bed.

He went out of his bedroom and along the corridor. The hall light had been left on and reflected dimly off the wall onto Aunt V's door and, farther on, the lodger's. He stood in front of Aunt V's for an age.

He twisted the knob slowly, in excruciating silence. He slipped in, pushing the door to almost behind him, but not letting the catch engage.

At first he could see nothing, then the tall rectangle of the wardrobe emerged, the pale oval of the dressing table mirror, the dark tunnel of the fireplace.

He walked there and reached down the glass statuette from the mantelshelf. It was heavy. To get a better grip he used both hands. He crossed to the bed. There was a dark, indistinct shape on the pillow. He raised the figure, his arms outstretched, until it was level with his forehead. He leaned back to increase the momentum of his swing. Then he brought the figure down with all his might.

There was no sound but a dull thud. He hit again. And again.

The door behind him swung open and the light showed the bed. There was something beginning to come from the hair to spread itself on the pillow. And as he looked, another head was raised from the side of that, and Aunt V, dark patterns on her white nightdress, was looking down at the work on the pillow and then back up at him.

"Yes, yes," she was saying. "You see what you have done. You have killed your mother. You see what you have done. You have disgraced us. They will hang you. The clock will strike. It is disgrace..."

*

In 1990, in Canada, sweat curled in the hairs on his chest.

"What is it? What's the matter?" Joanne was asking from her sleep.

His eyes focused on the ceiling that was barred with light through the blind's slats.

"Dreaming," he said. "I was dreaming I killed Aunt V."

"Um?"

"Only I didn't."

"Who?"

"Aunt V. She died years ago."

"Killed her?"

"It's only a dream. I've had it for years."

Still half asleep, she looked at his big sad pale face.

"Come here," she said and reached out. Hooking one arm heavily round his chest she pulled herself to him. "You're hot as hell," she said. She went to sleep again.

He lay awake for a while yet, staring at the light on the ceiling, then he too fell asleep.

Mark Asheton

The Entelechy Of Cyrus J. Porkbelly

Cyrus J. Porkbelly saw the name of Leibniz carved in his face. That is to say, he saw his face reflected in the plaque which identified the casket, propped against a bookshelf in his spacious study, as the final resting place of Leibniz, *the* Leibniz, whose books on calculus and monadism lined those very shelves against which his coffin now reclined. Mr. Foster, seated in a deep armchair opposite, saw his face suffused with a kind of fierce, possessive glee, as the man who had been introduced simply as Gur handed him a tumbler of bourbon.

They were an odd couple, thought Mr. Foster. Cyrus J. Porkbelly was a self-made billionaire, a scourge of boardrooms and money markets the world over, and a generous patron of the Arts. The layers of fat softened the effect of large, sturdy bones, and furled the skin on his neck, yet it could not obscure the power in his frame, not to mention his pockets. Like most men of his ilk, if he wanted something he would get it - he would buy it if possible, but if the previous owner refused to acknowledge the obligations of the poor to the rich, of the weak to the strong, Cyrus had no qualms about extracting it in a more nefarious fashion.

Cyrus had wanted the coffin of Leibniz, and Mr. Foster had got it for him.

"Did you have any trouble?" asked Cyrus softly.

"A bribe here, a threat there. Nothing heavy," replied Mr. Foster.

The contrast between Cyrus and Gur was startling. Gur was tall, wiry, unkempt. He dressed his dishevelled frame in a rough cotton robe and open-toed sandals, his beard deformed when he smiled, which was readily; he was every inch the Bohemian prophet, yet surprisingly there was no messianic gleam in his eyes, which in fact were an inexpressive grey. Instead, Gur manifested his closeness to divinity by putting flowers in ice-cubes. Mr. Foster watched as the cube in his glass fractured and cracked, and the little blossom bobbed to the surface. Gur smiled at him insistently, then turned as they heard a high-pitched metallic whine.

Cyrus was unscrewing the coffin lid. Mr. Foster spat out the flower against an engraving. Gur walked over to the desk and picked up a piece of cloth. He moved over to face the coffin lid as it came off and was slid to one side.

"Behold the man!" announced Gur.

"Behold the man," repeated Cyrus in a whisper.

"Behold the skeleton," muttered Mr. Foster.

It was, reflected Mr. Foster, just a bog-standard human skeleton. He could have dug it up anywhere. In retrospect, he wasn't sure why he didn't, rather than slog half-way across the world. Then he remembered: he was afraid of Cyrus Porkbelly. He would do it five times over if it was necessary to evade Cyrus' wrath.

Gur spread out the cloth over one hand. It glittered in the light, being woven with obscure, intricate, and - or so Mr. Foster felt - cabalistic designs. With his other hand, Gur reached into the coffin. The next thing Mr. Foster saw was a human skull gripped by the long fingers of Gur through the cloth, before the corners of the cloth were raised over the skull and fastened by a pin. Laying the cloth-bound skull aside, Gur nodded, and Cyrus rang a bell.

There was a knock on the panelled mahogany door.

"Come," called Cyrus.

A servant entered.

"Is the grave prepared?" asked Cyrus.

The Entelechy Of Cyrus J. Porkbelly

"Yes, sir," responded the servant.
Cyrus motioned to the coffin.
"Gur will show you what to do."
"Yes, sir."
After replacing the lid, Gur and the servant carried the coffin out.
"If that is all, I would like my payment and be on my way," said Mr. Foster nervously.
Cyrus reddened suddenly with temper, then sat silently behind his desk. He studied Mr. Foster, opened a drawer, and started piling money on the desk.
"You have performed a singular service for me. You will be discreet, I hope," said Cyrus.
Mr. Foster approached the desk.
He twisted violently as the air was pierced by a scream. The two moved quickly to where the sound was issuing. "My gallery!" wailed Cyrus as he saw the smoke curl from underneath a door which reverberated with frenzied thumping and screams that seemed to split the air, to make it visible just as within the gallery it was made visible by flames. The door sprung open and a small burning figure hurtled through the opening, scrabbled with agonised death-throes against the opposite wall, and was rudely extinguished.
"The sprinklers!" yelled Cyrus, turning to the burning room. "Turn on the sprinklers! My masterpieces!"
A crowd of people now crammed into the hallway, all immaculately dressed. What a shame, thought Cyrus. The evening had been going so well, until this ugliness had imposed itself. He looked down at the corpse; he saw a shaft of metal protrude from the left jaw.
Cyrus J. Porkbelly saw his daughter dead. He turned to his dinner guests.
"I'm sorry about all this. Please, try to enjoy the remainder of the evening as well you might. This gentleman here..." he motioned to Mr. Foster, "... is qualified to deal with the situation."
The guests filed away silently. Cyrus looked at the carnage of the greatest gallery in the world.
His face became grim.
"Bitch," he hissed.

*

Mona Lisa Porkbelly smiled enigmatically as she interrupted her father.
She often smiled enigmatically, in fact she could hardly do otherwise since Cyrus, as a present for her seventh birthday, wired servo-mechanisms into her jaw. He was turning her into a work of art, he said; he had photographers follow her and displayed pictures of her around the real Mona Lisa, displayed prominently in his gallery.
Cyrus and his fucking art. Mona Lisa hated her father. She ferried drinks around the dinner guests, all of whom were struck dumb by her appearance, being indistinguishable from Da Vinci's portrait, and smiled enigmatically. She rued the day she was born, and so, she determined, would Cyrus.
Her mother, Selina Porkbelly, had eventually escaped and committed herself to a sanatorium. She had tried to leave before by jumping off a cliff, but had succeeded only in crushing her left arm. Cyrus, installing his own medical staff on the estate, had ordered both of her arms amputated, and her body remodelled in imitation of the Venus De Milo. He had then admired her for at least several hours. She was, he told

Mark Asheton

her, now a thing of beauty, and should be grateful. The failure of her suicide attempt had resulted in immortality, as all great art is immortal.

How ironic.

Mona was surprised that he hadn't ordered a taxidermist. He probably just didn't think of it.

"What a lovely creature," she heard following her as she walked away with an empty tray.

Bastards, all of them. They acted as if they had a divine right to their wealth, since even divinity in their eyes assumed a material, corporeal form - they were simply unable to imagine anything else.

Mona cast a last malicious gaze over the assembly, made sure that her father, having been informed by her that there was a gentleman in the study with a coffin and some unfinished business, was in fact absent, and sneaked away from the party.

First the sprinklers.

She found the recess in the wall where the sprinkler controls were, and switched them off.

Now the gallery.

The room was filled with instantaneous sunlight. Natural sunlight was too mercurial and unpredictable, so the gallery was always lit by artificial light. Not ordinary artificial light, oh no, but artificial light specially modified to look natural, with the exception that it was entirely static and unchanging; it was almost like, Mona thought, a photograph of light.

The paintings were arranged around the walls in alphabetical order - Rembrandts abutted onto Renoirs, Gorkys onto Goyas. It was, thought Mona, a complete mess. Cyrus was completely lacking in aesthetic or spiritual sensibilities. He understood this, and like a true materialist decided to throw money at the problem. It was about this time that Gur had turned up. Looking dishevelled and quoting Leibniz, of all people, he had daily dispensed mantras and synthesized theosophy like a machine-gun gone berserk. Strangely, Cyrus and Gur were made for each other.

Mona went back out into the hallway.

She returned with a can of paraffin.

Mona Lisa Porkbelly doused the entire gallery with paraffin and smiled so much that the wires cut into the soft flesh of her mouth, but she was pleased, she liked the taste of her blood, she loved it like venom, she loved the overwhelming smell of paraffin which promised destruction to so much beauty.

Feeling the innocuous heat of a match, fire sped thunderously over the walls of the gallery.

"Father!" yelled Mona.

She watched, her smile now blurred by the profusion of blood around it, while wood burned, glass melted, and Rembrandts, Van Goghs, and Da Vincis slowly renounced their immortality, blackening and gradually becoming uniform.

"There are some things that not even money can put right" said Mona to herself.

She turned to leave.

The door! She was sure she had left it open! Mona ran to it... it wouldn't open.

"Help!" she shouted.

The room was becoming full of smoke now, embers swirled in their curls, the sound of the burning became louder, hotter.

"Help!" she screamed, nearly shattering her hands against the door as she

The Entelechy Of Cyrus J. Porkbelly

battered it. "Help!".

The fire was advancing on her now, its appetite not satisfied by paraffin and paintings, its flames not yet gorged on the nether regions of the alphabet.

X.

Mona screamed. The mechanisms in her jaw were now tearing her face apart; still nobody opened the door.

Y.

The bones in her hands were being crushed, but Mona was oblivious of anything but the oncoming flame and the smoke wreathing around her.

Z.

Mona was on fire.

She screamed, threw herself bodily against the door, again, again, the pain was unbearable. Then she burst forward... too late.

Mona was only dimly aware of the thrashings which accompanied her final heartbeats.

She was already dead.

*

"Everything is composed of monads, and each monad is a soul which mirrors the universe from its own perspective. Therefore no two monads are the same, save in one respect - all monads are immortal. They do not interact with each other, but are synchronised in pre-established harmony. Matter is an illusion. Everything is spirit."

Gur sat cross-legged on the finely-mown, 40 acre lawn. Opposite him, Cyrus sat on a servant. He still seethed with anger over his daughter's perfidy, the violation of so much perfection.

"So the monads, or souls, mirror the universe?" asked Cyrus.

"This is truth."

"And the universe is perfect?"

"It is the best of possible worlds, since God does nothing without sufficient reason"

"Then it is spherical?"

Gur smiled.

"You are forgetting relativity. The universe is cylindrical"

"So it is the cylinder which is the perfect shape, the shape which all great art should strive towards?" pondered Cyrus.

"The cylinder is the shape most beloved of God," Gur confirmed. "But I would like to get back to this idea of the best of possible worlds. God cannot do something illogical..."

Gur stopped mid-sentence as Cyrus clicked his fingers and ordered a servant to bring him a telephone. He cast a glance of ominous fixity at Gur as he tapped the buttons in practised succession.

"When you have as much money as I have," said Cyrus, " anything is possible."

*

Sluggish brown liquid slid ponderously through the tube into the mouth of Cyrus J. Porkbelly whilst another tube carried away the waste. He would have turned his head, but neither his neck nor anything below it could move, so he flicked his eyes around to survey his gallery. He had a good view of the gallery from his elevated position; he presided over it, he was its crowning glory. His sense of domination was not impeded but in fact reinforced by his lack of locomotion. Gur looked a diminutive figure as he entered the gallery carrying a large hold-all. Gur smiled.

"Mr. Porkbelly." Gur genuflected, then in a mockingly obsequious tone added: "You look like a cheese."

It was true. Surgeons and doctors of all descriptions had laboured for nine months to make the ultimate artistic statement; they had encouraged and trained, just as one trains a plant to climb a trellis, growths on Cyrus' body until the surface of his skin was smooth and differentiated only by the purplish veins which could still be faintly seen.

Cyrus J. Porkbelly was perfectly cylindrical.

"What do you think?" he asked Gur, referring to his gallery. "I've had the best forgers in the world working around the clock to restore it."

Gur looked up at Cyrus resting on his pedestal.

"The exhibit is complete," said Cyrus with satisfaction.

"Just the finishing touch," agreed Gur.

Cyrus' eyes bored into Gur, but found only a bland smile.

"You brought the skull?" inquired Cyrus.

Gur unzipped the hold-all and produced Leibniz's skull.

"The will?"

"On the top step," said Cyrus.

Gur climbed up to the pedestal, his smile widening as he approached the document. He would inherit everything.

Gur smiled at Cyrus.

"A pity Mona had to die," said Gur.

"No loss." Cyrus nearly shrugged. "She had no self-discipline. I made her into a work of art. She should have been grateful."

Gur set the skull on top of the will. Its effect had exceeded his expectations - it had been intended simply to fuel Cyrus' obsession, to invest it with a measure of fatality.

Gur then took something else out of the hold-all. It was long and black. Gur gripped one end and pulled at the other. Now it was long and... shining, Cyrus thought, coruscating with a lethal beauty... an antique samurai sword... Gur raised it over his head.

"Are you ready for entelechy?" asked Gur.

Cyrus blinked his assent.

He watched the sword.

The light of the artificial sun played along it, made it glimmer, made Gur hesitate as he saw a messianic glare reflected in the blade, and then it ignited the bright arterial blood that geysered from the top of the human cylinder. This is not sculpture, thought Gur. This is a firework. Gur waited until the bleeding subsided, cut the meat from around the spinal column, then, pushing the will into an inside pocket of his robe, he pushed the skull of Leibniz onto Cyrus' spine. He put the sword back in the hold-all, grasped the hair to lift Cyrus head into the light, and studied the rictus on his face.

"Have I got a skeleton for you," said Gur.

Rhys H. Hughes

The Troubadours Of Perception

Rosa is harsh and meaty, like an old glass of red wine. She wants to play duets in the dusky twilight. Alice is slow and cool, like a watermelon that takes several days to consume. She still has trouble tuning her instrument. Clara and Gabrielle wander the fretboard in the search for a fuller sound. I want to make love to Gabrielle but I am unsure of the fingering.

In the lounge of a pleasant suburban house in Solihull, I dally with Christine. The lamps are turned low, there is a real fire in the hearth. I bless the mirror above the mantelpiece that reflects my profile back at me. The shadow of an emerging beard, the long shiny hair that curls around my shoulders, the glittering of an earring. I have the accent down to perfection, the rascally shrug.

Christine is not really interested in the guitar. She wants to talk. She does not care that my own is strung with silver strings to give a sweeter sound. Her husband is away on a business trip. She suspects that he is losing enthusiasm for the relationship, that he has been bitten by the fleas of new desire. She has a similar itch, a need to be scratched. I sigh, I croon, I softly sing. The fleas that tease in the high Pyrenees. O Christine!

Afterwards we sip coffee and I listen to an account of their early life together. It had all been fun then. Or had it? Her doubts are growing, they are beginning to encompass the past. I ask her how she sees her role within the shifting mores of a modern society. In all this time, a single note has she played. But my fees will be the same. I can humour the dabblers, the dilettantes, but I cannot afford to indulge them. It is my way of life.

The bedsheets are chill around Christine's lithe body. Her musky scent reminds me of incense, honeysuckle, the taste of caramel. Candles float in little vases full of water. Her room is tastefully furnished, almost sparse. I trace delicate pathways along her stomach with my tongue. I used to teach the piano. I used to dream of possessing such women as Christine on the stool while our fingers explored their own crescendo. But I have learned from experience. Ivory and ebony keys do not turn locks of hearts; what is required are the chords that bind.

I leave Christine and catch the bus back into town. Dust and leaves swirl before me. I feel self-consciously romantic in my waistcoat, the white shirt whose huge flapping cuffs I must leave unbuttoned, face and hands never too clean. We trundle through streets dim and featureless to those who do not know. I have finally solved the enigma of these suburban boulevards, treeless avenues and bowbacked crescents. The language of the pavements is in my blood, my greasy veins. Behind each pair of William Morris curtains there are shattered fragments of secret lusts, shards of which have lodged in my heart.

Jessica presents a quite different prospect. There is a more subtle understanding between us. Her husband is possibly a little too devoted. It would be difficult for her to betray him without feeling guilt. Her frustration manifests itself in the sly look, the parted lips. She has become an expert in the ways of the flirt. Sometimes I think that I am imagining her responses, so skilfully does she proceed.

She also happens to be a very good player. With the possible exception of Catherine, she is my most talented pupil. It seems that soon there will be little more I can teach her. I will have to depart forever then, with the taste of a lost chance alone to remember her by. She sings as she plays, and her voice is surprisingly homespun among the exotic artefacts of her living-room, the indigo batiks, the wooden carvings and ethnic throws. Homespun from gold, her hair. I correct her fingering in one place only and I do this by taking her hand. She wants to know what it is like out there, life on the pavement. Thrilling, dirty, absurd, I tell her. She is not quite enchanted but she is tempted to smile. I have seen her smile, I know that it is radiant, trembling, all that my own smile is not. My own smile is wicked and charming. Wickedly charming.

Jessica is on my mind a great deal of the time. So too Amelia, a direct descendant of the last man to fight a legal duel in England. The victor, I assume; I have never questioned her on this point. So Amelia needs no work, no flash of chipped incisor. She is already mine, became mine right from the beginning, though in one way only. Her bosom heaves. It is very gratifying to learn that she shares my passion for the poet, the only poet. *Le ciel est triste et beau comme un grand reposoir.* We watch the clouds part for long afternoon hours. Over the crumbling brick walls of her semi-detached garden, the Clematis hugging tight to its lattice, the morning-glory, the sun drowns in its vermilion.

Out again into the dusk. Amelia does not dance. Amelia prefers to languish in a curiously undramatic way. It is Isabella who likes to dance. I play her a valse and a saraband and she is stately, graceful, a little sad among the frosty adjuncts of the kitchen, where she always affects to have her lessons. I guess that only here the neighbours may spy on her. She is cultivating her reputation.

Isabella's husband is a salesman, a surly fellow I once met and liked. But Isabella tells me that his manner is pure guile. He is contented with life, his cynicism is mere sophistication. He is also a devoted Adventist. His chosen method is to knock on doors, following much the same routes as myself, and to ask the occupants whether they would like to talk about God. Usually they say no. He then asks if he can sell them some double-glazing instead.

I watch Isabella stretch upwards, her eyes fixed on some remote point beyond the shelf of spice jars, her bare calves as smooth as a legato. I watch her weave between the oven and the washing-machine. Later, when the mood takes her, she will sit on the latter during spin cycle while I strum with hooded eyes. The neighbours will make notes. Her paramour is a parvenu, they will say. A roguish fellow.

With Isabella I play old Spanish airs. With Lydia I tour the *oeuvre* of Guiraut Riquier, still a neglected composer. Lydia is an exception to one rule of my calling. She does not share the general acceptance of the grime any true romantic must carry on his boots. She insists I remove my footwear on her threshold. Toes wriggle in chilly anticipation. Will I ever bear her over another threshold? Will I ever hear her loosen her restraints with a shriek as piercing as a split harmonic? I am working on Lydia, practice is what it takes. *Chapeaux bas!*

Out on the pavements, weaving their own destiny, there are others like me. They are colleagues, rivals. I see them trailing their worn instruments in the dirt behind them. Our paths frequently cross. Over all the cities of the land, the suburbs, we are engaged in absorbing the fantasies of a million wives. Our travels are netting the happy hamlets, the conurbia of mock-Tudor ideals, the security of the scrubbed, the pools of quiet desperation with their shallow bathers. We are

The Troubadours Of Perception

gouging the conduits of a freer life, evolving a whole nervous system down which emotions can flow like honeyed wine.

But it is not all certainty, this game of ours. The control can be lost easily enough. In the park, in winter, I often serenade the trees; an aubade to a false dawn. Hunched, cold, I neither welcome nor mock the sun. My fingers are like the highest twigs themselves, covered in sleet. The power slips between. Sometimes I meet my match, or more than my match. They are out there. No-one who takes this profession seriously can be deceived for long. Many of them, innumerable.

I fear them. I fear their strength and their mystery. There is Madeleine, who likes to bounce me on her knee while I play. There is Yvette, who speaks not a word and hides behind widow's weeds though her husband is very much alive, propped up in an old armchair, drooling, facing us as we trill. There is Arabella, who furnishes her house all in black and has set a worm-gnawed Grandfather clock in every room. There is Rebecca, who does not care for my silver strings. There is Melissa, who keeps a collection of love-letters in a coffin in her attic. Her house is full of a delicate mist, cobwebs. There is Leonora, who I am at a loss to describe because she stays always behind me, always, no matter how fast I turn.

Helena is the one who disturbs me the most. I would like to break off our arrangement, I would like to depart from her and never return. But there is a hold, a morbid influence that she exerts on me. Her house is full of jars. I ask her what she keeps in them. She taps her nose and winks. Dreams, she replies; the dreams of all her past lovers. She collects the residue from her own generous thighs after she has toyed with them. I have not succumbed. I feel drained with Helena, enervated, sucked dry. It is only a matter of time.

Something else is happening. There have been developments. Hazel, who has been separated from her husband for nearly a year, persuades me to pay him a visit. His house lies on the other side of town. I find that he wants to pay for lessons as well. So I am able to listen to his side of the story. He knows all about my experiments with Hazel. It has reawakened his feelings, anger and deep love. They are reunited because of me. Then they break off contact. Music was the food of love, but now they are full. They are devoted. Who am I to protest?

This is happening to others, I hear. Many of them now have more male pupils than female. What can this mean? Will we be forced to work for money alone? Will they all abandon me, one by one? Barbara, Candida, Deborah, Eulalia, Fiona, Faustina, Gwyneth? What will happen to my soul, my essential nature? Will Rosa no longer want to play duets in the dusky twilight? Will Alice learn to tune her instrument without me? Will Clara and Gabrielle succeed in their quest for a fuller sound?

A crisis meeting is called between all members of our fraternity. We gather in a crumbling café in the metropolis, an establishment that has served our kind for generations. We fill the place to bursting. There are more players in this tarnished age of ours than listeners. There is talk of returning to the piano. But I do not want to lose my hair, my patience. I do not want to have to wear tiny round spectacles. Are there really no alternatives? There is talk of finding a use for men, of somehow fitting them into our world-view. But what use can I find for men? I am lonely, lonely. I am so lonely.

Rhys H. Hughes

While we argue, debate, cajole, the waiter serves us all supper. We need to fortify ourselves for the tribulations ahead. But we must not be defiled. We are minstrels, the lyric poets of the garden cities. Music alone is the reason for our being, we require no other sustenance. In this particular café our needs are understood. Do not fret. We shall rebuild Carcassonne, we shall. Solemnly, in the sinister light that emanates from the charcoal ovens, we dine on manuscript stew and violin steaks and pick splinters from between our broken teeth.

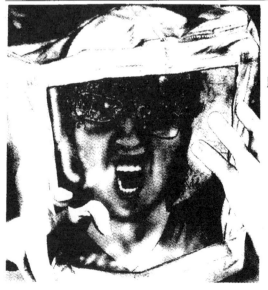

LAST RITES & RESURRECTIONS
16 extraordinary new stories · full colour paperback · 176pp · £5.99

Martin Simpson
Rick Cadger · Julie Travis
Lawrence Dyer
Kim Padgett-Clarke
Joel Lane · Nicholas Royle
James Miller · Simon Avery
Hick Turnball
Chris Kenworthy
Roger Stone · Mat Coward
Mike O'Driscoll
Neil Williamson
Conrad Williams

"A rich & varied anthology" Jonathan Coe

"Superb" Time Out

good shops or mail order

TTA Press, 5 Martins Lane
Witcham, Ely, Cambs

Michael Kelly

Monstrous Regiments

It is wrong to look. It is even more wrong to touch. Touching is the more difficult to manage so the wrongness of looking is more immediately to the point. "Don't stare, darling", "Look away", "You're not to look", were things his mother often told him. About drunks, accidents, intimacies, so many things of interest. She hated scenes. She hated what people would think, which meant notice. Anything private or emotional or unrespectable must be hidden away, its public non-existence pretended. Not seeing others' equivalent revelations more or less balanced repression at home. "Naughty naughty, John, don't peep," his nanny said, adjusting her knickers when the lavatory door swung open.

Yet his mother looked avidly at the stallions at stud. When she told him not to look he realised that she had well and truly seen first what she told him not to look at. He noted her flushed cheeks, her slightly swollen lips, her bright eyes, the enlarged pupils, when she tried to draw his attention away. Dogs mating, men fighting, lovers caressing, bathers changing, all excited her. He learnt to look at them secretly. They excited him too.

His nanny too liked to look at what she forbade him. She even liked to show. She looked at the man on the bank behind the trees with his hand in the woman's dress, at the male dogs panting and jostling to mount each other with pink prods poking from their outer parts. She looked at the old man whose towel fell off as he was changing on the pebbly beach, his long long penis dangling down his thigh. She looked at the pictures in his father's photography books of ladies and men with nothing on. "Ooh, they should be ashamed of themselves," she said about the ladies. She just looked at the men and stroked her own neck and went pink. He watched her in the shower and she said: "Naughty, naughty, don't watch. The men will come and cut your eyeballs out". But she stood with water dripping from her hair and squeezed the sponge on her tummy so that the water raced. And she flicked her towel open and shut so that he kept on looking.

His father did not make a fuss about looking. He never said it was wrong. But his father didn't work at home. And he was forever being told: "It's different for men. It's alright for men." He was kept in a womens' and ladies' world of superiority and inconsistency and ambivalence and secrets.

The milkman chased the Austrian maid, Gertrud, round the kitchen. She laughed and shouted softly and squealed. She waved her frilly apron at him. He was red faced beneath his tan. He pulled a chair out at the end of the table and caught Gertrud as she tried to climb over it. He held her from behind, one hand over her breasts, the other under her apron between her legs. She too was red-faced. Her frilly cap was askew. Her hair was untidy. The milkman kissed her neck and cheek and mouth. He saw their tongues, bright and pink, flicking and licking each other. The milkman opened Gertrud's dress. He squeezed her soft breast, pulling it out of her uniform. She saw him. "Not in front of the child," she said. Ze child. "No time to worry about that," the milkman muttered. "Push off, you little bastard. Go and look at something else," he said in a loud hard voice. "No, nein, it is not ze child's fault," Gertrud said. He loved Gertrud. She broke from the milkman and ushered him out of the kitchen. Her breast standing bare through her dress. Her kiss hot on his temple, her hair tickling him it fell so loose. "Hurry woman. Get rid of the little bastard," the milkman said roughly.

Michael Kelly

At lunch Gertrud looked neat and normal. If you looked and saw things, sometimes the changes afterwards made you wonder if you had seen what you had seen. People did not show the exciting things they had done or seemed to have felt. He felt that he was more marked by the glow of tension than those he had noticed.

His nanny took him for a walk through the park. He ran ahead to the summer house on the hillock. He ran quietly on the grass between the trees. He didn't like the gravel path so much as the grass. He followed a butterfly cautiously from tree shade to tree shade through the hot bright patches of light. As he weaved through the last clump of trees before the summer house he saw a movement in it. In the corner by one of the lattice pillar-wings, up which honeysuckle climbed, two people were clinging and struggling. When they moved into the light he saw that they were Gertrud and the milkman. Both of them were out of uniform. Gertrud's time-off dress was undone to the waist and the milkman was lifting her skirt right up her unstockinged legs. He held her bottom, squeezing it like modelling clay and turning her to face him with his other hand round the front of her thigh. Gertrud did not try to hide her hair from him. She pushed it at his face and he kissed it. He muzzled it, biting and licking. Gertrud helped him ease down his trousers and pants. The milkman's tom tiddler was sticking up, stiff and thick. But he scarcely saw it because Gertrud swung her leg over the milkman's lap and felt underneath her bare bottom to hide the milkman's prod. In her. He stared, enchanted at such desperate, obsessed, oblivious, frantic adult games. He looked to his nanny whose pebble-scattering progress up the path scrunched into his attention. Gertrud and the milkman did not hear anything. A pigeon's wings clattered violently. His nanny saw him by his tree. He beckoned her with a sshing finger to his lips. She joined him behind the tree. She looked round where he gestured. Gertrud's head was thrown back and jolted forward as she played a riding game on the milkman's lap. Neither of them sang. The game was so concentrated, so charged with absorption and inside savageness and feeling. Nanny gasped and squeezed his shoulder. Her fingers squeezed and relaxed, squeezed and relaxed. The milkman's bare thighs showed as Gertrud rode and pressed so fiercely. Once she looked at his glistening thing between them, linking them. Gertrud called out, thickly and thoughtlessly in German; the milkman gave a groan like a wordless call; the nanny gasped again. Gertrud and the milkman really lunged on each other and clung, their clasped bodies jumping and clenching together. Then they slumped. Gertrud's face disappeared behind the summer house pillar. The milkman lolled. His hard fingers slack on Gertrud's back where their streaky red marks showed on her skin. "Come away," his nanny whispered. Her face was as red as Gertrud's. She held his hand, moving with clumsy attempt to be quiet and unobtrusive, away from the summerhouse. Her co-ordination seemed to be affected by her excitement. She looked round several times at the summerhouse. They moved away from the path, to the side of the hillock further into the wood. Ahead of them he saw a movement. His mother. He ran to her without calling out. She had a sketch pad and a folding stool. She hurried nervously, irritably, into the wood, keeping her distance from his nanny. Her face was flushed. He pulled at the stool to slow her down. She stopped and allowed the nanny to catch up with them. He wanted to look at her drawings. She didn't want him to look under the elastic band which held the top sheet in place. She had drawn the summerhouse. It was empty. His mother said nothing to his nanny. Just stared her down. His nanny started to say; "Shocking. The brazenness. I've never seen ..." She trailed off in silence. They trailed back in silence through the trees until he saw some more butterflies and began to follow them, moving cautiously after them from tree shade to tree shade, through the hot bright patches of light.

When Hitler went into Austria Gertrud wept and wept and had to go home. She could not even see out her full notice. She hugged him. He promised he would not forget her. She was quickly replaced by a village girl. Mousey, sharp-faced but clumsy, who knocked into things and broke things. She soon joked with the milkman and sat on his knee, getting up flushed and jerkier than ever when he came into the kitchen. "Mum's the word, eh son," the milkman said, with a hideous smile and a frightening wink. In bed he thought about Gertrud and the bare bits of her body and her lost expression in her absorbed red face, so consumed, so inturned with sensation, and the milkman, and the new maid. He mixed them up in troubled dreams before sleep. Sometimes his nanny went on to the milkman's lap, looking at his prod with that almost unseeing intensity and handling it into her. Once it was his mother. Then he quickly changed the milkman into his father. With his nanny, Gertrud, the maid from the village. Somehow comforted, he laughed to himself and went to sleep cheerfully. He stopped thinking about what he had seen and looked at with such excited curiosity. For years he would forget it until he suddenly remembered.

*

Gertrud's breasts bare in the honeysuckle shade, the *contrejour* brightness of the summerhouse. Her legs and fleece bared with that sure, unselfconscious, sensation-centred speed. Her skin and hair moving, straining with such momentary beauty, all preoccupied with the present. Her skin, her hair. Their colour, changing in and out of the light. Their textures changing with the light. His nanny in the shower, peach-shaded, flirting with the transparent plastic curtain with its opaque fishes and its special smell. The dense hairs at the base of her round tummy. The full sponge pressed so that water washed through her hairs, straightening them and pouring through. As the water diminished the hairs curled back of their own sweet accord. She flirted with the towel for him, like a matador's movements with a muleta, irregular flicks and passes. In the orange pink light her yellow towel opened and shut and her breasts danced as the muscles of her tummy and legs danced and she showed and hid her hair and her eyes were bright and her lips were fixed in an excited smile. She had a servant's beauty and the silliness of the pretentious. His mother was even sillier. Gertrud was hardly silly, as far as his memories went, at all.

*

During the war they had to economise. In one of the houses they went to while his father's regiment was moved around the country, he had to share a room with his brother. Several times he had even to share his bed with his brother while a guest used the other bed. He remembered an ATS girl, a family friend, a county girl who was getting her moral and physical kicks by driving vans in a khaki uniform. Just after dawn she got up. He woke. In the dusk of the thin curtain she moved about in her nightdress sorting her clothes. She stood and crossed her arms down her nightdress to pull it off. She noticed him watching her. "Don't

Michael Kelly

look," she said; "You're not supposed to look. Gentlemen don't look. Put your head below the sheets." He did so for a moment. Then he looked out again firmly. She was naked, tousle-headed, dark-haired. Her body was rounded with the firmness of youth. Her breasts were big and large nippled. Her hair under her round tummy was soft in the dusky light. She was brown-lighted-skinned all over as if by pigment rather than sun tan. She rushed both hands between her legs. Her squeezed breasts altered shape. Lozenges. Like a frolicsome pear of flesh she leaned a little forward meeting his eyes with a long amused stare. "Oh you are naughty," she said: "What will I do with you? What will I tell your mother?" "I want to look," he said. "You are so pretty. If I don't look, I won't see you." She laughed. "Oh dear," she said. "Unanswerably disarming. Look then all you want." She held her hands above her head and pirouetted round. Her breasts moved, bonelessly beautiful. Her buttocks moved, full, muscular, beautiful. She stood still. They looked at each other. "Do you really think I'm pretty?" she said. He nodded, leaning back on the bedhead. "My God what a philosopher of the boudoir," she said. She came round the bed, arms crossed with light self-consciousness over her breasts, covering one, lifting the other so that the nipple showed in the crook of her arm at the elbow. She leaned on his bed looking down at him, her breasts hanging forward, moving between her arms as she breathed. She bent to kiss him. "Can I touch," he said, stroking both breasts. She jumped and stood up and away. "No, that would be going too far. At your age. At my age!" she said. She had jolted the bed. His brother woke. She stood there, her bush jutting forward, her hand on her chin, her other hand cupping her elbow, looking at the little boys looking at her. "Really," she said, laughing again. She went off to the basin, washed, dressed, made up. She came over to kiss them both goodbye. He held her round the neck. "Thank you," he said: "You are beautiful". She kissed him hard. "You've made my day right from the beginning," she said: "Pray that it lasts."

When the house was really full, he and his brother had to share his mother's room, when his father was away. Once an aunt shared his mother's bed. He and her son shared the camp bed. His brother was in his grown-out-of cot. His aunt's baby was in a carry-cot. In the early morning his aunt got up to dress for war work. He woke to find her searching for a case of clothes in her nakedness. She roamed about, looking, thinking, bending to open cases, rummaging, sorting, standing up, kneeling, squatting, reaching, replacing. In the grey twilight her body was white, her movements and postures, her positions, sharp and neat and distinct. And beautiful. He scarcely dared to breathe, guessing that she would not like to know that he could see her. She had his mother's silliness about noticing and pretending not to notice and denying noticing to others. She had less body hair than any grown-up he had ever seen. Her little breasts were delightfully pointed and dark nippled. They swung with her movements. When she curved, kneeling on one leg, the other bent for her to rest her elbow on and she reached for a case: her breast appeared below her armpit as her white arm stretched and her body tensed with her effort. She was entrancing. Her silliness kept his appreciation unsaid. She dressed briskly, unknowingly. "Goodbye aunty," he said as she looked round the room before leaving. "My goodness gracious," she said: "How long have you been awake? No. Don't tell me. I don't want to know." She laughed and pecked his forehead and went out.

*

They went to the seaside when his father was sent overseas with his regiment. Some friends lent his mother a cottage in Cornwall. A niece of the friends called Lavinia came with them. "Unhappy in love," his mother said to the new baby's new nanny: "We've got to offer. I do hope she's not a drip." His own nanny had gone off to do warwork. "Perhaps I'll meet Mr. Right," she had said. "Let me look at you one last time," he had said. "Look, you funny little man," she said. "No. You have to have nothing on," he said. "Don't be silly," she said: "It's dirty and silly to look at ladies with nothing on. And it's very very rude to talk about it." "But you used to," he said. "How dare you," she said: "You're a nasty-minded little boy and I shall tell your mother." He did not dare to say that she was a silly, nasty-minded liar. So he made a face at her and she smacked him. When she tucked him into bed she kissed him. "Let's be friends," she said: "I'm going tomorrow." So he kissed her. He feared she was going to be weepy. it was not the moment to remind her that he wanted to look at her. He woke when she came to bed because she was standing over him in her dressing gown and sensible nightdress, with curlers in her hair. "Ssh," she said: "Don't wake the others. I was looking at you while you slept. For the last time." He grimaced. "Look," he said, pulling down his bedclothes. She pinched his cheek. "You little monkey," she said: "What was it you were so shocking about this afternoon?" He grinned again. She looked at him a long silent look. Then she put the lamp down by his bed. Silently she undid her dressing gown and took it off and put it on the bottom of his bed. Silently she undid the neck of her nightdress and lifted it as carefully as possible over her curlers. Her stocky legs appeared below the slowly rising, shaking cloth. Then her hair, red in the night light lamp. She turned to get better leverage on the nightdress which had caught on one of her hair pins and showed him her big soft buttocks and the dimples above them in the small of her back. She patted her curlers, feeling if they were all in place, the nightdress still over her arm. Her breasts rose, stretching, as she reached her hand over her head. Not as beautiful as the ATS girl or his aunt or Gertrud but still beautiful. His nanny. Beautiful and loved for all her silliness. A bare woman. He knew there was nothing else so beautiful from as early as he could remember. She let him look then leaned and covered his eyes with one hand. "Oh John. Oh John," she said: "Remember me." "I'll never forget," he said. He reached to hold her breasts and she jumped and held his hands away. "No," she whispered fiercely: "You must be good. You mustn't spoil it." "But you feel so nice," he said. "That's as may be," she said: "You're a horror. I draw the line at touching. I really do. I don't know what came over me to make an exhibition of myself like this." Clucking she made a hen's quick gesture to pluck up her nightdress from the bed. "Don't be cross," he said: "Is it worse to touch than to look." "Much worse," she said, relenting, sitting naked on the bed near him, her breasts filling the shade made by her arms as she leaned forward, holding her knees. "Why?" he said. "Looking is naughty," she said, "but touching is wicked. It's dirty and nasty." He knew it must be the opposite on the strength of the complete wrongness of her views on looking, but now was not the time to upset her by arguing. She shivered. She kissed him. He kissed her. He went to sleep. In the morning she had gone.

Cornwall was wild and cliffy. Lavinia was drippy and moped for the first few days. Then she started eating again. She stopped going for walks on her own. She came to the beach with them. "What a waste of this lovely sun and water," she said, "to wear those stupid costumes. I'm going in in my skin. Keep watch for me," she said to his mother. His mother was shocked though the new nanny was even more so. Lavinia peeled off her dress and underwear and stood on tiptoe stretching to the sun and ran into the waves. He watched her buttocks bobbing as she ran and the sandy undersides to her feet and her mane of hair, trailing and flapping. His mother looked away from Lavinia and attended to him. "Don't stare, darling," she said: "Lavinia is a fine free spirit. But it is naughty to take advantage and stare." Lavinia splashed in the water, half crouching as if to defend her fragility against the sea, then dived and swam. She waved and shouted from the water. His brother and he raced to paddle. His mother wouldn't let them throw off their costumes. When Lavinia came to join them her nipples were thickened, condensed and pimpled and standing with cold. She had big goose flesh on her breasts and shoulders and hips and thighs. She played with them in the shallows, splashing and throwing water and catching them. "Take off those stupid things," she said and pulled down his costume. He resisted and she ducked him. His brother hared away towards his mother who was laughing in her tones of shocked politeness. Lavinia chased him but he squealed so earnestly that she let him go. She played with him some more, then she raced him to the towels. On the way he fell. She picked him up and carried him back to the water to douse the sand off him. Still carrying him close to her cold fleshy breasts she tickled him and as he struggled kissed his bare tummy. "Really," his mother grumbled as she dried him: "Lavinia is too unrestrained. Perhaps it's because she's Jewish."

On another day Lavinia danced naked in the surf and he and his brother danced with her, also naked this time, shrieking and laughing. A man watched them from the top of the cliff. The first person they had seen there apart from themselves. Lavinia waved. They waved. The man waved and wandered off.

Another day another man saw them. They waved again. The man waved and started down the cliff path towards them. "Oh my God, time for clothes," Lavinia said. They scampered to their towels. Like almost all the men not away at the war the man was elderly. "Very lovely too," he said. "Aphrodite and putti". "What do you want?" Lavinia said. "We were being private." The man laughed. "In public," he said: "And waving." "So what," Lavinia said: "Go away." "Don't be silly," the man said: "I haven't come to do you any harm or to insult you. I should merely like to know whether you have ever modelled and whether you would be willing to sit - or dance if you like - for me." He gave Lavinia still wet-haired and towelling her feet, a card. He bowed to his mother and went back up the cliff. "I wouldn't trust him," the new nanny said. "Dirty old beast. What call had he to come up and smarm. It's a trick." "I can't say I cared for his smile. Or his offhand way over introductions," his mother said: "Forward. He seemed gentlemanly enough and of a reasonable age but artists are notoriously bohemian and unreliable." He listened to them in amazement. "But Lavinia knew she had nothing on. She waved first," he said. "Don't be cheeky," his mother said: "Don't speak out of turn and don't try to talk about things you don't understand." "It could be interesting," Lavinia said: "Something to fall back on if the weather breaks." His mother put on her disapproving face. At bathtime the new nanny said, "That Lavinia has no shame. She'll live to regret it. It's because she isn't really English." His spirits soared. The very idea that there could be unEnglishness so unchecked as Lavinia even in deepest England made him feel much better. "I don't know what's got into you I'm sure," the nanny said while he sang and threw up the sponge and caught it in his mouth. "UnEnglish, unEnglish, unEnglish," he chanted, joggling back and forth so that his penis jumped up and down at the nanny. "Ttt, you're no better than a heathen," the nanny said: "All this baring yourself has gone to your head. It's disgusting." He calmed down. "Are you a servant nanny?" he asked. "Me? A servant," she said, shocked: "I'm Norland-trained. I'm a cut above any servant." Etc. His gathering hypothesis confirmed again. Non-servants were sillier about their bodies than servants. Friends and relatives were unpredictable. UnEnglishness helped.

*

Further confirmation, after a fallow period in exile at prep school, confined to boys, exiled by women from women, in Ireland. His mother claimed she was sending him away to school for his own good. To get him away from the blitz (strategy) and to make a man of him (policy). He invoked love. She wept. He wept. His brother wept. "In our class it has to happen," his mother said. He despised his class, the school, the teachers, the boys so happy to be away from women and girls, while he also feared the school, the teachers, the system. What could he do against them? He decided to wait, snatch enjoyment as he could, learn from within, not be corrupted or brain-washed. Long before the theory he became in practice a mole for anarchy, a non-confronter, an independent inhabitant of other's structures. Playing the systems, taking his private moments, not putting his cards on public tables. Ireland came up as a holiday alternative to war-burdened, rationed, depressed, bleak and boring England.

*

The house rambled, the park ran wild, shaggy grass, sudden bog, huge trees. Cottages were inhabited by witches and mad women. There were ghosts in ruins and burnt-out houses. Little people dance at full moon in the rath above the house. You had to take care pulling the curtains in case they fell apart in your hands. The china was cracked and chipped. A stair was missing on the back stairs. Bits of the barn loft were unsafe to tread on. Literature was to tell him this was Anglo-Irish. He found it entertaining and exciting, and beautiful. Particularly as his O'Connell name and his religion let him go to Them, the foreign Irish, his tribespeople, for all his English accent and ways, his Anglican mother, his Anglo-Church of Ireland relatives. In the church overspilling with grim jolly peasant people, poor and sudden in wit, horseplay, hospitality, he was at home. It was his church, for his faith, as it had been for his father killed in the war, and for Gertrud lost in Hitler. It was not for the superior, inconsistent, ambivalent, secretive, English women in his life.

The maid Theresa used to ride in the trap to Church with them but she got out before they reached the church to talk with her friends on the bridge. Which meant malarkying about with the young tearaways under the bridge according to his cousins' Irish nanny. Theresa was always tousled by the end of time for Mass and sometimes they had to take the trap on home without her because she could not be found. His uncle said her wandering left eye and her ability to drop the

Michael Kelly

undroppable and break the unbreakable were signs of simple-mindedness. John thought she was just over-excited to be away from home and to be discovering how to enjoy her body in its enjoyment by others. Entering adolescence he had discovered bliss in his body in dreams and then in waking exploration of those sensations. The priests called it masturbation. He knew it was the most beautiful experience he had found in God's creation. He guessed the fifteen year-old Theresa was finding something the same for herself.

His cousins' Irish nanny had a splendid deep-breasted body under her thick nightdress and uniform but she only cuddled his pre-adolescent brother. She let his brother into bed with her. "Ah sure, you're too old for such nonsense, a great hulking fellow like you," she said. His brother looked complacently out from her warm sheets. He looked out of the window at the horses and the trees. The greenness. The individual particularity of each branch and trunk and cluster of leaves. The grace and strength of the whole, the ensemble, and each final tracery of twig. At about that time he read in a novel on his mother's not for children shelf about a man going blind who regretted having looked at women so much instead of trees. Trees' beauty is incomparable. He thought either/or preferences like that silly. He guessed the man was not Catholic. Some sort of puritan snob.

Theresa saw him at his window. His brother was being bathed by the Irish nanny with their little cousins. Much splashing and shrieking and nakedness and soapiness and tickling. He imagined the Irish nanny undressing to join in. Her shy joy in her sensuality and in her beauty exposed with harmless excitement to a male not able to take advantage of her.

"No games for you," Theresa said. She stood in the doorway of his room in her afternoon-off dress. "Sure that Eileen is too fat. She'd be jumping and falling all over." "And you're not fat?" he said. Theresa stared at him. "I am not," she said: "You can see that yourself." She began to open her dress, backing away on to the landing and up the faulty stairs to the attic where she had her room. He followed her.

Theresa stood in the room she shared with the cook. It was stuffy and stark. "Am I fat? Am I an old saggy cow?" she said slipping her shoulders out of her dress, showing him her jutty little adolescent breasts. He shook his head. "Show me your skin," she said. They stripped. "Oh it's fine. It's fine. What a grand little man you are," Theresa said. "You're beautiful out of your clothes," he said. "You and your artistic pagan talk," she said. They softly touched each other, looking, gentle with delight rather than shyness, urgent and shivering. Her hair smelt of milk and hay but her body smelt of cheap soap and fish. She was smelly. Almost as soon as she touched his penis and hurried it into her he came. Too quick for the full joy he knew it could give. He felt suddenly desolate and tearful. She cradled him, bright eyed, rubbing her breasts on his face, kissing him, crooning. "Do you mind?" he said. "What would I mind? That you raced yourself makes you dear to me." "Do you think it's wrong?" he whispered. Theresa laughed. "Don't take notice of the priests," she said. "Isn't it what all the beasts do all the time?" When they unlinked, he reeked. She saw his expression. "Shall we bathe together?" she said. Her wandering eye twitching out of focus with the renewed spurt of her lust.

Within the week Theresa had been dismissed for breakages, insolence, fights with the nanny and the cook, smuggling the stable boy into the bed. He didn't know what he should think. He stormed and wept.

*

Years later Theresa's white skin and grey eyes with yellow green tints, their large bluish whites, her broad bright mouth, her entranced look and her fingers felt his skin, and she looked at him, and his fingers felt her skin and he looked at her, overlapped and mingled with Lavinia's sea-salty running, dancing, wetness, her flushed face and brown dark eyes, her full lips, her laughter at feeling sun and air and water all over her body, her playfulness. And somehow his aunt moving deft and bare and neat in the twilight, upright and reaching and bending and crouching like ballet, and his nanny letting him look, and the ATS girl showing herself, blended and confused among those images. And Gertrud desperate, wild, altogether preoccupied. Servant girl and bohemian and unEnglish, and semi-servant and upper class, they showed him what women could be in sympathy and beauty beyond the silly attitudes and clothed manners and movements and public expressions and conversational inanities and dishonesties he was told were superior.

*

The other day an African woman stood for him in her bathroom in London, well-lit by the summer morning through the frosted glass, as he watched through the open door from her kitchen. She stood naked for him. "I don't understand why you like to look," she said: "These are not beautiful," flipping her breasts - "This is not beautiful" - patting her brush - "These are not beautiful" - pushing down and pulling up her buttocks. "They are. You are," he said. She stared at him. Turned her hands outwards to him as they hung at her sides. Cultural sign of submission and gift. "Look then," she said: "But be quick because I shouldn't be late for work. We'll both look and we'll both touch this evening when I get back. Alright?"

An Englishwoman who had lived in the tropics said: "They'll never understand in this country how you can mean it when you write poems about nakedness as a matter of course, joy, a positive something to expect and celebrate rather than be rushed and secretive and exceptional about."

An African girl said: "Massa, how can you stand it? These your people dry. Man no de like life for here. Man no sabi life. The women vex and dry. The women like for dictate. They no sabi children or home or play small mischief or do the thing. No be you done see better thing? How can you bear it?"

An English girl said: "Africa has just compounded your childhood corruption. Hasn't anyone told you you mustn't look at people as if they were sex objects? I don't care if everyone who feels sex at all uses sexual bits and focuses on them. You're not allowed to look and touch in the open as if you meant it. Don't you know that looking at people is voyeurism and reductive and sadistic? You may think that's silly and bad faith but that's what everyone thinks today, or says they think. Do you really not realise that in this country touching is indecent assault? It's no good your liking to be touched as well as touch, you're just a very very dirty, very old, old-fashioned and beastly, old man. And it's no good your saying we're out of step with most societies and most of history and most of the human race. We, now, are in the culture of enlightenment, the liberation of women, and that is not ephemeral alibi-ing from the real problems of humans and creation. That is central. It is not hysterical self-indulgence. It is

Michael Kelly

not the peripheral neurosis of decadence. You don't believe in theories, and you don't believe in so many potentially attractive and likeable people - women, you mean, you old goat - smarting themselves up with tendentious and abrasive attitudinising! O bully for you. What you mean is you like uncompetitively easy-going crumpet spread out on your plate! You admit it! You're unspeakable. OK. I'll shut up and turn over and hold it. Afterwards, promise you'll take me somewhere nice and we can have a row or just moon about as usual. Looking and touching and feeling."

Richard Barlow

Things Of No Value

What happened was this.

*

At the end of the night shift the yard was washed down. When I arrived at the abattoir, the yard was empty and still wet. The iron gates were shut. I looked for the gatekeeper but there was no sign of him. This was not unusual. I tried the side gate, which should have been locked but, as so often, it was not.

I crossed the yard quickly, the soles of my shoes catching the grit that had not been washed away. As I reached the path I saw something glinting in the flowerbed. It was a pair of spectacles, unbroken except that one of the arms had been twisted and bent. I sighed despite myself. Now that I had seen them I would have to hand them in; that is how responsibility works. I have seen far too many people ignore what is before them. Their eyes slide away from things, leaving them unseen. What is not seen need not exist; and what does not exist is the responsibility of someone else, who might see it for what it is. For the moment I shoved the spectacles in my coat pocket; I was late enough already.

Martin, my department head - I hesitate to call him my boss, since that seems to suggest that I approve of him - looked up as I entered. He grinned in a manner that is often described, though not by me, as wolfish.

I have seen wolves, and they are not like that. They are creatures who have evolved to hunt and kill in order to live, and they do so without intention or feeling but out of necessity. That is their beauty. Beauty is not the wrong word. Beauty and evil cannot be misconstrued.

Martin looked, in fact, like the character in a children's cartoon who is just about to explain how his evil plan will work. I do not mean that Martin was evil; on the contrary, he was a good man. His dealings with me were always fair, as they were with all his staff as far as I know. It was just how he looked.

"Did you get the job?" he asked. This was his standard explanation for unexplained absence. His eyes shone, and I waited to see if his tongue would lick round his lips. It did not.

I said nothing and showed him the prescription the doctor had given me. Neither of us could read it but we both accepted it as a form of proof. Martin was immediately solicitous; as I said, a good man.

"How is she?" he said.

I wanted to tell him that her name was Elspeth, but I had told him many times before and still he never used her name.

"No different," I said.

"Progressing, then."

I nodded, though I thought he was talking nonsense in the way that most of what most people say is nonsense, but it fills the spaces that would otherwise fall between us.

We are all progressing, I thought. Not one of us is not. People mostly think we are striving forward, seeking improvement, betterment. I see an endless line of people shuffling along, falling off the end, not knowing why they joined the queue in the first place.

"That's all we can ask," said Martin.

I'd forgotten he was there, but I nodded sombrely to show him that, even

Richard Barlow

though I was oppressed in my daily life, I had reflected on his well-chosen words and had found comfort within them. At the same time I could see that my desk had been loaded with more pieces of paper than I would have been given had I not been more than an hour late.

"Someone's been busy," I said, which is as much as I allow myself in such circumstances. I looked at Martin, who gave a repeat performance of his wide-mouthed, mirthless grin. His desk was clear.

*

The main consignment of the day arrived, unaccountably early, some time before eleven. First the iron gates were banged aside, then the trucks rolled in. They manoeuvred into their assigned spaces, then stood with their engines idling. Footsteps shifted across the wet yard, voices could be heard, and then the beast were unloaded into the lairage pens. A low moaning filled the air. It was soft and full and muffled all other sounds, like a blanket thrown over a bed.

I had not heard this noise before. When I work, I am deaf to such things. This morning, starting late, I was unsettled. Normally, I am aware of nothing unless Martin puts his hand on my arm to arrest my attention. Touch is the most intimate of the senses. Hearing, on the other hand, seems to occur outside us, in another place. It happens, and it is gone. Unlike seeing, which takes place right up against our eyes, becomes a part of us. We ignore what we hear, but we cannot ignore what we see. We can only feign ignorance.

Martin was standing by the window, looking down on the scene below. It seemed to me that he did this every day, though I could not remember him doing so. But it had a settled feel about it, Martin standing there, watching the beast being herded into the lairage pens. I turned back to my work, but my attention was drawn by the man at the window. The beast made sounds like dull yawning, but mournful, as if they were aware of why they had been brought here and were patient. Martin gazed down at them. His face had the same passive quality. After a while, as the sounds and the movement died away, Martin turned from the window. He saw me watching him and hesitated, then turned back to the wet empty yard below. It was as if the sounds of the herded beast lay over us still.

Martin picked up his coat and stood for a moment, deciding whether he had to justify himself to me. Then he walked out, as he always did at about this time. He would be going to the delicatessen, a place much favoured by the men from the abattoir.

*

By working through my lunch hour I was able to clear my desk of all but the least important papers, and they could wait until those few quiet moments before the arrival of the second consignment towards the end of the afternoon. Not for the first time, it occurred to me that whoever decided that the transport of livestock around the country should be the responsibility of local rather than central government, had created a perfect system for corruption. Each transport contractor must be accredited by each authority within whose area he works. Each shipment must be approved, again by each authority. For a journey from one end of the country to the other there might be eight or nine sets of documents. Since the epidemic, there are some authorities which will not allow condemned meat to pass over their roads or, more accurately, through their unpolluted air, which results in lengthy detours and more documentation. The opportunities for bribery and falsification are endless, though not at my level. As in all areas of local government, what money there is to be made goes to the senior officials and the politicians. Almost their sole function is to hide this fact from each other, from the public, and from themselves.

Since the epidemic, of course, much of what comes into the abattoir is slaughtered and destroyed. But there are still those who would make a profit on a working animal no matter what its genetic line might be, and for these the abattoir serves as a staging-post or even a marketplace. It is a brisk trade. I have seen it grow from nothing. And from the papers which pass through this office there is much to be learned. But I have nowhere to take the information, and so it is valueless.

*

What I said about sound being less compelling than sight is not true.

I have dreams which consist of a single sound. It might be a tap at the window, a knock at the door, the thump of a drunk falling over in the street. I am fully awake now. I lie in my bed, knowing I have not heard these things but waiting to hear them again. The room is still and dark. The darkness seems to dissolve the walls of the house and my awareness extends out into the night. I am willing the sounds to enter my room. I know the direction from which they came. My eyes become accustomed to the darkness, but the silence still presses against me. There is not even the echo of the sound that I heard. The sound existed only in my sleep, it disappeared when I woke.

I ease myself out of bed. In her room Elspeth is asleep. Her room is at the front of the house and a pale light from the street washes through the curtains. In this pale light she is lovely. Asleep she smiles, peaceful, like any other person. She is not terrorised by her dreams. It is only awake that she is troubled.

I remember once we visited a farm. We walked around the barns and the fields. We saw cows and pigs and ducks and when she became tired I carried her. I carried her a long way and she clung to my neck and I was not tired until much later. At the end of our long walk we met the farmer who was about to take some children for a ride on a horse and cart. He asked if Elspeth would like to come. She clung more tightly and pressed her head against my cheek. I said perhaps another time. He said what fun it would be. I held Elspeth and looked at her and she looked at me and nodded very seriously. The farmer took her from me and carried her to the cart where the other children sat, then he swung her through the air and sat her on the horse itself. Elspeth gasped and her eyes sparkled. She rode away and around the field, the happiest girl in the world, and I stood by the gate and watched her and wondered how she might ever be this happy again.

I would have told Martin all this had he asked, but he never did. I would have told him anyway but the moment, if there ever was a moment, passed.

*

By the end of the day two consignments had been delivered, accounted for, processed through the abattoir or the market, and their documents despatched. There is a satisfaction in clearing my desk, but sometimes not much.

Martin had been away for most of the afternoon. He is a man of many responsibilities, not all of which confine him to the office, and he has a willing and competent deputy in me. When all the other staff had left I sat for a moment

Richard Barlow

or two in the silence. But I have responsibilities too, so I locked my desk and the filing cabinets and took my coat from the hook inside the door.

As I left the office I found the broken pair of spectacles in my coat pocket. It was too late now to do anything with them, everywhere would be closed. Just inside the front gate there is a pile of such things - shoes, spectacles, teeth - the things of no value that always get left behind. In all other respects the disposal of the beast is more tidily arranged than that. I threw the broken spectacles onto the pile and walked home.

Sarah Spiller
When Molly Met The Only Other People In The Whole World

There are only ten people in the whole world. The rest is done with mirrors.

Seven of these ten people knew Harry, Harriet and Sally, who were the other three people in the world. They knew them from the early days when Harriet had started fiddling her child benefit.

This dated from the time when Harriet had put down on her daughter's birth certificate that Molly's father was a traveller who had impregnated her in an *en passant* way, en route to Wales via Bath. In fact Molly's Dad was Harry. And he was a good person who shared half the child care, and was known to Molly as indeed 'Harry', or 'Dad', or sometimes as 'Primary Carer' or sometimes as 'A Penis', i.e. a reflection of men generally.

Molly is now five, and she can write and create beautiful collages of the clouds and the blue sky, and she nearly has a mind of her own. She says she will not eat olives because the brine contains lactic acid. She sometimes even reserves judgement about lentils. She is sharp about her nutritional requirements, and has decided of her own free will that she is a vegan.

Molly says do not eat this or that. Do not kill the rat in the outside lavatory in the squat. But she does not say to Harriet, her Mum, the secondary carer and woman, that she prefers to be with Harriet, although she loves Harry also.

She knows this might upset the applecart with her Dad, and with her Mum's lover Sally.

In effect then, there are sort of eleven people in the world, with Molly being a reflection of the other ten, surrounded by love.

And the rest is done by mirrors. Mirrors held up by society and occasionally by Department of Social Security investigators.

And this latter mirror was wherein the problem now lay.

Harry now wanted legal custody of Molly as the primary carer. But this could not happen because he had no legal rights on account of the fictional impregnating traveller, who did not exist, and was merely a reflection of Harry created for benefit fiddle purposes.

It could also not happen because it would mean Department of Social Security investigators might delve into past benefit payments, and finger anomalies, and this could be a very bad scene.

So the nine people out of the ten or eleven people in the whole world gathered to discuss this problem in a pub in Bath shortly before Christmas.

Molly stayed at home with Harry eating nutritious food, and getting ready for bed.

Harriet got the ball rolling by saying that she was in two minds as to whether Molly really wanted to go and live, full-time, with a penis, which, again, was Harry, and was his own problem because he was a man.

Sally agreed with Harriet.

The seven other people in the pub who were appointed as Molly's witch sisters or pagan parents, depending on their bag or their gender, were in their several different, but mutually reflecting minds too.

But the difficult question of the lack of legal status Harry might not achieve, took some time to be broached, despite the male penis reflection at the beginning.

Sarah Spiller

There first had to be the question of Christmas itself, looked at from all sides.

Upsettingly, Molly wanted a selection of Barbies for Christmas. Despite Molly's forward thinking on the question of her diet, she was inclined towards backward thinking on the question of her toys. She wanted two female plastic dolls, and a male plastic doll, and she had told Harry, who had told Harriet, who had told Sally, who had told the only other people in the whole world, that she wanted everyone to marry each other and live happily ever after.

This, obviously was not going to be possible. For the ten people in the world, the demands of the eleventh, who was after all a reflection of Harriet, were never going to be realistic.

They all understood that Molly was merely voicing dissatisfaction with the way her extended family had organised their lives, but the marriage thing, and the all-round-the-Christmas-tree-kissing-and-making-up thing were dodgy.

Molly's needs and anxieties, were in no small measure a reflection of the way society itself had forced its dubious mores on all their lives. This was an endlessly reflexive situation.

Harriet said Molly would get loads of toys for Christmas, but she would only get one doll. It would not be a repressed anorexic Barbie, it would be a lovely home-made rag doll, and Molly would be encouraged to think of this doll as a reflection of her, a strong beautiful female icon, an image of all the things her life could be.

Sally agreed, and bought everyone drinks from the ill-gotten child benefit payments and put Kurt Cobain's *I hate my life and I want to die* on the juke box to counteract all the cutesy carols that were assaulting everyone's ears.

Christmas sorted, the nine then moved onto the whole thing about responsibility and roles.

Everyone agreed that everyone loved Molly. Everyone also agreed that Harry was a top man on the childcare front. But everyone also expressed the opinion that Harry, through no fault of his own, merely as a result of his being a reflection of a penis, was a very controlling person.

And his request that he should be appointed legal custody of Molly would open a can of worms. It would mean that Harriet would have to come clean to the DSS and recant on the traveller story.

Harriet kicked off the debate about all this by saying that she wanted to spend her life caring for Molly and shagging Sally. She said, aggressively that if anyone had a problem with this, they could just fuck off on their own testosterone trip, and essentially die, as in *I hate my life and I want to*, which was now playing on the juke box again.

Sally agreed with Harriet, and everyone soothed Harriet by saying that of course they had no problem with Harriet's aspirations.

The reflection of a materialistic society in their lives had meant they, like everyone else in the whole world, had goals, which were of necessity not about materialism. Their expectations, along with those of everybody else, were about living and loving and sharing in a fair and equal and responsible way.

Thus Harry would have to come to some kind of accommodation about the custody stuff, which took in Harriet's desires too.

Harriet had a right to a life, and also, if she wanted, a right to be a secondary carer, although that did not mean she was not giving Molly a quality of love too.

When Molly Met The Only Other People In The Whole World

Molly was a great kid, with her lovely collages, and she was already expressing what she felt about living and loving in her vegan trip, which was in itself a reflection of the quality of love she got from Harriet.

Sally, who was also a vegan, agreed.

One of the pagan parents went to ring Harry, to keep him up to date on deliberations for reasons of fairness. Harry said that Molly was asleep, but had made this lovely collage before bedtime, which had a sunny blue sky, clouds, and then this little crowd of people sitting in a shack, around ten of them. It was beautiful and deep.

The pagan parent reported back, and everyone said that all this meant that Molly seemed to be overcoming the Barbie fixation, and also thinking in a really lateral way about seasons. Though it was dark in the lead up to Christmas, Molly was getting into light and renewal and looking towards summer.

Harriet returned to the theme of Harry being a top carer, but also being a controlling penis. She said that she was not going to go to the DSS and cop to fraud, and neither was she prepared to sign some state-orientated paper re Molly's future strong and beautiful life.

She said that she felt that Harry was really asking the other nine people in the world for a kind of gesture, to say that they all loved and appreciated what he was doing and his role in everything.

Everyone said that everyone saw this, and they all loved Molly, and there was no way that she should be used as a kind of emotional football to serve Harry's insecurities about himself, and his role and responsibility as a primary carer.

Harriet said that it was maybe all about labels. Society reflected this need for labels, and calling people stuff like Dad, Mum, etc, and this was the root of the issue they were now addressing.

Sally put on a Courtney Love song which went, I made my bed/I'll lie in it/I made my bed/I'll die in it.

Everyone thought that maybe through talking around this issue Harriet had hit on something which might resolve the legal status worry.

Harriet got combative again, and said that if Harry really wanted a label, maybe he should just change his name by deed poll to Molly.

Everyone laughed at this cool wheeze, but then slowly thought that maybe there was a really good idea in there.

Then there was a worry expressed that the deed poll thing was a kind of acceptance of state intervention, so maybe Harry should just call himself Molly, i.e. just say, "Hi, I'm Molly" as a matter of course.

There was a short pause whilst the only ten people in the world thought this through. Then the thought emerged, a reflection of everybody's concerns, that this was a kind of exclusive thing for Harry to do.

It labelled just him as Molly, whereas in fact everyone loved Molly too.

So, in fact, everyone agreed everyone should be called Molly.

They tried this out, as they ordered drinks, and though it was obviously a pretty confusing kind of strategy, because everyone was an individual, yet also part of this sharing, it seemed to work in a fun way.

Molly put on more Courtney Love, I made my bed/And I'll die in it, and whilst she was at the juke box Molly told Molly that she was going to go home and really love Molly and then tomorrow, on Christmas Eve Molly would collect

Sarah Spiller

Molly's child benefit from the DSS, and go and get Molly some toys.

From now on, Molly said that everyone in the world was Molly, even the DSS snoopers who were acting on behalf of the society which reflected in such a clear way into everyone's lives.

Molly phoned Molly at home to tell him about the conclusion that had been reached in the pub. Molly said it was great, and that maybe on reflection he had been wrong to keep banging on about the legal status thing, and it was a bad controlling male thing for him to have done.

He saw the error of his ways, and the fact that the custody number was a label thing, and it was up to everybody in the world, the ten people in the world, to take responsibilities for their own labels which, of course, they had now done.

Everyone went back to their places, well pleased, in a resolving way, with the events of the evening.

Molly stirs briefly in her sleep.

She is dreaming of a breakfast of warm spinach and a light sunny Christmas, and Barbie dolls, and spending more time with her Mum, although she also loves her Dad.

The pictures she sees behind her closed eyes are of blue skies and fleecy clouds, and of ten people, all like her, who are the only ten people in the whole world.

And the pictures Molly sees which are like her collages, will never never shatter into a thousand thousand other reflections of her life, because everything mirrors her. A five year-old girl called Molly.

Richard C. Zimler

The City For The Sea

My mother wakes me up with a phone call at eight in the morning to tell me that it's January 16, the feast day of Ferreolus, Bishop of Grenoble in the seventh century.

"You're ringing me up to tell me that?"

"He once excommunicated a loaf of bread which then turned black as coal," she announces.

If anyone else had told me this I'd have had a good laugh, even half-asleep. But my mother collects facts like these to use against me. I say, "Let me call you back later."

"Black as coal," she informs me. Her voice is threatening.

"Mom, I'm hanging up."

"What are you doing sleeping so late? Eugenia, are you sick?"

"It's Sunday, Mom. Remember the days of the week? Listen, I'll call you later." I hang up before she can say anything else.

At eleven that morning, she comes over. She says her legs hurt. It's arthritis. She slumps down at my kitchen table and picks at some crusted milk around its edge with a letter opener. My mother has two chins and hanging jowls. She wears a lot of make up. Jon thinks she looks like a clown. She fixes me with a big pink frown and says, "Couldn't you take a minute off to pick up the phone?"

"No, I couldn't. Anyway, tell me what the bread loaf did to merit excommunication from Bishop Ferreolus."

"Where's Jon?" she asks. She sticks her nose in the air like she might sniff him out.

"At the park."

"What park?"

"He's playing basketball."

She makes a face. "He leaves you alone?"

"Mom, give me a break."

"It was to make a point," she declares.

"Jon playing basketball?"

"No, excommunicating bread."

"And what point might that be?"

"That even a loaf of bread has to keep to the straight and narrow."

My mother emigrated to the United States from Brazil in 1967. She collects clichéd expressions like *straight and narrow* because she thinks they will help make her understandable to Americans like her daughter. I sometimes wonder if she'd make more sense if she spoke only Portuguese. I start drying dishes to escape her righteous stare and say, "You mean, so the other loaves of bread who happen to be unwedded wouldn't get themselves pregnant."

"Exactly."

"Mom, I'm already pregnant. Three months ago Ferreolus might have helped. Now, unless he can change the fetus into a slice of pumpernickel I don't think he's going to be of much use."

She crosses herself. "You shouldn't talk like that."

"It's 1994," I reply. "We live in Berkeley. Nobody here cares if I give birth to a baby out of wedlock as long as it isn't raised a Republican. And there's no

priest listening at the door to hear what I say."
"People are always listening. You don't understand."
"It's Berkeley, nobody cares."
"God hears everything we think."
"Then He's heard a lot worse from me over the years and nothing I could say at this point would shock Him."
She shifted to Portuguese out of frustration: *Você tem sempre uma resposta. Mas um dia destes Deus vai impor a Sua vontade...* You've always got an answer. But one of these days God will impose his will on you."
I hand her a dish towel. "Make yourself useful."

*

My mother watches television evangelists in the living room while I finish up the dishes. I do some laundry and read a bit of the Pink Section of the *Chronicle* at the kitchen table. Jon comes home about noon. He enters through the kitchen door because he undoubtedly spotted her car parked at the curb. He kisses me and pats my bottom. He doesn't say "hi" or anything else because he doesn't talk on Sunday. This started happening seven weeks ago. He saw a documentary on Channel 9 about a Buddhist monk in Thailand who took a vow of silence eighteen years ago. That very night, Jon announced in bed, "One day a week, I don't want to hear my own voice."

It seems to me that he thinks that not talking one day a week is going to make him a special person. Sunday was the only day it could be because has to talk workdays installing windows for Berkeley Glass. Saturdays he calls his parents and we do our shopping.

Since the documentary about the Buddhist monk, I haven't gotten a peep out of him on any Sunday. I really didn't think he could keep it up this long. I mean, he hasn't been able to quit smoking. And he'll never go back to art school like he promised he would. My friends say his vow of silence is weird. It doesn't matter to me one way or the other. It's only one day a week. Less even; between his playing basketball and taking avant-garde photographs with his new Nikon, I usually only see him on Sunday for a few minutes before bed.

Jon nods toward the living room and rolls his eyes.
"Yeah, Godzilla's here," I whisper.
He points to himself, then flutters his hand to tell me he's going to take a shower. We've worked out about twenty signs by now. I make believe I forget them sometimes because it doesn't seem fair I have to learn a new language just because he doesn't want to hear his own voice.

Jon tries to sneak up the stairs but my mother corners him.
"Hello, Jon," she says. "You were playing basketball."
I go to the laundry room where I won't be tempted to peek in.
"So you're not going to talk with me?" she says.
Silence.
"Do you think that's a way for educated people to behave?"
Silence.
"Don't just walk away! Jon...Jon!"
My mother waddles into the laundry room. "Your *friend* drives me crazy," she announces.
"E depois?" I say in Portuguese, meaning, "So what?"

She makes a face like she's eaten something rotten. "I'm your mother, he should talk to me."
"Mom, he doesn't talk to anyone on Sunday. It's got nothing to do with you. I don't know how many times I've told you."
"I'm sure he talks with other people."
"He doesn't. He doesn't even talk with me."
"You can't play basketball and not talk."
"You can."
"What if he gets faulted?"
"Fouled."
"Well?"
"I don't know. He stamps his foot or something."
"Doesn't it drive you crazy?"
"Sometimes."
"Then you should call it quits for him."
"Mom, he has a right not to talk if he doesn't want to."
"Nobody has that right. Do you see that right in the US constitution?"
I roll my eyes.
"Well, do you?"
The shower comes on upstairs.
"Mom, I'm not going to be in the middle of this. You want Jon to change then talk to him about it."
"That's the point, I can't. He's acting like he's *surdo-mudo.*"
"Deaf and dumb. He hears you perfectly."
"Might as well be *surdo-mudo* for all the good it does anyone."
"Mom, I'm not having this conversation for the umpteenth time. Talk to him."
"He's big trouble, your Jon."
"I don't want to hear any more. Talk to him, not me."
"I can't."
"You can. Next Saturday, come over here and talk to him. Or call him at work tomorrow. Do anything you want, only leave me out of it."

*

My mother doesn't call Jon, but instead shows up the next afternoon at the house on Spruce Street where he's installing aluminium windows. She got the address from Brenda, the receptionist at Berkeley Glass.

That night, Jon smokes a thick joint and tells me what happened between him and my mother in a lazy, amused voice. First, he took her outside to the back porch so that the client, who was typing his thesis in his study, wouldn't hear them arguing. The conversation went something like this:

"When the Portuguese rounded the Cape of Good Hope back in the fifteenth century, they were attacked by a cyclops named Adamastor," my mother began.

Jon replied, "What's the point, Edith?"

"The point is that you should start talking on Sunday or let my daughter go."

"Let her go?"

"Exactly."

"I don't follow the logic. I mean, how do you get from a cyclops to Jeanie to me letting her go?"

Richard C. Zimler

"I get from Adamastor to *Eugenia* to you because bad things happen to people who offend God."

"How have I offended God?"

"Look at Eugenia's belly."

"It's 1994."

"E depois?"

"It's America, Edith. You've been here what, nearly thirty years, and you still don't get it."

"And so when the baby comes along, you're not going to talk to it on Sunday? It's going to grow up ignored by its father? You know, I think you're crazy in the head. I've always thought so if you want to know."

"Listen Godzilla, I'm not going to change after the baby comes along. Not for you. Not for anybody!"

When Jon tells me this he looks me straight in the eye and nods like he's real certain. He says that he had his hands balled into fists by the end of the conversation. The last thing he told my mother was, "You know, Edith, one of these days I'm going to have to teach you a lesson with my belt."

This is a line he inherited from his father; there are scars on his bum from the beatings he used to get.

After Jon threatened my mother, she burst into tears and ran back to her Toyota.

I listen to all this silently, then go upstairs and lock myself in the bathroom. I sit on the toilet for a long time and stare out the window at the bougainvillea climbing up the drainpipe of the house next door.

*

I don't hear from my mother after that. Measured in Edith Cardoso days, seventy-two hours of silence is the equivalent of a whole lifetime.

The first day after her argument with Jon, I call her in the morning. No answer. I try again in the evening, just before my dinner shift at the Sixth Street Grill. I let it ring and ring. I think that maybe she's taken the phone off the hook. I figure that she needs to cool off, so I try to forget about her. But the second day, I call her after my lunch shift, at least a dozen times. The next evening, after trying her for hours and letting the phone ring on the last occasion exactly twenty-seven times, I drive to her house in the Sunset District of San Francisco. It's nighttime. The front door is locked. I call for her, knock at the back door. Then I use my key.

My mother is lying upstairs in her king-size bed. The lights are off, but I can see her head on her pillow because the curtains are open and there's a three-quarter moon. It smells foul, like a sickroom. I think, *first Dad, now Mom.* I run to her. Her cheek is warm. "Mom?!" I say. "Mom, it's me."

She wakes up. "Who is it?"

"Eugenia, Mom. Mom, what's wrong? Are you sick?" I feel her forehead. It's cool.

She sits up. Even in the gray light, I can see she's all mussed up. I turn on the light behind her head. Pink lipstick is smeared over her lips and cheeks. Her eyes are bruised with liner. Her dyed black hair looks like straw.

There are letters all over the bed - old handwritten letters on fine blue stationery.

"I've been calling for days," I tell her.
"Get me some water."
The door to her bathroom is closed. I go in. It smells like a kennel. I turn on the light. There's pee all over the floor, a small mountain of shit in the toilet. I flush it twice and toss a towel on the floor, then close the door behind me.
She gulps down the water as if she's been in the desert.
"Mom, what's going on? I've been calling for days."
"I've been reading."
"Reading! You scared the shit out of me!" I brush my hand through her hair to straighten it. I feel her forehead again. "You're cool," I say. "Have you had a fever? Maybe I should call the doctor."
"I've been reading letters," she says.
"From whom? Has someone sent you something that's upset you?"
"Letters from home," she says. She sits all the way up. She brushes the hair out of her eyes. She turns on the light above my father's pillows. She reaches for a page, scans it, tosses it away, then finds another. She hands me that second one. I read it. It's addressed to *Rosinha,* Little Rose, and is dated May 17, 1965. It's in Brazilian Portuguese. It's a love letter. It's signed, *beijinhos, Carlos* - kisses, Carlos.
Throughout the letter, he calls my mother *Rosinha.*
"It's from my brother," she explains. "Your Uncle Carlos."
"A love letter to you from your brother?! What are you talking about?"
"Not to me, to Rosa."
"Who's Rosa? Who's this Uncle Carlos?!"
"Carlos died years ago. In a kind of prison. It happened before you were born. There was no reason to tell you about it."
"Prison?"
"Brazil," she says. "People got murdered. No, that's not right. They got imprisoned and tortured and *then* they got murdered. By the government."
"Why'd you save the letters?"
My mother turns her right arm over. On the back and side of her wrist, there's a ring of scars which looks like an imprint left by thin leaves.
"Where you got caught on the ski lift," I say.
She shakes her head. "A chain. A metal chain. In Brazil."
"Mom, what are you telling me?!"
"They cut off Carlos' ears and sent them to my parents. The boy had his ears cut off. Who knows what else they took - probably his tongue. Maybe his fingers. We never got those. Maybe they sent them to Rosa."
I hold her hand. "I don't understand," I say. "Start at the beginning."
"There's no beginning and no end. You don't understand."
"Start anywhere you want then."
"It's not important."
"Listen, I'll make you some soup or something, then you'll talk."
My mother picks up some letters and stares at me. She says, "What was I supposed to do? Rosa didn't want them. My mother couldn't look at them. What was I supposed to do? Was I supposed to throw them out?"

*

I get home around midnight. Jon's still up. He's reading a magazine in the living room. I kiss his forehead, then tell him he's going to have to start talking on Sundays, at least to my mother.

"No way," he replies.

"It's just a small thing. She's really fragile, you know. You don't know what went on before I was born. Listen, you won't see her every Sunday. Maybe every two or three weeks, you'll have to say a few words after basketball. It's no big deal. Jon, we've got to be nice to each other."

"You wanta do some weed?" he asks.

"No."

He goes to the kitchen. We keep our stash of marijuana in a fake Coca Cola can that screws open. I stand in the doorway. "I want you to agree to talk to my mother. Ten words. I'm asking for ten words."

He takes a joint from the can. "I'm gonna watch stars at the Rose Garden. You wanta come, come. You don't, don't."

"Don't put me in the middle like this. Just ten words."

"You're putting yourself in the middle."

He stares at me like it's my move. I don't want to mention my pregnancy because I don't really see what it's got to do with this specific argument, but it seems to have to do with everything lately, so I say, "What about the baby?"

He slams the refrigerator door closed. "What about it?"

"It would be nice if its father got along with its grandmother."

"With Godzilla?"

"Don't call her that."

He rushes past me. Without looking back, he says, "The bitch calls her Godzilla and then yells at me! The bitch fucking taught me to call her that!"

"And don't ever threaten her again!" I shout.

I go and sit in the alcove by the bay window. I watch the lights of the Golden Gate Bridge from there. Jon starts up the car and screeches away.

I dial my mother's number, but there's no answer. I get my car keys.

*

Three years ago, just after we fell in love, Jon and I took a trip to Greece and Turkey. We were gone three months. He was out of work at the time. We used the money which my father left me in his will.

Jon used to like to show me off back then. He used to like to see the Turkish men with their thick mustaches smile and tell him what a catch I was.

In Istanbul, Jon had the idea that he wanted me to take photographs of him everywhere. It would be a kind of art project: Jon in Wonderland.

I took pictures of him in front of the Blue Mosque and Haghia Sophia; at the Saint Savior in Chora Church; in front of our hotel; in the outdoor restaurant of the Topkapi Museum; on the ferry up the Bosphorus. Jon was everywhere. We still have the results up in our bedroom.

I decided to put Jon out of focus in the photo I took of him in front of the Blue Mosque - to record a clear image of the mosque instead of him. It was dusk. Sea gulls were flying around the great dome. They were illuminated by the flood-lights lighting up the minarets. Luminescent gulls.

Driving over the Bay Bridge, I remember that photograph.

The thing is, when we got it developed, one flying gull was really clear. It looked lovely and free to most people. But even back then it looked lost to me. I said it looked like the bird had mistaken the city for the sea. Everybody thought I was nuts, especially Jon. My mother was the only one who agreed with me.

Pushover/Not A Pushover Quizzes

Pushover answer for Panurge 23 was Aldous Huxley. A £20 Book Token went to **Sally Zigmond** of Harrogate. Not A Pushover answer was **Pearl S.Buck.** She wrote an oriental cookery book and she was a Nobel Literature winner, unlikely as it sounds. No winner, alas.

Michael Zadoorian

Mystery Spot

We are tourists.
    I have recently come to terms with this. My husband and I were never the kind who travelled to expand our minds. We always travelled to have fun - Weeki Wachee, Gatlinburg, South Of The Border, Lake George, Rock City. We have seen swimming pigs and horses, a Russian palace covered with corn, young girls underwater drinking Pepsi-Cola from the seven ounce bottle, an automobile tire over six stories tall, a cycling cockatoo riding a tightrope.
    I guess we always knew.
    This, our last trip, was appropriately planned at the last minute, the luxury of the retiree. It is one that I'm glad I decided we take, although everybody (doctors, friends, children) forbade us to go. "I strongly, strongly advise against this, Ella," said one of my seemingly hundreds of physicians. But we needed a trip, more than we've ever needed one. Besides, the doctors only want me to stay around so they can run their tests on me, poke me with their icy instruments, spot shadows inside of me. And they have already done plenty of that.
    I decided to take action. Our van was packed and ready. We have kept it that way ever since retirement. So I kidnapped my husband John and we headed for Disneyland. This is where we took our kids, so we like it better than the other one. Besides, at this point in our lives, we are more like children than ever. Especially John.
    It is a lovely trip so far, quiet and steady. The miles are moving no faster than they should be, which is fine with me. When I see the sign, we are just about out of Nebraska and into some hillier terrain. It is along the rolling side of the interstate, a gaudy orange and yellow billboard, the kind that would have driven Lady Bird Johnson crazy, what with all her plans to beautify America.

VISIT THE AMAZING
"MYSTERY SPOT!"
43 miles

Amazing, indeed. I decide we should give it a try. On this trip, if something looks like fun, we stop. No more travelling in a hurry for us. There were too many vacations like that with the kids. Three days to get to Florida, four to California - *we've only got two weeks* - rush, rush, rush. Now there's all the time in the world. Except I'm falling apart and John can barely remember his name. That's all right. I remember it. Between the two of us, we are one whole person.

YOU CAN'T MISS IT
THE BAFFLING "MYSTERY SPOT"
20 miles

There are a lot of signs leading to this place.
    I watch for them and count them down like the kids used to do with the signs for *Stuckey's*. Every day on the road, travelling with Kevin and Cindy, we'd encounter at least one of those crazy places with their pecan logs and tepid coffee. Sometimes the signs would start a hundred miles away. Then there would be a

Tea Dance, King's Cross, 1990

Philip Wolmuth

Michael Zadoorian

new one every ten, fifteen miles. The kids would get all worked up and want to stop and John would say no, we had to get some miles under our belt. The kids would beg and beg, and finally, when we were a half-mile away, he'd give in. The kids would scream yay and John and I would look at each other and smile like parents who knew how to spoil their children just enough.

"Remember *Stuckey's*, John? I haven't seen one of those places in years," I say.

"Oh yeah," he says, nodding, staring blankly at the road. But he doesn't remember. This is something we have both gotten used to. Every once in a while, he knows enough to realize that he has forgotten everything, but these moments happen less and less these days. It doesn't matter. I am the keeper of the memories. It has been that way for quite some time. With John's mind, first the corners of the blackboard were slowly erased, then the edges, and the edges of edges, creating a circle that grew smaller, smaller, before finally disappearing into itself. What is left are only smudges of recollection here and there, places where the eraser did not completely do its job, memories that I hear again and again. It is surprising how well he still drives though. After all our car trips in the past, I don't think he'll ever forget how. And now, as the physical part of our person, it is one of his official duties. Anyway, once you get into the rhythm of long-distance driving, it is only a matter of direction (my job as well, mistress of the maps), avoiding those sudden, unexpected exits, and looking out for the danger that comes up fast in your mirror.

SEE FOR YOURSELF!
THE INCREDIBLE "MYSTERY SPOT"
This Exit

We get off the freeway and follow another car, a blue one, with its rear wheels riding way over to the left. "That man's car is so out of alignment, it looks like he's trying to pass himself," I say. After a half-mile or so, we end up in a huge gravel parking lot with about four or five other cars in it. There is a sign, brash and bright, like all the others:

"MYSTERY SPOT"
IT'S RIGHT HERE!

I'm glad to get there. My knees feel swollen and stiff. I need to stretch them and take care of my colostomy bag. After John parks the van, I grab my good four-pronged aluminium cane and we head on in.

After getting our tickets ($4.50!), we both stop at the bathroom. When I get out, John is waiting for me. Outside, there is a little shuttle bus idling, ready to take us to the Mystery Spot. I'm hoping there won't be too much walking after that, but I won't let it stop me. Not this trip. Inside the bus, there is already a family of four, (they have a son and a daughter, just like us) plus one man by himself. The single man is wearing a silly foreign sailor hat, a shrunken blue T-shirt, and big shorts with Budweiser beer emblems all over them. Slouched there, with his pale arms crossed, he looks like a big thirty-five year-old child. Luckily, he sits in the back, near the family. John and I are behind the driver, a young

shy-looking black man. In front of him, on the dashboard, there is a yellow stick-on note.
"I feel great & ready!"
YES - YES - YES

I wonder what he's ready for. I hope it's to drive safely. The young man puts the bus into gear, but before we take off, he gets on the PA. As if he is reading from a script, he says, "Hello and welcome to the Mystery Spot. It will be about a ten-minute ride to the area with the mysterious powers. So sit back and prepare to be amazed."

"He has a nice speaking voice," I whisper to John. He grunts, the way he's always grunted. This is one thing he has not forgotten, unfortunately. I shift around, try to get comfortable in my cramped seat. Finally, I give up and just read the brochure they gave us:

> At "Mystery Spot," you'll see many astonishing things that seem to defy the laws of nature, yet are simply natural illusions. It is a place where gravity seems to have disappeared, where your sense of balance seems entirely upset. Everything you know turns upside down and you are pulled in directions that never before seemed possible. It's entertaining for young and old alike!

"The key word here is 'seems,'" I say to John. He says nothing, looks out the window at the *Mammoth Gift Shop* passing by. John is well trained after years of spotting gift shops for me on the road. At one time, that was my favorite part of a vacation, the bringing back of things. My personal weakness was pottery. No matter where we travelled, I always came back with a little something. Indian pots from Wyoming and Montana, beautiful glazed vases from Pigeon Forge, Mexican bowls from the southwest. All beautiful, and most of it still packed away in boxes in our basement. A home, after all, only has so much room. These days, there might be a trinket or two brought back for the grandchildren, but we are done with all that. To possess, you need time. All those boxes. The kids are going to have quite a job ahead of them.

I peek behind us. The man in the Budweiser shorts is talking to the family. You can tell that the husband and wife are a little put off by him. The kids seem to like him though. I'm surprised he isn't talking to us. He looks kind of crazy and crazy people love old people. We're just good targets. Maybe because we can't get away as quickly. In the past ten years or so, whenever John and I have been in a city, it's isn't long before we're approached by bums, bunko artists or just plain kooks. "Glad he's sitting in the back," I whisper. I notice that John is taking a little nap. I let him rest. Driving is hard work. After a few minutes, the shuttle bus stops. We pull up by a bench at the edge of a field surrounded by trees.

The kids are the first out, the mother and father right behind them. I wake John up and have him give me a hand because my knees have stiffened up again. I try to keep myself from cursing as I get up. To top it off, the Budweiser man is waiting for us to get off the bus. We just ignore him and head for the asphalt path that leads through the trees.

Michael Zadoorian

THIS WAY TO "MYSTERY SPOT"

Half way into the woods, we stop at another bench for a breather. I'm hoping that the Budweiser fellow will pass us up, but he stops too, acting as if he is examining some nearby flora. While we rest, I read aloud to John from the brochure.

> *The nature of 'Mystery Spot' is baffling and mystifying. Exercise caution when entering the vortex of "Mystery Spot." It is an antigravitational electromagnetic force field and could cause reactions.*

I chuckle. "Remember that Wonder Spot in Wisconsin, dear? I think they said the same thing. The most dangerous part of it was the snack bar."

"Oh yeah," John says. "That was something."

I look up from the brochure. The path ahead is almost dark with foliage. At the end of it, I can see that there is a bright clearing. It's not that far really, but we still have a ways to go. As we continue walking, the Budweiser man stays fifty or sixty feet behind us. So John and I just walk along as briskly as we can. Rather, as briskly as I can. Along the path, there are signs:

ALMOST THERE!

"Hope I make it," I say to John. I keep up my pace. My hand is quivering a bit on my cane. Soon there is another sign:

YOU ARE ABOUT TO ENTER "MYSTERY SPOT"

We walk out into the clearing. It is wide and grassy and could be anywhere. "Looks like where we came in," I say, my breath coming fast and hard. But it's different. I realize this as we pause on the path. Not far ahead is a hill with a house, a little bungalow, settled on the side, as if it had slid down. The house could use a good coat of paint. The trees that surround it are like corkscrews twisted into the earth. I point them out to John as we walk. He just squints.

I look at the brochure. There is picture of a man and woman in "The House Of Mystery." The walls of the house are straight, yet the couple's bodies are slanted at an impossible angle. Their feet are back behind their heads, reluctantly staying put, while their bodies are being pulled toward something else. I turn to show the picture to John, but he isn't there and I drop the brochure. When I go to pick it up, I start to feel very woozy. I clutch at my cane, put my weight on it, and it keeps me from toppling to the asphalt, but I can't keep myself standing erect. I feel myself dropping slowly to my knees. I brace myself for the excruciating pain that will come as they meet the ground. It never comes. My knees aren't the least bit sore. Even with everything that is happening, I am amazed that my legs actually feel good. In fact, my whole body feels better than it has in years, freer, as if a small part of me has lifted, the part that feels pain. The only problem is that my head is lighter too. I can't get up.

Mystery Spot

"John," I say, kneeling now, on my painless knees, both hands on the handle of my cane.

I turn around and see John ten or fifteen feet behind me, off the path. I can see he feels something too, but not the same as me. He is in a daze, more so than usual. "Ella?," he croaks, looking the wrong way, toward the Mystery House. "Where are you?"

I call out to him again. He is quite lost. There are short periods like this at home. They used to be shorter. Now I watch my husband as he sits down on the lawn and starts to cry, every once in a while saying my name as he if he is mourning me here on the edge of Nebraska at the amazing Mystery Spot.

"John!," I yell as loudly as I can. My head is clear now, knees almost completely supporting me, but I still can't get up. Finally, I feel the presence of another person next to me. I know who it is.

"Are you two tourists?" asks the Budweiser man. Not "Can I help?" or "Should I get an ambulance?"

"My husband doesn't feel well and I can't get up," I say, sharper than I usually speak to anyone.

"But are you guys tourists?" His voice is all excited and skittery.

"Yes, we're tourists!" I screamed. "Now would you please help me up?"

The idiot just stands there. He pulls a notebook from the pocket of his baggy shorts.

"I knew you were tourists because that's the only people this happens to. It doesn't bother us people who live around here."

I take a deep breath, swing my cane and hit him right where it counts. He goes down like a sack of bricks. While he is on the ground, writhing, I scream into his right ear. "Will you help us?" I have my cane poised over his head. I am pretty annoyed by this time. He frantically shakes his head yes. "Good," I say. "Now help me up."

The Budweiser man, holding his stomach, a little unsteady, slowly rises to his feet, then helps me to do the same. Surprisingly, once I am up, I don't need much assistance. I am still a bit dizzy, but my knees feel sturdy and strong, like a twenty year-old's. We head over to John. I take one arm, the Budweiser man takes the other. John seems to be able to walk all right. He's just very disoriented.

Back on the path, John keeps opening his eyes wide like something is startling him, but he is walking more on his own. This is good, because the further we walk, the harder it gets for me to hold him up, even a little. My knees are starting to feel how they usually feel. Worse. I look over at the Budweiser man. This man, whom I just smacked in the balls, has my husband on his arm and is walking very straight and proud, like we are all on the promenade at Atlantic City.

"You come to this place, even though you live around here?" I say to him.

"Sure. It's fun."

"You mean it's fun watching the tourists pass out."

He looks down at his shoes, like a child. "It doesn't happen to everyone. It's just that the nearer you get to the vortex, the less gravity there is. Plus the magnetic fields and all."

We get through the woods. John is walking now without any help. He seems fine, but my whole body hurts like hell. My knees are throbbing. John now starts

Michael Zadoorian

to help me. The Budweiser man, finally untethered from the two of us, will not shut up.

"We're lighter here," he keeps saying. "There's not so much pulling us to the earth. But on the other hand, there's not so much holding us either. Some say it's a sort of deflection of gravitational force. But according to "Newtonian theory - "

"Excuse us, but we've got to catch the shuttle. Thank you for the help," I say to him.

"Uh-huh," says John. He seems like his old self. Well, maybe not his old self, but at least his recent self. And I will settle for that.

"Good*bye*," I say firmly, to the Budweiser man.

It is just a little further to the bench at the shuttle stop. Our friend reluctantly turns and starts back through the woods. I imagine he will continue his search for disoriented tourists in the area with the mysterious powers. We have already made his day. At the bench, we sit quietly. Then for no reason, John takes my hand and holds it in his.

We are the only ones on the shuttle and in the same seats as before. The same young man is driving. This time, he does not say anything over the PA. I wonder if he still feels great and ready. I know there are times when I feel ready, then I look at John and wonder how he will get along. I think about what the Budweiser man said, that there is not so much holding us to the earth. Still, we hold on for as long as we can, for whatever our reasons. The driver drops us off by the ticket office.

As we head back to the van, John walks much faster than he usually does. I know he just wants to get out of there, but I can't keep up, so I stop in the middle of the parking lot. Standing there, surrounded by all this gravel, I try not to feel what I am feeling. I look over at John. He is almost to the van when he notices that I am not with him. There is a flash of alarm in his eyes. Then I know that this is where we are heading, our own Mystery Spot, the eventual destination of all marriages, where one is without the other.

Finally, John looks over to where I am standing. After a few seconds, I start walking again. As I go around to my side of the van, I notice that someone has put a bumper sticker right above our license plate.

WE'VE BEEN TO
THE AMAZING "MYSTERY SPOT"

Amazing, indeed.

Back on the freeway, there is no traffic. We drive like hell, try to put some distance between us and that place. And we do. Occasionally, I catch a glimpse of one of the signs in my rear view mirror, but I avert my eyes. Soon, there are no more signs. The miles just roll past us, carry us, as if we are pulled by a force that we cannot possibly resist.

We are at Disneyland by the next morning.